DEAD BEFORE DARK

WENDY CORSI STAUB

DEAD BEFORE DARK

ZEBRA BOOKS
KENSINGTON PUBLISHING CORP.

ZEBRA BOOKS are published by

Kensington Publishing Corp.
119 West 40th Street
New York, NY 10018

ISBN-13: 978-1-60751-903-4

Printed in the United States of America

*This book is dedicated to my dear friends
Chris and Anita,
Lucas and Gabriela,
and to Mark, Morgan, and Brody,
with love.*

*With gratitude to William Rasmussen
for his endless patience
with my endless queries about FBI procedure.
Any errors in that regard are my own—
and Bill gets the credit for all that rings true.*

Bill, I couldn't have done it without you.

Prologue

Attica, New York
June

They called him the Night Watchman.

Back in the late sixties, he stole into women's homes after dark on nights when the moon was full and they were alone. He slaughtered them—and always left an eerie calling card at the crime scene.

The authorities never publicly revealed what it was.

For over a year, the killer engaged in a deadly game of cat and mouse with the local police and FBI, the press, and the jittery populations of cities he so sporadically struck beneath a full moon, claiming seemingly random female victims.

No one ever did manage to figure out how or why he chose the women he killed.

The only certainty was that he watched them closely in the days or weeks leading up to their deaths. Learned their routines. Knew precisely where and when to catch them alone at night, off guard and vulnerable.

Out of the blue, the killing stopped.

Months went by without a telltale murder. Then years.

The Night Watchman Murders joined a long list of legendary unsolved American crimes, perhaps the most notorious since the Borden axe murders almost a century before.

Unsolved? Of course Lizzie was guilty as hell. She was acquitted based only on the Victorian presumption that a homicidal monster couldn't possibly dwell within a genteel lady.

Back then, few suspected that pure evil was quite capable of lurking behind the most benign of facades.

A hundred years later, as the Night Watchman went about his gruesome business undetected, even those who knew him best had yet to catch on. He—like others who would come after him: Ted Bundy, John Wayne Gacy, Jeffrey Dahmer— was a monster masquerading as a gentleman.

Unlike the others, though, he was never apprehended. Not for the Night Watchman murders, anyway.

A theory came to light, when the bloodbath was so suddenly curtailed, that the killer had either died himself, or been jailed for another crime.

As the decade drew to a close, the lingering public fascination with the Night Watchman faded and was finally eclipsed by interest in the elusive Zodiac Killer.

Years went by, decades dawned and waned, the nineteen-hundreds gave way to a shiny new millennium.

Once in a while, some unsolved crimes buff would turn the media spotlight on the Night Watchman.

For the most part, though, he remained shrouded in shadow, and has to this day.

Ah, well, the darkest night always gives way to dawn.

He emerges into the hot glare of summer sunlight on what happens to be the longest day of the year.

Fitting, isn't it?

He smiles at the final uniformed guard standing sentry over his path to freedom.

The guard doesn't smile back.

They never have. They simply keep a joyless, steady vigil,

scrutinizing the most mundane human activities, day in and day out, night in and night out.

Night in and night out . . .

Ha. No joy in it for prison guards, anyway.

Street clothes are on his back for the first time in three and a half decades; bus fare home is stashed in his pocket . . . if he had a home to go to.

Thirty-five years is a long time.

But finding a place to live is the last thing on his mind as he walks toward the bus stop, free at last, with nightfall hours away.

New York City
August

"Five minutes," a cute twenty-something production assistant announces, sticking her short, chic haircut into the green room.

Lucinda Sloan promptly pulls out a compact, snaps it open, and finds a stranger looking back at her.

Oh, for the love of . . .

The reflection shakes its head.

Thanks to the morning show's makeup artist, she's wearing more makeup than usual.

A *lot* more makeup.

More makeup, quite possibly, than she's ever worn in her life—or at least since her sixth grade coed dance at the Millwood Academy, a milestone occasion for which she also stuffed her bra with toilet paper. Twenty years later, that's hardly necessary, but if it were, she wouldn't bother. These days, she's strictly a lip gloss and blue jeans kind of girl.

But if Lucinda Sloan has learned anything at all in this forty-eight hour media feeding frenzy, it's that pre-camera primping is de rigueur here in the big leagues. All national television news show guests are plopped into the hair and makeup chair, regardless of whether they're a movie star or a run-of-the-mill psychic who just helped snag a notorious Jersey Shore serial killer.

Though she belongs to the latter category, Lucinda looks, at the moment, like the former.

It's the lipstick. Definitely. Her mouth is slicked red, the very shade of fresh blood. Maybe that was the intent, given the macabre topic of her impending segment.

Blood.

Lucinda suppresses a shudder, remembering the gore she encountered at a secluded Monmouth County farmhouse just a few days ago. Thank God the only blood shed at the final crime scene belonged to the killer, slain by the cops to save the would-be victim's life.

Fourteen-year-old Tess Hastings is now laid up with a broken leg at home in Montclair. Her parents, Camden and Mike, have protected her from the press so far, but they're here in the green room themselves.

Mike, handsome in a suit, sits with a protective arm around his pregnant wife, as though someone is going to snatch her away. And no wonder, after their ordeal.

Your family is safe now—the lunatic can't hurt you, or anyone else, ever again, Lucinda wants to tell him.

Trouble is, that wouldn't help. Once you've encountered violent evil, you never feel safe in this world again.

Who knows that better than Lucinda? Her life's work has taken her to the darkest places imaginable, has shown her that human beings are capable of inflicting unspeakable cruelty.

She learned long ago not to let any of it get to her—at least, not on the outside. She's not about to spend her life looking over her shoulder.

She's a Sloan, after all.

Generations before her have traditionally valued a stiff upper lip almost as much as they have their material possessions. Lucinda might have eschewed the trappings of wealth in her adult life, but when high pressure hits, her own facade is stolid as the stone mansion where she grew up.

She sighs and snaps the compact closed.

"Don't worry . . . You look great."

The compliment—courtesy of Detective Randall Barakat—inspires an unwanted spark of satisfaction.

"Thanks." Feeling his eyes on her—and not about to return the gaze—she busies herself wiping imaginary lipstick off her teeth.

An imminent live on-air interview is nerve-wracking enough. Sitting so close to Randy that she can smell his Tic-Tac breath takes that stress to a whole new level.

The Hastings case brought them together again after three years . . . but only professionally.

Randy's married now, living seventy miles away from Philly on Long Beach Island, and Lucinda's long over him.

Not.

But hey, she's one hell of an actress.

Randy, on the other hand, wouldn't win any Oscars for his performance since their paths crossed again last month. Lucinda doesn't have to be psychic to know that he, too, has unresolved feelings. But she wouldn't tap that vein if it were made of gold.

"Hey—what about me?" His voice conveniently barges into her thoughts.

"Huh?"

"What about me?" Randy repeats. "Do I look okay?"

Reluctantly, she glances up at him.

Black hair, blue eyes, dimples, bronzed skin. Yeah. He looks okay, and then some.

"Lucinda, can I borrow your mirror for a second?" Camden Hastings asks, and Lucinda hands it over.

Cam, an attractive olive-skinned brunette, has also been glammed up for the cameras. Her lipstick, though, is a subtle pearly pink.

Lucinda should be wearing pink lipstick, too, or a nice summer peach shade, or—*Hey! Here's a thought: how about no lipstick at all?*

Wistful, Lucinda figures that right about now on an ordinary Monday morning, she'd be home wearing an old T-shirt, dishing up her usual breakfast: Cap'n Crunch or Frosted Flakes, coffee, and a can of Pepsi.

Then again, the green room spread isn't too shabby. She was able to snag two glazed donuts and a Pepsi before heading into the makeup chair for the works, from foundation to curled eyelashes.

Next, she visited the hairstylist, who chattily tamed her auburn waves. Lucinda typically lets her hair hang down her back unfettered; it now nests sedately in a jeweled barrette at the nape of her neck.

Her hair is behaving itself, and the lipstick hasn't yet made its way onto her teeth, so she's good to go. Not bad for a lip gloss and blue jeans kind of girl.

Yeah, and she can't wait to ditch the barrette, scrub her face, and stick this little black Chanel dress back in her spare closet. Way, way back, where it belongs, hanging beside the other relics of her society girl past. She's kept only a few designer items; they come in handy for occasions like weddings, charity functions, funerals, lunch with her mother—only slightly more appealing than funerals—and national television appearances.

This happens to be her fifth national television appearance in the last forty-eight hours, and in her entire life. She's starting to get the hang of it, though.

Her family isn't.

In Bitsy and Rudolph Sloan's world, a woman's only proper place in the newspapers is on the society pages—or the obituaries. Her parents were horrified to see their only child splashed all over the news. They've left several messages to let her know.

"Do you ever pick up the phone for them?" Cam asked when her mother's number popped up on her cell earlier.

"Pretty much never."

"That's so sad."

Cam's reaction caught Lucinda off guard.

It's been years since she questioned her relationship—or lack thereof—with her parents. Years since she went from being a poor little love-deprived rich girl to a self-sufficient woman whose life is enriched by friends and work—a vocation that, ironically, led to the communication breakdown with her parents in the first place.

"Tic Tac?"

Randy again. He produces a plastic box, gives it a little shake.

"No, thanks." Lucinda can't resist adding, as he pops yet another green pellet into his mouth, "I don't want to go on TV with a green tongue."

"I have a green tongue?"

"I've seen worse. But hey, your breath is minty fresh."

Cam returns the compact and checks her watch. "Hasn't it been more than five minutes?"

"Not even two." Mike rubs circles in the small of her back. "Take a deep breath and relax."

"You make it sound so easy."

Cam has been looking at her watch repeatedly for the last twenty minutes—anxious, Lucinda knows, not to get the latest interview underway but to get it over with.

With their daughter safe and sound, their recently troubled marriage back on track, and another baby on the way, the Hastings have no interest in being on TV. They wouldn't be here at all if it weren't for Ava Neary. It was Lucinda who alerted Cam that her older sister's long-ago death might not have been a suicide after all.

Maybe I shouldn't have told her . . . or at least, not so soon after what happened to Tess.

But Cam needed to know, after all these years of trying to reconcile her own turbulent past, that nineteen-year-old Ava didn't jump from the top floor of a Manhattan building that long ago day. She was pushed to her death.

Lucinda expected Cam to dispute—or at least question—that claim, based as it is on nothing more than a psychic vision of Ava struggling with a hooded figure before the fall. But Cam didn't dispute it. Maybe deep down, she already suspected the truth.

All this media attention over the serial killer is a golden opportunity to shed light on Ava's case. Whoever took her life might still be out there. Someone, somewhere, might know something.

The Hastings agreed to all these interviews with the stipulation that Ava would be prominently featured—and that Tess would not.

The press would have a field day if they knew that the rescued girl's mother—like Lucinda—is a clairvoyant. But Cam's abilities are under wraps, and it was officially Lucinda's ESP that led the police to the killer. Only Lucinda, Mike, and Randy are aware that Cam was having visions of her daughter's abduction long before it became a frightening reality.

Lucinda returns the compact to her bag, a vintage Hermès Kelly—named after the late princess of Monaco who, like Lucinda herself, was a product of Philadelphia's Main Line.

First Hollywood, then a real-life Prince Charming, whisked Grace Kelly away from all that. Granted, her fairy-tale ending had a fatal postscript. But at least the dashing Rainier claimed her as his royal bride.

Not so for Lucinda Sloan. Her would-be prince married Carla Karnecki, the proverbial truck stop waitress with a heart of gold.

She was already Randy's live-in fiancée back when Lucinda met him.

Yet Lucinda felt an instant tug of attraction the moment they met and sensed that it was mutual, despite his being engaged.

Of course she fought it. So did he.

But working together day after day, night after night, under the most exhausting, heart-wrenching of circumstances, their emotions on edge. . . . Maybe it was inevitable that Lucinda and Randy would wind up in each other's arms sooner or later.

It only happened a few times, and they both hated themselves for it.

Meanwhile, an oblivious Carla was blissfully planning the wedding, dutifully saving her tips for her dream house, and caring for her dying mother, Zelda.

Randy wanted to break the engagement. Lucinda told him not to do it, not for her sake. She never really understood why she reacted that way, and she later regretted it, thinking of what might have been.

But at the time, it was a gut reaction, and she always trusted her instincts.

Maybe she was so drawn to Randy because he was unavailable. Maybe she was too independent back then, freshly sprung from her gilded cage, not ready for all that their relationship would entail if he were free. Maybe she just couldn't handle what his leaving Carla would do to her conscience. Maybe she was afraid of needing him. Needing anyone.

Maybe, maybe, maybe . . .

So much uncertainty. She loathes uncertainty, and it dogged every move she made with Randy—even after it was over.

Did she expect Randy to tell her she was wrong about them? Did she want him to fight for her, make her change her mind?

As if anyone ever could.

But if anyone could, it was him.

Didn't he know that?

No. He didn't know.

Anyway, girls like Carla deserve a fairy-tale ending, right?

Randy transferred to an out-of-state job on the Jersey shore. Married Carla.

Lucinda built a nice little life for herself and put the past behind her.

Now that Not-Prince-Charming is back on the scene, though, she's got her work cut out for her. With three more joint press interviews scheduled in the next two days, Lucinda can't escape Randy just yet.

"Okay, let's go! Cell phones off, everyone. You're on right after the author interview." The production assistant is back to herd Lucinda, Randy, and the Hastingses down the hall toward the studio.

People stride importantly past them in both directions, clipboards and props in hand. The scene is becoming familiar. Lucinda knows what to expect beyond that soundproof door: on-air talent who are household names, authoritative producers, bustling stagehands, jeans-clad cameramen, bright lights, a clip-on mike, arctic air conditioning. . . .

The door opens, and in they go.

Yup—right again.

Lucinda is getting to be an old hand at this TV stuff.

"Nervous?" Randy whispers as they're led to the interview chairs.

"Nah. Are you?"

"Uh-uh."

"Liar."

He shrugs, grins. "We can't all be as cool and composed as the Comely Clairvoyant."

She rolls her eyes. He's quoting yesterday's *New York Post*, which Lucinda's friend Bradley Carmichael, who lives in Manhattan, called and woke her to tell her about at five-thirty A.M. when it was hot off the press.

"You're a tabloid star, darling!" Bradley, on his way to the gym, has always been oblivious to the fact that some people aren't up at dawn to work out. "Just like Paris and Britney."

Not quite.

But the press has been all over this story, particularly her role in it. She's pretty much been portrayed as a Sexy Sooth-sayer Superhero—that being this morning's *Daily News* tagline beneath a particularly flattering photo of her.

"The *Daily News* says you have a smokin' hot Jennifer Aniston bod and a Demi Moore bedroom voice."

"Bedroom voice?" She laughed at that. "If I'd been in a bedroom lately I wouldn't have this voice."

"Meaning . . . ?"

"Meaning I always get hoarse when I'm over-tired," she informed Bradley.

"Well, the world doesn't know that. The world thinks you're a smoldering femme fatale."

Forget the world. Lucinda can't help but wonder what Randy's wife thinks of all this. Is Carla at home watching right now? If so, will she suspect that her husband and the Comely Clairvoyant slash Sexy Soothsayer Superhero were once a hot item?

Probably not.

Anyway, what does it matter? *Once* is the key word.

Once upon a time . . .

Yeah. Unlike Princess Grace and Carla Karnecki Barakat, Lucinda Sloan only got the fairy-tale beginning.

Middlebury, Vermont

"Never, ever, *ever* turn on the television in the daytime. You do, and it's all over."

That was the advice Vic Shattuck's former colleague David Gudlaug gave him upon his mandatory retirement from the Bureau's Behavioral Studies Unit last summer.

Dave had already been retired for a good decade by then, and was full of other nuggets of advice, which didn't, thank God, include buying an RV.

Vic's had his fill of travel over a twenty-five-year career with the FBI. Not so with Dave, who's on yet another cruise with his wife this month, somewhere in the Mediterranean.

Vic found that out from Dave's son, who answered the phone when Vic called this morning to ask, with regard to turning on the television in the daytime, "*What's* all over? The day? Life as I knew it? What? Is it really so bad?"

Vic's wife Kitty had left for work a little while ago as he settled into his chair in front of the TV.

"What are you going to do today?" she asked.

"Same as I do every day. A whole lot of nothing."

He saw the look in her eyes. Kitty can say less with silence than most women can say with a week's worth of words.

Vic has never been big on television—daytime, or otherwise. He managed to follow Dave's advice, at first. Re-settled with Kitty to their native New England after years living near Quantico, he golfed every day the weather would allow. Kitty, who doesn't golf, went stir crazy after a few idle weeks and found an accounting job at the university. On rainy days, he kept busy with Kitty's lengthy Honey Do list around their new—albeit centuries old—saltbox home, mostly landscaping.

But then winter settled over the mountains of New England, and there wasn't much to do—around the house or otherwise.

One morning, Vic turned on the television to see if it was going to snow—it was, big surprise—and wound up watching the entire morning newscast waiting for weather updates.

The storm held off till the next day, so he tuned in again to check the local closings and cancellations list—not that he had anywhere to be. And not that a winter storm in the mountains of Vermont was out of the ordinary in the least.

But it was good, sitting there in front of the wood-burning stove with a cup of coffee, catching up on what's been going on in the world.

Not as fulfilling as working, of course. But he didn't have

a choice about that. You reach fifty-seven, and ready or not, there you go. You miss your job and the people. You try to stay busy. You think about the things you did right and the things you'd do differently and, always, about the one that got away.

When spring came, he started golfing again—until he threw out his back. Two specialists and one surgery later, he's been ordered to stay away from the golf course until it's fully healed.

So here he is, on a beautiful summer morning, watching the morning news as has become his daily habit. He'll follow it up with a couple of lame talk shows targeted toward women, and channel surf after lunch, avoiding the shopping networks.

The way he sees it, as long as he stays away from home shopping, he's not pathetic.

And as long as he remembers to keep dirty dishes out of the sink and fold the laundry, Kitty doesn't seem to think he's pathetic, either. At least, she doesn't say it.

Maybe it was better when he was pleasantly oblivious to the news, though. Between the political coverage out of Washington, a passenger airliner crash in South America, and another hurricane bearing down on the Gulf Coast, things are looking pretty grim.

Vic looks around for the remote to turn the channel.

"This morning," the beautiful anchorwoman says, "we're going to talk with a New Jersey woman who as a child overcame the tragic suicide of her older sister, only to have her young daughter abducted by a serial killer just days ago. Meet the police detective and beautiful psychic who teamed up to rescue the teen and apprehend the killer—and learn why they are seeking new information on the decades-old so-called suicide."

So-called suicide?

In other words, they're looking into the possibility that it might have been a homicide. Interesting.

Vic stops looking for the remote.

"But first," the anchor continues, "we have the author of a new book on the disappearance of aviator Amelia Earhart, and he claims to have solved the mystery at last."

Ah, Amelia Earhart. One of the great unsolved mysteries of all time.

Solved?

Vic watches the segment with interest. The author is a journalist who has spent the past two years with a team of scientists digging up convincing forensic evidence on an island in the South Pacific.

"What made you decide to write this book?" the author is asked as the interview winds to a close.

The journalist shrugs. "I've just always been obsessed with what happened to her."

"I know the feeling, buddy," Vic mutters.

It was an obsession with an unsolved case that led him to FBI work in the first place.

He'd gotten interested in crime back when he was a psych major and a notorious murderer was terrorizing the Northeast—the one the press called the Night Watchman. He became so fascinated by newspaper accounts of the murders that Kitty—who was just his girlfriend at the time—had a suggestion for him.

"Why don't you solve the case?"

"Because I'm not a detective."

Kitty just looked at him.

The next thing he knew, he'd changed his mind about becoming a shrink.

With Kitty's support, he filled out applications, endured tough interviews, passed incredibly difficult tests. Eventually, he found himself in a four-month FBI training program in Quantico.

As an agent in the seventies, when a rash of what his future mentor Robert K. Ressler coined "serial killing" took hold across the country, Vic grew even more fascinated by the criminal mind. Curious about what made human monsters tick, he found that his earlier interest in psychology came in handy on the job.

For four years, he took college courses in deviant psychology by night, hunted down the bad guys by day. It might not have been the dream situation for a happily married father of four kids—the youngest being twins—but he and Kitty made it work.

It all came together when he earned his master's and was assigned to the FBI's BSU as a criminal profiler. There, he studied the complex cases of known killers—including the most notorious of all time, Charles Manson—and applied what he learned to active, unsolved cases.

And to inactive cases.

Revisiting the long-exhausted evidence on the Night Watchman murders, he pored over every detail and conjured a profile of the perpetrator. He anticipated what the unknown subject's next moves were likely to have been, and came up with a proactive plan to lay a trap for him.

All the while, he imagined the satisfaction he would find in solving one of the most notorious cold cases in Bureau history.

It didn't happen.

He profiled the killer as an organized, highly intelligent white male. He was young, probably in his early twenties at the most when the crimes occurred. His relationships with women were unfulfilling. He felt no remorse after killing and was in no hurry to get away; on the contrary, he meticulously staged the victims and left a distinct calling card at the scene.

Yes, Vic knew *who* they were looking for.

He just didn't know *when*—or *where*—or *whether*—the unsub would strike again.

He didn't.

Still, not a day goes by, even after almost forty years, that Vic Shattuck doesn't wonder what happened to the Night Watchman.

All those brutal killings—and then nothing.

Vic has a theory, of course—just like everyone else who ever had anything to do with the case. The killer either died, or went to prison for some unrelated crime.

For years after the murders had ended, the evidence boxed away, pending inactive, Vic held his breath. He waited for him to reemerge, waited for another woman to turn up dead at the hands of the Night Watchman.

There were a number of crimes with a similar M.O.: woman who lives alone is killed by an intruder in the night. One, years after the last known Night Watchman murder, was even an obvious—and flimsy—copycat crime. It was a domestic abuse case that ended in murder, and the husband tried to make it look otherwise.

No one bought it for a minute, not even the press.

The moon wasn't even full that night.

But for the investigators, the dead giveaway—as it were— was that the Night Watchman's calling card, the one that had never been revealed to the public, was conspicuously absent at the scene.

The victim's lips hadn't been smeared with red lipstick.

It's the red lipstick that gets him.

It always has been.

She's a beautiful woman, yeah. Great body—skinny with big boobs. Just the way he likes them. Who doesn't?

But that luscious red mouth has him mesmerized, even before he actually hears the words spilling from it in a hauntingly throaty voice, or reads the caption superimposed over her image.

LUCINDA SLOAN, PSYCHIC DETECTIVE

Fascinating.

Utterly fascinating.

"Yes, I've been involved in missing persons work for years

now," she informs the handsome interviewer in a throaty voice, "but they don't always turn out this way."

"In other words," the interviewer says, "you don't always catch the bad guy—or woman, as the case may be? This was just a lucky break?"

She appears to weigh her response carefully before acknowledging, "It was absolutely a lucky break in the sense that Tess Hastings's life was saved. But two other girls lost theirs to a ruthless serial killer."

"I understand you were working with the police to find those missing kids and had had visions of their deaths before Tess Hastings was kidnapped?"

"Yes."

"And you tend to use a process called psychometry, is that right? You make physical contact with something that belonged to the person you're trying to find—say, a piece of jewelry or clothing—and you are then able to glean information about the person?"

"That's right."

Psychometry.

He finds a scrap of paper and a pen, writes the word down along with

Lucinda Sloan, Psychic Detective.

"And that's what you did in the case of those two missing girls?"

"Yes."

"Did you ever think there was hope of finding them, Ms. Sloan?"

For a moment, she bites her luscious lower lip. Then, shaking her head, she says, "I didn't, no. It's not an exact science, but in my line of work, I'm brought in after the fact, so with my visions, I tend to see things after they happen."

"In other words, when it's too late."

She nods.

"Do you ever get immune to dealing with human anguish on a daily basis?"

"Not immune—I guess accustomed is a better word."

"How do you cope?"

"It's never easy. You have to be able to compartmentalize your life—you know, remove yourself from it."

"Remove yourself." The reporter nods. "I understand that you were supposed to be on an Alaskan cruise vacation right about now, but you missed the boat, so to speak, in order to help find Tess Hastings."

"That's right." She shrugs. "It's not a big deal."

"Detective Barakat, hindsight is twenty-twenty, but I'm sure there are some on your force who might have criticized you, at the time, for putting any stock into a psychic's visions?"

Regrettably, the camera shifts to a man whose caption reads *DETECTIVE RANDALL BARAKAT, LONG BEACH TOWNSHIP*.

"Well, it's not like I went around broadcasting it."

"How did her involvement come about? Was it official, or unofficial?"

"Unofficial—I mean, I've known Lucinda for years. We used to work together on missing persons cases when I was back in Philly. I've seen her do some amazing things."

Oh you have, have you?

The detective's gold wedding band is clearly visible as he fidgets with his lapel. The guy is married—not to the amazing Lucinda with the luscious red lips, or the caption would undoubtedly say so.

But something in the man's blue eyes—a flicker of admiration, a flash of regret, a glimmer of lust, perhaps—conveys that Detective Randall Barakat has more than casual interest in Lucinda Sloan, Psychic Detective.

Hmm.

Interesting.

"They're calling Lucinda a superhero these days, Detective Barakat. Do you agree?"

"Sure. You know, danger goes with the territory when you're a cop. But Lucinda, she's fearless. Nothing ever fazes her."

The camera darts back to her as the interviewer asks, "What do you say to that, Lucinda? Is there anything at all you're afraid of?"

"The dark," she says promptly—almost glibly, with a jittery little laugh and a sidewise glance at the detective.

Again—interesting.

"You're afraid of the dark?" The interviewer looks amused.

But she's not kidding. She means it. I can tell.

"Ever since I was a little girl. I guess I always figured bad things couldn't happen in broad daylight, you know? When the sun goes down, the boogeyman comes out."

His gaze narrows.

He stares thoughtfully at her until the camera cuts away again, to a man and woman identified as CAMDEN AND MICHAEL HASTINGS, PARENTS OF KIDNAPPED GIRL.

The interviewer drones on, questioning them about their ordeal. His mind drifts until the screen shifts again.

In sheer disbelief, he finds himself looking at a vintage photo captioned *AVA NEARY, SUPPOSED 1970 NYU SUICIDE, SISTER OF CAMDEN HASTINGS.*

"Now that Mr. and Mrs. Hastings's daughter has been found, they—with the assistance of Lucinda Sloan, are looking into the death of Mrs. Hastings's sister, who supposedly jumped to her death from a building at New York University over thirty-five years ago."

Well, well, well.

What a small world.

Lucinda Sloan's red mouth announces, "We're asking anyone who knew Ava Neary at NYU and might have any information on the period leading up to her death to please come forward."

A small world indeed, he thinks, as an idea ignites in the mind once deemed, by a court-ordered psychiatric evaluation, competent to stand trial for matricide.

Tried, convicted, sentenced, rehabilitated.

Time served.

Case closed.

No longer a threat to society.

Or so it was assumed last June, when the Night Watchman was unwittingly released after serving thirty-five years in prison.

PART I

5:40

Chapter One

When it's over, he stands back to survey his handiwork.

Almost.

He reaches out with a gloved hand to adjust the sleeve of her pajama top, pulling it lower on her wrist.

Better.

He pushes back a few strands of her hair, the better to assess the frozen grimace on her mouth.

Ah. Very nice, indeed.

He pries open the corpse's clenched right fingers. First, he slides the silver signet ring from the pinkie and puts it aside. Then he unzips the pocket of his down jacket and pulls out a plastic Ziploc bag.

Painstakingly, he deposits the contents of the bag in the palm of her hand. Then he closes her fingers again to form a fist.

Good. This was a last minute idea—a nice little twist to keep them all guessing. To let the almighty Lucinda Sloan know that she no longer has control of her own life.

That he controls her now. He controls everything.

Picking up the pinkie ring, he dredges it through the puddle of blood. He seals it into the Ziploc, dripping red, and puts the bag back into his pocket.

And now, the grand finale.

He takes out a tube of lipstick, uncaps it, gives it a twist, and pauses to admire the slanted, waxy tip.

Then he runs it over the dead woman's lips, staining them a scarlet shade to match the pool of blood in which she lies.

There.

You're perfect, darling.

Her gaping eyes seem to be fixed on his face now in vacant, terrified recognition, belying the fact that she never saw him coming. Not until the last moment.

They never do.

He takes one long, last look; then, satisfied, he leaves her.

Just before closing the door behind him, he snakes a black glove around the doorjamb to turn off the light, leaving her alone in the dark.

She won't mind. Not now.

Maybe she wouldn't have before, either.

For all he knows, she was never afraid of the dark.

But some people are.

Some people are terrified.

Outside, he takes her house key—a duplicate of the one he'd brazenly borrowed from her purse in an unguarded moment—and slides it under the WELCOME mat. Just to make things a little easier, when the time comes.

You really have thought of everything, he congratulates himself.

He pauses momentarily at the foot of the driveway to leave behind another calling card, placing it in a spot where it probably won't be discovered right away—if ever.

But it's there.

He always plays by the rules.

At least, when it comes to his own little game.

He chuckles softly as he slips away into the night beneath the light of a full moon.

* * *

Gazing out the passenger's side window at the Federal brick row houses lining the cobblestone street, Lucinda reminds herself that she loves her new neighborhood.

Really, she does.

Philadelphia's Society Hill is safe, convenient, historic, beautiful . . . and very few people know to look for her here. That's the important thing.

In the midst of the media attention following the Hastings case, her phone number and address were leaked on the Internet. She was inundated with phone calls and drop-in visitors seeking her help. Families of missing persons from all over the country, private detectives—even a few furtive law enforcement agencies that made it clear she was their last resort.

She moved last month, got an unlisted number and a new e-mail address.

It isn't that she no longer wants to work as a psychic detective—or that people haven't offered exorbitant fees for her services.

On the contrary, she doesn't charge at all. She doesn't have to, thanks to family money. She lives very comfortably off the interest of her trust fund.

But there are only so many people she can help, and she intends to stick with the old routine: Inspector Neal Bullard of the Philadelphia Police Department tells the families of missing persons about her, and brings her on board if they're interested.

They usually are, regardless of whether they believe in this stuff. People whose loved ones have vanished are desperate enough to try anything in order to bring them home.

"Here we are," Jimmy Molinero, at the wheel beside her, announces as they pull up at the curb beneath the exceptionally dim yellow glow of a lamppost.

Some people probably find the district's old-fashioned street lights charming. Lucinda will take the bright white wattage of modern fixtures any day.

"Home, sweet home." Jimmy puts the Mercedes into park and gestures up at the three-story brick townhouse.

Lucinda murmurs in agreement, reluctant to admit that she feels about as at home here as she did on the Dutch Antilles island of Curaçao, where the two of them just spent the long President's Day weekend.

Their rented Caribbean villa was picturesque and upscale. But it wasn't . . . comfortable. She wasn't comfortable. She couldn't quite relax, despite day after leisurely day spent in abundant warm sunshine with attentive staff doling out cocktails mixed with the island's namesake liqueur, the same inviting shade as the sparkling Caribbean Sea.

Truly, there was no reason for her not to feel as though she had landed in paradise.

It wasn't the place, though.

It was the company.

She gazes out the window at her building, bathed in the soft white glow of a waning moon and a luminescent dusting of snow.

She's been anxious to get back here practically from the moment she left. Now that she's arrived, she finds herself inexplicably on edge.

But—like it or not—this is her home now. And it was almost like coming full circle, settling into the second floor apartment of a nineteenth century townhouse in one of the oldest—and probably wealthiest, too—neighborhoods in the Northeast.

Not that Lucinda herself has ever lived in this particular area before. But she's willing to bet that her Sloan ancestors once inhabited these elegant, centuries-old homes, going right back to Philadelphia's Colonial days.

"Your mother will be thrilled when she finds out where you've landed," her friend Bradley commented when he helped her move in.

"That's why I'm not going to mention it."

Bradley knew the deal with her family, having also grown

up in—and been expelled from—Main Line society, albeit decades earlier.

He peered at her over the cardboard dish carton he was holding. "Pretty childish of you, don't you think, darling?"

"Absolutely. But I can't help it."

Bitsy Sloan has a way of bringing out her daughter's unreasonable, petty side.

"I don't suppose you've got any of that pretty blue liqueur hanging around your kitchen for a nightcap?" Jimmy asks her, obviously interested in prolonging their long weekend.

"Fresh out," Lucinda says quickly—maybe too quickly, judging by the hurt dismay in his eyes.

"I was just kidding. I didn't actually think you had—"

"Oh, I know. Listen, I do have coffee," she offers. "If you want to come in for a cup."

After all, Jimmy went all out this weekend: plane tickets to the island, meals at the nicest restaurants, a chartered diving trip to Bonaire. . . .

Poor guy.

He means well.

He just isn't . . .

An image of another man flashes into Lucinda's brain.

She sighs inwardly.

Okay, so Jimmy isn't Randy.

But Randy isn't here; he's a two-hour drive away from Philadelphia, on Long Beach Island. And God knows he isn't available.

Jimmy—a good-looking, twice divorced corporate lawyer with two teenaged daughters—is.

He deserves a chance, remember? That's why you made yourself go out with him in the first place.

She and Jimmy met entirely by chance, literally bumping into each other on the courthouse steps a few days after New Year's. They both had their heads bent against a bracing wind, both happened to be running late, both apologized profusely—and moved on.

"We've got to stop meeting like this," she heard a voice say a few days later in a Starbucks a few blocks from there, as she was waiting for her triple shot mocha with triple whipped cream.

She looked up and—surprise!—there he was again. What a coincidence. They chatted over coffee, and she was pleased when he asked her out. Particularly since he had no idea who she was—heiress to the Sloan fortune, or otherwise.

In the wake of last summer's media splash, she's had her share of attention from guys who wanted to date a Sexy Soothsayer Superhero. All of them had turned out to be opportunists in one way or another, not unlike the gold diggers who pursued her in her privileged youth.

Jimmy was pleasantly clueless. He didn't recognize her from the papers or television, and when she told him her last name, he didn't ask, "Are you one of *the* Sloans?"

It wasn't until she left Starbucks that she started having second thoughts about accepting Jimmy's invitation to go to dinner. As the date drew nearer, she found countless excuses why she shouldn't date him. She actually called to cancel at the last minute, but lost her nerve when his voice mail picked up.

The first date was fine. It led to an impulsive second—and more retrospective reluctance on Lucinda's part, but she convinced herself she was just out of practice. Dating one of the most eligible bachelors in Philadelphia wasn't such a horrible idea, given the state of her love life.

And now, six weeks later, here they are.

Not necessarily a couple . . . but a little too close for Lucinda's comfort.

"Coffee sounds good. Do you have decaf?" Jimmy asks hopefully. "Because I don't drink caffeine after four o'clock. It keeps me up all night, makes me crazy."

We wouldn't want that.

"No decaf, sorry."

It's the truth, she notes, defending herself . . . to herself.

Not that she can't offer him some other decaf beverage . . . but to his credit, Jimmy gives up more easily than she expected.

"Then I guess I'd better get going. I should call my kids and tell them I'm back in town, and I've got to unpack and repack for a business trip."

Maybe he, too, is aware that there's just no chemistry.

He insists on escorting Lucinda and her luggage inside, leaving the silver Mercedes idling at the curb. Not necessarily a great idea in any urban neighborhood, but if she points that out, he might take it as an invitation to turn off the ignition and stick around after all.

Anyway, she's noticed that he treats all the trappings of his wealth with the same casual disregard. He's got money to burn—that's what Neal Bullard said about Jimmy when Lucinda introduced the two men just last week.

She hadn't necessarily expected the crusty old detective to hit it off with a guy whose idea of dressing down is exchanging black wing tips for black Gucci loafers. In fact, maybe that's why she had impulsively suggested that her longtime colleague—and, okay, father figure—join her and Jimmy for lunch at Morton's that day. Maybe she wanted a good reason to stop seeing a perfectly nice guy.

Neal, who has lived all his life over in Two Street, and for a good part of it raised a large, tight-knit family on a police detective's shoestring budget, wasn't thrilled to see Jimmy leave most of his Porterhouse entree on the plate.

"Erma could turn that hunk of beef into cheese steak sandwiches to feed all my kids and grandkids for a coupl'a days," he later grumbled to Lucinda, who is well-acquainted with—and impressed by—Mrs. Bullard's domestic thrift.

Naturally, she welcomed the criticism with a quick, "You're right, I should stop seeing him."

"I didn't say *that*." Neal raised a bushy white eyebrow at her.

He knows her too well. Knows Randy, too. The three of

them worked dozens of missing persons cases together back in the old days, before Randy moved away to Long Beach Island.

She told Neal all about what happened out there last summer, of course. All except the part about sparking old feelings for Randy.

But she didn't have to elaborate.

Neal is a wise old guy.

And Jimmy is a nice, not-quite-as-old—though nearly a generation older than Lucinda—guy, and in the end, she couldn't come up with a good enough reason not to go away with him. He's well-traveled, well-mannered, well-spoken. A natural athlete, he skis, plays tennis and golf, and owns a sailboat he keeps moored—coincidentally—on Long Beach Island.

"You'll have to come sailing with me when the weather gets nice," he said, and she imagined herself there with him, running into Randy.

Then she wondered whether she's going to spend the rest of her life doing this—comparing every man she meets to the one who got away.

Lucinda flips a light switch and picks up her mail in the lobby, then she and Jimmy climb the steep, narrow staircase. At the top, she pulls her keys from her pocket, juggles the mail under her arm, and reaches for her bag.

"I can take that from here, thanks."

"Oh, I've got it."

"But your car is running."

"That's good for the engine, after sitting idle in the cold parking lot for days. And what kind of jerk would I be if I made you carry your own bag?"

"It's not that heavy," she reminds him—echoing his own words when he lifted it from her bed before they left for the airport on Friday night.

"I've never seen a woman pack so little for an entire

weekend," he comments now, with admiration—still carrying the bag.

She shouldn't be irritated that he didn't hand it over. He's just being polite.

But Lucinda likes to do things for herself.

She gets the impression that Jimmy's two ex-wives and teenaged daughters do not. And that they travel with suitcases full of resort wear in tow, unlike Lucinda, who figured a weekend in the Caribbean required nothing more than a couple of pairs of shorts, flip flops, and a bathing suit. Which was true. Although, when she found herself wearing the same T-shirt to the pool a few days in a row, she figured she might have underdone it, just a little.

Jimmy didn't seem to mind that Lucinda hadn't been entirely outfitted by Tommy Bahama before the trip. In fact, he kept complimenting her on whatever she was wearing. He also complimented her on being so low-maintenance. And, one night when she'd had too much rum, he actually complimented her on her dancing—which, in retrospect, casts serious doubt on his overall sincerity.

Too many compliments.

There are worse problems, she reminds herself.

As a rule, she doesn't do guilt. Yet somehow, Jimmy manages to bring it out in her.

"What does your week look like?"

"Crazy, as usual." Not really. She sticks the key into the deadbolt. "How about yours?"

"Crazy, as usual. I've got to fly away again tomorrow."

Right. His business trip. He's mentioned it a few times over the weekend. She should probably ask him where he's going, but that would prolong the conversation and she's tired.

And I don't really care.

Why, oh why, can't she make herself care? Life would be so much easier if she fell in love with Jimmy. He's the kind of guy she could even bring home to her mother.

And that, in a nutshell, is probably why you'll never let yourself fall in love with Jimmy. Nice, Lucinda.

Very healthy.

Very mature.

"Let's get together for dinner next weekend," he says.

It's more a suggestion than an outright invitation, so she can't exactly say no. You can't answer a question nobody's asked.

Whatever. She should probably see him at least once more. Let him down easy.

And, hey, you never know. Maybe he'll start to grow on you.

He leans in and kisses her on the lips.

Nah.

"Thanks for everything, Jimmy." She reaches around the doorjamb and turns on an interior light. "I had a really nice time."

"So did I. I'll call you."

Something snaps inside of Lucinda. Before she can stop herself, she hears herself saying, "I don't think we should see each other anymore."

Jimmy's dark eyebrows shoot toward his equally dark hairline—both expertly salon dyed, she suspects.

"I'm so sorry," she says helplessly. "It just doesn't feel right."

She debates adding a cliché line to soften the blow. Like "It's not you, it's me"—or maybe something about wanting to stay friends.

But that's not true. She doesn't want to stay friends. It would be awkward. And it *is* him. He's not her type. She can't change that.

"I'm surprised you feel that way, Lucinda. I thought things were going well, and you just said you had a nice time. . . ."

I lied.

I'm an idiot.

"I'm sorry," she says again. "You're a great guy, and I'm really glad we met. I just . . . can't. Do this."

"It's okay." With a sad smile, he waves a black leather gloved hand at her and heads down the stairs.

Lucinda steps into her chilly apartment, kicks the door closed, leans against it, and heaves a tremendous sigh of relief.

Jimmy will be fine, she's sure.

Maybe it was cruel to cut him loose on the heels of a lavish weekend trip, but spending so much time together made it obvious to her that it wasn't going to work. Wouldn't it have been more cruel to lead him on even a little while longer?

Maybe not. Who knows?

"I stink at relationships," she announces to the empty room. "But it had to be done."

"Oh, geez, now I'm talking to myself," she adds. "Pathetic."

She pushes her weight off the wall with her foot and turns on a lamp before turning off the overhead light.

There. The place seems a little cozier and more welcoming . . . although she still isn't entirely comfortable. Turning up the heat will help . . . but that's not all that's missing.

On the plane this afternoon, she felt anxious to get back to Philadelphia. Now she wonders why. This quiet place feels isolated compared to her old neighborhood.

That's not all. Something else is bothering her tonight, here. She can't put her finger on what it is.

She's certainly used to coming home to an empty apartment. She's been doing it all her adult life. In fact, she's always reveled in it, after years of living under the tight reins of her parents, her nannies, and teachers at the Millwood Academy.

Tonight, though, she feels uneasy about being alone.

Guess what? You're probably lonely. Admit it. You need someone to talk to. Someone other than Jimmy.

Someone like Bradley, who hasn't been back to Philly in over a month. He's not one of her oldest friends—well, other than age-wise—but he is one of her fondest, ever since they met at his cousin's society wedding and hit it off instantly as fellow pariahs.

He was sitting alone, and so was she. The next thing she knew, they were laughing, then cutting up the dance floor.

"How is it that we've never met before?" he asked as he whirled her around.

"Oh, I don't go to these things very often if I can help it—even if I happen to be invited. I'm the family black sheep."

"So am I!" he exclaimed delightedly. "Disowned eons ago. You?"

"Not disowned, exactly. More like . . ."

"Shunned?"

"Exactly." She didn't bother to tell him that she was both shunnee, and shunner.

"What was your crime?"

"My parents couldn't accept who I am, or my lifestyle."

"Same here! You're gay, too? And in the theater?"

"No . . . psychic."

"I love it!" he screamed.

Bradley's extended family—those in his own generation, anyway—have apparently felt no monetary obligation, though they do keep in touch. Not that anyone made an effort to speak to him at the wedding, Lucinda noticed.

Yes, she misses Bradley, she acknowledges as she removes the rubber band from the bundle of mail in her hand and flips through it.

She misses Cam Hastings, too. She's away this week on a ski trip with her husband's family—one that, as she privately admitted to Lucinda the last time they spoke, she wasn't particularly looking forward to.

Lucinda and Cam forged a fast friendship, the way people do when they're thrown together under unique circumstances. Like boarding school, or summer camp, or . . .

Or using psychic impressions to catch a serial killer.

All in a day's work for Lucinda. For Cam, not so much.

She'd never talked to anyone about her so-called gift. Nor had Lucinda, really. Not on an intimate, note-comparing basis. It was a relief to both of them to realize that someone understood.

Lucinda drove up to Montclair every couple of weeks throughout the fall to visit her and Mike and Tess. Then, just before Thanksgiving, Cam gave birth to a baby girl. She got busy, the weather got bad, Lucinda moved to her new place. . . .

She hasn't seen the Hastings family since Christmastime, nor spoken to Cam in over a week.

Thank God for Neal, Lucinda thinks as she throws her coat on a hook. He's right here in Philly, and he's not going anywhere—even though his wife Erma retired last June and has been begging him to do the same.

"What would I do with myself if I retired?" he frequently asks Lucinda.

"You'd relax, and spend time with your family." Neal has six grandchildren, including a newborn, with yet another on the way.

"I already spend time with them. Constantly. And I don't like to relax. Relaxing makes me nervous."

Typical Neal.

And typical me. Lucinda isn't big on relaxation, either. She moved into this apartment mere weeks ago but has long since been unpacked, put away, organized, even decorated— if you can call hanging a few framed black-and-white prints on the wall *decorating*.

There's still a lot to do, but she'll get it done. She's always been full of nervous energy—fueled, no doubt, by liberal daily doses of caffeine and chocolate. Not the healthiest of habits, but hardly the worst.

She makes a mental note to take her iPod out of her coat pocket later. She should return it to the docking station Bradley bought her for Christmas, after she mentioned that she was always losing track of it.

What a waste to bring it to Curaçao. She had downloaded
a couple of new playlists in advance of the trip, hoping to
relax and tune in on the plane, on the beach, on the ocean-
front balcony. . . .

But Jimmy likes to talk. A lot.

Yes, cutting him loose was definitely the right thing to do.

She kicks off her sneakers and leaves them beside several
other scattered pairs on the mat next to the door. Then, carrying her luggage and the mail, flipping on a couple of lights
to dispel the shadows, she detours to the kitchen. There, she
sorts through the mail and finds a cardboard sleeve from an
online media store, addressed to her.

She orders books and DVDs from there pretty frequently,
but not in the last week or so. Was something back ordered,
and she forgot about it?

She opens the envelope and pulls out a DVD.

She reads the title aloud, perplexed. *"Moonstruck?"*

She saw it years ago, and it's on television all the time.
She definitely didn't order it. Must be a mistake.

Looking at the invoice, she sees that it was ordered online
through her account, and billed to the credit card she keeps
on file there.

Must be a mistake. She puts it aside to deal with later.

The only other thing of interest is a letter from Norwegian Cruise lines.

Lucinda's eyes widen as she reads it.

Well, how about that.

Last summer, when she called customer service after she
missed her scheduled Alaskan cruise, she'd been told that
because she hadn't purchased trip insurance, she was out the
several thousand dollars she'd paid for seven days in a luxury suite.

Looks like customer service was wrong.

According to this letter, she's been rebooked on a cruise
for this summer, in the same luxury suite. All she has to do is

call the customer service telephone number listed on the letterhead, give the reference number, and confirm the dates.

I'll do it right now, before I forget.

She picks up the phone and dials the number.

"Norwegian Cruise lines," a cheerful male customer service rep says. "How may I help you?"

"I just got a letter about rebooking an Alaskan cruise for this June because I had to cancel last year at the last minute. I was originally told that I wouldn't be able to rebook, so I was a little surprised by this."

"When last year was your cruise scheduled?"

"In August, on the *Norwegian Star*."

"We only sail to Alaska during the summer months, and we're usually sold out through September. Whoever you spoke to should have explained that it was too late to rebook for last summer, but we can certainly get you on one of this summer's first Alaskan sailings."

"Oh, well, she didn't explain that. I thought it was a lost cause."

"I apologize. Do you have the name of the person you spoke to? I'd be happy to look into it for you."

"No—it's all right." Lucinda probably should have asked more questions. "Let's just confirm the new date."

"I'll be glad to do that for you. Do you have a reference number?"

She gives it to him, hears him clicking away on a computer keyboard.

All these months, she'd thought the trip was a loss. Typical misinformed customer service reps.

"All right, Ms. Sloan, we have you in suite 11520 on the *Star*, same as before. The new sail date is June fourteenth, and your confirmation number is IP061411520."

She grabs a pen and pad and jots it down. "Thank you. Do you need anything else from me?"

"No, you're all set. We'll send your confirmation and

your new ticket a few weeks before sailing. All you need to
do is show up. You have a good night now."

"You, too."

Wow. That was easy. Thinking about Alaska in February
isn't particularly appealing, but she'll definitely be looking
forward to it by June. Too bad it's such a long ways away.

She grabs a Three Musketeers bar from the freezer before
heading into the bedroom.

Even without shoes, her footsteps seem to echo through
the drafty rooms. The place has hardwood floors, high ceilings, and lots of tall windows that probably need draperies,
if Lucinda can bring herself to obscure some of the scarce
winter daylight.

There's no daylight now. There is moonlight, which she'd
be able to see if she turned off the interior lights. But she
won't, of course, so there's only glare on the glass.

She'll have to do something about the windows soon.

And about the leaky faucet she can hear in the bathroom.

Odd, because she could swear she turned it off tightly to
stop the dripping before she left Friday night. She even used
a wrench. Now, when she stops to examine the faucet, she
finds that the handle turns easily.

How did that happen?

When she takes the wrench from the gilt-mirrored medicine cabinet and forces the handle as far back to the right as
she can—the way she did Friday night—the dripping ceases.

Frowning, she waits a few minutes to make sure.

No drips.

Wrapping her fingers around the handle, she tugs it hard
enough to turn the faucet on, then turns it off just enough to
stop the flow, the way one might if he or she were unaware of
the leak.

After a moment, a droplet of water plunks into the sink.
Moments later, another.

*Okay, you don't honestly believe someone came into the
apartment while you were gone and used the sink, do you?*

Maybe it loosened on its own, then. Whatever.

Shaking her head at her own dubious expression in the ugly gold-framed mirror, she tightens it once more, stashes the wrench in the cabinet again, and leaves the bathroom.

Back in the hall, she turns up the heat on the thermostat, and hears a prompt hissing through the registers. There. That's better. With the chill gone, and lights on, she'll feel more at home.

It's really a nice apartment. Nicer than her last place. Just not Lucinda's style. The crown moldings and antique fixtures—major selling points in the real estate ad, along with newly replaced wiring and—ha—upgraded plumbing—are a little too fussy for her taste. And the place has a musty yesteryear smell she's still getting used to. It reminds her of rainy days and old books and her grandmother's cedar closet. Not unpleasant. Just . . .

Not my style.

It's getting to be a refrain.

The apartment, Jimmy . . .

What is my style?

No, she immediately cautions her wayward brain, *don't you dare go there again. Married men are not your style.*

In the bedroom, she turns on two more lamps, then drops her bag between the wicker hamper and the bureau.

As she transfers her clothing from suitcase to laundry or drawer, she clenches the unwrapped candy bar between her front teeth. Every so often she bites into the crisp chocolate and frosty nougat, then expertly reaches out to catch the candy bar before it drops to the floor. In no time, she's devoured the whole thing, her suitcase is empty . . . and she's still feeling unsatisfied. Unsettled.

Well, there's a lot to do.

I need to start a load of laundry. I need to check my e-mail. I need to find my charger and charge my BlackBerry.

But before any of that, she needs another Three Musketeers. She starts for the kitchen again.

Then, seeing something out of the corner of her eye, she stops short.

Slowly, she turns back toward the bed.

Lying in the center of the puffy white duvet is something that wasn't there before she left on Friday.

The truth hits her, hard, even before she steps closer to see what it is.

Someone was in her apartment while she was gone.

Chapter Two

Lucinda doesn't call Neal about the intrusion right away.

She wants to—desperately—but she hates to disturb him at home, at night, on a holiday weekend.

That's part of the reason.

The rest of it has to do with her own irresponsibility.

She should have changed the locks when she moved into the apartment. Any fool knows to do that.

Recklessly, she ignored that basic precaution.

And now, she's paying the price.

She might as well deal with it on her own, the way she's dealt with pretty much everything else that comes her way.

This isn't a leaky faucet, though. Nor is it a cupboard mouse, or a flat tire—both of which she has also recently handled on her own, thank you very much.

This situation is far more disturbing. Maybe even dangerous.

This time, she needs help.

From whom?

Not Bradley. He's in New York.

Not Cam. No need to alarm her yet.

The police?

Neal *is* the police. He'll know what to do.

At last she allows herself to pick up the phone and dial his number. Erma will answer, of course. She always does, usually on the first ring. She's the chatty type. Neal hates the telephone.

But it's his gruff voice that greets Lucinda, and only after several rings.

"Neal, I'm sorry to bother you. . . ."

"Are you okay?"

Hell, no.

"I am, but . . . somebody broke into my apartment while I was—"

A piercing scream erupts in the background on Neal's end of the line.

"Hang on a second, Cin." She hears a rustling against the receiver as he covers it with his hand. Then his voice, only slightly muffled, bellows, "Cut that out, Maeve! Poppy is on the phone!"

He returns to the line with a brusque apology.

"I didn't realize you had the grandkids there," Lucinda says, wishing she hadn't disturbed him. "I'll let you get back to babysitting, Neal, I didn't mean to—"

"No, it's okay. Someone broke into your place, you said? How did they get in?"

She hesitates. "I have no idea. I can't tell."

But chances are, they had a key, unlocked the door, and walked right in.

"Did you call the police?"

"I called you."

"A robbery should be reported, Cin."

"I know, but . . . it wasn't a robbery. They didn't take anything. They actually . . . *left* something."

"What is it?"

Lucinda hesitates, looking at the scrapbook still sitting in the middle of her bed.

"Maybe I should show it to you in person," she tells Neal. "I know you're busy, but maybe tomorrow, if—"

"The hell with tomorrow. Come on over. Or do you need me to come there instead?"

"No, I can come," she says hastily. He has the kids, and anyway, she doesn't want to spend another moment alone in this apartment.

She hangs up the phone, still not entirely convinced she's alone here, even though she's checked all the closets, under the bed, and behind all the doors and the shower curtain—armed with a chef's knife, trembling, like a soon-to-be victim in one of those teen slasher movies.

The only difference is that the frightened females on-screen always, inexplicably, go from room to room in the dark.

Not Lucinda.

Every lamp, every overhead fixture, every bare closet bulb in the entire apartment is now ablaze.

There are no more shadows. There is no place for the boogeyman to hide.

But he was here.

With a shudder, she grabs her coat and her keys, then remembers to pull on her gloves again before picking up the scrapbook. Years of working police investigations made her do that even before she touched it the first time. Fingerprints.

Leafing through the album, she was initially bewildered by the chronology of photocopied newspaper clippings mounted to the thick paper pages—each one featuring a beautiful college-aged woman who had committed suicide.

They appeared to have lived, and died, months, years, miles, worlds apart; Lucinda had no idea how they were connected to each other, much less to her.

Then she spotted a familiar face in one of the photos, and the latter became clear.

It was Cam's sister, Ava Neary.

*   *   *

Not far from Society Hill lies the leafy South Philadelphia neighborhood now known—post revitalization—as Pennsport.

Lifelong resident Neal still refers to it by its bygone name, Two Street—when he isn't reminiscing, fondly, about the "shanty town" of his distant youth. Or grumbling about the new crop of up-and-comers who have commandeered the early nineteenth century homes, installing solar panels, hot tubs, stainless steel, and granite.

"The whole neighborhood is a construction zone," he frequently complains to Lucinda. "A man can't even drive down his own street because of all the contractors' trucks parked all over the place."

Neal bristled when his elderly next door neighbors put their home on the market last fall. Tonight, after emerging from the subway and covering the short distance to Neal's house, Lucinda notes the FOR SALE sign has disappeared from the adjacent lawn.

Either the place sold, or the neighbors changed their minds about moving. For Neal's sake, she hopes for the latter.

A bracing wind stirs the tree branches overhead, heavy with the scent of wood smoke wafting from the Bullards' brick chimney and most of the others in the neighborhood. Shivering and hugging the scrapbook against her chest, Lucinda remembers why she's here.

The same ripple of fear that had her constantly looking over her shoulder on the way over causes her to keep a furtive eye on the shadowy shrub border as she hurries to the front door of Neal's modest two-story home.

A total stranger answers the door.

Oops.

"I'm sorry. . . ." Lucinda steps back to look up at the house number, illuminated in the glow of the porch light. "I must have the wrong house. I was looking for—"

"The Bullards? You're in the right place." The man—balding, graying, somewhere around retirement age, wearing denim overalls—holds the door open for her. "Come on in. You must be Lucinda."

"Yes." And he must be . . .

She really has no clue.

"I'm Garland Fisher," he explains, shaking her gloved hand. "I just moved in next door."

"Oh! It's nice to meet you."

"You, too. Say, that's some moon up there, isn't it?"

She looks over her shoulder to briefly admire, beyond the bare tree branches, the fat white orb hanging low in the sky.

Just like in the movie *Moonstruck*, she finds herself thinking—the memory triggered by that DVD that mistakenly arrived earlier.

Though tonight's moon, in its waning phase, looks as though someone sliced a crescent from its curved surface.

"Neal's trying to get the grandkids into their pajamas," his neighbor informs her as she steps over the threshold. "Said for me to tell you that he'll be right down and for you to make yourself at home. Told me to do the same thing when I popped over a few minutes ago, but really, I just need to borrow a wrench. Got a leaky faucet in the kitchen. Old houses . . . You know how it goes."

She does. . . . But how does he know that?

Of course there's no hidden meaning in his words—no hint of a knowing expression in his pale blue eyes as they gaze at her from behind a pair of wire-rimmed bifocals.

He's just a nice man making conversation, nothing more.

He certainly didn't break into Lucinda's apartment while she was away, tamper with her own leaky faucet, and leave behind a scrapbook filled with dead women. Of course not.

"Was out all day, and walked in a little while ago to find my sink full of water," he confides, plopping himself down on the couch in the Bullards' familiar gold wallpapered living room.

Familiar to Lucinda, that is. She can't help but notice that newcomer Garland Fisher really is making himself right at home amid the family photos and 1970s era furniture, with the air of one who belongs.

"All my tools are still packed—just moved in last week— and darned if I didn't open half a dozen boxes, looking for a wrench, before I decided it would be easier to just borrow one. But it looks like poor Neal has his hands full with those kids. Sounds like it, too," he adds, casting a glance at the ceiling as running footsteps scamper overhead.

"I'm sure he does."

"Got a couple of grandkids myself," he confides. "They live with my son and daughter-in-law out in California."

"Is that where you moved from?"

"Oh, no. Lived in Philadelphia all my life."

Watching Garland Fisher cross his legs and drape an arm along the back of the couch atop Erma's homemade doilies, she again notes that he's a little too comfortable here for someone who's so new to the neighborhood.

"Lost my wife last spring," he adds. "She was just sixty-six. We were high school sweethearts, had been together forever."

"I'm so sorry."

He nods. "Couldn't stand living in our house without her. People say a widower shouldn't make a move for at least a year, but me, I've always thought a change of scenery is good for the soul. Helps you heal. So here I am. New house, new neighborhood, maybe even new career. Always wanted to be a writer, and now I've got a couple of stories accepted by a magazine."

"Really? Congratulations. Which magazine?"

"You probably never heard of it. One of those literary short story publications. Pays in copies, not cash—but hey, my name and my work will be in print. That's what counts, right?"

"Absolutely," she agrees, discarding her paranoia in favor

of the theory that he's simply an exceedingly affable, harmless, lonely old guy.

Mentioning a leaky faucet and a wrench wasn't a veiled message that he was behind the album in her hands. That's ridiculous.

Although when his eyes flick down at it, held stiffly on her lap in her gloved hands, she finds herself growing tense all over again.

"That a photo album?" he asks.

Technically it isn't, but she nods anyway and fights the urge to put it behind her back.

"Come over to show Neal some pictures, did you?"

Footsteps pounding down the stairs save her having to reply.

Neal's twin redheaded, freckled grandchildren, Maeve and Sean, skid into the room wearing footie pajamas.

"Hi Lucinda!" Sean—whom his grandfather calls a shameless little flirt—looks thrilled to see her. "Guess what? I lost my front teeth!"

"I see that. Very cool!"

He grins broadly, then hollers, "Poppy! Lucinda's here!"

Maeve has already busied herself over by the fireplace, picking up a poker and jabbing it into the dying embers beyond the folding glass door and screen.

"Whoa there, I don't think that's a good idea, young lady!" Garland, surprisingly spry, is on his feet and taking the poker out of the child's hand before Lucinda even realizes what she was up to.

"No! I want that! It's mine!" Maeve protests, grabbing at the poker.

Garland staunchly holds it out of her reach.

Sean looks at Lucinda. "Want to know a secret Maeve told me? The tooth fairy isn't real."

Lucinda shakes her head. "Maeve, guess what? A secret isn't a secret unless only one person knows it."

"Ah, truer words have never been spoken."

Lucinda looks up to see Neal in the doorway.

As always, she's momentarily taken aback at the sight of him in casual clothes: a flannel shirt, jeans, and suede slippers. What's left of his salt and pepper hair tufts on the crown of his head, probably courtesy of a child's playful fingers, and his green eyes, deeply set beneath bushy white brows in a weathered face, are tired.

"Maeve! You stop that," he scolds, and takes the poker from Garland's grasp.

"I'm a cowgirl. I have to cook my supper over the fire."

"You already ate your supper, cowgirl, and fires are dangerous." Neal sets the poker in the wrought iron stand on the tile hearth, then glances over at Lucinda.

"I hate to bother you when you have your family here, Neal. I didn't know they were coming this weekend."

"Neither did I. Erma and I went to visit them in Scranton Saturday, and Patty and the kids decided to ride back with us for a few days. Then tonight Erma decided they needed some mother-daughter time, so they went out to dinner and left the kids with me."

"Even the baby?"

"Not the baby. Her, they took with them. Why not? She doesn't do anything but sleep, eat, and crap. But these twins are a handful lately."

"Where's Jeff?"

"Back in Scranton, on E.R. duty all weekend." Neal turns his attention to his new neighbor. "I'll go to the basement now and grab that wrench you wanted, Garland. Sorry about the wait."

"No rush. Take your time."

"After that, Maeve and Sean, you two can sit here and watch Noggin and keep yourselves out of trouble while I talk to Lucinda in the other room." Even as he says it, he glances worriedly at the fireplace.

"Don't think that's a good idea." Garland voices the thought on Lucinda's mind—and probably on Neal's as well.

"All right, then, Lucinda and I will talk in here, and you two kids will go wait in the kitchen."

Right. With the stove and the knife block and all kinds of food they can choke on. Lucinda opens her mouth to tell Neal she'll just catch up with him tomorrow, but Garland speaks first.

"Neal, how about if I sit here and watch TV with the kids while you and your friend go talk in the kitchen?"

"You don't have to—"

"What else have I got to do?" Garland shrugs. "My leaky sink can wait. When you're done with your visit, I'll take the wrench and be on my way."

"Thanks, Garland."

Lucinda follows Neal to the kitchen, past a glass cabinet that holds Erma's collection of Willow Tree figurines, a table cluttered with little wooden Cat's Meows, and a shelf lined with thimbles from around the world. Not that Erma's been any of those places—she asks friends to bring them back to her.

Neal is always grumbling about Erma's many collections, but Lucinda notices that he seems to enjoy adding to at least one of them on every gift-giving occasion. Just last week on Valentine's Day, he'd shown Lucinda a silver bracelet dangling with dragonfly charms he'd bought for Erma, who—of course—collects dragonfly jewelry: pins, earrings, pendants.

The Bullards' affectionate marriage is so different from her own parents'. The only thing her mother collects is designer handbags, and every time Dad buys her one, Lucinda suspects, he also buys one for his longtime mistress.

Neal kicks the swinging kitchen door shut behind them. "Sorry about the mess in here."

"It's not so bad."

Erma ordinarily keeps a neat house, but the remnants of supper—and perhaps lunch, too—are on the countertops and sink. Crumbs litter the floor, several apple magnets have fallen off the fridge door—Erma collects apples—the throw rug in front of the stove is askew, and one of the blue gingham check curtains that frame the back door window is missing a tie-back.

"Want some tea?" Neal asks, turning on the flame beneath the copper kettle on the stove. "I'm making some for myself."

"Thanks. . . . We should make this quick, though, so that your neighbor can be on his way."

"I just hope we don't go back into the living room and find him roped to a chair with a fire burning at his feet."

She can't help but grin at that. "The kids aren't so bad."

"No, they're just . . . creative. With active imaginations. That's what Erma keeps telling me. Good thing Mr. Fisher hasn't been hanging around here all day, or he wouldn't have offered to keep an eye on them."

"He's a nice man."

"Seems that way. Little too folksy for me, though," Neal adds in a whisper, and she can't help but smile.

Folksy about sums up Garland Fisher, from the overalls to his pronoun-dropping speech pattern.

Folksy—and harmless.

"Have a seat and I'll be right back. I want to go grab that wrench from my tool box before I forget." Neal disappears through a doorway and down the stairs into the basement.

Lucinda sits at the table. She's shared many meals here with Neal and Erma, a motherly homebody with an innate need to feed people.

Quite the opposite of the fashionably skeletal Bitsy Sloan, who exists mainly on lemon water and watercress and believes others should do the same.

Back from the basement, Neal puts the wrench on the counter beside an open loaf of Wonder Bread and jar of peanut butter, then sits opposite Lucinda.

"Let me see what you have there." He gestures at the scrapbook.

Lucinda lays it carefully on the kitchen table between them. "I found this on my bed when I got home—I was away this weekend, remember?"

"With that guy Jimmy." He nods. "Someone broke in while you were gone and left this?"

"Well, I don't know that they 'broke in.' I mean, the door was locked, so . . ." She pauses, hearing running footsteps and giggling. Uh-oh. The kids are on the move.

Neal ignores it, focused on the matter at hand. "So someone has a duplicate key."

"It looks that way. Or maybe they came in a window. Some of them don't have locks, and there aren't any bars, or anything. And—well, the thing is, I didn't have the door locks changed, either, when I moved in," she admits, and waits for him to scold her.

"Lucinda, don't tell me that after all these years of living in the city you—"

"I know, I know. I'll talk to Peggy tomorrow."

"Who's Peggy?"

"The super."

"A woman super?"

"Yes, and we can vote, too." She opens the scrapbook. "I want to show you—"

She breaks off at the sound of a loud crash somewhere at the front of the house.

"What the devil . . ." Neal bolts from the kitchen, with Lucinda on his heels.

A shattered vase lies on the floor beside a table in the front hall. Garland and Sean are on the stairway, peering over the bannister.

Seeing them, Neal asks, "Where's Maeve?"

"Don't know. . . . She kept asking if we could play hide and seek. Told her no, we were watching TV, and the next thing I knew she was gone. Sean and I were just looking for her."

"Maeve! Where are you?"

"I didn't do it, Poppy," a small voice announces, and Lucinda spots Neal's granddaughter peeking around the doorway in the living room.

She looks so traumatized that Neal's expression immediately softens. "It's okay, Maeve. It was an accident."

"But I didn't break it. The man did."

They all look at Garland. "You did me a favor," Neal says. "I never liked that vase, and Erma has so many knickknacks around here that you can't make a move without—"

"Not *that* man."

"Wasn't me."

Simultaneously interrupted by both Maeve and Garland, Neal breaks off, confused, looking from one to the other.

"The other man did it, Poppy," Maeve explains, still half-hidden—almost cowering—behind the door frame.

"Which man?"

"He was scary. I was hiding over there." She points at the corner behind a coat tree draped in winter garments. "He didn't see me."

"Who?"

"The scary man," she says impatiently.

"What scary man?"

"The one who opened the door. He knocked the vase off the table and then he closed the door."

Neal looks at Lucinda. "Active imagination is right," he mutters, and she smiles sympathetically at both him and Maeve.

When Lucinda was young, she herself was often accused by her family of having an active imagination. That's what you get when you see things nobody else can see and know things you can't possibly know.

Lucinda is pretty sure Maeve isn't a budding psychic, but she feels a kinship to the child nonetheless.

Neal goes over to Maeve and crouches beside her. "I don't mind that you broke the vase, but I do mind that you're lying about it."

"Lying is bad," Sean announces from the stairway above. "Mom says liars don't get dessert."

"I'm not a liar, Sean!"

"You are too!"

"I am not!"

Lucinda begins picking up the shards of broken pottery as Neal referees and Garland surveys the situation, probably grateful that his own grandchildren live across the continent.

During the first lull, he clears his throat and announces, "Really should get going. . . ."

"Oh, Garland—" Crouched beside a frustrated Maeve, Neal looks apologetically up at his neighbor. "I'm sorry, I left the wrench on the counter in the kitchen. Go ahead and grab it."

"Thanks, Neal. I'll let myself out the back door then." He takes a down jacket from the coat tree, shrugs into it, and pulls on a knit navy blue ski cap and matching gloves. "Nice meeting you, Lucinda."

"You, too." She waves with the hand that isn't full of broken shards.

Neal goes back to trying to reason with the kids as Garland disappears into the kitchen. A moment later, Lucinda hears the back door open, then close behind him.

Neal gives up on trying to reason with Maeve, who is still insisting she didn't lie, and Sean, who is still insisting he's going to tell their mother. He sends the kids back into the living room and Noggin, then turns to Lucinda, still picking up pieces of the vase.

"I'll get that, Cin. You'll cut yourself."

"It's fine. I've got it. Lucky thing I never took my gloves off, see?"

He nods. "We'll take that photo album to be dusted for fingerprints tomorrow."

"I knew you were going to say that."

"It'll have to wait until afternoon, though. I have to drive Patty and the kids back to Scranton."

And none too soon, she suspects. "Do you really think

they'll find any prints—any that match anything in the data-
base, I mean?"

Neal shoots from the hip, as always. "Hell, no. But you
know we have to check."

"I know."

Lucinda straightens and heads toward the kitchen with
the broken pottery, suddenly exhausted. She isn't eager to
head back home to her apartment after what happened, but
what choice does she have?

As if he's read her mind, Neal falls into step behind her,
saying, "Stay here tonight with us, Cin."

For the briefest moment, she entertains the possibility.

"No," she tells him, "I can't. You already have a houseful,
and anyway, I have to go back there sooner or later."

"You can't be sure it's safe."

"This time, I'll lock the windows. And I'll chain the
door." *After* she checks under the bed and in the closets
again, just to be sure she's alone.

"Wait for Erma, at least, so that I can come back with you
and check things out."

Again, she shakes her head.

Tempting as the offer is, she can't let herself take him up
on it. He's been through enough tonight, and he has a long
round-trip drive ahead of him tomorrow.

"I really want to get home to bed," she tells him. "I'll take
the album with me. Call me when you—"

She breaks off, staring at the kitchen table.

The scrapbook is gone.

On the table, in its place, is a piece of paper.

Stepping closer, Lucinda sees that it reads:

74.2
39.6

That's it. Just a pair of decimal numbers, one on top of the
other, in the center of the page.

* * *

"But why would Garland have stolen the scrapbook?" Neal asks Lucinda, shaking his head as he hands her a mug of strong hot Irish tea. "It doesn't make sense."

"I know it doesn't. All I'm saying is that he walked through the kitchen on his way out the door. No one else was in here, and we would have noticed if one of the kids had left the room."

"Possibly."

"Probably."

Neal shrugs and sits across from her, sipping his own tea.

Lucinda has never been a big believer in circumstantial evidence. Too many times, her own intuition has led her to look beyond the obvious—with fruitful results.

Too bad her intuitive gifts seem clouded by her own involvement in this case. Aside from having sensed something wrong when she walked into her apartment earlier, she hasn't had any psychic impressions of who left the book in her apartment, or why someone stole it away again and left the cryptic message in its place.

"I still think the sheet of paper fell out of the scrapbook when you put it on the table," Neal tells her.

"But I went through it a couple of times, and I never saw it."

"Maybe you missed it."

Maybe she did. But if it had fallen from the album's pages, it might have landed upside down, or on the floor. . . .

The way it was found, lying face up, margins almost precisely perpendicular to the edge of the table, makes it seem far more likely that someone deliberately placed it there.

"Why don't you tell me what was in it, before we jump to any more conclusions."

"There were articles and pictures of several young women who died years ago. They were all college students. And they all committed suicide, supposedly."

"Supposedly."

"Right. Ava Neary was one of them. Camden Hastings's sister—remember?"

"Yes. You were all over television, talking about that case."

"Don't remind me." She sighs. "I was trying to help. I thought maybe somebody who knew something would see it and come forward."

"Looks to me like somebody did." Neal's face, creased with age yet still handsome, is grim. "I don't like this."

"You're not the only one."

"So the scrapbook was filled with newspaper articles?"

"Not original clippings. They were photocopies. Someone probably made them from a microfiche of the old newspaper pages or printed them off the Internet."

"All suicides are initially investigated as homicides, Cin. You know that, right?"

"I do, but the cops investigating them didn't have the big picture. They're all isolated cases, handled by local police in seven different jurisdictions. It doesn't look like anyone even connected the victims—other than in this scrapbook."

"It was a lot easier to miss patterns in the days before computers, and to miss signs of foul play. Forensics back then might as well have been nonexistent compared to what we have today."

"I know. And there were similarities in these cases that might have raised a red flag if anyone had connected them."

"Like?"

"Like all of the women were young and pretty, with long, straight hair parted in the middle."

"It was the early seventies, right? That's what everyone looked like."

"They all used particularly violent means to kill themselves. One drove her car off a cliff, a couple of them hung themselves, some jumped to their deaths, one even shot herself in the mouth."

"That's unusual. Men tend to kill themselves using violent means. Not women. Women swallow pills. Shut themselves in a garage with the motor running. That sort of thing. There are exceptions, but . . ." He shakes his head.

"Exactly. And in every one of those reports, if you look at the quotes from the people who knew the victims, nobody around these girls saw it coming. The suicides happened out of the blue. Some of them left notes, but they were typewritten."

"Isn't that a surprise."

"Neal, if the same person who killed Ava Neary killed the rest of them . . ."

Neal nods. "We might have a serial killer on our hands."

"Well, *we* don't. I mean, this all happened decades ago. But it does seem like someone wants us—*me*—to tie it all together."

"Let's just hope whoever managed to get into your apartment didn't play an active role in any of it."

"I doubt it. Why would the killer want someone to solve the murders?"

"Some serial offenders leave clues or even communicate with the authorities, as if they consciously—or subconsciously—want to be caught. But that's usually not really the case. More likely, what they want is attention. Even anonymous attention. They're starring in their own scripted drama."

"More like pulling the strings in a puppet show."

"Exactly. They want to demonstrate that they're in control. That's what it's all about. Control. Power. They'll tease the authorities into coming close, dangerously, oh-so-close—and then slip away again, to show who's in charge."

But I'm not the authorities, Lucinda thinks.

And anyway, forty years have passed since the first so-called suicide was committed. Hearing from the killer now doesn't fit a typical pattern . . . does it?

"Maybe it wasn't the killer who left me this scrapbook, Neal. Maybe one of the victims' family members saw me on television, and wanted me to know that Ava wasn't the only one."

"I don't buy it. Even if the person wanted to remain anonymous, he could have just called the police hotline number."

"Seeing all those women together in a scrapbook was pretty powerful stuff, though."

"Then why not mail it to you?"

"I don't know."

"I do. Someone wanted to scare the hell out of you, Cin."

"Well, they didn't succeed."

Neal just looks at her.

"All right, maybe they succeeded just a little."

She sips her tea, hating that this happened to her, hating that she's scared.

"How much do you know about this guy Jimmy you've been seeing?"

Startled by Neal's abrupt question, she considers it—and realizes it's one that's been in the back of her own mind ever since she found the album on her bed.

"For one thing, I'm not seeing him anymore."

"I thought you just—"

"I told him tonight when we got back that it's not going to work out."

"That's good. I wasn't crazy about him."

"No way, really?" She smiles faintly, but only for a moment. "You don't think he did this . . . do you?"

Neal throws up his hands. "After all these years in this business, Cin, I wouldn't put anything past anyone. You know that."

"Jimmy was with me all weekend, though. He picked me up Friday night to take me to the airport, and he brought me home again tonight."

"Okay . . . so you had your eyes on him the whole time he was in your place?"

"Tonight, yes. The other night . . ."

"The other night, what?"

She shakes her head. "I'm not sure. We were running late for the flight, and I was making sure I had my passport and watering the plants and all that last minute stuff. . . . He was in my room because he carried my bag and that's where I had it, but . . . I just wasn't paying attention. I can't remember if I was in there after he was, or not."

"So if he was the last one out of your bedroom, he could have left the album on your bed."

"He could have . . . but it would have been pretty damned risky, don't you think?"

"You know as well as I do that some people—dangerous people—thrive on the thrill of taking risks."

"Jimmy isn't one of them. Trust me."

But how can you be sure? You only know what he's told you. What he's shown you. You've never even met anyone else in his life, never seen his kids or heard them call him while you were with him, never seen where he works, or lives. . . .

How do you know any of it is true?

"Just be careful around him, Cin, if he tries to get in touch again."

"I will." The mere thought that Jimmy could possibly be behind this—as a prank, or something more sinister—is far more disturbing to her than she lets on to Neal.

She's always been a good judge of character. Goes with the territory when you're a psychic. She's reasonably sure Jimmy didn't do it.

But not a hundred percent sure, are you?

Lucinda has never had much trouble falling asleep, despite all her nervous energy. Or, perhaps, because of it. Most nights, she falls into bed exhausted and is typically out cold within minutes of hitting the pillow.

Not tonight.

She can't stop thinking about the missing scrapbook.

She has no idea what the numbers mean, but one thing is clear: Lucinda is being followed. Watched.

That alone is enough to keep her awake into the wee hours.

Not that she fears a stranger is lurking in the apartment with her now. She examined every inch of the apartment when she got back here, holding her BlackBerry with a worried Neal connected on the other end of the phone line.

"No Boogey Man," she assured him before hanging up, forcing an upbeat tone into her voice.

She's pretty sure Neal didn't buy it, because he asked her, one last time, if she was sure she wanted to spend the night here alone.

"I'm absolutely positive, Neal."

And she absolutely was.

Still is.

This is, quite simply, how she operates. Lucinda Sloan doesn't run scared, and she doesn't rely on other people to bail her out of tough situations. Where would she be if she did that?

Back on the Main Line, living off her parents' money, and under their thumbs.

No, thank you. She's been taking care of herself ever since the day she moved out of their stone mansion for the last time, after years of coming and going from boarding schools and college dorms.

Whatever is going on here, she'll handle.

Even if I am secretly scared shitless and have to sleep with the light on.

She rolls onto her back and stares at the cracks in the plaster ceiling, once again going over every detail.

One thing keeps nagging at her: Maeve's comment about a man breaking the vase.

There's no doubt that the child has an active imagination.

But what if she was telling the truth?

*   *   *

He smiles as he leafs through the scrapbook, this time with bare fingers chapped blotchy red from the relentless cold.

He had forgotten, over all those insulated years in prison, how harsh the elements can be. Had forgotten how wind off the water can slice like a knife; can rub raw the skin over joints until it splits and bleeds.

Maybe he should wear gloves more often—not just to prevent leaving fingerprints.

No need to worry about that now that the scrapbook is back in his possession, though.

No need to worry about anything from here on in.

Things have fallen into place like clockwork in the past couple of days.

Clockwork.

His grin broadens at his own cleverness.

What did she make of his first little clue: the numbers?

Could she possibly have figured out what they mean?

No . . . but she will, soon enough.

And soon enough, she'll discover the second clue he left her. Not tonight, though.

First thing tomorrow morning. He'd bet his life on that. He's been watching her long enough to know she's a creature of habit.

Standing abruptly, he carries the scrapbook over to the hearth. After moving the screen aside, he jabs at the logs with a wrought iron poker, stirring the red-hot embers back to life, enjoying the crackling sound.

When the blaze is good and ready, he opens the book one last time, to the page that shows Ava Neary's photo.

"Thank you, sweetheart," he softly tells her.

Then he tosses the scrapbook onto the fire and watches the ferocious flames lick her smiling, unsuspecting face.

Chapter Three

On this dismal winter morning, there's no real sunrise. The rectangles of sky beyond Lucinda's bedroom windows simply go from black to charcoal and finally to a sodden gray, signaling that it's safe for her to turn off the bedside lamp.

Feeling as though someone took a loofah to her eyelids, she gets out of bed and laces her fingers at the nape of her neck, stretching. Her entire body aches with tension, but sleep is a lost cause.

She dozed off at some point in the night, but not for long, and it was a restless sleep marred by a reoccurring dream she's had lately.

In the dream, she's always working a big wooden jigsaw puzzle. It's almost done, but for some reason, she can't tell what it's supposed to be; the picture has worn off the box. She fits one piece after another until she gets to the end—and realizes one piece is missing. She looks everywhere for it, but it's nowhere to be found, and without it, she can't tell what the picture is.

It makes no sense, of course. One missing piece wouldn't make a puzzle picture ambiguous. But dreams have little logic;

unless she finds the missing piece, all her work has been for nothing because the puzzle has no meaning.

Whenever she wakes from this particular dream she feels exhausted—though today, she'd probably feel that way regardless.

Grateful for the light of dawn, dim as it is, Lucinda goes into the bathroom to brush her teeth.

Her reflection in the medicine cabinet mirror catches her off guard. The fluorescent lighting is harsh, emphasizing the dark circles beneath her eyes and the haunted expression in them.

She quickly opens the mirrored door to get the toothpaste and leaves it open as she brushes her teeth and splashes water on her face, not wanting to look at herself.

An immediate caffeine fix is in order.

She goes to the kitchen, opens the fridge, grabs a can of Pepsi, and chugs some. Not exactly the breakfast of champions, but the sweet fizz is just what she needs first thing every morning—particularly this morning.

When she ordered it for breakfast the first morning in Curaçao, Jimmy looked at her as though she'd just asked the waiter to score her some heroin.

"*Pepsi*? At this hour?"

"We're in a different time zone."

"Yeah, an hour ahead of Philly."

"Whatever. I drink Pepsi for breakfast. Sue me." That was the first time she wished she were back in the slushy, muddy Northeast, but it wasn't the last.

Remembering what Neal said last night about Jimmy, she decides it's a very good thing she impulsively broke it off last night. Just in case . . .

Just in case he happened to have killed Ava Neary and a bunch of other innocent girls back in the sixties and seventies?

That's hardly likely. How old can he be? A couple of

decades older than she is—but he's been pretty vague about his age.

For all she knows, he was twelve when Ava was killed.

Or maybe he was twenty—around Ava's age.

Troubled, Lucinda takes a stack of fluted white paper filters from the cupboard and separates one.

Wishing Cam weren't skiing somewhere out West, where it's still the middle of the night, Lucinda is planning to call her cell phone later. Cam should be told about the scrapbook. Told, warned—just in case someone has been prowling around her as well. At least she's safely out of town for the time being.

As Lucinda fits the filter into the black plastic basket she tries—as she's been doing all night—to remember the details about some of the women who appeared in the scrapbook before it was snatched away.

She clearly recalls two of the victims' entire names.

One is Sandra Wubner. The girl bore an incredible resemblance to Ava—even more so than the others. Lucinda read her story with particular interest.

Sandra Wubner hung herself while she was babysitting for a little girl, who found her body. The child's mother told the police her daughter said Sandra's boyfriend had been over that night, which he later denied, even providing an alibi.

Lucinda can't remember his name, or that of the family for whom Sandra had been babysitting, but she's pretty sure it was Italian. And she's positive Sandra Wubner lived—and died—in Buffalo.

The other memorable so-called suicide victim was Elizabeth Johnson. Lucinda had known an Elizabeth Johnston back in boarding school. When she was skimming the scrapbook the name jumped out at her, and she did a double-take before seeing that it was Johnson. No T.

Common name.

She can just imagine how many hits she'd find on a search engine. At least she knows that this Elizabeth—like her old friend—was also from suburban New York City. Westchester, maybe, or Connecticut. She wishes she could remember where, but she can't. One of the shore towns. Rye? Darien? Where was it?

Yawning deeply, she measures coffee grounds into the filter basket. Instead of making half a pot—all of which she drinks herself on an ordinary morning—she decides to go for the full twelve cups. She'll need it.

About to fill the glass carafe at the tap, she notices something inside, resting on the bottom.

Frowning, she opens the lid.

What on earth?

It's a ring.

She pulls it out to examine it.

A signet ring, engraved with an elaborately swirled letter *Z* and caked with something dried and brown.

As Lucinda holds it, a vision sweeps her thoughts.

A woman.

She's lying on a tile floor in a pool of blood, face frozen in terror. . . .

Familiar face.

Eyes wide open . . .

Familiar blue eyes . . .

As quickly as it came over her, the vision disappears.

Gripping the edge of the sink, Lucinda realizes she's just seen the corpse of Randy Barakat's wife, Carla.

Cam gently settles the pink-wrapped bundle into the cradle.

"There," she barely whispers. "Go back to sleep now. It's early."

She touches her baby's face to make sure the fever hasn't come back. No—she's over the worst of it: her first cold.

Cam tiptoes into the hall and closes the door to the baby's room, right next door to Tess's room. If only little Grace would sleep as soundly as her big sister does.

Teenagers, Cam knows, are biologically disposed to sleeping in. But half past noon—which is what time Tess came downstairs yesterday—is a little extreme, even for a weekend.

Of course, Tess was then up until all hours last night, rattling noisily around the house and waking the baby after her midnight feeding.

As a result, Cam threatened to wake Tess at the crack of dawn today—if only to ensure that she'll be good and tired tonight.

Then again, it's nice to have the house quiet, all to herself for a change. Maybe she'll let Tess sleep just a little longer.

Cam pads back downstairs in her robe and slippers and wonders whether to bother making a pot of coffee. She got out of the habit for all those months when she was pregnant and she and Mike were separated—and got back into it when he moved back home, especially after the baby came.

Grace is a fussy baby, and a light sleeper, snoozing only for a few hours at a time even now that she's over three months old. The pediatrician said she's no longer waking in the night because she's hungry, but Cam isn't about to let her lie there and cry.

So she continues to get up around the clock, and whenever she does, she feeds her daughter—because the baby always takes it and maybe the doctor is wrong.

Standing in her big, beautiful kitchen—stainless and granite and custom cherry cabinetry, all appreciated daily and a far cry from the dingy apartments where she was raised by a single father—Cam yawns deeply and surveys the coffeemaker.

It seems like so much trouble to brew a whole pot just for one person.

Mike is away, skiing in Utah with his parents, brothers, and their families. Cam and the girls were supposed to go with them, but then Grace got sick, and the pediatrician thought the plane trip might be painful for her ears with all the congestion. Tess, who ordinarily would have jumped at the chance to go skiing, jumped instead at the chance to stay home and "help." Cam has no illusion there. Her daughter wasn't looking forward to being away from her boyfriend for a week. Now she doesn't have to.

Mike, too, would have stayed behind, but Cam wouldn't let him. How could she? His family's annual February family trip was, last year, the bone of contention that ultimately triggered their marital separation. Trouble had been simmering for years, though: a bitter brew of resentment, secrets, and booze.

Cam drank to block out the visions that had tormented her since childhood: visions of people, mostly kids, in danger. She didn't dare tell anyone, not even Mike, afraid he would decide she was nuts, just like her mother had been, and that he would leave her—just like her mother had done.

It had been hard enough for Mike to defy his father's expectations and marry a girl like her in the first place. Staying in the marriage, despite Cam's drinking and the labyrinth she'd constructed to protect her secret, wasn't easy for him.

Now the walls have come down, and she hasn't had a drop of liquor in almost a year, and although the troubling visions continue to pop up, she deals with them—with Mike's support and understanding.

Her marriage is back on track. Not perfect, not easy, but working for them both—much, Cam assumes, to her father-in-law's dismay.

Mike's father has never liked Cam—never liked anyone, really, as far as she can tell, but her family background made her lower than low on his list. Michael Hastings, Senior, was hardly thrilled when his son married a Jersey girl with a hard-living bar band rocker for a father and a mother who had disappeared onto the streets of Camden, New Jersey, when her younger daughter was barely out of diapers.

Last summer, Cam found out what happened to her mother after she left them. She now knows where Brenda Neary lived—and where she died.

But the nagging questions about what had happened to Cam's mother were almost immediately replaced with more disturbing questions about her sister.

Revisiting Ava's death after all these years—in such a troubling manner—came completely out of left field. But Cam doesn't doubt Lucinda Sloan's claim that her beautiful, capable older sister—who had everything to live for, and who promised never to leave Cam after their mother did— didn't really kill herself.

She does believe that Ava was murdered.

Difficult as it was to face the media spotlight in the wake of Tess's encounter with a homicidal lunatic last summer, Cam was hopeful that it might lead to the truth about Ava. That somebody, somewhere, would recognize her picture on television. That Ava's fate, too, would be laid to rest.

They did hear from a couple of people who had known Ava at NYU. Cam and Lucinda had spoken to all of them; while they expressed how shocked they had been by her suicide, no one had solid information indicating that it had been anything else.

There were false leads, too. More than a few crackpots came out of the woodwork. Now, months later, there has been nothing at all. After getting her hopes up, Cam has come to accept that she'll probably never find out who was responsible for her sister's death.

She's grateful to know, at least, that it wasn't Ava herself. That Ava hadn't broken her promise never to leave Cam.

Not like her mother.

Not like her father, Ike, who did his best to raise her, but who was more attached to the band and the bottle than he was to being a dad.

Not like Mike.

"You have some serious abandonment issues," her marriage therapist told her in a recent session. "Everyone you've ever depended on has left you at one time or another."

Even Mike.

Of course he came back, and they're in a good place now—
better than ever before—but there will always be a nagging
fear, in the back of Cam's mind, that everything they have
could disappear tomorrow.

"You can't think that way," Mike told her when, in a counseling session, she confessed the persistent shred of misgiving.

"I can't help it. People come and go—sometimes by choice,
and sometimes not." She was remembering how close they had
come to losing Tess. "You can't guarantee that you'll be here
forever, Mike."

"If it's up to me, I will be."

But it might not always be up to him. Life is precarious;
you can't know what lies in the future—or even right around
the corner.

Ironic for a psychic to have come to that realization.

So really, all Cam can do when it comes to the people she
loves—all anyone can do—is hold on tight, and hope.

But when it comes to Ava—maybe all she can do is let go.

Had it been a decent hour when his cell phone rang,
Randy might have recognized the Philadelphia area code on
Caller ID and had the presence of mind to ignore it.

Instead, groggy with sleep, he finds himself answering it.

"Randy. It's Lucinda."

The sound of her voice catches him off guard. Or maybe
it's not her voice as much as his own reaction to it. Even
after all these years.

Years? It's been mere months since he last spoke to her.
He called just before Thanksgiving, ostensibly to see whether
she'd had any news on the Ava Neary case.

She hadn't, of course. She'd have let him know if there
had been any new developments . . . wouldn't she?

Maybe not.

Maybe she had concluded—as he initially had—that they
were better off keeping a safe distance from each other.

How many times did they attempt that in the old days before falling into each other's arms again?

It was Neal who pointed out the obvious back then. Neal, who had pretended to look the other way for so long; Neal, who rarely said much of anything that wasn't directly related to their police work.

Long-married, fiercely devoted family man Neal.

"You have to go," he told Randy one day. Man of few words. One minute, they were discussing a case—or rather, Neal was talking, and Randy was pretending to listen while watching Lucinda through the glass window of Neal's office.

"Go where?" Randy figured he'd missed something, that Neal wanted him to go investigate some detail of the crime.

"Away. For good."

"What are you talking about?"

"You have to go. Because of her." Neal, back to the window, jerked his thumb in Lucinda's direction.

Neal was right. If Randy couldn't have her, he couldn't be near her. He had to move on.

And he had tried. For years.

When he called Lucinda that cold November day, he'd been planning to feel her out, maybe to suggest that they see each other so that she could fill him in on the case and he could fill her in on his own life.

But she rushed him off the phone, saying she was on her way to see Cam and Mike's new baby.

Ever since, amid all that's been going on, he's been waiting for the right time to reconnect.

He never expected Lucinda to beat him to it.

"Hey, what's up? How are you?" he asks, trying to sound casual.

There's a pause on the other end of the line.

"I just . . . Is Carla there with you?"

She knows, he realizes. *That's why she's calling.*

Or does she?

How would she?

His heart pounds. "No."

"Are you at home?"

He hesitates.

"No," he says again. "She is, though. I'm in Tahoe. Skiing. I came out for the long weekend with a couple of buddies."

Silence on the other end of the line. "When was the last time you talked to her?"

Oh, hell. He doesn't really want to do this right now. Not from here. Not like this.

"Last night," he lies. "Why?"

She ignores the question, asking another of her own. "When are you going back home?"

Never.

"In a couple of days."

"Randy . . ."

She knows he's lying.

She knows the truth.

Why else would she be asking these pointed questions?

"Yeah?" He holds his breath, waiting.

But the confrontation doesn't come. She says only, "I'll let you get back to your . . . skiing."

"Lucinda, it's five in the morning here. I'm not skiing."

"Oh! Right. I'll let you get back to sleep then. I never would have called if I had known you were in a different time zone. Sorry, Randy."

"No worries."

No worries?

Where did that come from? He's never used that phrase in his life.

He's noticed Californians say it all the time, though.

And you are in California, he reminds himself.

Never mind that *no worries* hardly describes his current frame of mind. Let Lucinda think he's having a good old time in his rented Tahoe chalet and hanging out on the slopes.

For now, anyway.

Sooner or later, she'll learn the truth.

Restless, Cam moves around the kitchen, making coffee after all.

Her gaze falls on a stack of mail on the counter, unopened for at least a couple of days—probably since Mike left on Friday.

She had forgotten, in fifteen years, how chaotic it can be to have a newborn in the house. How the most mundane things—opening mail, unloading the dishwasher, returning phone calls—can be neglected for days on end.

After pouring water into the coffeemaker and pressing start, she sits at the table, determined to at least sort the pile so that she can weed the junk—credit card offers, catalogues—from the "real" mail, which in this age of electronic correspondence will all be bills, of course.

Bill, bill, bill . . .

Ah, something that's neither a bill nor, as far as she can tell, junk.

The envelope is postmarked in New York City and affixed with a typed white address label that, oddly, bears her name. Her whole name—Camden Neary Hastings.

That's the odd part—the *Neary*.

Most people in her life these days don't know her maiden name. Those who were in her life back in the old days when she used it, have long since drifted away.

Frowning, she turns the envelope over, looking for a return address.

There isn't one.

When she opens it, she finds out why.

Lucinda had been so sure she'd find Randy at home with Carla; that her vision had been a terrible mistake.

Or had she?

Come on, Lucinda. There's a ring in your coffee pot, for God's sake!

A ring in her coffee pot and a corpse in her mind, as vivid as if she'd stumbled across it in person.

Never in her life has her sixth sense shown her a dead person who wasn't already dead . . . or soon to be.

Why would you think that might have changed now?

She knows the answer to her own question.

When she'd first seen Ava Neary being pushed from that rooftop in a vision, she had mistaken her for Cam's daughter, Tess.

Then Tess went missing, and Lucinda knew, beyond a shadow of a doubt, that there would be no happy ending.

But there was.

Maybe there will be again.

But what are the odds that Carla Karnecki Barakat has a lookalike who happens to have been murdered on a bathroom floor somewhere?

Her head spinning, Lucinda looks at the signet ring.

Where did it come from?

And what is that brown stuff on it?

Could it possibly be . . . blood?

But it can't be Carla's ring, can it?

Not with the initial *Z* on it.

Neal—I have to call Neal.

He's still got the grandkids today, and that long round-trip drive to Scranton, and it's still so early.

Bradley. He'll be up. He'll know what to do.

She quickly speed dials his cell phone from her Black-Berry, noticing, as she does, that her battery is down to one bar. She forgot to charge it last night.

The phone rings a few times, then goes into voice mail. "You've reached Bradley Carmichael. Please leave a message, and I'll call you back."

Dammit. He's probably on a treadmill or something.

"Bradley. It's Lucinda. Call me."

She knows he checks his voice mail religiously. An aging musical theater actor, he's been out of work since before the holidays, other than a department store Santa gig.

For years, he performed on Broadway. He loves to share anecdotes about the hit musicals he's been in: *My Fair Lady, Guys and Dolls, Mame*. Now his audition prospects are growing fewer and farther between, and he needs every job he can get.

Lucinda turns off her BlackBerry to conserve the battery and starts opening drawers, looking for the charger.

She plugs in the phone, then paces some more.

She could call Neal . . . but after last night, she'd feel terrible if she disturbed him without a good reason.

A ring in your coffee pot is a damned good reason!

Yet maybe her vision of Carla means nothing.

Maybe it wasn't a true vision at all.

There's only one way to find out, Lucinda realizes, and heads for the bedroom to get dressed.

Still in his robe and slippers, carrying a cup of coffee, Vic makes his way to the den, bypassing the television set and his recliner, where he spent all those idle months last year before Kitty came up with her brilliant idea.

"Why don't you do that?" she asked one night over dinner, as he told her about the investigative journalist he'd seen interviewed on the news program that morning.

"Why don't I do what? Solve the Amelia Earhart disappearance?"

"No," Kitty said patiently. "Why don't you write a book about one of the unsolved cases you worked on?"

"I can't do that."

"Why not?"

"Because I'm not a writer."

Kitty just looked at him.

He rubbed his unshaven jaw, looking back at her.

The next morning, he sat down in front of the computer instead of the television.

And so it began.

"Even if I never get this thing published," he told Kitty, a couple hundred pages in, "at least I feel productive again."

"You'll get it published."

Over Thanksgiving, they visited their daughter Melody in Manhattan. One of her friends happens to be a literary agent. At Melody's urging, and with reluctance, Vic suspects, she agreed to take a look at his work in progress.

He sent it to her a week later and promptly found himself negotiating with a major publisher by Christmas. Press releases went out after New Year's, announcing the upcoming publication of his book, *On the Night Watch*, chronicling his career obsession with a notorious serial killer.

The book isn't slated for release until next year, and his official deadline is still months away. But he's almost finished with it. Before it goes to his editor, it has to be submitted to FBI headquarters for a review, to make sure he isn't venturing into classified territory.

Vic only wishes he could write a different ending—one that doesn't involve the Night Watchman fading into the shadows, eluding capture.

"Mom? What are you doing?"

Hearing Tess behind her, Cam gasps.

Her coffee—her third cup—sloshes all over her robe and the slate floor of the sunken sunroom off the kitchen, where she's been patiently waiting for a decent hour to call Lucinda Sloan—or Mike, in the mountain time zone.

Actually, she tried Mike's cell earlier, heedless of the hour, but he must have been sleeping too soundly to hear it. She couldn't bring herself to call the main line of the condo he's sharing with his family. Waking everyone before dawn would require some kind of emergency, and that's not what this is.

"Geez, Mom, sorry. I didn't mean to scare you to death."

Tess is wearing sweats and sneakers. Her hair is pulled back in a somewhat stubby pony tail, with loose strands escaping to frame her hazel eyes. For months now, she's been growing out the layers of her thick, light brown hair, but it's a slow process. Cam suspects that her boyfriend is the motive for Tess's trading her longtime sporty style for something a little more feminine.

They've been dating since the ordeal last summer that brought them together.

He's a good kid, with the maturity to actually look Cam in the eye when she enters the room, and call her Mrs. Hastings.

But Tess with a boyfriend—at fifteen—has taken some getting used to.

At least she no longer goes to school with him. As committed as Cam and Mike were to public school, they opted to transfer her back to private last September. It wasn't just because she'd had a falling out with several of her closest friends—or because they wanted to keep her away from her new boyfriend.

But after all she'd gone through—from being abducted to breaking her leg to being the focus of all that media attention, even if she never appeared on-air herself—they concluded that a fresh start was in order.

She didn't return to the prestigious Cortland Acadamy not far from Montclair, where she'd gone to school through eighth grade.

Instead, they'd sent her to an even more prestigious—but somehow, much lower key—all girls school in Manhattan. She joins Mike on his commute to the office every day. Rather than wait around for him after school, she takes the train back home again, and Cam picks her up at the station.

Initially, they had set her up with a car service, desperate to keep her safe at any cost. But after a few weeks of that, Tess begged to be allowed to take public transportation.

"All the kids do it, Mom," she informed Cam, the hold-out.

Cam doubts that. But Mike thought some independence was a good idea, and so did the child psychiatrist Tess was still seeing back then, to help her process all that had happened.

In the end, Cam relented. If Tess wants to be independent, the more power to her. After all she went through, they're lucky she didn't emerge a cowardly basket case. No one would blame her if she were.

"What are you doing?" Tess asks now.

"Where are you going?" she asks Tess in return, because it's easier than explaining that she's waiting to call Mike and tell him that something very strange—and frightening—showed up in the mail over the past few days. Which day, she hasn't a clue.

She hopes it won't matter later.

She hopes this is just another prank, sent by another loser belatedly coming out of the woodwork.

"We're going for a run," Tess explains.

Cam doesn't have to ask who the other half of "we" is.

"It's freezing out, Tess." Cam bends over to wipe the spattered coffee from the floor with the sleeve of her terry cloth robe, which is already covered in baby spit-up and going into the dirty clothes hamper, anyway.

"The physical therapist said that running is good for my leg as long as I stretch before and after."

True enough.

"You wanted me to get up early."

Also true, but . . .

"You didn't even eat breakfast." And the world is full of crackpots. And some of them are dangerous.

"You know you're not supposed to eat right before you run, Mom."

She does know—not that she's been doing much running lately.

She probably should be.

She has another twenty pounds of baby weight to shed. Apparently, it doesn't come off without a struggle when one is pushing forty.

When she said as much to Dr. Advani at the last checkup, the Ob-Gyn reminded Cam, "You're only thirty-seven. Be patient. It'll come off."

Maybe.

Right now, she has other things to worry about.

And having Tess out of the house for a while might be a good thing.

"Go ahead," she says. "Be careful."

"I'm always careful, Mom."

Yes, she is. Now. She learned the hard way.

Cam listens to Tess leave, and the house settles again. Not a sound but the hum of the refrigerator in the next room and the mantel clock, ticking away the minutes.

It's still too early to call Mike . . . but not Lucinda.

Cam dials her apartment and gets the voice mail.

"Lucinda, it's Cam. I . . . need to talk to you. Call me when you get this."

She hangs up, tries Lucinda's cell. Voice mail again. She leaves the same message.

Uneasy, she hangs up the phone and reaches into the pocket of her robe, making sure it's still there, that she didn't imagine it.

No.

Still there.

A photocopy of Ava's obituary—and block lettering scrawled across it:

I KNOW WHAT HAPPIENED TO HER. SOLV IT AND IF YOU ARE WRIGHT YOU WILL FIND ME.

Yes, it could be yet another crank—yet another one who can't spell very well, at that.

But—call it a psychic impression, call it paranoia—something about this note feels different to Cam.

Maybe it's the timing—coming months after the media coverage of Ava's case.

Or maybe it's the unsettling fact that the note wasn't type-written, or even done in ink.

No, it appears to have been written—oddly enough—in red lipstick.

Chapter Four

The sky hangs low and bleak over Long Beach Island today; wisps of mist waft in the air like wraiths drifting about a midnight graveyard. Down beyond the dunes at the end of the block, the windswept sea reminds Lucinda of a child's crayon scratch art: hints of purplish blue and greenish gray color barely visible beneath a black surface.

Randy's house, a low, gray-shingled ranch, gives off an air of desertion not unlike neighboring cottages that have been obviously abandoned for the winter.

But here, there are signs of off-season life: storm windows. A shovel and a bucket of Ice Melt on the step beside the front door. Several newspapers wrapped in mud-spattered blue plastic bags sit ominously at the end of the driveway, behind a Toyota bearing a New Jersey license plate that reads RBNME.

Obviously a vanity plate, but it takes a moment for Lucinda to find the presence of mind to decipher it.

RBNME . . . ?

Oh.

RBNME . . .

As in *R.B. 'n me . . .*

Randy Barakat and me.

Carla's car.

Lucinda parks behind it.

Randy, who once drove a Jeep with the top down and music blaring, drives a dark-colored sedan these days.

Lucinda knows this because she's ridden in it—but only on official business, when they were looking into the disappearances on Long Beach Island.

Sitting beside him in the front seat last summer, with the radio playing—not blaring, but loud enough—and the windows rolled down and the salt air in her hair, she was sometimes tempted to close her eyes and pretend, just for an instant, that they were involved in something other than police work.

But she never really let herself do it.

Nor did she take Randy up on his invitation for her to come stay here with him and his wife, when she checked out of the less-than-comfortable Beach Haven bed and breakfast.

"Don't you think that would be a little awkward?" she asked him at the time.

"For whom? Carla doesn't know."

"For you," she told him. *"For me."*

"I wouldn't feel awkward at all," he informed her.

Ouch.

Apparently, that meant he was over Lucinda.

Or so she assumed at the time.

Randy wrote down his address and home phone number for her before they parted ways the day he invited her to stay.

"In case you change your mind," he said.

"I won't," she said, pocketing it anyway, and she didn't.

Not long after, though, she came to realize that she wasn't the only one harboring old feelings. Nor was she the only one behaving herself despite them.

What would she have done if Randy had thrown caution to the wind and made a pass at her?

She doesn't like to think about that.

When she allows herself to, she concludes that she's only human, and if he had made a pass, she might not have resisted him.

But he didn't.

Which, ironically, only makes him more attractive.

Integrity.

She respects that quality in a man. He's not going to cheat on his wife. Good for him. Good for her. Good for Carla.

Carla.

Fighting the urge to back out of Randy's driveway and speed back to Philadelphia, she turns off the engine and looks at Carla's car.

So she's at home.

Why hasn't she answered the phone? Lucinda tried calling a few times from her BlackBerry as she drove out here, all but killing what's left of the battery.

Maybe Carla's screening calls.

Maybe she won't answer the door, either.

You have to at least try, Lucinda tells herself. *You drove all this way. You have to make sure she's okay.*

If she is, you have to warn her.

And if she's not . . .

She shakes her head and grimly climbs out of the car. She stoops to pick up the newspapers and tucks them under her arm as she walks up to the door, head bent against a stiff northeasterly wind.

This is crazy. What is she doing here?

There's no going back now, though. For all she knows, Carla is inside, watching her through the window.

God, I hope so.

She steps onto the black rubber mat with its nearly worn WELCOME stamp in white block letters.

Taking a deep breath, she pushes the doorbell and waits for the reassuring sound of footsteps on the other side of the door.

All is still. Too still. Eerily still.

* * *

He followed her all the way to Manahawkin, stopping just short of the causeway leading to Long Beach Island.

That's where she was headed, though. He watched her car until it disappeared into the island mist.

Incredible.

His little test proved that it really does work like she said that day on television.

Psychometry, it's called. He's been researching it.

But he can't say that he was much of a believer until now.

Bravo. Very impressive, Lucinda.

It will be interesting to see what else your magic powers tell you.

With his binoculars trained on her kitchen window, he watched her find Carla Barakat's blood-caked signet ring where he'd left it in her coffee pot, knowing she wouldn't miss it there. The first thing Lucinda does every morning is attend to her caffeine addiction.

She must have seen something when she touched that ring, or felt something, or whatever it is that happens when a psychic touches a dead person's belonging.

His first inkling that his experiment might have been a success was the look on her face when she held that ring with her eyes closed.

Then she snapped into action.

She made a quick phone call—to whom?—then threw on her clothes and headed for the door, leaving him barely enough time to scramble to follow her.

Having anticipated that she might do just that, he had a rental car ready and waiting around the corner. He'd considered simply borrowing a vehicle from an unsuspecting owner to avoid the hassle and expense, but the last thing he needs is to be chased down by a cop on the lookout for a stolen plate.

Personally, he doesn't much care for surprises—pleasant, or otherwise.

When it comes to surprising others, though, he's in his element. What better feeling is there than to see all of his laborious manipulations come to fruition in an instant: wide-eyed shock blasting across a woman's face when she realizes she's not alone after all.

Once, though, the tables were turned on him.

He'll never forget the night that his mother came walking in the door when she should have been at work, and found him washing Judy Steinberg's blood from his hands.

He didn't hear Mother come in.

"What have you done?" she began shrieking, out of nowhere.

Regrettably, his reaction to that little surprise had cost his mother her life—and ultimately cost him thirty-five years of his.

So, no, he doesn't appreciate being blindsided by a woman. Not when he's spent months of his time and energy planning and executing every intricate step, having anticipated every possible obstacle, every loophole.

That's the beauty of studying a woman's routine the way he has Lucinda's, and Carla's, and others before them.

Where once, so very long ago, he did it just for voyeuristic pleasure, now his surveillance is an important tool to be used in gaining total control. If he can anticipate a woman's movements and reactions in any given situation on any given day, he can manipulate her like a human puppet oblivious to its own strings.

Seeing Lucinda Sloan barreling toward Beach Haven on this ugly Tuesday morning has been enormously satisfying. Here is the proof that he's gained the ultimate control over her, manipulating not just her surroundings and her movements, but her thoughts themselves.

What lies ahead is going to be far more rewarding than he ever imagined.

* * *

Lucinda rings the bell again, fearing that it's too late.

Dammit.

Dammit, dammit, dammit.

Lucinda rests her forehead against the Barakats' front door, waiting in vain.

You should have told Randy what was going on when you spoke to him earlier.

She'd been about to, but she stopped herself.

She couldn't bring herself to do that to him. Not with him helpless, all the way on the other side of the country. He's familiar enough with Lucinda and her visions to have been thrown into a panic if she called out of the blue to tell him she'd had one involving his wife.

Come on. That's not the only reason you didn't tell him, and you know it.

Okay.

Maybe she was worried that he'd think she was making up stuff about Carla, because of her lingering feelings for him.

Or, worse yet . . .

Maybe she thought he'd believe the vision had been real, but that it had stemmed from her subconscious jealousy of his wife. From wishful thinking.

Maybe I believed that, too.

Did she really want something horrible to happen to Carla? Of course not.

Not consciously, anyway.

Riddled with more unaccustomed guilt, she didn't call Neal to tell him about the disturbing vision, or that she was driving out here, or about the ring.

Nor did she call the Long Beach Township Police Department to have them check on Carla. How could she? Randy's colleagues there would have been on the phone to him in a heartbeat, telling them some woman was worried something might have happened to his wife.

Whatever. Now I just need to make sure that Carla is okay, go home . . . and get myself into therapy.

She never resorted to that in the past, but if her subconscious mind is killing off her ex-lover's wife, she definitely needs help.

Still, a dark cloud hangs over the Barakat residence like a funeral shroud, and Lucinda suspects that it has nothing to do with her and her forbidden feelings for Carla's husband.

She should leave.

She should call the township police despite Randy's connection to them.

She should go home and call Neal and tell him about the strange signet ring.

She should do a lot of things—story of her life—but she doesn't.

What Lucinda does is reach for the knob and turn it, tentatively.

It's locked, of course.

After all that happened here in Beach Haven last summer, did she really expect anything different?

Now what?

At a loss, she looks around—then down at the worn WELCOME beneath her feet.

Nah.

After a moment, though, she stoops to lift the rubber corner.

It would be so easy, too easy, if . . .

There it is.

Stunned, she pulls a house key from beneath the mat.

After all that happened here in Beach Haven . . . ?

How could you let your guard down like this? she scolds Carla and Randy.

Particularly Randy. He's a cop. He worked the local case. He, of all people, knows that evil can dwell where you least expect it.

As she puts the key into the lock, she sees a fleeting image of another hand turning it—a man's hand, wearing a black glove.

Trembling, Lucinda turns the key.

Oh, Carla . . . please be okay. Please don't be dead.

Why did you hide the damned key under the doormat?

The island has always been a safe place. And with last summer's killer no longer on the loose, is it any wonder the locals have been lulled into a false sense of security?

False?

Can you really blame them?

What are the chances that lightning will strike twice in the same place?

Lucinda sucks in her breath and opens the door, then steps gingerly over the threshold.

The house is warm, and still.

This isn't good.

She can feel it.

She exhales shakily, and when she breathes in again, she knows.

The putrid miasma of death chokes the overheated air.

Gagging, she hurtles herself back out into the cold, fumbling blindly in her pocket for her BlackBerry.

As he follows the highway back west toward Philadelphia, his mind is on what lies ahead: packing and making the other necessary preparations for his trip.

It's time to take this show on the road.

Still, he really was tempted to follow Lucinda the rest of the way out to the island.

How he'd have loved to see her make an entrance on his carefully dressed scene, to hear her protesting her innocence, even as the police collect evidence that will indicate otherwise.

But for now, much as he'd love to be there to watch the drama unfold from a nice, secluded seat in the wings, he has to keep his distance.

He doesn't dare take a chance. Not with the police and Lucinda the psychic on the scene. All it would take is for someone to spot him, and . . .

Curtains for you, old boy.

Wouldn't that be a shame. After all the trouble he took with props . . . not to mention makeup.

He's been setting the stage for months.

Months?

Years, really.

All those years spent in a six by nine concrete cell, with nothing to do but think.

And remember.

And plan.

He emerged from prison ripe for action . . . and then Lucinda Sloan popped up on his television set, with those red, red lips, and there was Ava Neary—*Ava Neary!*—and he knew it was meant to be.

Why? Carla Barakat asked him, over and over, sobbing hysterically. *Why are you doing this to me?*

The last two words were key.

To me.

She didn't ask—as investigators had, all those years ago, when they were trying to determine whether he was competent to stand trial—why he felt the need to kill.

She asked why he was killing *her.*

Caught up in the pleasure of carrying out the long-planned execution, he didn't bother to explain that she was no random victim. That he simply had no choice. She had to die in order to set the plan in motion.

He probably should have told her.

Even a condemned prisoner on death row is officially informed of the reason for his sentence. It's only fair.

Carla Barakat went to her death without realizing her sentence had been set the August day he—and the rest of the world—saw the unmistakable connection between her husband and Lucinda Sloan.

Ah, well. He won't make that mistake with the next one.
He'll tell her exactly why she has to die, if she asks.
It's only fair.
But first, he has to find her.

Hearing the rumble of the mail truck on the street, Vic
hits Save, leans back from the keyboard, and stretches.
Break time.
He picks up his long-empty coffee cup and brings it to
the kitchen, leaving it in the sink with the breakfast dishes.
Today, he'll try to empty the dishwasher and reload it before
Kitty gets home. Yesterday, he lost track of time.
"It's okay," she said, wiping waffle crumbs off the counter
at seven o'clock last night, still wearing her suit and pumps
from the office. "You're on a deadline."
God, he loves his wife.
She's going to be so proud when his book comes out. His
publisher is already talking about sending him on a book
tour. Newspaper interviews, television appearances, store
signings . . .
That will be exciting.
It would be even more exciting if he could do all of that
as a hero, with the Night Watchman behind bars at last.
For all he knows, the unsub is already there, or died
thirty-five years ago.
It would be nice to know.
Nice?
It would be the culmination of his life's work, and one
hell of an epilogue.
Vic opens the front door as the red, white, and blue postal
truck rolls toward his driveway. The yard and tree branches
are blanketed in a feathery coating of white, the driveway
marred by a pair of dusted-over tire tracks from Kitty's car.
He didn't even notice that it had snowed.
"Sorry it's not shoveled," he calls to Smitty, the mailman,

as he heads up the walk carrying a bundle of letters. "Guess I'd better get to it."

"You're a rich book author now," Smitty replies with a grin. He, like everyone else in the world, saw the articles written about Vic and the Night Watchman case when the Associated Press picked up on the publisher's press release. "Get someone else to do the dirty work."

Vic doesn't tell him he has yet to receive the advance, and that it will hardly make him rich when he does get it.

With any luck, though, the amended contract will be in today's mail. His agent said she sent it to him for his signature before the long weekend.

"How's the book coming along?" Smitty asks, handing over the mail.

"It's coming along." Vic breathes white puffs of frigid air.

"Well, get back to it. See you later."

With a wave, Smitty is on his way. Vic shuts out the cold and carries the mail back toward the kitchen, stopping to turn up the thermostat.

He probably shouldn't, oil prices being what they are this winter.

But who knows? Maybe, once the book comes out, he really will be a rich author. His agent is trying to negotiate movie rights.

"It might be an easier sell if they'd caught the guy," she told him. "Like Helter Skelter. But there's a certain marketable mystique to this killer still being out there, walking among us. The guy who wrote about the Zodiac got a major movie deal out of it."

Wouldn't that be something. Vic and Kitty have gotten a lot of mileage out of fantasizing about who might play them on film.

"I think Brad Pitt should play you," she told Vic, who snorted.

"He's too young." He added dryly, "And not good-looking enough."

"He's not playing you as you are now," she pointed out. "He's playing you in the past, when you were on the case. You were young then."

Right.

Yet another reminder that nothing of note has happened on the case since.

Vic couldn't care less about marketable mystique. He doesn't want to cash in on the fact that the killer might still be out there, walking among them.

But when he said that to his agent, she told him to leave the business end of things to her.

Sitting at the kitchen table, he pushes aside the dirty breakfast plates and utensils and goes through the mail.

No contract today.

There's a brochure from Norwegian Cruise Lines, courtesy of Dave Gudlaug, who's been trying to convince Vic that he and Kitty would love cruising.

Vic said he'd think about it, but that was back before the book. Now he's got better things to do than sail around, learning to salsa dance or playing bingo or eating at buffets or whatever it is that people do on cruises.

He puts the brochure aside.

Beneath it is a legal-sized white envelope addressed to VICTOR SHATTUCK, FBI AGENT.

The label is typewritten and the envelope was postmarked in New York City, without a return address.

Vic picks up a butter knife from the table, wipes the greasy toast crumbs from the blade, and uses it as a letter opener.

He removes a single sheet of paper, unfolds it.

Two words are written in the center of the page in what looks like red lipstick.

I'M BACK.

Chapter Five

Huddled tearfully on the WELCOME mat, still clutching the Barakats' newspapers, Lucinda has no idea how much time has passed before a squad car comes wailing up to the house.

Probably only a few minutes, but it feels like hours since she called 911.

The sea air seems infused with the stench of rotting flesh and her own vomit wafting up from the shrubs beside the steps. It has taken every ounce of her strength to stay here, waiting for the authorities.

Now, thank God, they're here. She wipes her eyes on her sleeve, vaguely recognizing one of the two uniformed officers who dash from the car.

The male— who looks exactly like Harry Potter, minus the forehead lightning bolt—was around police headquarters last summer. Randy introduced him to Lucinda then, but she can't remember his name.

With him is a stocky blond female officer Lucinda's never seen before. But now isn't the time for introductions, or reintroductions.

"Look in the bathroom," Lucinda instructs them, then

buries her face in a trembling hand as they hurry past her, into the house.

Alone again, she forces herself to stay calm, to keep breathing, to stay here, on the scene.

You can do this. You can see it through. You've done it before. So many times before.

In her line of work, death scenes are inevitable.

But she isn't working. And this time, death has struck too close to home.

Oh, Randy.

He's going to be devastated.

How could this have happened?

The thought that's been flitting through her traumatized brain settles at last:

What if this has something to do with that scrapbook filled with dead women?

Did Carla's killer leave it for Lucinda—and then snatch it away?

And the signet ring she wrapped with care and locked in her glove compartment? Could it have been Carla's after all? Covered in Carla's blood?

Lucinda darts a wary glance around at the yard, the neighboring houses, the street. Everything seems deserted.

But that doesn't mean he's not here even now, watching her.

He?

It could be a she. . . .

No. It's not.

She doesn't know how she's so sure about that, but she is.

Her own intuition?

Or is it because of Maeve's scary man?

Maybe a bit of both.

The door opens behind her, and she looks up to see the female officer step out of the house, looking green. The woman gulps some air.

"Are you all right?" Lucinda asks.

"Absolutely." But when she rakes a hand through her stubbly blond hair, Lucinda sees that it's shaking.

She's probably new on the force. Not used to dead bodies.

Not like me.

Yet, does one ever really get used to the smell of death? Or the sight of it?

Thank God she didn't have to see Carla. Not in person, anyway. It's bad enough to have glimpsed the bloody scene in her vision.

"Is she dead?" she asks the cop, but the words clog in her throat, barely emerging a whisper.

"My partner's trying to locate the next of kin."

Next of kin.

Randy.

She can't speak.

"I'm Sergeant Van Aken, ma'am, and I'm going to need some information from you."

Numb, Lucinda nods. Of course. She's a witness.

A witness who has no idea what's going on.

She watches the female officer stride to the squad car.

Again, Lucinda thinks about the scrapbook, wonders if there can possibly be a connection.

The scrapbook . . . the piece of paper . . . the ring . . .

It doesn't make sense . . .

It does make sense. . . .

Oh, hell, she can't even think straight.

Sergeant Van Aken returns with a clipboard, her radio squawking at her hip. It's her partner's voice, Lucinda realizes, hearing Randy's address. The officer inside the house is radioing for backup.

"Got a 10-54 here," he's saying, and of course, Lucinda knows the code.

10-54.

Possible dead body.

"Were you a friend of the victim's, ma'am?"

"I'm a friend . . . of her husband's. Sort of. I mean, I know him."

Someone has to tell Randy, she thinks dully, and wonders who's going to do it, and when, and how, as the officer writes down her name, address, age, and other statistics Lucinda is able to provide with robotic precision.

Then Sergeant Van Aken asks, "So you drove all the way out here from Philadelphia . . . to visit?"

Lucinda's autopilot shuts off abruptly. She hesitates, conscious of the woman's steely gaze fixed on her face.

"I . . . I, um . . ."

How the hell is she supposed to explain her presence here?

Should she tell her about the ring, and the vision?

But that's so complicated.

"Ms. Sloan?"

"Yes, I came to see Randy," she hears herself say—and immediately regrets it.

Randy is in Lake Tahoe.

If they check her phone records, they'll see that she called him this morning, and it'll be pretty obvious that she knew he wouldn't be home.

Why would they check my phone records, though? I'm not a suspect.

She shifts her weight uneasily, realizing what Sergeant Van Aken is thinking.

I need Randy here to set her straight. Or Neal. I don't know how to answer these questions without making myself look suspicious.

"What was the purpose for your visit here, Ms. Sloan?"

"Just . . . to say hello." Knowing enough not to elaborate, she bites down on her bottom lip and waits for the next question.

"And you had a key to the house?"

"No, I . . ." She looks up, sees the key still sticking out of the lock where she left it. "I found it under the doormat, I swear."

The officer, who had started to write that down, looks up sharply at her last words. "Why do you say that?"

"What?"

" 'I swear.' It sounds like you're trying to convince me that you found the key under the mat. Why wouldn't I believe you?"

"Because . . . I mean, a key under the mat?"

"A lot of people hide keys under the mat."

"I know, that's why . . . Never mind," she mutters uneasily, and shifts a nervous gaze back toward the house, wishing Harry Potter would come out and vouch for her.

If he even remembers her, that is.

But of course he must. It's not every day that a police psychic blows into town to help solve a missing persons case.

"So, Ms. Sloan, let's recap. You got here, you opened the door with the key, you went into the house, and then . . . what?"

"Then I called 911."

"You found Mrs. Barakat and you called 911."

"No, I didn't find her. I called 911, and then—"

"Without seeing the victim?"

She nods. "It smelled like . . . I mean, I knew, when I walked in. So I came back out, and I called."

The officer writes that down. "Just to be clear, then, you called without seeing Mrs. Barakat."

"That's what I said."

Watch it, Lucinda. Don't get prickly. That won't help, and she's just doing her job.

"And what, exactly, did you do while you were in the house?"

"Nothing," she says promptly. Defensively. "I was barely *in* the house. I didn't get more than a step or two past the front door."

Sergeant Van Aken digests this. "Have you ever been in the house before?"

"No. Never."

"Not in the past?"

That's what before means, isn't it?

"Never," Lucinda bites out.

"And not today."

"*Never.*"

"Yet when Detective Lambert and I arrived, you told us to look in the bathroom. Correct?"

Lucinda curses silently and fights the urge to close her eyes or look up at the sky, instead fastening her gaze on the police officer's.

"Yes," she says simply, "that's what I told you."

"And you knew this because . . . ?"

"Because I'm a psychic."

The woman waits, apparently, for a more acceptable answer—thinking Lucinda is some kind of wise ass.

Happens all the time. But usually, the stakes aren't this high.

A gust of salty wet wind blows her long auburn curls across her face. As she rakes a restless hand through her hair she does her best not to look longingly at her car. She's not going anywhere. She's got to be here for Randy when he arrives. Forget their past, forget her vow to keep her distance. He's going to need all the support he can get.

Sergeant Van Aken clears her throat. "Ms. Sloan, I asked how you found the victim if you hadn't been inside the house."

I know you did. And I answered you.

She swallows the ache in her throat and repeats wearily, "I knew because I'm a psychic. Look, it's true. You can ask your partner."

"Excuse me?"

"I met him," she gestures at the house, "last summer. They know me on the force. Seriously, ask your partner—

Detective Lambert, is it?—to come out here, or . . . You know what? Just ask Randy Barakat. He'll explain."

Belatedly, she realizes the absurdity of that suggestion. Explaining Lucinda's psychic abilities is going to be the last thing on Randy's agenda when the Beach Haven police reach him.

Poor Randy, she thinks again.

Noting the suspicion in Sergeant Van Aken's eyes, she thinks, *And poor me.*

Sergeant Van Aken still looks a little pale, obviously not over what she found in the house.

All at once, Lucinda realizes something.

Fresh corpses don't smell. It takes at least a day or two before putrefication starts to set in, bringing with it the stench of rotting flesh.

But when she reached Randy this morning, he said he'd spoken to Carla last night.

Obviously, he was lying.

Why?

Sitting in construction traffic outside Winslow, he turns on the radio to look for a local station, wondering if there will be any news on the discovery of a body in Beach Haven.

Nothing but music.

Music—that reminds him. He smiles, wondering whether Lucinda has found the little serenade he left on her iPod yet.

Fat, wet snowflakes begin to plop onto the windshield.

Pity, he thinks, as he flicks on the wipers, that he's not headed for a warmer climate at this time of year.

But there is no room for deviation in this plan. He's painstakingly laid out every step in advance and of course knows exactly where, and when, he'll make his next appearance.

Soon enough—if she's as smart as he thinks she is—so will Lucinda Sloan.

That, for him, is the very best part.

In fact, maybe he'll make a little detour, now that he knows she's not home. Give her another little clue to keep her guessing.

Sooner or later, she's bound to figure it out.

And when she does, the fun will really begin.

He laughs just thinking about it.

Laughs good and long and hard, laughs until his sides hurt and the traffic begins to move again and he can barely see to drive.

"Lucinda. Of course I remember you." Summoned to the front steps by Sergeant Van Aken, Detective Dan Lambert nods. "You're Randy's friend."

"That's what she told me," Van Aken informs him, as yet another investigator, this one carrying photography equipment, hurries past them and into the house. "I just wanted to double-check, because—well, you know."

Yes. Lambert knows.

And so does Lucinda, who was rapidly being made to feel like a suspect in the murder of Carla Barakat.

"Lucinda is the psychic detective who helped out on the case last summer, before you got here," Lambert tells Van Aken.

The case. No need to specify which one on an island where the police spend far more time handing out parking tickets than investigating abductions and homicides.

"Psychic *detective*?" Van Aken slants a bushy blond eyebrow at Lucinda. "You didn't say you were a detective."

There are a lot of things Lucinda didn't say.

"You're based out of Philadelphia, right?" Lambert asks.

"Yes."

"And *what* was it again, that brought you here?" he asks, as though he and Lucinda have already discussed the situation.

They haven't, but she has a feeling he and Van Aken have.

"I had a vision," she says simply. "It made me worry about Carla."

"She said that's how she knew to find the victim in the bathroom," Van Aken puts in.

Lucinda notices that even with Lambert here to back up Lucinda's psychic background, the female cop doesn't seem entirely convinced of her abilities.

Most people are skeptical upon meeting her and hearing what she does. That's typically the least of Lucinda's worries.

Not today.

Not as the only witness at the murder scene of her ex-lover's wife.

"Look, someone left a ring in my kitchen, and I found it this morning," she tells Lambert and Van Aken as a couple of paramedics exit the house and brush past, carrying unused equipment back to their van.

"A ring? As in jewelry?"

"Yes. And it was coated in something that looked to me like dried blood."

The two cops look at each other.

"Did you call the police when you found it?"

"No. When I picked it up, I connected it to Carla right away."

"It was her ring?"

"I don't know. . . . I didn't think so. It was a signet, but the initial was wrong. It was a *Z*."

Lambert's eyes widen behind his oval glasses. "That was Carla's ring; I've seen it. She wore it all the time. It used to belong to her mother."

Her mother . . . of course. Zelda.

Lucinda feels as though someone just vacuumed the air out of her lungs.

If it was Carla's ring . . . covered in Carla's blood . . . then it had to have been left in Lucinda's apartment by Carla's killer.

"Why didn't you call the police when you found this bloody ring and had this disturbing vision about Mrs. Barakat?"

She can't tell Lambert that she didn't trust herself—that she thought her subconsciousness might have conjured the image of Carla, dead, out of some deep-seated resentment. How can she admit that to anyone, especially a friend of Randy's, especially now?

You were a fool, Lucinda. You're always a fool where Randy is concerned. You let your feelings get in the way of sound judgement. How could you?

It's so obvious in retrospect that she did everything wrong, from not calling the police to her careless handling of the evidence.

"Lucinda?" Lambert prods—now watching her nearly as warily as Van Aken has been all along.

"I called Randy," she tells them. "But when I found out he was away, I didn't want to alarm him."

"Did you say anything at all to him about his wife?"

I asked him when he last talked to her, and he said last night.

Oh, Randy, why did you lie about that? What are you hiding?

"Not really," she tells his colleagues. "I just . . . I decided to come on over here and see if everything was okay."

Come on over, as if it's right around the corner.

"Where is the ring right now?" Lambert asks.

"In a plastic bag in my glove compartment."

"A plastic bag. All right, good." He gives her a little nod of approval.

Van Aken, less approving, asks, "Did you wear gloves when you handled it?"

"No," she admits. "Not the first time. Not until I realized what it might be. My prints will be on it."

Lambert is already walking toward her car. "With any luck, so will someone else's."

Twilight is falling by the time Neal Bullard arrives at the Long Beach Township police headquarters on Long Beach Boulevard.

Never in her life has Lucinda been so glad to see anyone.

Being a man of few words—particularly over the telephone—Neal didn't say much when she reached him earlier with the news. He told her he was just leaving Scranton, and promised to get to her as quickly as possible.

He also asked if she knew whether an investigator named Frank Santiago was on the case.

"I think so. Why? Do you know him?"

"I did. A long time ago."

Neal didn't elaborate. She didn't expect him to.

He did ask her how she'd come to be on Long Beach Island.

"Long story," she told him. "I'll tell you when you get here."

Grateful to see him at last, she rises from her chair as Neal strides past the desk sergeant, who looks up only briefly before going back to a phone call.

"I'm so glad you're here."

"I was just going to say that to you." He gives her a swift, hard hug. "I've been trying to call your cell. I thought maybe you'd left."

"Where would I go? The battery died after I called you." She sinks into her chair again, facing the Beach Buggy permit sign she's read and reread for hours now, brooding about Randy.

"Are there still reporters out front?" she asks Neal.

"What do you think?" He sits beside her, stretching his long legs in front of him. He's wearing jeans and sneakers. He really didn't waste a moment's time getting here. "Does the press know you're involved?"

"I don't think so."

"They're going to have a field day when they find out."

"Maybe they won't."

"Have a field day? Are you kidding?"

"I meant maybe they won't find out."

"You're kidding, right?"

She sighs and shakes her head.

"Oh, I bought this for you when I stopped for gas." Neal pulls something out of his pocket.

"Thank you." She gladly accepts the jumbo-sized Twix bar, surprised by the lump of emotion in her throat.

Neal takes care of her—even when she doesn't think that she wants—or needs—to be taken care of. Which is, pretty much, always.

"I figured you might be hungry."

She is hungry, she realizes, though she hadn't even noticed until this very moment. Aside from the Pepsi and coffee she gulped down before hitting the road, she hasn't had a thing to drink, much less eat, all day.

He watches her take a huge bite of chocolate-coated caramel.

And then another.

"So is Randy . . . ?"

"He's on his way."

Again, she thinks about Randy's lie, and the candy bar turns sodden in her mouth.

But she can't tell Neal. She can't tell anyone.

Not without at least talking to Randy first.

"How is he?" Neal asks.

"I don't know. I tried calling his cell phone again before mine died, and there was no answer. Maybe he's on a plane."

"What time is he getting in?"

She shrugs. "All I know is that someone called him. I heard them say that he was going to catch the first plane back. But he's out in Tahoe—I don't even know if there's an airport there."

"Reno. He'll have to drive there, or maybe Sacramento, and make a connection."

"How do you know that?" she asks, having often heard Neal's claim that he's never been west of Pennsylvania.

"Patty and Jeff went skiing at Squaw Valley a few years ago, and they left the twins with us. Maeve ended up in the ER with pneumonia, and they had a hell of a time getting back. Randy will be lucky if he gets here before tomorrow."

"I figured it would be a while."

"You're not planning to wait all night, are you, Cin?"

"If that's what it takes. I want to be here for him."

He gives her a long look.

"No matter what happened between us in the past"—*and no matter what reason he had for lying to me this morning*—"Randy's my friend. How can I walk out on him now?"

Neal says nothing to that, asking instead, "Did you get any more information on what happened to Carla?"

"I have no idea. Nobody's telling me any of the details."

"Did they at least mention whether there are any suspects?"

"Just me."

Neal's green eyes widen.

"Well, not really," she says quickly. "Not anymore, anyway."

She explains about the ring, and how she came to be here, and what happened back at Randy's house.

She keeps her voice low, even though they're the only two people sitting here. The desk sergeant has his hands full with incessantly ringing phones. The press has clearly gotten wind of another murder on the quiet little island.

"You should have called me the second you found that ring," Neal tells her, just as she'd known he would.

"I should have done a lot of things. I'm sorry. I hadn't slept much, and I wasn't thinking straight. I don't think I am even now." She sighs, rubs her eyes, exhausted. "I don't suppose you bought me some coffee at that gas station, did you?"

"Sorry. I should have. Let's go out and find a diner or something."

"What about the press out there?"

"You'll have to leave sooner or later. Maybe there's a back door."

"What if Randy shows up?"

"He won't. Not yet. Come on. I'll buy you dinner, and then we'll come right back."

She hesitates. "Okay."

Standing, she tosses the candy bar wrapper into the trash can, then picks up her coat. Several blue plastic bags drop from the folds onto the floor.

"What are those?"

"The Barakats' newspapers," she tells Neal, gathering them. "I picked them up from the driveway when I got there, and I forgot I had them."

She starts to throw them into the trash, but Neal stops her.

"If we're going to sit here all night, I'll read them."

"Old news?"

"Not the news, but I'll take all the sports sections. You can throw the rest of it away. I missed the last few Sixers games because I had the kids with me, so I've got to catch up." Neal, a rabid basketball fan, holds out his hand.

Lucinda takes the papers out of their protective plastic bags and begins sorting through the sections. Something flutters to the floor.

Neal bends to pick it up as she separates yesterday's sports page from the rest of the paper.

"Cin."

"Mmm hmm?"

He doesn't reply.

She looks up to see him holding up a white sheet of paper.

Typed precisely in the middle of the page, in bold black type, are two numbers:

87.7
41.9

Chapter Six

"Morning, Joe."

"Night, Larry."

Both men smile as they pass each other with their usual greeting, Larry Blazer carrying a janitor's bucket and mop, ready to erase the sticky remains of another night at the bar; Joe Armano with a down jacket thrown over his dress shirt and loosened tie, car keys in hand, heading home after the closing shift.

If he's lucky, he'll get home in time to kiss his wife Mary Lou hello and good-bye as she leaves to start her early morning nursing shift at Methodist Hospital. Sometimes he catches her; sometimes he doesn't. It all depends on how many times she hits the Snooze button on the alarm.

She works hard, Mary Lou. So does he. With two sons in college and a daughter planning a wedding for June, they have no choice. After being forced into early retirement from his job as a telecommunications manager and cheated out of ten percent of his pension, Joe has no choice but to do what he can to make ends meet.

He likes bartending better than his other current job, driving for an airport car service. Drunken revelers tip a lot better than harried businessmen on ever leaner corporate expense accounts.

Any other time of day, the streets are buzzing in the Rittenhouse Square area, filled with people coming and going from upscale restaurants, expensive shops, fancy hotels and apartment buildings. At this hour, though, even the club kids have gone home, and with freezing temperatures and sunup still a few hours off, all is quiet.

Joe's footsteps sound hollow as he walks the familiar route up South 18th Street toward the garage off Market Street where he pays a small fortune to park his car every night. He parked on the street when he first started working down here, but after a few tickets and a few break-ins, he wised up.

Not that the streets around here aren't safe.

But you leave a decent looking BMW—even the older model, used one that Mary Lou fondly continues to call his 'midlife crisis' splurge years later—on the street anywhere in the wee hours, and you're going to see some damage.

Damn, it's cold tonight.

Joe crosses against the light—not a car in sight—and starts up the next block, where a couple of older storefronts hug the sidewalk.

Someone steps from the sheltered doorway of one of them, directly into his path, facing him.

Startled, Joe stops walking and prays that the man is bundled in a parka zipped to his nose and a ski cap pulled low over his eyes because of the temperature. If not, Joe wonders if he can fight him off and run. The guy is the same height as he is, and looks about the same weight, though it's hard to tell with the bulk of the parka.

But Joe used to be a wrestler. He's still strong, and he knows some moves. . . .

He sees the gun, and his guts go liquid.

"Give me your wallet."

Joe's gloved hand, trembling, goes to the back pocket of the nice gray dress pants Mary Lou gave him for Christmas, saying he needed to dress more fashionably if he was going to work at an upscale bar near Rittenhouse.

He hands over his wallet.

The mugger, wearing black leather gloves, opens it and looks inside.

"Take it. You can have whatever's in it. Just don't hurt me. Please."

The mugger gives a nod as if he's satisfied, snaps the wallet closed, and tucks it into his pocket.

"Sorry, Joe," are the last words Joe Armano hears before his brains are blown out.

"Ms. Sloan?"

She looks up to see the young cop who's been working the desk phones since beginning last night's late shift. "Yes?"

"Would you like one?" He offers a box of Krispy Kremes, adding, "I know what you're thinking. Cops and donuts. Cliché, right?"

"Clichés are clichés because they're true." She manages a faint smile and gratefully accepts a glazed jelly donut.

He returns to his post, and she devours it in two bites, wishing she'd taken two. She hasn't eaten a thing since the Twix bar Neal brought her last night, right before they found the paper bearing the strange numerical sequence.

They immediately turned it over to the police, along with the newspapers and plastic bags.

"Which newspaper was this with?" was, of course, one of the first questions from the detectives who came on duty when Lambert and Van Aken went off.

Her answer—"I'm not sure"—was hardly satisfactory, another strike against Lucinda with a fresh crop of Long Beach Township investigators.

She should have given Lambert and Van Aken the newspapers in the first place yesterday, but it never occurred to her that—beyond the ring—she was harboring evidence from a crime scene.

It should have. You're not exactly new to this; yet somehow, you've bungled one thing after another.

In her defense—as Neal pointed out to the police—she was upset, and tired, and anyway, hindsight is twenty-twenty. How could she have guessed that Carla's killer might have left a clue with the newspaper?

How, indeed?

She gathered the papers, carried them away. In the grand scheme of things, that wouldn't exactly be second nature. She's pretty sure that was no accident.

No, because her brain is wired to pick up on things most people don't.

She was subconsciously drawn to those newspapers because she herself has some oblique connection to Carla's killer, the most frightening prospect of all.

"Is there any way this note wasn't in with the papers when you picked them up off the driveway?" Neal asked her last night on the heels of their discovery.

"What do you mean?"

"I mean, maybe someone is following you and left it in the newspaper after you picked it up. Did you let the papers out of your sight for even a moment today?"

"I forgot I even had them with me!" Her nerves were fraying fast at that point, thanks to exhaustion, low blood sugar—and, though she would never admit it to anyone but herself, sheer fright. "I probably left them here with my coat a couple of times when I went to the ladies' room."

"So anyone could have come in and left this note."

"I guess so . . . but would someone really do that in a police station?"

Probably not.

In the end, both she and Neal concluded that the killer had probably left the note at the scene of the crime, that he was the same person who left the album and the ring in her apartment, and that he might have something to do with Ava Neary's death as well.

The Long Beach Township police didn't seem as convinced. They asked to see the other sheet of paper, which was back at Neal's house. He left after midnight to drive back to Philadelphia to get it and to meet a couple of other detectives from the Philadelphia police department at her apartment to dust for prints.

"I should go with you," she said, but he shook his head immediately.

"You're safer here."

"On an island with a murderer on the loose?"

"In the police station on an island far away from your apartment—which, let's not forget, he visited *after* the murder to leave the bloody souvenir. I'd be surprised if he's hanging around Beach Haven now—but we might be able to pick up the trail in Philly."

Neal was right, of course.

Anyway, she wanted to wait for word about Randy. She spent the night mostly staring into space but occasionally dozing into a fitful sleep, dogged by the familiar unfinished puzzle dream.

Now, glancing toward the glass doors, she sees that it's still dark outside. The sun should be coming up soon, though; it's past six A.M.

She stretches and stands. This time, she takes her belongings with her when she goes to the restroom, hanging her coat and purse on a door hook as she splashes some cold water on her face.

Looking into the mirror above the sink, she sees blatant evidence of two sleepless nights and a murder in between. Beyond the predictable dark circles around her eyes, her wavy hair is out of control; her skin is dry and her lips are cracked from being exposed to the elements outside Randy's house yesterday.

She checks her purse for something that might help—lip balm, a comb, lotion, a barrette. Nope. She isn't the type to primp away from home. In her coat pocket, though, along with the iPod she forgot to remove the other night, she finds a stray rubber band. Not a coated hair elastic, but the plain old office supply kind—from the bundle of mail she took from her box when she returned from Curaçao, she realizes.

It'll have to do.

She finger-combs her curls the best she can, gathers them into a ponytail, then winces as she snaps the band around it, the rubber tugging painfully at a few strands.

Better, though, she decides, looking into the mirror.

Back in the waiting room, she returns to her lonely vigil.

Remembering her iPod, she removes it from her pocket and inserts the white ear buds. Maybe music will make things a little brighter in this darkest hour before the dawn.

Oh, who is she kidding?

Even music isn't going to let her forget Carla's death for one instant.

Still, what else has she got to do?

As her thumb reaches to work the scroll wheel, Detective Lambert appears.

"Ms. Sloan?" His gaze is solemn behind those storybook wizard glasses.

She yanks out the ear buds. "You can call me Lucinda."

"Lucinda." He nods. "Randy's back home. He took a red eye. I told him you've been here all night. He wants to see you right away."

A beach town in the off-season is the perfect place to commit a crime, Lucinda concludes as she turns onto Randy's deserted street a few blocks from the beach.

There's no one around, really, to part the blinds and make note of a strange car prowling the street. No one would have heard terrified cries for help even if the sound made it past the storm windows, even if the wind and surf didn't sweep them away.

Still . . .

Someone, somewhere, might have seen something. Heard something.

Experience has taught Lucinda that someone usually does.

A squad car sits again—or, perhaps, *still*—in front of Randy's house.

Lucinda parks a few doors down and walks past the mostly deserted homes of the Barakats' neighbors, holding two cups of deli coffee balanced against her hip on a spongy beige cardboard carrier. One is laced with lots of sugar and half and half; the other black and unsweetened.

She knows, of course, how Randy takes his coffee; they drank a lot of it together during those late night investigations.

Filmy sunlight has broken through the clouds. The wind off the ocean feels colder, though, than it did yesterday, permeating Lucinda's body and blowing her hair across her face. The strands tickle her cheeks, and she slaps at them like a joyless kitten pawing at dangling yarn.

Randy's car, mud-spattered and coated with road salt, is parked behind Carla's in the driveway. Lucinda walks past it, approaching the Barakats' front door for the second time in twenty-four hours.

A uniformed officer answers her knock. She recognizes him, having seen him around the station yesterday. He's considerably more friendly now that she's being admitted to the inner circle.

"Lucinda Sloan, right?"

"Yes."

"Here, want a hand with the coffee?"

"No, thanks, I've got it."

"Randy's waiting for you. He's in the kitchen. Go on in—it's that way."

As she moves beyond the threshold, she can smell Lysol and bleach, but nothing more. The windows are cracked open. Randy's fellow officers must have worked to air out the house after Carla's body was moved to the morgue yesterday.

Lucinda can't help but notice that the house isn't the charming dream house she imagined. A cursory glance as she moves through the living room and dining room shows that while the place is nicely furnished—mostly in blond wood and beige upholstery, with a couple of pastel prints in metallic frames hanging on the walls—there are none of the little personal touches that make a house a home.

She can't help but compare the place to Neal and Erma's, with its family photos, tchotchkes, and collections galore. Or even to her own apartment, which feels a lot more lived in—even though she's alone, and has only been there a month.

So Randy and Carla aren't into *stuff*. So what?

That doesn't mean this isn't a happy home.

No. . . . But it doesn't feel happy.

Well of course the house gives off a bad vibe. Carla died here.

But it feels like there's more to it than that.

Pausing in the kitchen doorway, she spots Randy and immediately curtails the little argument with her psychic self.

He's sitting with his back to her, slumped forward with his head resting on his forearms folded flat against the table.

Lucinda watches him for a moment, a fist of regret squeezing her heart. He's a good guy; the best. He doesn't deserve this pain.

What is he going to do now? How is he going to live with this?

And why, why, *why* did he lie about the last time he'd spoken to Carla?

What if—

No. You know he didn't have anything to do with it.

Of course he didn't.

He couldn't have.

But it's been such a long time. . . . How well do you know him now?

Frustrated by the track her thoughts are taking, she clears her throat. "Randy."

He lifts his head and turns, tears running down his sorrow-scoured face. "Somebody killed her, Lucinda. Somebody killed her."

It's a little-boy wail, and it pierces her soul, sending her to his side.

This is Randy. She knows him. Trusts him.

She blindly puts aside the hot coffee cups and bends over him, holding him, stroking his hair as he shudders and soaks her shoulder with tears.

"I'm sorry," she says, over and over.

When the tide of despair begins to ebb, she finds her way into a chair, pulling it close beside his, an arm draped around his shoulder.

"I can't believe she's dead. I have to go down to the morgue. . . ." His voice breaks.

"Can't someone else do that for you?"

"No, no, I have to do it, because . . . I just can't believe it."

"I'm so, so sorry, Randy."

He nods, plucks a tissue from the box on the table, blows his nose.

What more is there to say?

"I know how hard this is. I know how much you loved her."

In the midst of crumpling the tissue, he glances up at Lucinda. Something flickers in his blue eyes, giving her pause.

But then it's gone, and he slumps in his chair, shaking his head. "This can't be happening."

How many times has she heard those words from the families of doomed missing persons?

Over time, the stunned disbelief gives way to grief, and

anger, and eventually—if their ordeal ends with the discovery of a body, which many do not—grim acceptance.

All of those emotions abrade Randy's handsome face now, along with blatant exhaustion and none of the hope families of missing persons struggle to keep alive until the end, should they be fortunate enough to find closure.

Randy's journey was over before it began, and closure— the certainty that his wife will never come home again— brings no relief.

Neal arrives at Lucinda's apartment before the detective team.

Wearing rubber gloves, he pockets her keys and closes the door behind him, wiping the slush from his sneakers.

As a detective, he's entered unoccupied homes on countless occasions. All in a day's work.

Why, then, does this feel so wrong?

Because I know her, and somehow, I feel like I'm invading her privacy. Even though this is a crime scene now.

He looks around. The apartment has come a long way since he came with her to give it a second look on a blustery December day, at her request.

"I like it, but I'm not sure about it," she'd said. "I need another opinion."

"About the neighborhood?"

"God, no. About the place itself. It's an old building. Really old."

He asked where it was, and when she told him the cross streets, he understood the "God, no."

As Philadelphia neighborhoods go, Society Hill is among the safest.

It's also the last place he'd expect Lucinda Sloan to settle. She's never liked to talk much about her past, but Neal knows she likes to keep some distance between herself and her blue blood roots.

She always did, anyway.

But maybe, the older she gets, the more she feels the need to reconcile the past.

Her mother, her father, Randy . . .

Randy.

Carla.

Fresh shock courses through Neal. What the hell is going on?

He walks into the living room, looking for signs of an intruder. There are none that he can see, but how would he know? He's only been here once before, on that first day, before she moved in.

"The apartment is great," Neal told Lucinda, after a walk through and a cursory inspection of the pipes and the outlets. "I just have one question: why here?"

"You mean, this neighborhood?"

"I mean, this neighborhood."

She shrugged. "It's convenient, and it's nice, and it's affordable. Why not?"

"The next thing I know, you'll be calling your mother for lunch." He winked at her, and she gave him the finger.

He's never met her parents, but he'd heard of them even before he met Lucinda. Who hadn't? Charity golf events, black tie fund-raisers, on the board of this and that foundation . . . Bitsy and Rudolph Sloan, and their forebears, have long been fixtures in Philadelphia society.

Back when Neal first encountered their daughter, fresh from her parents' home—or clutches, as Lucinda preferred to phrase it—she bore the remnants of what struck him as adolescent rebelliousness.

Not only that, but she was full of crap—or so he believed. A staunch Irish Catholic, he was predisposed to skepticism when a family he was working with brought a so-called psychic on board to help locate a missing teenager.

She advised the investigators to concentrate the search in an industrial area east of the city, despite the fact that the girl had last been seen near the Amtrak station and was widely believed—within the police force, anyway—to be a runaway.

Lucinda claimed that the girl had been boldly abducted from a city street by two men in a black pickup truck, raped and kept alive for nearly two weeks before they decapitated her and buried her head in a box near an abandoned brick factory.

Neal took all that with a grain of salt. He and the other investigators humored her, though, and looked where she said to look.

Lucinda was correct, as it turned out. Right down to the fact that the box was from an electronics store.

Who was he to argue with facts, extraordinary as they might be?

Neal found a new and instant respect for the wayward heiress who wore defiance like gang colors. Yet there was a sensitivity there, too, a vulnerability, somewhere beneath the brash and jaded facade.

Patience brings payoff. The detective's credo has served Neal well where Lucinda Sloan is concerned.

Early on, they crossed paths again and again in an effort to locate missing persons, evolving into colleagues, then friends, and now, perhaps *family* is the most appropriate term for their relationship. Lucinda has become as close to Neal as his own daughters are—perhaps even more so, because he doesn't have to share her with Erma, and because he and Lucinda have been to hell and back together more times than he cares to count.

This is a brutal business.

You can't help but grow hardened over time until you're almost immune to the victims' pain, to their loved ones' pain, even to your own. You know it's there—the pain—but you can't let yourself feel it because if you do, you'll never be able to get up the next morning and do what has to be done.

This time, Neal is dangerously close to emotional involvement. He needs to take a step back, pull himself together, regain professional detachment. For Lucinda's sake, for Randy's, for Carla's.

He remembers Randy Barakat's wife as a sweet, if needy girl.

Not woman.

Girl.

He remembers thinking—the first time he realized that something was simmering between Randy and Lucinda, which was pretty much the first time they ever came into contact with each other—that Carla Karnecki didn't stand a chance.

Lucinda was no girl.

She was woman enough for Randy, and he—unlike scores of others—was man enough for her.

It wasn't just that Randy was a cop, and a damned good one. She'd dated, and discarded, plenty of cops before.

It wasn't that he was as fearless as she, as extraordinarily good-looking as she, with just as sharp a sense of humor, or that he was as masculine as they come, with old-fashioned manners.

It wasn't even that his family background had bred in him a steely core similar to her own, though for different reasons. His mother was an Irish Catholic, his father an Arab—coming from fiercely religious backgrounds into a marriage that was denounced by both families.

His strength appealed to Lucinda, but as Neal saw it, the main reason Randall Barakat captured her heart was that he never once questioned her uncanny ability. Not skeptical or fascinated or even all that curious, he simply accepted her for who she was.

Neal wasn't the only one who'd noticed the way Lucinda and Randy clicked.

"Those two are written in the stars," Erma commented on the one and only occasion she saw the two of them in the same room.

"I doubt that," Neal said, though he was secretly impressed

his wife had picked up on it too. "He's engaged to someone else."

"Then I feel sorry for her."

"For Lucinda?" he'd asked, surprised, because feeling sorry for Lucinda Sloan was not customary by any means.

"No," Erma said. "For the someone else."

Randy had married her, though, in the end. Carla.

And now she's dead.

And her bloody ring was in Lucinda's possession.

And Ava Neary—where does she fit into all this?

Neal has been going over every detail, running the facts through his head like a computer processing forensic evidence, looking for a match.

So far, he hasn't come up with a connection.

In the kitchen, Neal sees the empty coffee pot sitting on the counter, where Lucinda left it. They'll dust the whole area for prints.

The whole place.

Careful not to disturb anything, he moves through the apartment, past a couple of closed doors to the bedroom at the end of the hall.

He stares at the unmade bed for a long minute. This is where the album was found.

Backtracking down the hall, he opens a door.

Linen closet.

Neatly stacked towels and sheets, everything in perfect order.

He opens another door.

The bathroom.

"Sweet Jesus," spills from Neal's lips, and he stares in disbelief.

Chapter Seven

"Here . . . You should drink this." Lucinda slides the take-out coffee cup toward Randy.

"Where did it come from?" He sips it.

"I brought it. It's probably cold by now." As if he notices, or cares.

"Thank you." He sets down the cup and looks at her. "I'm glad you came. When they first told me that you were in town, I was shocked for maybe the first few seconds. Then I thought, *of course she is. Of course she's here.* For some reason it made perfect sense."

"It did?" Because it still doesn't entirely make sense to her.

He nods. "I have no idea how you got here, but Lucinda, I need you."

He needs me.

And I need to be here for him.

"Have your parents been here, or your sister?" she asks him.

"My parents were spending the winter in Florida. They're trying to get home. Julie was getting her kids off to school and finding someone to watch them later, and then she has to go pick up my parents at the airport."

"I can go to the airport, or I can watch the kids," she offers. "So that your sister can be with you."

"No. . . . That's sweet, but no. Thanks."

"Does she still live in Cherry Hill? Because it's really no problem for me to—"

"Yes, she still lives there. But I need you here more than I need her. She's freaking out. You can imagine."

Yes, she can. Randy's sister, a divorced single mom, is notoriously excitable. The drama queen, he always called her.

Lucinda realizes that while there's so much she doesn't know about his life now—so much that's changed—there is still a lot that hasn't.

"Well, what can I do, then?" she asks him.

"Just be here with me. Please. I don't want to be alone right now."

"You won't be," she promises, patting his arm. "I'll stay as long as you need me."

She has to tell him about the ring, but she's not sure where to start, or whether it'll upset him.

He looks as though he's about to say something, too.

Is he going to bring up the lie?

The phone rings.

"Do you want me to get it?"

"No, I will." Wearily, he picks it up.

It's one of the detectives working the case.

Lucinda sips her own coffee as he talks, knowing the caffeine won't do a thing to assuage the ache of exhaustion gripping her body.

When was the last time she got a decent night's sleep? Not even in Curaçao, on that cloud of a fancy resort hotel bed. Not with Jimmy sharing it.

Uneasily, she allows herself to consider, once again, Neal's suspicion that Jimmy could have possibly been behind the scrapbook on her bed. If she were willing to believe that, she would also have to be willing to believe he could have killed Carla Barakat.

I have no idea who he really is.

This isn't the first time she's realized it, but the truth is more pronounced now that she's here with Randy.

Randy—she knows exactly who he is. Knows him inside and out, even after all these years apart. Being with Randy feels natural in a way that nothing else in her life ever has.

Being with other men, or with her family, or even alone . . .

None of that feels right the way this does. Even here, even now, even being with him under the worst of circumstances—she belongs. It feels right.

Which is wrong. Especially here, especially now.

But it is what it is.

And you don't do guilt, remember?

They know, Randy realizes, going through the motions yet again with people who have dropped in to pay their respects.

They all know, except Lucinda.

He has to tell her.

He meant to, sooner or later. Maybe this isn't the ideal time, but, remarkably, she's here.

Or maybe not so remarkably.

"I had a vision that something happened to Carla, so I drove out to check on her when I found out you were out of town," she explained earlier in her matter-of-fact way, sitting beside him at the kitchen table.

A vision. Of course.

"It just came to you out of the blue?"

She shook her head. Told him about the ring, Carla's ring, now in the possession of the police as evidence.

She told him, too, about the strange pieces of paper found at both the murder scene and on Neal's kitchen table Monday night.

"Why didn't you tell me?" Randy asked her, chilled by the ominous linkage of Lucinda to Carla.

"I just . . . I couldn't. You couldn't have done anything about it from there anyway. And I could have been wrong."

"So you're the one who found her?"

"No. I called the police, and they did."

He's glad. He's glad Lucinda wasn't the one who walked in on what must have been a bloodbath in the bathroom.

Lambert told him—when he pressed for details he probably didn't really want to know—that Carla's jugular vein was severed, and she'd bled to death.

He knows Lucinda has seen worse—much worse.

But her being the one who found Carla would have complicated things even more than they are. Or are about to be, anyway.

Standing in the kitchen, surrounded by chattering acquaintances and enough Saran-wrapped platters to stock a high school bake sale, Randy longs to pull her aside and tell her the truth.

But there are too many people around, more pouring in every time the damned doorbell rings, people he didn't realize even knew Carla and people he can't believe even care that she's dead.

Whether they do or not, all appear genuinely shaken. If nothing else, an air of *there-but-for-the-grace-of-God* mourning permeates the house where Randy's wife bled to death.

He doesn't want to see her.

He has to, though. Has to officially identify her down at the morgue and sign the papers so that the death certificate can be issued. Lambert offered to have someone else do it, but Randy said that wouldn't be right.

He can do this. It won't be easy, but he owes her this much.

For now, though, it's enough to go numbly through the day, accepting condolences and bundt cakes, and to catch Lucinda's eye every once in a while, wishing he could be alone with her so that he can tell her the truth at last.

Sitting in the glider chair in the baby's room, nursing her little girl, Cam worries.

Where, where, *where* is Lucinda?

Cam could have sworn she'd said last week that she was only going to Curaçao for the weekend, but maybe she extended the trip.

She must have, because in the last twenty-four hours, Cam has left a couple of messages each on her home and cell phone voice mail, and Lucinda has yet to return the call. She can't have heard them yet, because Cam was increasingly adamant, when she spoke into the phone, that it was really important to connect.

What if . . .

No. Lucinda is fine. Of course she is.

Cam stares out the window at the bare-branched trees against an ice-blue winter sky, wishing she knew that for sure.

But she can't allow her thoughts to take her to the dark place, can't allow herself to consider that something might have happened to her friend. Something that has something to do with Ava, and the strange lipstick note she found in the mail.

Mike, when she reached him yesterday morning, was concerned enough to tell her he'd cut the ski trip short and come home.

"No!" Cam protested impulsively—though when she called, she supposed, she'd been hoping he'd offer to be on the next plane.

But if Mike left the trip early, he'd miss out on something he looks forward to all year. Plus, she'd never hear the end of it from her father-in-law.

Mike's father isn't one to withhold a grudge. He still

blames Cam for, as he put it, "nearly getting my grand-daughter killed."

As if only he has Tess's best interests at heart. As if Cam, or for that matter, Tess, had been incredibly reckless.

And then, of course, he was mortified by the press coverage, which—as he put it—"drags all the dirty linen out of the closet for the world to see."

Dirty linen, meaning Cam's murdered sister.

"Ignore him," Mike advised her. "What else can you do? He's always been a jerk, and he always will be."

For Cam—who was always prepared to give Mike, Senior, the benefit of the doubt for her husband's sake—ignoring the man hasn't been very challenging. She hasn't even seen him lately—other than when he and Mike's mom came to see the baby in the hospital, and a chaotic Christmas dinner in Connecticut.

As far as she's concerned, if she doesn't see them until next Christmas, it'll be too soon.

Well, Mike's father, anyway.

His mother, she adores. Too bad they're usually a package deal. Cam has been inviting her mother-in-law down to stay for a week but Mike's father doesn't believe in women traveling solo, and claims he doesn't want to drive on winter roads to get her here.

No, but he doesn't mind driving up a winter mountain road in Utah to go skiing.

Whatever.

"Daddy's right," she tells baby Grace, as she props her against her shoulder to burp her. "Grandpa is a jerk. But don't tell anyone I told you, okay?"

She's always careful never to say a bad word about her father-in-law in front of Tess.

Or about her own father, for that matter. Ike Neary has his faults, too, of course, brought on by an addictive personality and compounded by all the tragic loss he's suffered in his life.

Pop isn't doing so well lately. He's been in and out of hospitals since last fall, having been diagnosed with Alzheimer's. He has his good days, but there are more bad now. Often, when Cam goes to visit him, he thinks she's her mother.

"Brenda," he'll say, "where the hell have you been? I've been worried sick about you."

Once, when Cam came into the room just as he was waking up, he even thought she was Ava.

Rather, Ava's ghost, apparently, meeting him at the pearly gates.

"You're alive, Pop," Cam kept telling him, over and over. "I'm not Ava; I'm Cam."

He nodded, finally getting it. "You're Cam. Did you hear about Ava?"

"Hear what?"

"She's dead." He wiped tears from his eyes. "Killed herself, poor thing."

No, Pop. She didn't kill herself.

Somebody killed her.

And now somebody might be trying to tell me what really happened.

"It's really no big deal, Mike," she told her husband on the phone, nonetheless, about the strange note in the mail.

"It was a big enough deal to scare you. I'm coming home."

"You do, and I'll be really pissed at you."

He laughed.

"I'm serious, Mike."

"That you'll be really pissed?"

"That you shouldn't come home. Listen, this is just another stupid prank thing. Like all those hang ups we got before we changed the phone number, and people who said they were Ava, or calling for Ava . . ."

"That's different. That was kids, playing around."

"I'm sure this is, too." She must have sounded convincing, because he agreed to stay in Utah through the end of the week as planned.

Then he proceeded to call her every waking hour in the last twenty-four.

"Just checking in. Everything okay?"

"Status quo," she tells him, every time.

The house is quiet today. Tess is at the mall—with a girl-friend, for a change. Her boyfriend doesn't have a school break in February, which spares Cam having to wedge some healthy distance between the lovebirds 24/7 this week.

She stands, pulls the shade, and carries her drowsy baby across the plush white carpet. She lays her in the white cradle and winds the mobile hanging above it. A quartet of characters from the Hundred Acre Wood begin dancing slowly above Grace's head to tinkling Winnie the Pooh music.

"Take your nap, Precious." Cam presses a kiss against her downy hair. "Mama will be back to check on you. But right now I have to check on someone else."

She closes the door behind the baby and goes into the master bedroom.

When Mike moved out last year, she avoided spending time here. She hated seeing the half-empty closet and barren dresser top, hated having the king-sized bed all to herself.

Now that it's a happy, cozy room again, she's glad to retreat here with a book or her journal when the baby naps. She's even been writing again lately—poetry and short stories, not that any of it's very good, or that she's willing to show anyone. Not even Mike, who has been encouraging her to try publishing something.

Maybe someday.

She picks up the phone on the bedside table and dials Lucinda's home number.

Voice mail again.

"Lucinda, it's Cam. Now I don't just need to talk to you—I'm worried about you. Please call and let me know you're okay as soon as you get this."

* * *

"Oh, she's perfectly okay," he assures Camden Hastings's disembodied voice. "She will be for quite some time. But I can't guarantee anything past . . . oh, let's say, June."

He laughs aloud.

Hard.

It always feels good to laugh. It's a release.

Sometimes, in prison, well after lights out, some random thought would amuse him, and he'd let loose with a rip-roaring belly laugh that would echo down the C block in the dead of night.

The others would stir and start banging on the walls and barred windows of their cells, hollering at him to shut up, and then the guards would show up to investigate, shining lights in his face—which he found even funnier.

"You know I've always loved the spotlight," he'd say and writhe and clutch his gut as howls exploded from him, laughing until his ribs ached and there was a knot of pain at the back of his throat.

"What the hell is so funny?" they'd demand—almost suspiciously. Just as his teachers had when he was a kid.

As if he were hiding something. As if humor were some kind of threat.

He never told anyone why he was laughing because most of the time, he really didn't know, and it really didn't matter.

He only knew that it felt good, had always felt good, to let it all out, to purge until he was spent: laughter.

And sometimes, rage.

"To hear this message again, press one," a mechanical voice advises him. "To save it, press two. To erase it, press three."

He wipes tears of mirth from his eyes and presses one, just for the fun of it.

"Lucinda, it's Cam. Now I don't just need to talk to you—I'm worried about you. Please call and let me know you're okay as soon as you get this."

He relishes the urgency in her voice, glad to have this opportunity.

Getting into her PIN-protected voice mail, e-mail, and computer files was tricky, but not impossible for someone like him: schooled in the old C block. He'd emerged with plenty of connections in the outside world, along with fresh knowledge and training in areas that would come in handy in his business, courtesy of the state prison reforms.

In Lucinda Sloan's case, all it took was a keyboard sniffer installed on her laptop while she was out one day. The software is readily available for purchase, and cash is not hard to come by when one has no qualms about where and how one obtains it.

He learned Lucinda's voice mail access code the old-fashioned way: by observing her from the rooftop next door with a pair of high-powered binoculars.

People entering PINs in the so-called privacy of their own homes don't attempt to shield the movements of their fingers from prying eyes the way they do at ATMs. All he'd had to do was watch for her to come home each night, knowing that the first thing she'd do was check her voice mail. It took a few weeks for her to stand with the phone at exactly the right angle in exactly the right spot in front of one of the apartment's many windows, but he had all the time and patience in the world.

The whole thing, really, is a waiting game.

How many nights had he reminded himself of that, watching from his rooftop perch as she slept, bathed in the glow of the bedside lamp?

Never before had he had such an opportunity, not with the others. No one else slept all night with the light on.

Had he not known all along of Lucinda Sloan's weakness—her fear of the dark—he might have interpreted that bedside lamp as a beacon. He might have been tempted—the night he slipped into her apartment through a window to borrow her keys and make a duplicate set—to let her blood ooze across those nice white sheets, right then and there.

But he knows her secret.

And of course, he possesses a level of self-control and intelligence unmatched in any other human being he's ever known.

Killing her right then and there wouldn't be nearly as satisfying as what he has planned.

It's so nice to have something to look forward to, really.

And so, he slipped away with her keys, made himself a set, and returned them well before dawn.

Grinning, he reaches into his pocket, unfolding a well-worn newspaper clipping.

SEXY SOOTHSAYER SUPERHERO screams the kitschy tabloid headline.

And there she is, smiling out at him in sepia-tones, aside from the little adjustment he couldn't help making.

Photoshop would have been more effective, but this will do.

"See you soon, Lucinda," he tells her, admiring the delicate arch of her brow and the sassy gleam in her eye and, above all, the lips he carefully stained red with a whittled nub of lipstick. It refused to stay defined but instead bled across the newsprint, giving her a garish clown's mouth.

No matter.

Soon enough, he'll have another chance—with the real thing.

Whistling, he tucks the clipping back into his pocket and picks up his suitcase.

He has a flight to catch.

All morning and late into the afternoon, as people come and go, Lucinda remains at Randy's side.

"I need you," he said simply when, earlier, the doorbell started ringing incessantly and strangers—to her, anyway—

started filling the house and she offered to give him some space. "Please don't leave me."

So she's still here, trying to stay helpful yet out of the way as the investigators do their thing and friends and neighbors stop by to offer condolences. They stand in little knots in the kitchen and speak in hushed voices, and when they leave, they always say, "If you need anything, Randy, just call."

He thanks them, and somehow, he keeps his composure through it all, even when they don't. It's obvious he's built a life here on the island; that he and Carla are—were—a part of the community.

Lucinda brews endless pots of coffee and keeps a list of who brought what. Randy might want it later, so that he'll know whom to thank. She figures the names and faces must be a blur for him now.

A few of the visitors are obviously closer to him than others, some of whom strike Lucinda as ghoulish curiosity seekers. Yet even they seem truly shaken by his loss.

As the day wears on, though, Lucinda notices that even among the inner circle, there's an undercurrent of something other than just sympathy.

Resentment? Nosiness? Whatever it is, it seems to have something to do with her presence.

Randy introduces her, over and over, as an old friend, yet she senses closer scrutiny than a platonic relationship merits. Particularly from the women: a few who are middle-aged locals, and a couple who are considerably younger and must be friends of Carla's.

It's likely they recognize her from last summer's media blitz, but as Lucinda finds herself being sized up repeatedly, something tells her there's more to their interest than that.

Is it possible that her secret past with Randy is common knowledge here on the island?

Or is it already public knowledge that she's the one who called the police before they found Carla's body?

Neal is finally about to head back here with the evidence,

after spending a few hours overseeing the investigation at Lucinda's apartment.

"I want you to be careful there, Cin," Neal warned from his cell phone when she reached him a little while ago.

"Neal, it's broad daylight, and I'm surrounded by people. Oh, and P.S., a lot of them are cops. What can possibly happen to me?"

"Just be careful."

"Why? Did something else happen?"

There was a telltale pause.

"I'm on my way. I'll talk to you when I get there."

"Did you remember to get my BlackBerry charger?"

"Got it," he said, and hung up before she could ask him anything else.

Standing in Lucinda's living room, Neal gazes out the window at the squad cars parked on the street below, wondering if Carla Barakat's killer can see them too.

Is he lurking somewhere nearby, keeping an eye on Lucinda's place, waiting to strike again?

Detective Lenny Rozyczka—Roz, as he's known around the station—finishes yet another cell phone conversation, hangs up, and walks back over to Neal.

"Sorry about all the interruptions. Crazy day."

"What's going on?" Neal asks, not really caring.

"They think they might have an ID on that John Doe from this morning."

"That's good." Neal had heard about the case earlier: an older male had been found over on South 18th Street, shot once through the head, apparent robbery victim. His wallet was, of course, missing.

"Yeah. We've got a worried wife, Mary Lou Armano, who called to report her husband missing. His name's Joe. He works as a bartender at a club over by Rittenhouse Square. Never came home last night. His description fits Doe: gray hair, brown eyes, medium build, bit of a gut."

It fits a lot of men, including Roz himself, Neal can't help thinking.

"Good," he says again. "About this . . ." He sweeps a hand toward Lucinda's bathroom down the hall, where a couple of officers are dusting for prints.

"I'll have them e-mail the photos right out to you, and you can access them when you get out to the island."

"What about—"

"I'll go get it. Hang on."

He steps away to talk to one of the investigators in the next room.

Neal thinks about Frank Santiago, who's leading the case in Beach Haven. He's a good investigator. One of the best cops to come out of Neal's class at the police academy all those years ago.

Not exactly a friend, though. Their personalities didn't mesh. Frank was arrogant, Neal thought. Swagger didn't appeal to him.

One stormy January night after class, Frank's car wouldn't start. Neal tried to give him a jump, but that didn't work. He wound up driving Frank all the way home to Reading—over an hour in the opposite direction, but it took two because of the weather, and three back.

"I owe you one," Frank told Neal the next day. "I won't forget it."

"Don't worry. I won't let you."

He didn't.

Frank left Philadelphia soon after, landing in Atlantic City homicide. Neal kept track of him. After years in the gritty trenches, Frank is winding down his career in Beach Haven.

Neal finally called in the favor a few years ago.

"Are we even?" Frank asked, when the deal was done.

"Hell, no. I'd say you owe me an even bigger favor now."

"How's that?"

"You just got yourself one hell of a good cop."

Randy Barakat.

Neal hated to lose him, but he knew it was best that he move on, knew he'd better do it in a place that was far removed from Philadelphia—and Lucinda.

"Here you go." Roz is back. He hands over the manila envelope containing a photocopy of the sheet of paper found on Neal's kitchen table. They're keeping the original here, of course, as evidence.

"Thanks, Roz. Keep me posted, will you?"

"You bet. Drive safe."

Neal nods and heads out the door.

The streetlights are flicking on when Lucinda sees the retired couple from down the street to the door, followed closely by a trio of guys from Randy's summer softball league, then the white-collared priest from the local church.

Finally shutting the door behind her, she realizes they've reached a welcome lull. The house is quiet at last. Probably not for long, though.

In the kitchen, she rinses the last acrid bit of coffee from the bottom of the carafe and is refilling it, thinking again about Carla's ring, when Randy comes up beside her.

"How are you holding up?"

"*You're* asking *me*?"

"You look exhausted."

"I'm fine. How are *you*?"

"Not fine."

"I know." She turns off the tap. "Do you want to go lie down or something? If anyone shows up, I'll tell them—"

"No. Just—sit down. I want to talk to you."

Heart pounding, she sits. So does he.

Something is up. Paranoia seeps in.

Could he possibly be questioning her involvement in what happened here yesterday?

Or is he going to acknowledge that he lied about speaking to Carla *after* she'd been killed?

Unwilling to let him see her concern, Lucinda rests her chin in her hand and waits.

Not for long, though. "There's something you should know."

She nods.

Randy curses as the doorbell rings yet again.

"Do you want me to get that?" she asks, starting to push her chair back.

"No." He grasps her wrist. "Dammit. I want to tell you this."

"Okay. Tell me."

"Carla and I . . ."

The doorbell again.

Detective Lambert sticks his head in. "Want me to get it?"

"I guess you have to," Randy says tersely, eyes focused on Lucinda. "See if you can get rid of whoever it is, Dan."

Lambert nods, disappears.

Fixated on Randy's face, Lucinda coaxes softly, "Go ahead. I'm listening."

"Carla and I . . . We've been separated for a while. I moved out last September."

Chapter Eight

Located on almost four hundred acres of picturesque woodland at the United States Marine Corps base forty miles southwest of Washington, D.C., the F.B.I. Academy complex looks for all the world like a secluded college campus.

As Vic strides through the glass corridors connecting the buildings, he takes it as a positive sign that nothing has changed during his nearly eighteen-month absence. It's almost as if he never left—aside from the fact that he can no longer come and go with a flash of official ID.

For a good portion of Vic's career, the Behavioral Science Unit was located in the bowels of the Academy. But they've since moved up in the world. By the time he left, Vic had a relatively spacious window office.

He passes its closed door on the way to his destination, and feels only a mild pang of regret-tinged nostalgia. He has a feeling it would probably be much more pronounced were he still sitting around watching television day in and day out.

But writing the book has captivated him in a way his FBI work once did. Apparently, the media attention has captivated the unsub as well.

A secretary takes his coat, then ushers him into the meeting he scheduled yesterday morning, immediately after opening the mail.

"Good to see you again, Vic." Supervisory Special Agent Annabelle Wyatt stands and shakes his hand across her file-stacked desk. Funny—all those years he worked with her, Vic never noticed how much Annabelle reminds him of a much thinner Oprah, with the same dark beauty, the same authoritative demeanor.

That's because you'd never seen an episode of "Oprah" when you were working here. You had other things to do.

As he does now.

"I hear you're keeping busy with your book," Annabelle tells him, and he can't tell by her tone whether she approves or disapproves of the project.

He does know that it's either one or the other, though. If he learned anything about Annabelle Wyatt when they were colleagues, it's that she has a strong opinion about everything, though she'll usually keep it to herself.

"I was told you had something to show me, Vic. Highly sensitive evidence."

"Yes." He reaches into the pocket of his suit coat and removes the envelope, now encased in a plastic bag.

She immediately puts on a pair of gloves, opens the envelope, removes the paper, and unfolds it.

"The Night Watchman," Annabelle says without hesitation. "Where did you get this?"

"Yesterday's mail."

"Who have you told?"

"My wife. And you."

"Thank you, Vic. We'll get right on it."

"Either he just committed a murder, or he's about to. We need to start cross-referencing every homicide case we can find across the country that has a remotely similar M.O. to the Night Watchman cases we have on file. Check all the murders that happened when the moon was full."

Annabelle gives him a long, hard look. "We may do that, Vic." Her emphasis on the first word is unmistakable, as it is on the next. "You're retired now, remember? Go home and enjoy it."

He had anticipated her response, of course.

Once you're gone, you're gone.

It isn't unheard of for the FBI to reach out to a retired agent to assist on a cold case, but that would be a matter of don't call us, we'll call you.

Still, it stings just a little.

"I've been up to my eyeballs in research on this guy for months now," he reminds Annabelle. "If you need me to—"

"We'll call. Thanks, Vic."

This isn't the first time Lucinda has been inside this small, windowless room in the Long Beach Township Police Headquarters.

Six months later, it all comes rushing back to her.

Tess Hastings had just gone missing, and Lucinda was here to tell the authorities about a vision she'd had—a vision she was certain involved Tess being thrown from a Manhattan rooftop.

Of course it turned out to have been Ava, the look-alike aunt who had died decades before Tess was born.

Tess was far from safe that night as Lucinda and Randy and the other detectives sat strategizing in this room. But she survived.

Tonight, as on that August night, the mood is somber; yet there is no sense of urgency as they all take their seats around the big table.

Like last time, files and papers and coffee cups litter the room.

Unlike last time, Neal Bullard is present, waiting for them there when they arrive.

He drove straight here when he got into town, then called Randy's house and asked that the two of them meet him at headquarters. Lucinda welcomed the interruption, still reeling from Randy's announcement that his marriage had been over for months now.

Right after Randy dropped the bombshell, Lambert escorted Randy's sister Julie into the kitchen. She was sobbing, and after a few minutes, Lucinda could tell that her emotions were setting Randy's even more on edge. He left the room, and Lucinda did her best to calm Julie, who stayed for a good hour, pretty much crying inconsolably the whole time.

By the time his sister left to go pick up their parents at the airport in Newark, the moment between Randy and Lucinda had passed.

Just as well. She isn't sure how to feel about what Randy told her.

Even if she'd known long before now, she would hardly have been jumping for joy. The end of a marriage is no cause for celebration, regardless of the implications it might have had given Lucinda's feelings for Randy.

Now, with Carla's death, she can't relate to it on a personal level at all.

No wonder the house felt so barren. No wonder she sensed an awkwardness when all those people offered Randy their condolences. No wonder they were intrigued by Lucinda's presence.

Knowing he had left Carla, they must have been suspicious about the nature of his relationship with Lucinda. They probably thought her being there was inappropriate.

Who knows? Small town gossip travels fast. Maybe the locals somehow even knew that she and Randy were once more than friends.

But that's all we are now.

The lead investigator, Frank Santiago, made it clear that

she and Neal are in this meeting because they're directly involved in the case. But he emphasized that they won't be
privy to the ongoing investigation. Not on this end, anyway.

"How are you holding up?" someone asks Randy as they
gather around the table.

"I'm okay. Better, now that the shock is wearing off."

They all nod, and Lucinda wonders what they're thinking.

Does the fact that Randy and Carla were separated make
the loss any easier for him to bear?

Maybe.

Already, he wasn't planning on spending the rest of his
life with Carla, so the impact on his day-to-day life will be
lessened.

Even so, her death is no less tragic within its own context.
Her life was brutally taken.

"I want you to know we're going to put every resource we
have into solving this crime." Santiago, a tall, lean man with
an aquiline nose and sharp-edged black goatee, leans forward, pressing his palms authoritatively on the table. "We're
going to get the son of a bitch who did this, Randy. I promise
you."

The other law officers nod in mute agreement as Santiago
breaks off to cough, wheezing with the effort.

"Sorry," he says, "I've had pneumonia this winter."

He pulls a handkerchief from his pocket to cover his
mouth, and his eyes collide with Lucinda's. Seized by the
sudden impression that he isn't well, and that it's more complicated than pneumonia, she feels a flash of empathy for the
man.

Cancer, she realizes. *Poor Frank. Does he even know?*

Looking away from her, he makes brief introductions of
those seated around the table. When he reaches Lucinda, he
says, "I'm sure some of you remember Lucinda Sloan, the
psychic investigator who worked with our team last summer
on the Pearson case."

"So you're going to be working on this case, too?" one of the young uniforms asks.

"If I'm needed." Lucinda's voice is thin, starting to rasp a little. That always happens to her when she's tired. If she's not careful, it'll go into full blown laryngitis.

She can feel Santiago's black-eyed gaze on her, and doesn't dare meet it.

Last summer, when he was on the periphery of the Pearson and Hastings cases, she always sensed a disapproving vibe coming her way. It didn't really bother her then—she's used to territorial, skeptical, even chauvinistic investigators.

She tries not to let it bother her now, either.

Santiago, after another brief coughing bout, begins by telling them all what Lucinda had already guessed: the medical examiner had estimated that Carla had been dead for several days when she was found.

"Lambert said you're going to ID her, Randy."

"Yes."

Santiago peers at him with concern. "Do you want to have someone else do it?"

"No." Randy swallows hard. "I can do it."

"Okay. Lambert, drive him over to the morgue after this."

Santiago lays two sheets of paper side by side for everyone to see.

"One of these was found by Ms. Sloan and Detective Bullard on Detective Bullard's kitchen table Monday night. The other was bagged with one of the newspapers lying at the foot of the driveway, Randy. I realize the neighborhood is quiet at this time of year, but I'm still surprised that no one at least checked to make sure Carla was okay with all those papers piling up."

"But Carla never picked up the paper," Randy responds. "I kept meaning to stop the subscription, since I was the one who paid for it and I was the only one who ever read it. She lets them pile up out there for days. She walks right by them to get into her car. If I didn't stop by and get them, she'd dump them when she put out the cans on trash day."

Wheezing a little, Santiago rubs his beard. "Do these numbers mean anything to you?"

Randy shakes his head.

"Anyone else?"

Silence.

Santiago looks pointedly at Neal, who clears his throat and turns to Lucinda.

She feels her body instinctively clench, going into defensive mode.

"I wanted to show you this first, privately," Neal says, "but I didn't get the chance."

"Show me what?" Her heart is pounding.

He slides a blown-up photograph toward her. Everyone leans in to look.

The picture was snapped looking into a mirror. Neal's torso is visible in one corner, topped by a circle of flashbulb glare.

The mirror is gilt-framed.

Scrawled on the glass, in what looks like blood, are garish numerals:

87.7
41.9

"This," Neal announces to the room as renewed dread screeches through her mind, "is Lucinda's bathroom mirror. I found it earlier when I stopped by her apartment back in Philadelphia."

"Is that . . . blood?" one of the officers asks.

"Red lipstick."

Lucinda looks up just in time to see a look pass between Lambert and Van Aken, seated directly across from her. Shifting her gaze to Santiago, she notes that he's shaking his head a little at Lambert and Van Aken, as if to warn them not to say anything.

Anything . . . like what?

She checks Randy's reaction. He glances from the photo to Lucinda herself, wearing an expectant expression.

"It wasn't there when I left yesterday morning," she manages to say—needlessly. "Someone must have gotten in again while I was gone."

"For what it's worth, Cin," Neal says, "there was no indication that someone broke in. Who's had access to your keys?"

"Besides you, you mean?" she quips humorlessly, knowing what Neal's thinking.

It could have been anyone, over time, because she had never changed the locks. A past tenant, a friend of a past tenant, an acquaintance of the landlord, one of the electricians or plumbers who came and went during the upgrades . . .

It could have been Jimmy, too. He could have slipped her keys out of her bag and made a copy. He's not the only one—but he's certainly had ample opportunity.

Neal—and the others—wait for a response. She doesn't dare look at Randy, but she can feel his eyes fixed on her, can feel his concern.

"Um, my friend Bradley has the keys." She exhales through puffed cheeks. "I gave him the spare set when he helped me move in, because he was coming and going without me there. But there's no way he—"

"Who," interrupts Sergeant Van Aken, still not exactly Lucinda's best bud, "is your friend Bradley?"

"Bradley Carmichael." Bradley Carmichael IV, but who's counting? "He's a friend from New York. I met him at his cousin's wedding last year, and we got to be good friends."

Really good friends. Fast friends, the way it was with Cam; two strangers thrown together under unique circumstances.

"Look," she tells Neal—tells all of them, feeling their dubious stares, "I trust Bradley."

"You haven't known him for very long," Neal points out.

"I've known him long enough to know he would never hurt me—or anyone else."

Neal nods, though his eyes ask her if she's absolutely sure about that—and so does a little voice in the back of her head.

"What should I wear?" Jaime Dobiak asks her friend Nancy above the Coldplay song blasting from the iPod plugged into the dock on her clock radio. She holds up two hangers from her closet. "The red or the black?"

Sprawled on Jaime's blue bedspread, Nancy doesn't bother to look up from the latest issue of *Cosmopolitan* she'd found on the nightstand. "Red. You could use a little color in your life."

"I have plenty of color in my life." Jaime gestures around her newly painted bedroom. Blue walls, blue curtains, blue bedspread. Even blue tissues in the box beside the bed. "And look what I bought yesterday." She holds up a bright yellow silk Hermès scarf. With the sale price and her employee discount at Bloomingdale's, it was a steal. "Do you like it?"

"I love it," Nancy tells her. "Are you going to wear it?"

"Not with this." She holds it against the black dress. "I'd look like a bumblebee."

"Don't wear that. You wear too much black."

"But black is slimming."

"True."

Heaven knows Jaime could stand to lose ten pounds—although the weight charts always say she's in a healthy range for her height.

Too much beer, not enough exercise. But between a full time job as a secretary and a part-time one at Bloomies on Michigan Avenue—the only way to afford her wardrobe and the rent on this great apartment off West Division Street, in walking distance to all her favorite clubs—who has time for the gym?

Granted, she might if she cut out the nightly partying. But not yet a year out of college and on her own for the first time in Chicago, Jaime Dobiak has no intention of taming her social life just yet.

She tosses the yellow scarf over the bedpost. Standing in front of the full length mirror, she holds one dress up to her chin, and then the other, swaying in time to the music.

"I love this song." She turns up the volume.

"What?"

"I said, I love this song!"

"The neighbors are going to call the cops!" Nancy glances up at last.

"No, the walls are really thick. Like, soundproof."

"*What?*"

"Soundproof walls!"

That's what the landlord told her when she moved in last summer. That—along with the prime location, near all Jaime's favorite hangouts on West Division and Rush Streets—was a big selling point. Not because she's a light sleeper, or concerned about the neighbors' parties. Rather, because she's worried that the neighbors are light sleepers and might complain about her frequent after-hours parties.

No one ever has.

Because they don't hear a thing.

The song ends. Jaime turns down the volume and compares the two hangers again. "I need a verdict, Nance."

"Wear the red. You look good in red with your coloring."

Blond hair and blue eyes go with everything in her closet, as far as Jaime's concerned.

Whatever. She'll wear the red.

She even has the lipstick to match, having stopped by the makeup counter at Bloomies before Valentine's Day to pick up a daring new shade.

It's called Blood Red.

Her Valentine's Day date said it looked good on her.

She'll wear it again tonight.

They don't call this the Windy City for nothing.

He shivers and pulls the collar of his black overcoat higher around his neck as he walks along State Street, rolling his dark blue Samsonite bag along behind him.

No one gives him a second glance; he's one in a cast of thousands: businesspeople in town for meetings and seminars and whatever the hell it is that businesspeople do.

He had the cab driver from O'Hare drop him at a different hotel: the enormous, upscale Renaissance over on Wacker. Just in case.

"Here for the conference?" the cabbie—a talkative, older guy with a flat Midwestern accent—asked.

"That's right," he replied, and wondered what kind of conference it was.

He hoped the cabbie wouldn't ask any specific questions, because then he wouldn't be able to answer them, and he'd have to get rid of the guy, and really, he's too busy for that right now.

Luckily for him—for both of them, really—the cabbie didn't bother to ask, just collected his fare and tip with a "Hey, thanks for all the ones. I can use 'em, I've been breaking twenties all day, a lot of short trips, being it's so cold out."

"No problem."

He tipped the doorman who came over to open the cab door with yet another dollar bill from the tremendous wad in his pocket.

"Thank you, sir."

Sir. He grinned. "No problem."

He made his way through the sea of professional types in the busy lobby, bought some mints and a newspaper at the lobby shop, visited the men's room. When a good fifteen minutes had passed he left, crossing Wacker and heading across the river.

Always cover your tracks.

"Right this way, Randy."

He nods, and with his friend Dan at his side, follows the

medical examiner's assistant—Sherri is her name—through a set of doors. A pert little blonde, Sherri is wearing a snug white ribbed turtleneck tucked into a snug black tweed skirt, with heels that tap tap tap along the tile floors.

They know each other fairly well: professionally, of course. He's escorted a number of people into the small viewing room at the morgue: distraught families of car wreck victims, mostly. How many times has he half-walked, half-carried, a hysterical mother back through these doors with her screeching "My baby"?

Now it's his turn to be escorted to that awful room.

"Do you want me to come in with you?" Lambert asks, laying a hand on Randy's shoulder when they reach the door.

"No. It's okay." He takes a deep breath. "Let's just do this."

Sherri opens the door with a jangling of her charm bracelet. Her nails, Randy notices, are long and polished bright red, with little gold hearts painted on the tip of each one.

The gaudy, cheerful manicure seems wrong here.

Maybe it's not.

Who knows? Maybe it's better, in this place where death hangs in the halls like a killing frost, to have a reminder that somewhere out there, life goes on. Somewhere out there, pretty girls polish their nails. Wear charm bracelets. Celebrate Valentine's Day. Stuff like that.

Then Randy is in the room with his dead wife.

She's lying there on a steel table with her eyes closed, looking just like all the other corpses he's seen—skin an unearthly gray shade, almost a dark blue around her lips, features concave, hair pulled back from her face. The smell of death assaults his nostrils, but it isn't overpowering. They've cleaned her up the best they can.

When he leaves, he knows, the process will begin. They'll undress her, and cut her up for the autopsy. Officially determine what killed her when the evidence is right there, beneath an enormous gauze bandage shielding her neck.

"Randy?" Sherri asks softly.

"It's her. It's Carla."

Sherri nods. After a moment, she hands him a clipboard.
He signs the papers.

Just a formality.

"Do you want a minute with her?"

He nods.

Sherri steps somberly into the hall. He can hear her voice,
low, and then Dan's.

Hot tears pool in his eyes, then spill over.

He looks at Carla. Forces himself to really look. One last
time.

"I'm sorry, baby," he whispers raggedly, and touches her
cold, blue hand.

She isn't wearing her wedding band—she wouldn't be.
She took it off in September. He did the same with his.

Of course, she isn't wearing her mother's sterling signet ring,
either. She wore it every day, on the ring finger of her right
hand, because it's too big for her pinkie. Every night that Randy
lived with her, when she got ready for bed, she would take
off her earrings and her watch and whatever other jewelry
she had been wearing during the day, and she would put it in
a little tray on her dresser.

But she never removed the signet ring.

The wedding band, either.

Not until September.

Her murderer stole the signet ring and left it for Lucinda
to find.

Did he steal her other jewelry as well?

Randy looks to her earlobes, mottled and dark.

The piercings are bare.

Oh . . . She's wearing pajamas. He's seen them before: blue
top with three-quarter length sleeves, and blue and green
striped pants.

That's why her jewelry is off. She had already gotten
ready for bed when she died.

That doesn't necessarily mean that it was late. Sometimes

Carla got ready for bed before the sun even went down and ate dinner in her pajamas.

He'll have to look, back at the house, at the little tray on the dresser for her earrings and whatever else she'd had on the day she died. Make sure nothing else is missing.

Randy hears a stirring in the hall and looks up. Both Sherri and Dan are looking in at him.

"You okay?" Dan asks.

Of course not. He's here with his dead wife.

"I'm okay."

He sighs and reaches out to touch her hand, one last time.

Her extremities are purplish blue. Her hand feels weirdly thick and cold and hard.

"I'm sorry, Carla," he whispers, bending to press a kiss against her hand.

That's when he sees the watch around her wrist.

Chapter Nine

Lucinda left her car back at Randy's house when they headed over to the police station earlier.

"Just leave it there and ride with me," Neal tells her now, as he stands, buttoning his coat, just inside the doors at police headquarters.

"No, I want my car." She tries to fight a yawn.

"Look at you. How are you going to drive for two hours after days without sleep?"

"I'll manage."

"At least let me drive you over there to get it, then, and we can follow each other back. We're going to the same place."

Yes. To Neal's place.

She's already agreed to stay in the Bullards' guest room for a few days—and not with much reluctance. Returning to her own apartment is, of course, out of the question for the time being.

87.7
41.9

What do those numbers mean? She's been running them through her head ever since Neal showed the photograph, to no avail. Santiago said they've run them through search engines and come up with countless references to—among other things—weight, weather, and air temperature. Nothing makes sense in terms of what is going on here.

They're going to analyze them, possibly even call in a numerologist.

The meeting lasted almost two hours, with countless interruptions. That was the way it always went in an active investigation. Unfortunately, they had no new information or potential leads by the time they left. Santiago asked the homicide investigators to assemble again later.

Of course. To go over all the details that couldn't be revealed to Lucinda and Neal—or even to Randy, as a victim of this crime, rather than an investigator.

Lucinda half-expected Neal to protest when they were dismissed, but he was anxious to get on the road. Erma had called him during the meeting, worried because the forecast along the shore calls for sleet, with snow inland.

Meteorology—and her own exhaustion—be damned, Lucinda is in no hurry to leave. Not without making sure Randy's okay after having gone to the morgue to identify Carla's body.

"I told Randy I was going to wait here for him to come back. Go ahead, Neal. I promise I'll be fine."

"Call my cell when you get on the road."

"I will."

"And don't wait too long."

"I won't."

Ten minutes after Neal departs, Randy is back from the morgue, looking shaken.

"How are you? Are you okay?"

"Not really." He accepts the cup full of Poland Spring water she pours him from the cooler.

How can she leave him like this?

They ride back over to the house in Officer Lambert's sedan. Randy sits in the front seat, drawn and quiet; Lucinda in the back, wishing she could comfort him somehow.

"We're going to find out who did it, Randy," Lambert tells him. "You know Santiago will be on this thing like a pit bull until he's got someone in custody."

"I know."

"Is he sick?" Lucinda asks them, remembering what she sensed earlier, in the conference room. "Santiago, I mean."

"He's had pneumonia," Dan says.

"No, something more serious than that. I felt it. I saw it." Realizing Frank might not want anyone to know—or might not even know himself—she shakes her head. "Never mind. I could be wrong."

But I'm not.

Randy's phone rings.

It's his sister Julie calling to say that their parents' flight had been delayed because of the weather in Newark. Their plane is still sitting at the gate in Florida.

"Forget about driving them all the way out here tonight when they get in, Julie," he says. "*If* they even get in."

Sitting in the back seat, Lucinda can hear Julie protesting into his ear.

"No, just tell them I'll see them first thing tomorrow," he says. "It's okay. I'm okay."

Julie is audibly crying on the other end of the telephone line, and talking. A lot.

Randy listens.

Tries to interrupt.

Listens some more.

"Yeah," he manages to say at last, "I'm sure I'll be fine tonight. I'm exhausted. I just want to get some rest."

Lucinda can relate to that. Her body feels numb with the lack of sleep, and she's starting to feel as though her brain is headed in the same direction.

Randy hangs up just as the squad car arrives in front of the Barakats' house, darkened for the night other than the doorstep light and a single lamp Randy left burning in the living room.

Lucinda and Randy climb out. The wind is blowing incessantly and a fine mist is already in the air, not yet sleet but it can't be far off.

"Do you want to come back to my cottage with me and have a cup of coffee before you head back?" Randy asks as they stand beside her car, both with their own keys in hand.

"Where is it?"

"Just a couple of blocks away."

She hesitates. "Okay. Sure."

Going to his apartment is probably a bad idea for more reasons than she cares to think about, but she can tell he doesn't want to be alone yet.

Anyway, she could use a cup of coffee for the road. It's a long drive.

"Good. I just want to check the house one last time, and then you can follow me over."

Lucinda climbs into her car to wait, starts the engine, and turns the heat on full blast, wishing the frigid interior would warm up. She's cold, and she's tired, and she's unnerved by the dark and by the unbelievable sequence of events that led her to this moment.

Cam.

With all that's gone on, Lucinda forgot to call her.

I can't let it go.

I've got to call her as soon as I get over to Randy's.

As she hugs herself and stares out the windshield, a figure appears on the sidewalk, eerily illuminated by the misty glow from the headlights.

It's a man—or it could be a larger woman—wearing a parka and walking a dog. The person's hood is pulled up and zipped tight around the face. Obviously one of the neighbors. For all Lucinda knows, she poured coffee for this person at Randy's this afternoon. Yet she can't see enough of the face to rule out a stranger, and if the person recognizes her, he or she is not letting on.

Lucinda can feel him—her?—staring in this direction with

more than casual interest. Is it concerned, neighborhood watch-type interest in light of the fact that a woman was murdered a stone's throw away? Or is it nosy, gossipy interest stem-ming from the fact that the dead woman's estranged husband might be seeing another woman?

The figure passes slowly, more slowly than is necessary as the dog strains at the leash. Randy comes out and gets into his car without glancing toward the street, and the dog-walker watches him, too.

Randy pulls up alongside Lucinda and gestures for her to roll down her window.

"Follow me," he calls above the wind. "It's only a few blocks away, off Bay Avenue."

Certain his voice carried along the sidewalk, she wonders if she should tell him she's changed her mind and is heading back.

Just because some busybody is snooping around?
Please.
Who cares what people think?
Randy is her friend—a friend in need.
"I'll follow you," she agrees, and promptly shifts into Drive.

He's reached the towering Westin on North Dearborn.

Like the Renaissance, it's a sleek, upscale hotel, its lobby also filled with businessmen in overcoats with rolling lug-gage. Candles flicker pleasantly.

"Checking in, sir?"

He looks around to see a uniformed bellman.

"Yes."

"Need a hand with your bag?"

"No, thanks." No way is he taking any chances with let-ting it out of his sight.

But he hands the bellman a dollar anyway. The kid looks a bit mystified, but pockets it and walks away.

He likes being called sir, he decides, as he heads for the

reception desk. It's about time he earned some of the respect he deserves.

He waits his turn to check in, pretending to check e-mail on his BlackBerry like everyone else. Of course it's just for show.

If you're playing a role, you must, of course, have the right wardrobe and the right props. You want to look like a Construction Worker, you need jeans, steel-toed boots, one of those insulated lunch bags. Soccer Dad, you get your hands on a great camera, khakis, and a polo shirt. And so it goes.

He stole the BlackBerry just a little while ago at O'Hare, lifting it boldly right out of the pocket holster of a business-man waiting to board a plane in the overcrowded terminal. With luck the person—*normalwe@aol.com*—didn't realize it was missing until he was on the plane, and it'll be a few hours before he can do anything about it.

By then it'll be lying in the bottom of the Chicago River which, he noticed while crossing the State Street bridge, is conveniently *not* frozen over.

"Okay, you're all set. We have you in room 1421." Smil-ing, the clerk hands back his credit card and a room key. "Thank you, Mr. Armano. Enjoy your stay."

The cottage Randy's renting is strictly no-frills: living room; bedroom—marked by a brass plate that reads Cap-tain's Quarters tacked above the door frame; a kitchen with a similar sign that announces the Galley and literally is one, barely large enough to hold the requisite stove, sink, and fridge. The bathroom, naturally, is marked Poop Deck.

"Charming, isn't it?" Randy tugs the front door, trying to get it to close tightly.

"It's very . . . kitschy." That's the kindest word she can think of. "At least it's furnished."

Not exactly Ethan Allen, though. More like the kind of stuff you buy in a box with instructions and put together yourself.

Lucinda looks around at the bookshelves shaped like up-ended rowboats, end tables made from ship's wheels, lamps with lighthouse bases. The sailboat-sprigged blue couch and chair slipcovers have that dank, beachy mildew smell that reminds Lucinda of canvas lawn chairs left moldering too long in a sealed shed. On the knotty pine walls are framed nautical charts and a seascape painting Lucinda immediately pegs as a paint-by-number.

"Kind of makes me want to sing 'Anchors Away,' " she tells Randy, and she is rewarded by a faint smile.

"You're too hoarse to sing," he tells her. "Want some tea with honey instead of coffee?"

"No, thanks. Need the caffeine."

"Tea has caffeine."

"Not enough for me. You know I like the strong stuff."

"How about a shot of whiskey in the coffee, then? My mother would say that'll cure all that ails ye," he adds in an expert brogue.

"I have to drive. Plain old coffee's good. Do you mind if I plug in my BlackBerry while I'm here? The battery's dead, and I need to make a call before I get on the road."

"There's an outlet somewhere here. . . ." He moves aside several cardboard boxes stacked in a corner. "There it is. Hand me the cord."

She inserts her phone into the other end and hands it to him. "Are you still moving in?" she asks, eying the boxes.

"No, that stuff belongs to the people who own the place. They didn't want to haul it back up to the city over the winter."

"What *is* all that?"

"Who knows? Probably seashells and lobster traps."

She flashes the obligatory smile, but hates that Randy is living like this, in a drafty kitschy cottage that's barely been winterized, surrounded by other people's boxed up belongings and press board furniture.

"Maybe you can move back home to your house now,"

she suggests as he fumbles around with the cord, trying to get the plug to stick in an outlet that won't seem to grip it.

"I need to plug this in someplace else," he mutters, and straightens.

She follows him to the kitchen—more knotty pine, and seagull-printed vinyl wallpaper. The lone wall outlet is occupied by a can opener and coffeemaker. He yanks the can opener cord to vacate a receptacle, plugs in her phone, then takes the carafe from the coffee pot and turns on the tap at the sink.

"Randy? Maybe you can move back home," she repeats, thinking he might not have heard the suggestion before. Her voice is wearing away quickly.

The answer comes immediately this time, and she realizes he heard her the first.

"I don't want to move back."

He fills the carafe, his back to her.

"I didn't mean right this second—I know it's too soon to make any decisions, but that's your house, and—"

"No, it's actually her house." He turns off the water and faces her. "I mean, it *was* hers."

"*All* hers?"

"When Zelda died, she left Carla some money and her condo. Carla rented it out for a while, but then she sold it and bought the house out here."

"You didn't buy it together?"

"No." He dumps the water into the coffeemaker. "Things have been bad for a while, Lucinda. A long while. I guess we both knew it wasn't going to last."

"For how long?"

"Let's see—right after we walked down the aisle. Or maybe even before."

Then why did you marry her? she wants to ask, but talk about a loaded question.

Now is not the time to ask it.

"Don't get me wrong—I loved her. But I knew it wasn't in the right way, and I knew it wasn't ever going to be enough. Eventually, we were basically going through the motions—both of us, not just me."

"What happened?"

"I fell out of love with her," he says simply. "And she fell in love with someone else." As he methodically measures coffee grounds into the filter basket, he adds, "When I look back, it's hard to tell which of those things happened first."

"She had someone else?"

He nods. "Jack Ramsden."

Jack Ramsden.

She heard that name earlier. Santiago asked Lambert if they had tracked him down yet, and Lambert said they were still trying. No one elaborated for the benefit of Lucinda and Neal, and she didn't want to ask many questions.

"He's a fisherman on the island," Randy tells her now. "Been dating my wife for . . . oh, I'd guess almost a year, give or take. The first few months of it behind my back, obviously."

"But you knew they were seeing each other?" She follows him back to the living room as the coffeemaker begins to hiss.

"Not right away. Unlike me, Carla was a damned terrific liar." Randy sits on the sofa. The springs creak noisily. He looks at her. "I can't believe I'm saying any of this. I mean, right now. Speaking ill of the dead is . . ."

"You don't have to explain yourself to me, Randy." Lucinda sits, too, keeping a full cushion between them. It's tempting to rest her aching neck and back against the cushions as a wave of weariness washes over her.

"I was shocked when I found out what happened to her, and I was sick about it."

"I know you were. Of course you were."

"She was my wife. She was a good person."

There's a *but* coming. She can tell by his tone.

Well, of course there is. Randy isn't your typical grieving

widower—not with a marriage that has long since crashed and burned.

"I cared about Carla. But the truth is, Lucinda, it was long over between us. We haven't lived together since September, and it feels like a lot longer. That was just when I finally got myself out."

"That had to be so hard for you to do. Leave, I mean."

"I wish I could say it was. But we both knew it was over way before then. And I wasn't going to tell you this, but . . . what the hell . . ."

Her heart pounds. She has to force herself not to break eye contact, much as she longs to avoid what she sees in his eyes.

". . . It was seeing you again last July, out of the blue, that made me realize . . . a lot of things."

"Please don't say you left your wife for me, Randy, because—"

"No, I didn't leave her *for* you. I left her *because* of you. There's a difference."

"I know." She gets it—really, she does.

She knows what he's trying to say.

But he shouldn't be saying it.

Now is not the right time.

Not when she's so tired she can't think straight and she's going to lose her voice any minute.

Not with Carla lying dead in the morgue and Lucinda, in the most bizarre twist imaginable, somehow involved.

"I didn't know if I was ever going to see you again," Randy tells her. "After last summer, I mean. But knowing that when we reconnected—that I could still feel that way about you, after all those years—about someone who wasn't my wife— well, it pretty much told me all I needed to know. It made me take the initiative to get out, because I knew she never would."

"Not even for—what was his name? Jack?"

"I doubt it. Carla has never been one to make decisions

and changes. She lets herself be propelled. I mean—she *did*," he amends, and Lucinda glimpses a flash of sorrow in his eyes.

"So where is Jack now?"

"Away. He's divorced, and his kids live somewhere in the Midwest—I'm not sure where. But Lambert said that when they checked with his neighbors, they all said they hadn't seen him in a few days and he's been visiting his kids on their winter break. They're trying to track him down."

"You don't think there's any chance that he . . ."

"Jack? No."

"Based on what? Do you know him well?"

"Not really. He hasn't lived on the island very long. But based on sheer gut instinct as a cop—and the evidence we have so far—this is something bigger than Carla being killed in some lovers' quarrel. It feels to me like . . ."

When he trails off, she completes his sentence. She knows where he's going. She thinks of Ava Neary, of all the pretty dead girls who supposedly took their own lives.

"It feels like a serial killer."

"And if it is," Randy tells her, "he's going to do it again."

Lucinda nods, sickened by the realization that he's already been in her apartment. He may still be watching her, following her. . . .

Stalking his next victim.

Before leaving for the airport, Vic was interviewed by a couple of agents who wanted to know whether he'd had any other recent contact from the anonymous person who'd sent the note, whether he'd seen anyone suspicious lately, whether he'd had phone call hang ups—all the usual questions he himself would have once asked someone in his situation.

He had nothing to tell them, other than that the note had arrived out of the blue.

They assume, as Vic does, that the recent publicity about

his book smoked the deadly phantom out of his hiding place. And that it might trigger him to start killing again.

"We can only hope that's not the case," one of the agents told him before he left.

The local field office will be involved now, they told him. They'll send agents out to Vic's house to investigate, and probably keep tabs on him to determine whether anyone is lurking.

The long-ago profile he'd helped to create in the early years of the BSU will be resurrected, re-examined.

They'll be looking for a nocturnal loner, intelligent, organized.

A careless set of footprints found on the muddy grass leading to the sidewalk at an early crime scene—before he perfected his M.O.—indicated that back then, he'd weighed about two hundred pounds and worn a size eleven loafer.

That particular crime had been committed on a busy suburban avenue, at a time of night when others would have been on the streets. Yet he had walked—not run—away from the scene. Clearly, he was ordinary-looking enough to have managed to blend into the setting without anyone's giving him a second glance.

That image has haunted Vic all these years: an average Joe sauntering away into the night after hacking a woman to death in her own kitchen.

The crime would be no less heinous were he a frenzied madman racing from the scene, but he sure as hell would have been easier to catch.

Now, sitting in a crowded gate area at Dulles airport, Vic thumbs through yet another newspaper, searching every headline.

There are plenty of homicides in the news today, but none so far that match, at a glance, the Night Watchman's M.O.

That doesn't mean he hasn't struck again, or isn't about to.

Vic figures that chances are slim of his randomly stum-

bling across a murder that fits—particularly without the resources he'd have were he still a part of the Bureau—but
what else has he got to do?

What he really needs is the Internet, so that he can check
in a more methodical manner, beginning his search on recent
dates when the moon was full, and working backward.

But he doesn't have his laptop, and the business center
here at the airport is closed.

So he keeps looking, going through one paper after another from the stack he bought at Hudson News on the concourse after he learned that his flight has been delayed yet
again.

Weather is wreaking havoc up and down the East Coast.

He has a feeling he's going to be stuck here all night. It
shouldn't matter. Kitty isn't even home. He asked her to stay
with a friend while he's away. Just in case.

"Just in case he's watching us?" she asked matter-of-
factly.

"He's probably not watching us," he told her.

But chances are, he's watching someone.

Ordinarily, on a night like this, with a storm blowing in,
Frank Santiago would be focused on what lies ahead, counting on the department's being flooded with calls regarding
car accidents, downed trees, that sort of thing.

But tonight, the storm is the last thing on anyone's mind.

Tonight, they've got a murder on their hands, and every
bit of manpower, every resource they have, is aimed at figuring out what the hell happened to Carla Barakat.

That Neal Bullard has become involved has really thrown
Frank for a loop.

But then, it's no coincidence.

It was Neal who asked him to hire Randy in the first
place.

"Why?" Frank asked suspiciously. "Is he in some kind of trouble there?"

"No, nothing like that."

"It has to be something, or you wouldn't be calling me."

"He just needs a fresh start."

"He's burnt out?"

"No. He's planning to get married. Wants to get away from the city, buy a house, raise a family someplace safe—you know the drill."

Yeah. Frank knew the drill.

Detective work takes its toll on a guy. On his health. On his marriage.

Frank knew.

It just so happened that Frank had an opening on the township force at the time. Otherwise he really could have given a shit about repaying a decades-old favor.

He had other things to worry about. Chemo, radiation, endless tests, and then waiting for the numbers.

Numbers—it was always about numbers.

Still is.

The numbers measure his blood levels, and his tumors. The numbers essentially tell Frank Santiago—who never smoked a cigarette in his life, yet somehow found his lungs clogged with cancer cells—whether he will live or die in another couple of months.

They continue to do so.

The news isn't always good.

Frank detests numbers. Fears them.

And so the irony hadn't escaped him today when Neal Bullard blew back into his life like a nor'easter, with numeric evidence to turn everything upside down.

From the start, though, Frank had assumed they were dealing with a domestic case. Everyone knew Carla Barakat had a lover—and at first, no one knew where Jack Ramsden was, other than that he was unaccounted for.

Lovers' quarrel gone bad. That was what Frank figured.

But Jack Ramsden turned up in St. Louis with an airtight alibi right around the time Bullard showed up with the evidence.

Evidence that, along with the bloody ring, soundly links the Other Woman to the crime, as far as Frank's concerned.

Lucinda Sloan.

Lucinda Sloan who, he had realized earlier, in the meeting, really might be a psychic after all.

He's always had his doubts about that.

But when he caught her looking at him in the meeting, some flash of empathy—or maybe sympathy—in her eyes told him that she knows his dark secret. Somehow, she picked up on the one thing he hasn't told anyone—and doesn't intend to, until it's absolutely necessary.

Damn her, he'd thought when he realized she knew. *Why does she have to be involved in this case?*

Why, indeed?

He has his suspicions. Had them before she barged into his private hell.

Why would she just hand over the ring, though, if she were involved in Carla's murder? Why wouldn't she have hidden it?

It doesn't make sense.

But if Frank looks hard enough, it will. Of that, he's certain.

Lucinda, after all, is the reason Randy Barakat was so hot to get out of Philadelphia.

Any skilled detective—hell, any human being with eyes and ears—could figure that out after spending five minutes in the same room with the two of them. Frank had certainly done his share of that last summer when she was in town working on the Pearson and Hastings cases.

It was no accident that the Barakats' marriage crashed and burned weeks later.

And it was obvious—if anyone cared, which Frank really

didn't at the time—that Randy Barakat and Lucinda Sloan must have picked up right where they left off.

They've managed to cover their trail remarkably well until now.

Now that Lucinda Sloan has found reason to kill off the competition in an elaborate set-up—making it look like the work of a homicidal stranger—all bets are off.

Anything is possible.

For all Frank knows, Randy was in on it.

Lambert probably doesn't think so. They're buddies. And Lambert is an earnest type, which sometimes serves him well in police work, and sometimes does not.

Which is why Frank is going to have to sit him down and make it very clear that he is not to involve Randy in this investigation.

It shouldn't be necessary, but he has a feeling it is.

Frank already briefly cautioned him, before Lambert left to take Randy over to the morgue, not to reveal any of the details of the case that weren't already revealed earlier in the meeting.

"There are things we can't have getting out," Frank told Lambert, who certainly knows the drill. That's how it always works with a homicide investigation. You keep certain details from the public and the press, details only the killer and those at the scene could possibly know.

Like the bright red lipstick Carla Barakat was wearing.

Lipstick she sure as hell didn't apply herself, unless she was trying to look like a demented clown.

"You didn't tell Randy about the lipstick she had on, did you?" Frank asked Lambert, just to be sure.

"Are you kidding? She was his wife."

Was being the key word.

"I didn't tell him anything like that. Why would I want to upset him even more?"

"That's good," Frank said, knowing Randy wouldn't see the lipstick at the morgue.

It had, of course, been washed away, along with the blood, when the corpse was prepared for viewing. You do your best never to let the family members see anything upsetting when they get their last look at their dead loved one.

But photographic evidence remains.

Other evidence, too. Plenty of it.

Frank fully intends to keep the specifics from being revealed to anyone outside the immediate investigation. Including Neal Bullard and Randy Barakat and Lucinda Sloan.

Just in case the official shadow of suspicion falls on one— or for all he knows, more—of them.

Chapter Ten

"Sorry, I need to answer this," Randy tells Lucinda, after checking Caller ID on his ringing cell phone.

"It's okay." She stretches, rubs her eyes. "I should go."

"No. Not yet." Is it wrong for him to need her so badly tonight?

Her company, her comforting presence . . . and more. More than that.

Yes, it's wrong, but he can't help it.

"It's getting late." She starts gathering her things.

The phone is still ringing.

Randy has to get it.

But first, he has to make her stay. "It's not that late."

"It feels like the middle of the night."

"But—you need coffee."

"That's okay—"

"No, I already made it. Just let me take this call, and then we'll have coffee."

"Okay," she says around a yawn, and leans back.

Relieved, Randy snaps open his phone. "What's up, Dan?"

"Where are you?"

"Home. Why?"

"Home . . . where?"

"The cottage."

"Are you alone there?"

Randy hesitates. "No. Why?"

There's a long pause, as if Lambert is wondering whether he should ask who might be there with him.

As if he doesn't know.

"I was going to swing over there. There's something you should take a look at."

"Want me to come down to headquarters?"

"No," Lambert says quickly. "You're home, stay put. The weather's crummy. I'll just tell you about it."

"Tell me about what?" he asks, conscious of Lucinda beside him, trying to act as though she's not listening to his side of the conversation—as if she can help it.

He supposes he can go into the next room to take the call, but really, he has nothing to hide from her. Not anymore.

"You're never going to believe this, Randy."

"What?" He rakes his hands up his forehead, overtired, losing patience.

"You know how you mentioned after we left the morgue that Carla was wearing a watch with her pajamas, and that was unusual? I went back over there after I dropped you off, and I checked out the watch. It was a Freestyle. Are you familiar with that brand?"

"No."

"Nothing fancy. The strange thing is, the battery was dead. The hands were stopped at five-forty."

Randy can feel Lucinda trying to catch his eye, but he can't even look at her, his heart racing.

Why would Carla wear a watch with a dead battery?

"And Randy—the watch was engraved. On the back."

"Engraved."

"Yes."

"What did it say?"

Dan clears his throat. "Just the date she died and numbers. That's all. Decimals. 74.2 and 39.6."

"74.2 and 39.6," Randy repeats, with chilling recognition as Lucinda snaps blatantly to attention beside him.

A quick perusal of the local publications in the hotel room tells him that West Division Street is where all the action is.

Looks fairly easy to find, according to the map. He could take a cab—God knows he's got plenty of ones to pay the fare, courtesy of the dead bartender's wallet loaded with tips.

But he has all the time in the world tonight, and he wants to relish every minute. He'll stroll over.

This has always been his favorite part: the anticipatory stage.

The search: trolling for the perfect woman, considering and discarding potential candidates, waiting for the one who speaks to something inside him when he spots her, the one who fits the bill.

He was cheated out of that last time. Carla Barakat was a necessity, but she didn't fill his needs, really. Not the way all the others had.

He had expected the kill to be diminished because of that. Had wondered whether he might even have misgivings about it after it was over.

Like with his mother.

But that was different.

With her, there was no anticipatory stage, no search, no plan.

Mother was never meant to die. Not at his hands, anyway.

Unlike those who came before her.

Unlike Carla, and those who will come after—including Lucinda Sloan.

For a good fifteen minutes, Lucinda and Randy have analyzed the numbers—where they've appeared, what they might mean, what message Carla's killer is trying to convey.

"I feel like my brain just isn't working," Lucinda finally admits, sagging against the cushions, fighting yawn after yawn, aching with exhaustion.

"Mine isn't either. I'm wiped out."

She nods. She should get moving. Grab that cup of coffee, call Cam, go.

Get moving, then.

But her energy has been utterly depleted.

She just needs to sit here a moment longer before facing the long drive.

"I still can't believe it," Randy says again—mostly to himself. "I can't believe someone just walked into that house and killed her."

"Did Carla say anything at all to make you think she felt like she was in danger?"

"Carla didn't say anything at all to me, period. We exchanged a few e-mails, stuff about the lawyers, accounts, that kind of thing. But we didn't talk anymore."

"That's so . . ." She shuts her mouth, thinking better of what she was about to say.

"What?"

"Just . . . It's so ironic that you weren't even speaking to each other in the end, and yet . . . you were her next of kin."

"It would be different if we were divorced, but that was still a ways away. The thing is . . . I'm not just her next of kin, I'm her sole heir. I spoke to Gregg Genett today—he's her lawyer—and he told me she hadn't updated her will in a few years."

"Was she planning to, do you think?"

"Probably. But like I said, she wasn't one to take much initiative, and anyway—she didn't have close family left, and her friends . . . Well, they kind of came and went over the years, so—" He breaks off as what sounds like a bucket full of marbles patters against the house.

"What was that?" Lucinda jumps up and follows him to the window.

Randy flips off the inside light so that they can see out. "Sleet," he says unnecessarily.

For a moment, they're both silent.

Side by side in the dark, they look out at the frozen precipitation slanting from the sky on a misty wind that rocks the tree branches.

"You can't go out in that."

Lucinda was just thinking the same thing. "I'll be fine."

Not very convincing, but she has to go. She can't stay here with him.

"You won't be fine. Stay with me tonight."

"No."

"Lucinda, there's not a reason in the world you should go out in that."

Yes, there is.

Standing here alone in the dark with him is just as unnerving as the storm outside, and—

The sudden ring of a phone pierces the air.

Her cell.

Randy flicks the light on again. She goes to the kitchen to answer the phone, leaving it plugged into the wall, knowing the battery has barely begun to charge.

It's Neal. Of course. Wondering why she hasn't called.

"Hi, Neal, what's up?"

"Are you okay? You sound sick."

"That's just my voice. You know how it gets when I'm tired."

"Are you on the road yet?"

"No," she admits, watching Randy fill two mugs with steaming coffee.

"Then don't go anywhere. It's miserable out here. The causeway's glare ice. Cars spinning out and off the road everywhere."

"Oh, no."

Randy shoots her a questioning look—wondering, no doubt, whether there's been some new development in the case.

"The roads are bad," she tells him. "Neal doesn't want me to leave here."

"That makes two of us."

Ignoring the comment—and his blue, blue eyes—she turns her back a little, telling Neal, "I'll wait it out for a while, then."

"Wait it out until tomorrow. It's going to get worse before it gets better. The temperature will keep dropping overnight."

"What about you?"

"I'll make it home. I've driven through worse."

"I'm sure I have, too."

"You stay where you are. Do you hear me?"

Bristling at his authoritative tone, she reminds herself that he's only trying to keep her safe.

Here alone overnight with Randy.

Yeah, that's safe.

Hanging up the phone, Lucinda covers a yawn.

"You can have the lovely Captain's Quarters." Randy arcs a hand toward the bedroom. "I'll sleep on the couch."

"I'm not putting you out of your bed tonight. I'll take the couch."

"No, you won't." As she opens her mouth to protest, he stops her, saying, "I'm going to stay up a while, and you look ready for bed."

"I have to make a phone call first."

"I forgot. Do you still want coffee?"

She eyes the two cups he's just filled.

Coffee will keep her up. It'll keep them both up.

Sleep. Sleep is safe.

"I guess there's no need for coffee if I don't have to drive."

"I was just thinking the same thing." Randy pours the coffee out in the sink. "What I could really use is a drink."

"I was just thinking the same thing," she admits, and smiles faintly.

Randy reaches up into a cupboard.

Standing behind him, still holding her phone, she tries

not to watch his sweater ride up, revealing the muscles of his lower back.

He pulls down a bottle of Jack Daniels and plunks it on the counter, then looks at Lucinda. When she nods her approval, he wordlessly throws a couple of ice cubes into two glasses and pours.

The phone in her hand beeps as she reaches for her drink. "Another call?"

"No," she tells Randy. "It means I've got messages."

No surprise, after a couple of days with no battery.

She sips her drink, relishing the burn of bourbon sliding down her throat.

"I need to check my voice mail before I make my call," she tells him. "Is it okay if I go into your bedroom?"

Randy nods and gulps his drink, as befits a man who's been through hell in the last thirty-six hours.

Cam has always loved a good storm—when Mike is home, and nobody has to go anywhere. When they can cuddle by a roaring fire in the brick-walled sunken sunroom that stretches along the back of the house, watching the snow fall past the tall windows and French doors.

If Mike were here tonight instead of still out in Utah, she'd feel cozy as opposed to uneasy, listening to the wind howl and toss freezing rain at the windows.

Well, maybe not cozy.

The baby's been fussy all evening. Every time Cam thinks she has her settled, she wakes fitfully ten or fifteen minutes later, crying.

"Maybe it's just from her cold," Tess suggests, walking her wailing sister across the floor as Cam hunts for the infant thermometer to see if the fever is back. "Her nose is still kind of runny."

Thermometer in hand at last, Cam checks the baby.

She's got a fever.

"Poor little thing. Hang onto her, Tess, while I see if we've got enough Tylenol drops to get her through the night."

Cam looks in the medicine cabinet in the half-bath off the kitchen.

The Infant Tylenol is almost gone.

If Mike were here, he'd run out to Rite Aid.

If Mike were here, if Mike were here . . .

How did she ever get through all those months without him last year?

The phone rings just as she returns to the kitchen to take the whimpering baby from Tess.

"That's Daddy," she says with absolute certainty.

When two people have been a couple for as long as they have—and through as much together as they have—they don't have to be psychic to know when they're needed. "Can you grab the phone for me and tell him I'll call him back in a few minutes, when I get Grace settled down?"

"Sure."

Cam walks her miserable daughter into the next room, rubbing her back and bouncing her a little. "It's okay, Grace. Mama's here. . . . Mama's here. . . . Shhh. . . ."

"Mom? It's for you." Tess appears in the doorway with the phone. "It's not Daddy. It's Lucinda."

Lucinda.

Cam wondered when she was going to hear back from her. Then the baby grew fussy and Cam got busy with her, and forgot.

Telling Lucinda about the note in the mail seems a lot less urgent now.

But she takes the call anyway, handing Grace over to Tess.

"Walk her up to her room and show her the stuffed animals. She likes that."

Grace sobs, and Tess gives Cam a dubious look. "Whatever. Come on, Grace. Let's go see lamby and kitty cat!"

Cam returns to the kitchen with the phone.

Of course she didn't tell Tess about the anonymous message in the mail. She's not going to bring it up now, when Tess finally put last summer's nightmare behind her.

We all have.

But it refuses to die.

"Lucinda?"

"Cam!" The voice on the other end of the line is raspy. "Is everything all right?"

"Everything's fine. Are you sick?"

"No. Just tired. I got all those messages, and I thought something awful must have happened."

"No, nothing like that. I'm sorry. I didn't mean to—"

"My cell battery died, and . . . I've been in the middle of something the last few days."

Something tells Cam that whatever *something* is, it's not pleasant.

"Are *you* all right? Other than being tired, I mean?"

"Yes. Long story, and I've been meaning to call you and tell you about it, but—first tell me why you called me."

Cam opens the drawer and reaches toward the back, where she stashed the envelope. "It's about my sister, actually. . . ."

She hears a gasp on the other end of the line and, startled, stops rifling through the drawer.

"What's wrong?" she asks Lucinda.

"Nothing, just . . . What about your sister?"

"Randy?"

Sitting on the couch, empty glass in hand, he finds his morbid thoughts taking an abrupt detour when he looks up to see Lucinda standing in the bedroom doorway.

He had been wondering about the arrangements that will have to be made when Carla's body is released.

Now his bourbon infused brain wonders what it would be like if he'd never married Carla at all; if Lucinda were his wife; if that bedroom over her shoulder belonged to the two of them instead of to the captain; if he could sweep her right back in there and hold her and never let her go.

"We've got to call Santiago right away. And Neal. We've got to talk to Neal."

The urgency in Lucinda's hoarse voice and the grim look on her face swipe errant thoughts from Randy's mind.

"What happened?"

"That was Cam Hastings. She got a note in the mail—a picture of her sister Ava, and a note that said 'I know what happened to her. Solve it and if you are right you will find me.' Cam said there were a bunch of misspellings."

He considers that—does his best to, anyway, wishing he hadn't finished a glass of bourbon while she was on the phone in the bedroom. His analytical powers are shot, dammit.

Still, remembering all the kooks and cranks who popped up after he and Lucinda and the Hastings did their round of media interviews last August, he says, "It might not have anything to do with—"

"It was written in red lipstick."

He curses under his breath. "Like your mirror."

"Did Carla . . . Did she wear red lipstick?"

He shakes his head.

"Never?"

"No. Never."

"You're that sure?"

"Positive. It was a *thing* with Carla. Makeup. My mother-in-law worked at one of those department store cosmetics counters."

Sssssssstore cossssssssssmeticssss counterssssssssssssss . . .

Is he slurring?

"Zelda figured out Carla's best colors," he forges on, "and she always wore pink lipstick. Always. Pink. And blue eyeshadow. I hate it. Blue eyeshadow. Looks cheap. But you know what? She wears it anyway. She says it goes with her eyes. *Said*," he amends, remembering.

Blue eyes.

They both had blue eyes, he and Carla.

Back when he still thought they had a chance in hell of making it together, he had imagined the blue-eyed children they would have. Basic genetics. Blue eyes plus blue eyes equals blue eyes.

"What do you think it means?"

He looks at Lucinda. She's not talking about all those little squares—what the heck do you call those little squares?—in biology class.

Lucinda has brown eyes.

Big brown eyes.

One pair of big brown eyes plus one pair of blue eyes—*his*—equals . . .

What does it equal?

Blue?

Brown?

He should have paid more attention.

No. He shouldn't be paying attention at all, not to her eyes, not to his feelings for her. Not tonight.

"Randy?"

"Yeah?"

"Are you okay? Really?"

"Yeah."

"Then . . . what do you think it means?" she asks again.

What does he think it means?

What does he think *what* means?

He leans his head back against the couch cushion, attempting to backtrack along the conversational path, but his thoughts are hopelessly entangled.

Damned bourbon.

"The red lipstick," she reminds him. "It was on my mirror, too. And—I swear, Randy, when Neal mentioned that today when we were in the meeting, Van Aken and Lambert exchanged a look, as if . . . I swear it meant something to them. Does it to you?"

Does it to you. . . .
Does it to you. . . .
Red lipstick. She's talking about red lipstick.
"Hell, no."
She looks at him for a minute. "Are you okay?"
"I'm . . . drunk," he says helplessly.
She nods. "I'm going to call Neal."
"Okay." He closes his eyes, just to rest them for a minute.

Beneath an overcast, moonless sky, he walks through the cold along Rush Street toward West Division, past restaurants and bars crowded with patrons even on a weeknight, most of them young, some spilling out onto the sidewalks to smoke.

He buys himself a beer in one of the bars—not because he wants to, but because he has to. He buys a pack of cigarettes. Same reasoning.

He drinks the beer with his back to the bar, and then he goes outside and he smokes a few cigarettes and he tries not to shiver in the bitter cold.

He'd rather not linger too long inside, where the bartenders and wait staff, at least, are sober. Watchful.

He watches the carefree patrons, many of them inebriated, not even shivering as they smoke and laugh and talk in the frigid Chicago night.

They don't see him.

No one gives him a second glance.

Not the guys, who are focused on the girls.

And not the girls, who are focused on the guys their own age, unaware of the predator in their midst.

Lucinda stands over Randy, wondering what to do.

She shook him a few times, but there's no waking him. His

head is thrown back, mouth open, chest rising and falling in slow, rhythmic breathing.

He needs sleep.

So does she.

Neal reminded her of that just now, before they hung up.

"Get some rest," he said, after they'd discussed the latest development. "We'll go over everything tomorrow."

"You get home safely." She was worried about him, still on the road from the shore to Philadelphia.

It's slow going, he told her. Accidents everywhere.

"I'm glad you stayed there, Cin."

So is she.

Especially now that Randy's asleep and she doesn't have to worry about . . .

Well, anything.

Her throat aches with the effort of forcing sound; another sip of bourbon soothes it a little, but she pours the rest into the sink. She needs sleep. *Now.*

She goes back into the bedroom and takes the quilt—embroidered with nautical flags, of course—off the rumpled bed. Back in the living room, she covers Randy with it, gently tucking the edges around his shoulders and legs.

He doesn't stir.

She props a life preserver-embellished throw pillow beneath his head. He's still sound asleep, but at least he looks more comfortable.

Encouraged, she kneels and takes off his boots.

Okay, better yet. But that's as far as it goes.

He'll be fine.

She stands and watches him sleep for a moment, remembering that she did this once before. Years ago.

She watched him sleeping on the final night they were together and shouldn't have been, the night when she came to the realization that she had to end it. She extracted herself from his naked embrace, got out of bed, and snuck away, but only after giving him a long, last look, memorizing everything about him. She knew they would see each other again, that they would go on working together for as long as they had to, but was certain she would never again experience the intimacy of watching him sleep.

She was wrong.

But never in a million years could she have imagined the incredible series of events that had led them from that moment to this.

Shaking her head, she goes into the bedroom and slips between sheets that smell of Randy, resting her head on a pillow that smells of Randy.

She leaves the light on.

Outside, the wind roars, hurtling pellets of ice against the house.

After a few minutes of listening to the storm's fury, she gets up and digs her iPod out of her coat pocket.

Settling back in bed with the earbuds in her ears, she presses the scroll wheel, hoping to find some soothing music on one of the playlists she uploaded before Curaçao.

Wait a minute. . . .

What's going on?

Where is all her music?

How can Beethoven's Piano Sonata 14 be the only song file on the iPod?

She didn't put it here.

She did, however, load the iPod with hundreds of other songs . . . all of which are somehow missing.

Did she accidentally erase all the files somehow?

She must have.

But then, how the heck did Sonata 14 end up on here? She's not big on classical music. It's not that she doesn't like it. She just knows absolutely nothing about it.

Could she possibly have picked up someone else's iPod by mistake?

Must be.

An iPod that belongs to someone whose only song choice is classical piano written over two hundred years ago.

An iPod that's encased in an identical mint green leather skin.

Okay, that might be the only thing that makes sense, but it's a reach.

It's also not the case. Because when she slips the iPod out of the skin to check the back of it, she sees her initials and telephone number etched there.

The engraving was free when she ordered it from the Web site on her last birthday, a gift to herself.

So it's definitely her iPod.

Without her music.

With unfamiliar music.

Or maybe, she realizes after she presses Play, not so unfamiliar at all.

Lucinda's heard Sonata 14 before, many times.

Even she, with her limited knowledge of classical music, knows the famous piece, only not as Sonata 14.

She knows it by its more familiar name: *Moonlight Sonata.*

It's freaking freezing out here, and it's getting late, and as much as he'd hoped to find her on this first night and not waste any time, he finally decides to call it a night.

He stomps out his cigarette on a sidewalk scraped dry and clean of snow, and he starts to walk away.

That is when it happens.

A cigarette butt, still smoldering, lands by his feet.

A butt stained scarlet at the tip.

He looks up, slowly.

And there she is.

A buxom blonde in a red dress, laughing with her friends, oblivious to him as she shakes another menthol out of her pack.

He watches as she purses the cigarette between luscious lips the dense, sugary red of a summer tomato.

As she lights up, he smiles a satisfied smile.

The clock has just started ticking, the countdown begun again.

Lucinda stares at the framed nautical map of Long Beach Island on the wall opposite the bed, wondering how she can possibly still be awake.

It's not the storm—that's died down quite a bit in the hour since she climbed into bed.

And it's not that she's not tired, because her body aches with fatigue and it's all she can do to form coherent thoughts.

It's not that the light is on, because she's used to that.

It's the iPod.

Someone tampered with it. Someone was on her computer, accessing her music files. Someone replaced them with a haunting Beethoven sonata that means nothing to her.

Should it?

She can't seem to shake the nagging feeling that she's missing something. Maybe not anything to do with the iPod, but some clue that's right under her nose.

Was it something Cam said when they spoke earlier?

Or Neal?

She's gone over both conversations repeatedly, coming up with nothing.

Neal was intrigued by the letter Cam had received, particularly because it was written in red lipstick.

"There's something about the lipstick, Neal," she told him. "The local cops here aren't telling us everything."

"Of course they aren't. They were humoring us by having us there. Humoring Randy, really."

"Not really. We're the ones with the evidence. And they're going to be working with the police in Philly. You *are* the police in Philly."

"But I'm personally involved. No one on the investigation is going to trust me—or you, for that matter—with any information we don't already have. For all they know, we could be involved."

By *we*, he meant she.

"Do you think they're still suspicious of me, Neal?" she asked worriedly.

"Why would they be? You have an alibi. You were away all weekend. Jimmy was with you, and he can vouch for it. Don't worry, Cin. They're not suspicious of you." There was a click on the line, and he said, "I have to go. That's Erma calling me. She's worried sick about me out here on the road."

"So am I. Please get home safely."

By then, her voice was a mere whisper. Efforts to clear her throat brought mere squeaks of sound.

Hopefully it'll be better tomorrow.

It will be if you get some rest.

Lucinda punches the too-flat loose down pillow beneath her head and tries desperately to fall asleep.

Nothing doing.

Cam Hastings was rattled, to say the least, to hear of the possible connection between her sister's death and Carla Barakat's.

"It's too huge a coincidence, don't you think?" she asked Lucinda. "To think that whoever killed my sister killed Carla."

"Not if whoever killed your sister read or saw on TV that we were looking for more information about Ava's death. You and I and Randy were all out there—our names, our faces. We were on national TV, Cam. Do you know how many people we reached?"

"And you think one of them was responsible for Ava's death."

"Or knew something about it."

"What about Carla, though?"

That's just it.

What about Carla?

What if her killer is still here on the island?

What if he followed Lucinda and Randy over here tonight and is hovering somewhere nearby right now?

She looks at the map on the wall, gauging the distance between this cottage and the Barakats' house. . . .

Between this cottage and the police station.

Is there a legend? What's the scale?

As she searches the fringes of the map, something jumps out at her.

Shocked, she sits up in bed, leans closer, gets out, and hurries over to the wall to examine the map.

Can it be?

Lucinda gasps, clapping a hand over her mouth in utter astonishment.

"Oh my God," she whispers, then tries to scream, "Randy!"

The effort is futile. Her voice is shot.

She hurries to the next room, frantically whispering, "Randy, wake up!"

PART II

7:05

Chapter Eleven

Weeks' worth of paranoia come rushing back to haunt Jaime Dobiak the moment she walks into her bedroom to see him standing there.

"Hello, Jaime."

All this time, she'd been feeling as though something wasn't right. As though someone might have been in her apartment. Things were moved around. Things were missing; her new yellow scarf seemed to have vanished overnight from the bedpost where she was certain she'd left it.

Yet even now, she wants to believe he is whom he'd claimed to be all along—a harmless new neighbor from down the block, whose path has occasionally crossed hers these last few weeks.

"What are you doing h—" She breaks off, seeing the knife.

She tries to run, but he's got her by the arm, his strong bicep pressed against her face, muffling her cries for help.

At twenty-two years old, Isaiah Drew was on the cusp of becoming the first one in his family to graduate college—Ivy League, no less—when he disappeared off a South Philly street over the weekend.

This isn't the first time Lucinda's been called in to investigate a missing student at the University of Pennsylvania.

Typically, someone goes off on a bender or a spontaneous road trip or caves under the rigorous academic pressure and simply checks out for a while. Those cases tend to have happier endings than most.

This one won't.

"Drugs," she tells Neal, who's standing in the doorway as cops and campus security behind him keep curious dorm residents at bay.

Neal shakes his head slightly. "No."

"I'm not asking you, Neal, I'm telling you. He was involved in drugs."

"I'm not saying I don't believe you," Neal responds, "but that would be news to his roommate and his R.A. and his friends. Every person we've talked to who knew Isaiah says he was a good kid. Clean."

"I don't think so."

"But you're not sure?"

Lucinda hesitates.

Ordinarily, she wouldn't. Ordinarily, she'd trust her instincts and tell Neal that yes, she's sure.

This evening, though, she's not able to focus one hundred percent of her energy on her work. She feels as though a pall is hanging over her—has felt it all day, even before Neal called to summon her to the campus.

She rests her hand on the pillow where Isaiah reportedly took a nap before heading out onto the street and vanishing.

Nothing comes to her.

It isn't just this evening; her perceptive abilities simply haven't been up to par since she received an odd package in the mail the other day.

The package bore a typewritten label and no return address. It had been postmarked in Chicago.

She turned it over to the police without opening it. Inside, she learned, was a yellow silk Hermès scarf. That was all.

Lucinda wanted so badly to believe that there was no connection, after all, between the brutal murder of Carla Barakat
and the strange communication over the same period of days.

Now, of course, it's clear that was no coincidence.

She's known that from the moment she was compelled to
look at that nautical chart of Long Beach Island in Randy's
rental house almost a month ago.

74.2
39.6

The precise longitude and latitude of Beach Haven, New
Jersey.

The second set of numbers proved to be the longitude and
latitude of Chicago.

Are they—and the scarf—meant to indicate that the killer
has struck there, as well? Or that he intends to?

Lucinda is taking no chances.

Neal had her laptop examined and found that someone
had disabled her spyware and installed a keyboard sniffer:
surveillance software that is notoriously difficult to detect
unless you're looking for it—and sometimes, not even then.

She hasn't let her guard down, not even when she's alone
in her apartment.

Plagued by insomnia, she asked the doctor for a prescription sleeping pill when she was recently there for the flu. She
filled the prescription, but hasn't been able to bring herself
to take a pill just yet.

"Why on earth not?" Bradley asked her over the phone
the other morning, when she confessed to yet another sleepless night.

"Because I don't like medication. I'm afraid I won't be in
control if I take it."

"Lord knows you like to be in control," he agreed. "You
know, you'd sleep a lot better if you'd just turn out the lights
like the rest of the world."

"How do you know that I don't?"

"Honey, the whole world knows you're afraid of the dark."

"What do you mean?"

"You said it in one of those interviews you did on television. Don't you remember?"

She shrugged. She said a lot of things in those interviews. None of them yielded a solid clue to what happened to Ava Neary.

If the police have re-opened the investigation into her death—as Lucinda had expected them to—they've given her no information. For all she knows, they consider it a dead end.

Solve it and you will find me.

It's such an odd phrase. It's been nagging at her. So has the scrapbook.

If only someone else had gotten a good look at it. Sometimes she wonders if anyone even believes what she saw in it.

Anyone other than Neal, that is. Or Cam.

Lucinda gave her as many names and details as she could recall. Cam said she was going to look into it.

Lucinda plans to get involved too, just as soon as she's able.

But right now, she has other things on her plate.

And right now, she's not supposed to be thinking about Ava Neary.

She closes her eyes, tries to concentrate.

Isaiah Drew.

The first time Jaime met him, he was strolling by her building.

He kindly held the door open for her when she came home with a rare armload of groceries. He even carried the bags up the stairs, where they chatted pleasantly while she unlocked her door. He kind of reminded her of her grandfather—back when Grandpa Dobiak was a little younger, and not so sick.

A few days after that, he was canvassing the neighborhood with a petition and asked her to sign it. Something about air pollution.

Of course Jaime signed. Who wouldn't? Who isn't against air pollution?

Okay, maybe she did think it might be a little hypocritical, since she happens to be a smoker, but seriously, what do her measly cigarettes and some occasional weed matter in the grand scheme of things?

"Thanks so much," said her harmless new neighbor, looking at her signature. "What's your name? Jemima?"

She laughed. Bad handwriting. "It's Jaime. What's yours?"

"Joe," he said, and from that blustery early March day on, they were on a first name basis whenever they passed in the street.

"Hey, Jaime."

"What's up, Joe?"

Just her harmless new grandfatherly neighbor.

"Please," Jaime begs him, panting in terror, cowering on the floor beside her bed, watching the knife in his black gloved hand. "Please don't hurt me."

"I wouldn't waste my breath if I were you," he advises calmly. "You have so few left."

Isaiah Drew.

Lucinda pictures his face. Sees his brown eyes, furtive— and the pupils are dilated. Sees his hand, practiced, steady, cutting white powder on a mirror with a razor blade.

She opens her eyes and shakes her head. "I'm definitely getting something about drugs, Neal. This room should be searched."

"It's already been searched."

"For residue?"

"For anything at all."

"So search again. Bring in drug-sniffing dogs."

"Cin, I don't think—"

"Are you saying I don't know what I'm talking about?" she snaps—and immediately regrets it. "Look, I'm sorry. I'm having an off night."

"Really?" he asks dryly. "I hadn't noticed."

"Sorry," she says again. "I'm just giving you what I'm getting. I know it doesn't mesh with who you think this kid was, but it's what I feel in this room. Okay?"

Neal looks at her for a long time, as if he wants to ask her something. Something that has nothing to do with Isaiah Drew.

But he merely shrugs and says, "Okay. We'll bring in dogs."

He allows the tip of the knife to jab—but just barely—the skin on her neck.

"No," Jaime sobs. "Please, no."

"Oh, for the love of Pete. You're not crying, are you? Didn't your mother ever tell you that only babies cry?"

"Please . . . Please don't hurt me."

"All right. Not yet." He moves the knife back and glances at the window above her head—or the digital clock on the nightstand—or both. "We still have some time."

"Why are you doing this?" she sobs hysterically. "Why?"

Joe tilts his gray head. "Why. Good question. And you know what, Jaime? I'm going to answer it for you. It's only fair, and like I said, we still have time."

"Cam Neary? Ava Neary's little sister? Girl, is this really you?"

"It's really me," she says into the telephone, wishing she found the voice on the other end of the line the least bit familiar. She'd been so young, though, the last time she'd heard it. Too young to remember the voice, but not the name.

"How are you, Bernice?"

"I'm doin' all right, doin' all right."

Bernice Watts, Ava's best friend all the way through high school, had grown up across the street from them in Camden, a fellow latchkey kid in a neighborhood filled with single parent families.

Bernice's widowed mother was a good cook, a real churchgoing, family-focused maternal kind of woman, unlike Brenda Neary. Mrs. Watts was always good to Ava, a fixture in the Watts household from the time she was old enough to cross the street alone—by their parents' lax judgement, anyway. Cam remembers often toddling along with her, and eating homemade cookies at the Watts's kitchen table with a horde of other kids—most of them Bernice's siblings.

Ava and Bernice spent a lot of their time together studying, both determined to go to college. It paid off in scholarships, and when Ava went off to NYU, Bernice enrolled at Rutgers.

It was through their alumni association that Cam managed to find her—married, with children and grandchildren, living in Trenton.

"Why you callin' me after all these years, girl?"

"It's about my sister."

"Lord rest her soul. You know, not a day goes by that I don't miss Ava Neary."

"Same here, Bernice. She's the reason why I'm calling."

There's a pause. "I thought so. I saw you on the news, back last summer."

"You did?"

"For a split second, when you first came on that screen, I would have sworn I was looking at Ava."

"She was only twenty the last time you saw her, Bernice. I'm almost twice her age."

"But you look exactly like her. It was like looking at a ghost. I thought about calling that hotline number they set up, you know . . . but then I lost my nerve."

"Why were you going to call?" Trying to maintain her composure, Cam jerks open a kitchen drawer to look for a pad and pen. "Is there something I should know about my sister?"

"Maybe."

Cam bites her bottom lip to keep from asking why on earth Bernice hadn't called her. She doesn't want to scare her off now.

"Back when it happened, and they said it was a suicide, I just figured that was the truth," Bernice tells her. "It was hard to believe Ava would do that to herself, but a lot of things are hard to believe in this world, you hear what I'm sayin'?"

Cam murmurs that she does.

"Ava and I used to write letters when we were both away at school. That was what people did back then. None of this e-mail-text-message-IM stuff like my grandbabies are doing. I remember your sister telling me in some of those letters not long before she died that she got herself involved in something she shouldn't have. At the time, I didn't think it was a big deal, but when I saw you on TV with those detectives, saying she might have been murdered—well, I thought maybe I was wrong."

But you didn't tell me! Why not?

It's too late for admonishment. All Cam can do is listen, and hope that she's on the verge of a breakthrough at last.

"What was she involved in, Bernice? Drinking? Drugs?"

"No, nothing like that. It was a man."

"You mean Ava had a boyfriend?"

"For a while. Not a boy. A *man*, like I said. One of her professors."

Cam raises her eyebrows. None of the others who had

known her sister in college had mentioned anything of the sort.

But then, Bernice was like a sister to Ava. More like a sister, really, than Cam was, being so much younger.

That would probably have changed as they grew older. They'd probably barely notice the age difference these days, if only Ava were still alive.

If only.

"What was this professor's name?"

"Lordy, hon, I don't even remember what I had for breakfast today."

"So she was involved with him when she died?"

"I don't think so. I think she wrote me that it was over. Or maybe she just told me that—we used to speak on the phone once in a while, too. That was about as high tech as things got, back then." She chuckles.

"Do you still have the letters, Bernice?"

"You know, I've been wondering about that. I never was one to throw stuff away—a pack rat, your sister called me. She always liked things nice and tidy, Ava."

"She did? Really? My daughter's like that."

"Oh, yes, Ava was Miss Perfect. Organized, neat as a pin."

Funny—that's something Cam never knew about her sister. Back then, she was too young to pay attention to that sort of thing.

The unexpected new insight into her sister's personality makes her acutely aware of just what her family has lost—rather, what was cruelly stolen from them.

"Do you think you could look for the letters, Bernice?"

"I already did. I looked around the house a while back, after I saw you on TV, but I couldn't find them. I suppose if I kept them, though, they wouldn't be here. I probably would have left them behind at my mother's house."

"Do you think they're still there?"

Bernice chortles. "You haven't been back to the old

neighborhood in a while, have you? Cam, the house isn't even there. It burned down years ago. Pretty much the whole darn block burned down."

Her heart sinks.

"'Course, that was after my mother moved out."

"Where does she live now?"

"With the good Lord in heaven. We lost her about two years ago."

"I'm sorry," Cam murmurs.

"It was her time," Bernice says simply. "But it wasn't Ava's."

"No."

"Before my mother died, she was living with my brother DeK'wan down in D.C. That's where all the stuff from our house in Camden went. I'll call down there and see what I can find out."

The bare-branched trees of Locust Walk are still strung with white starburst bulbs at this time of year. They, along with the full moon, glowing lamppost globes, and light splashing from windows of the Collegiate Gothic buildings along the way, are meant to dispel the shadows of this cold March evening.

But Lucinda, walking along the brick pedestrian campus thoroughfare with Neal after leaving the dorm, can't seem to shake the aura of gloom.

Oddly, she isn't entirely sure it has anything to do with the missing student. The sense of foreboding feels almost personal, as though something terrible is about to happen to her—or someone close to her.

Not to Isaiah Drew who, as far as she can tell, has already met his fate.

"Do you think he's still alive?" Neal asks her now, as if he's read her thoughts.

"No. I don't."

From the moment she walked into Isaiah's dorm room, she's had the sense that he won't be coming back.

"Any idea where he might be?"

His remains, Neal means. All that's left of a boy who held such promise, a boy whose family believed he was going to make the world a better place.

"I'm not sure."

"Any chance you could be wrong about his being dead? And about the drugs, too?"

"I don't think so. Sorry."

They walk in silence for a minute or two.

"Why don't you come home with me for dinner, Cin?"

"Oh—that's sweet of you, Neal, but I can't just show up at the last minute."

"Sure you can. Garland Fisher does it all the time."

Garland Fisher—his neighbor. The one who was there the night the scrapbook vanished from his table and the numerical clue appeared.

"Will he be there tonight?" she asks, wondering if seeing the man again will trigger her sixth sense about whether he could possibly have had something to do with it.

"No, he's been away. Why? Still suspicious?"

She shrugs. "You're not. And you know him a lot better than I do."

"I checked out his background, Cin. I told you that. He is who he says he is."

Is anyone?

"You're going to come for dinner tonight." Neal pulls out his phone. "Erma's been asking about you. I'm going to call and tell her you're coming home with me. Okay?"

Lucinda knows a losing battle when she's in one. "Okay. Thanks."

Neal dials home, talks to Erma.

Something cold and wet plops onto Lucinda's forehead. She looks up to see that the moon has slipped behind a cloud and a few snowflakes are beginning to come down.

"Oh, no," she mutters, looking down at her thin leather flats. "I'm so sick of winter."

"Winter's over as of today." Neal pockets his cell phone again.

"Yeah, well, looks like someone forgot to tell Mother Nature."

It really has been a crummy March, weather-wise.

A crummy March for Lucinda's health, too—she came down with the flu on the heels of Carla's death, and since then, it seems, her resistance is down. She's been battling one bug after another.

All the travel hasn't helped. She's been driving between Philly and the Poconos, helping local police there track down a pair of hikers who disappeared into the mountains.

Really, it's been a crummy March all around—except for the fact that Randy is back in her life.

Not romantically.

Nothing has happened between them, and neither of them has mentioned that anything once did—or might again.

Maybe it won't.

Or maybe they're both waiting for enough time to pass, waiting for the raw pain of Carla's death to heal, waiting for the tide to turn naturally and carry them from friendship and support to something more.

Waiting.

Sometimes, Lucinda wonders if she and Randy will ever get the timing right.

The first time around, it was too late.

This time, it's too soon.

Still, they've seen each other quite a few times over the past month—whenever neither of them is working or traveling or sick. Mostly, he drives into Philadelphia to get away from the island and all the fallout from Carla's as-yet unsolved murder.

It's not a cold case by any means—the township police are reportedly following a few leads, hoping forensics will yield something, but the results aren't in.

Lucinda herself had to provide a DNA sample, having

been present at the scene and inadvertently having handled evidence. Routine police procedure.

Meanwhile, there have been no new clues, and no official suspects, as far as she knows. The Philly detectives were unable to pick up a single print from her apartment that didn't belong to her. Even Jimmy, her only visitor, had apparently left no prints behind.

Which would of course be strange at any other time of year. But it was cold the night he came to pick her up for the airport, and again when he dropped her off. Lucinda is certain that he never took off his coat, and, as she told Neal, he probably didn't take off his gloves, either.

"You didn't notice?"

"Why would I? That was before I had any reason to be suspicious of him, Neal."

She still isn't. Not really.

Lucinda's instincts—which God only knows might very well be off the mark—are telling her that Jimmy is nothing more than a very nice, very busy lawyer.

Jaime watches him reach over to the table beside her bed, past the blue tissue box and her clock radio, toward the ashtray she meant to empty this morning before she left for work.

Holding the knife in his clenched right hand and plucking a lipstick-stained cigarette butt from the ashtray with his left, he dangles it over her. "It's all because of this, Jaime."

"Because I smoke?" Incredulous, she remembers the pollution petition he asked her to sign. What is he, some save-the-earth freak? Is he trying to scare her into quitting?

Please let that be it.

Please, God, let that be it.

"Because you smoke?" He starts to laugh. "Oh, no, my dear. I don't give a damn if you smoke. Smoking does kill you, though. I bet your parents told you that, didn't they?

Don't start smoking, because it can kill you. See, now?" He waves the knife over her. "They were right."

He laughs harder, maniacally.

If only someone would hear and come save her. But the walls in this old Division Street building are well-insulated. Nearly soundproof, the landlord said.

No one can hear a thing.

"You know what, Jaime?" he interrupts his laughter to ask. "You should have smoked more. Three, four packs a day instead of one and a half."

How does he know exactly how much she smokes?

"You're going to die young anyway. Hey, how about one last cigarette? Even the guys on death row got to have a last cigarette."

More laughter.

He yanks open a drawer on the nightstand, pulls out a pack of menthols and a lighter. Somewhere in the back of her frantic, fear-clogged mind, she realizes he knows exactly where she keeps them.

He's been here before.

She was right to be paranoid. She kept telling her friends she could swear someone had been in her apartment, rifling through her things. They rolled their eyes and told her she watched too much "C.S.I."

A montage of grisly scenes from the show flashes through her mind as the man she knew as Joe the harmless new neighbor stands over her with a pack of cigarettes and a knife.

She's going to die, like all those characters on the show— the ones who turn up with fixed, gaping, vacant eyes in litter-strewn, desolate vacant lots.

He sighs, the way one does after a good laugh.

"You might as well have a smoke," he advises her, waving the cigarettes. "You still have another"—again, his gaze flicks to the bedside clock—"seven minutes to live. That's enough time for a cigarette, right?"

His laugh is shrill, like a woman's.

An insane woman's.

The sound chills her blood.

"Oh, wait, first . . ."

He grabs her face, cupping her chin in his gloved left hand, squeezing painfully hard.

"Stay still."

He brandishes something toward her.

For a terrible instant, she thinks it's the knife, that he's going to slash her face.

But she's wrong.

It's a tube of bright red lipstick, uncapped and jabbing at her quivering lips.

"Another round?" the bartender asks.

"No, thanks," Lambert tells him. "Randy?"

Rolling his half-full bottle of Bud back and forth between his palms, Randy shakes his head at the bartender, who goes back to watching "Wheel of Fortune" at the other end of the bar.

Slow night at the Sandbucket Grill. They all are, at this time of year.

After Memorial Day, you can't get close to a bar stool for happy hour.

But from now until then, it will be a smattering of locals, most of them around the pool table. Beyond it, the outdoor tables are stacked in the corridor near the restrooms, and the big glass doors that lead to the outdoor stage are winterized with thick sheets of transparent plastic to shut out the draft.

"Maybe if you can just talk to Frank again," Randy tells Lambert, going back to the conversation they've been having all evening.

All month, really.

"I've talked to him. He won't budge, and Randy, I wouldn't expect him to. You know you can't get involved in the case."

"I'm not even talking about me. I'm talking about Lucinda.

If she could just see that watch, or take a look at the ring again, Dan, she might pick up on something. It's what she does."

Dan sips his beer, looking intently at "Wheel of Fortune."

"Dan."

"I heard you, Randy. Frank's not going to let her do that."

"How about you, then? You have access. You can let her see it. I don't even have to be there. Frank doesn't have to know."

"I want to be there for you, man, really I do. But you've got to stop asking me to break the rules. We're doing our best to solve this thing."

"And coming up cold."

Dan levels a look at him. "How do you know that?"

"Because you'd tell me if you had something."

"I can't tell you anything and you know it."

"So you have something."

"I didn't say that." Dan plunks down his bottle, raises his arm to flag the bartender. "I'll have another one after all, Jerry. Give him one, too. Maybe that'll make him shut up and stop bugging me."

"It won't," Randy tells him when the bartender walks away. "For God's sake, Dan, her life is at stake here."

Dan shakes his head and touches Randy's arm. "Finding out who killed her won't bring her back, Randy."

"You're talking about Carla. Do you think I don't know nothing's going to bring her back?"

"You're not talking about Carla?"

"No."

"Lucinda."

"Yes. Whoever killed Carla might come after her next, Dan."

Lambert looks at him for a long time. "That's not going to happen, okay?"

"How do you know that?"

"I just know."

"What are you saying, Dan? Or what *aren't* you saying?"

For a moment, his friend looks as though he wants to tell him something.

But then the bartender returns with their beers, and Dan breaks eye contact, pulling out his wallet.

When the beers are paid for and they're alone again at their end of the bar, Randy says, "Something's going on, Dan."

"What do you mean?"

"Something's going on with the investigation. Do you have a suspect under surveillance or something? Is that what it is?"

"We're working on it."

"On a suspect?"

He shrugs. "Just be careful, Randy. I'm worried about you."

"I'm not worried about me. I'm worried about Lucinda."

"Don't. Just move on, okay? Move on, and forget about her. There's a reason you married Carla instead of her."

Yeah, there is, Randy thinks.

It's because he was a fool.

Agony explodes through Jaime Dobiak's body the first time he stabs her, in the stomach.

Agony that turns everything a blinding white; her eyes are closed but then they're wide open, and she still sees the white, white spattered with red paint. . . .

Some part of her brain not consumed by hysteria registers that she's staring at the white ceiling or the wall, and it isn't spattered with red paint, it's red blood, her blood, Dear God, her blood. . . .

And then the monster looms with the knife, and feral shrieks fill her head, her own anguished shrieks, and he stabs her again, in the stomach, and she knows that he's killing her, and this can't be happening but it is, he's really killing her, she's going to die.

She's going to die.

No, please . . .

Another savage stab.

This time she didn't see it coming, didn't hear it coming.

She only feels the detonation of pain as the knife strikes her arm, feels the river of red hot, sticky blood, feels her nerve endings shattering, burning.

Then the knife thrusts fiercely again, her pelvis, and again, her chest, and there is no pain, only a dull, jarring sensation each time it thuds into her dying flesh.

She opens her mouth to ask, again, the question he told her he would answer, but didn't.

Not in a way that she could understand.

All he said, when she asked him why, were three cryptic words.

"Because of Scarlet."

And then he laughed.

Is laughing still as he stabs her, as he kills her, maniacal laughter that is the last sound she hears before silence absorbs her.

Standing on his back deck, Vic Shattuck gazes at the full moon glittering in the black night sky.

Somewhere, he's certain, a cold-blooded killer is aware of it as well.

Vic has spent weeks trying to find time to write his book in between pinpointing possible Night Watchman murders—from the comfort of his own home, of course, via e-mail and telephone. He can hardly go traipsing around the country looking into every homicide that took place over the last few months on nights when the moon is full.

On paper, quite a few of them started out as potential leads: women ambushed at night when they were home alone.

But a closer look at the details—and, in some cases, cur-

sory contact with the local police—ruled out the Night Watchman in all but a few cases.

Of the ones that seemed to fit, only a couple are still open,
but those appear close to being solved, too.

One, involving a high school girl in St. Louis, now appears
gang related.

Another, the murder of a cop's estranged wife on the Jersey Shore, appears to be domestic, and they've already targeted a suspect, according to the lead investigator.

When Vic asked the cops in both those cases whether there
had been any unusual signatures to the crimes—anything that
might, for example, indicate the work of a serial killer—the
answer on the St. Louis case was a resounding no.

The Jersey Shore investigator first asked why he wanted
to know, then said he wasn't at liberty to discuss details of
the homicide that hadn't been released to the public.

"Why don't you give me more information?" he invited,
"and I'll let you know if any of it applies."

Vic did his best. "The Night Watchman always struck at
night, during a full moon."

"A lot of killers do."

True.

"And the moon is full once every twenty-eight days,
right?" the investigator, Frank Santiago, went on.

"Twenty-nine."

"So any killer has a one in twenty-nine shot of striking
when the moon is full, right?"

"If you look at it that way but—"

"I do. And I appreciate the help, but we have forensic evidence we expect to implicate one of our leading suspects."

Frustratingly, Vic couldn't come right out and ask whether
the victim had been found wearing red lipstick. He wasn't at
liberty to divulge that evidence, known only to the killer and
a handful of witnesses and task force investigators.

Without it—or Vic's guidance—it would take an almost impossibly shrewd local investigator to connect a modern victim to the Night Watchman's victims of almost forty years ago.

Even if a local force were diligent about entering unsolved crime information into the Bureau's computerized Violent Criminal Apprehension Profile—most aren't, and it's only required in three states, including New Jersey— the data banks only go back a couple of decades. Everything before that is hard evidence, boxed away in case files. It would take a lot of deliberate digging to unearth any of it now.

Behind Vic, the slider opens. "Ready to eat? I brought home a pizza."

He turns to see Kitty there, backlit by the kitchen light. She's changed from her suit into jeans and a hooded sweatshirt. Her face is scrubbed clean of the makeup she wore to work, her short dark hair is tucked behind her ears, and she's traded her contacts for glasses.

To him, she's the most beautiful woman in the world. He's a lucky man.

And if you never finish the damn book, he reminds himself, *and never unmask the Night Watchman, you'll still be a lucky man.*

He takes one last look at the full moon before heading back inside, locking the door behind him, and pressing the keypad on the brand new alarm system.

Chapter Twelve

Sitting in the Bullards' cozy kitchen, with the radio tuned to Neal's favorite old show tunes station in the background, Lucinda feels almost content for the first time today.

Almost.

"More mashed potatoes?"

"No, thanks, Erma. I'm stuffed." She pushes back her plate, where all that remains is a smear of golden gravy, a couple of stray peas, and some chicken bones. "This is the best meal I've had in a long time."

"You should have been here a few nights ago," Neal tells her. "No one makes corned beef and cabbage like Erma."

Saint Patrick's Day.

Lucinda spent it with Randy, drinking too much green beer and trying to pretend—to herself, to him, to the rest of the world—that they're still just friends.

"Not everyone likes corned beef and cabbage, Neal."

"Lucinda does," he tells his wife. "Lucinda likes everything."

She has to grin both at Neal's comment, and at the scolding look Erma gives him before carrying the bowl of mashed potatoes back to the stove.

She's glad Neal forced her to come, glad she managed to

push aside, for at least a little while, the oppressive feeling that dogged her earlier. Maybe she was wrong. Maybe it did have to do with Isaiah Drew.

"It's a compliment, right, Cin?"

"Mr. Bullard, I'm afraid commenting on a lady's appetite is never appropriate," Lucinda chides in her best Bitsy Sloan imitation. "And anyway, I don't like *everything*."

"What don't you like?"

"Salad, for one thing."

"How can you not like salad? Everyone likes salad."

"Not me."

Even Erma is shaking her head—and eyeing the untouched bowl of it beside Lucinda's plate.

"It's good for you, honey," she says. "You should eat it."

"No, thanks."

"When was the last time you tried it?"

"Every couple of years, I try it, thinking I might have changed my mind. I never have."

"Every couple of years? I'm guessing you're due. Take a bite," Neal tells her.

"Neal—"

"It won't hurt you to try it." That comes from Erma, watching with interest. "Go ahead—I made the dressing and croutons myself."

"In that case . . ." Lucinda takes a bite.

It isn't bad.

In fact . . .

"It's good."

"See? What'd I tell you?" Neal shakes his head. "Sometimes you're too stubborn for your own good."

"Look who's talking." Laughing, but looking pleased, Erma pours the gravy into a plastic tub.

"Maybe the reason I've never liked salad," Lucinda tells them, "is that for years, it was all my mother ate. Without croutons and dressing."

"Speaking of your mother," Neal says, "weren't you supposed to have lunch with her this week?"

"Tomorrow, and it's brunch, and don't remind me. I'd rather talk about salad. Or corned beef and cabbage."

"Well, Erma makes the best. You should've seen the way Garland Fisher gobbled up three helpings when he was here."

"Poor man must not cook for himself." Erma shakes her head.

"Does he come over for dinner a lot?" Lucinda asks.

"He'd come every night if we invited him," Neal tells her.

"He's away right now, visiting his grandkids." Erma scrapes some scraps from one plate onto another. "I'm picking up his newspapers and mail—and that reminds me, Neal, I have to show you something."

She puts the plates in the sink, wipes off her hands, and goes through a plastic supermarket bag hanging from the back of a chair.

"What is that?" Neal asks.

"I told you. Garland's mail and papers. Look what came!" She pulls out what looks like a paper pamphlet. "Isn't this exciting?"

"*Meanderings* 19.03," he reads on the cover, then shrugs, not looking particularly excited. "What is it?"

"It's a literary magazine."

"From 1903?"

"No! That means volume nineteen, issue three. Neal, don't you listen to anything?" Erma shakes her head. "Honestly."

"I'm listening, but I'm not hearing anything that makes sense."

"Garland told us he sold his first story to *Meanderings* magazine, remember?"

The look on Neal's face tells Lucinda that he doesn't, but he wisely gives a nod and murmurs, "Oh, that's right. Well, good for him."

"He's going to be very happy when he comes home to this." As Erma replaces the magazine in the shopping bag, then turns back to the sink, Neal winks at Lucinda.

She can't help but smile at the way the Bullards always manage to keep their marital peace.

"All righty." Erma bustles back over to the table for more dishes. "Who's ready for dessert?"

"Oh, Erma, don't bother with that. It's getting late." Lucinda pushes back her chair reluctantly.

Before she can pick up her plate, Erma whisks it from her grasp. "You can't leave without dessert. I made Neal's favorite sour cream coffee cake. You sit and chat with Neal. I'll clean up."

"How about if *you* sit and chat with Neal and I clean up?" Lucinda returns, taking the plate from Erma and carrying it over to the sink.

"How about if the two of you—" Neal breaks off as the cell phone in his pocket rings. "Never mind. How about if the two of you clean up while I go take this call?"

"Opportunist." Lucinda sticks out her tongue.

Neal grins before slipping out of the room, pulling the phone from his pocket.

It's been hours since he left Jaime Dobiak gurgling in a futile effort to draw air through blood-drowned airways, but the euphoria has yet to wear off.

Too exhilarated to return to the solitude of his rented room—which isn't nearly as nice as the Westin where he spent his first night here—he walks the streets of this glorious city aglow with streetlights and headlights, neon signs, a glorious full moon.

It will be a shame to leave Chicago tomorrow. He's gotten to like it here.

But that's okay. He has something to look forward to: paying a little visit to Lucinda, back in Philadelphia.

She's disappointed him.

When he slipped into Jaime's apartment tonight using his stolen key, he was half-expecting to find Lucinda waiting for him.

He'd sent her Jaime's scarf, certain she would touch it and know where to find him. He would have let her watch what he did to Jaime, and then he would have let her go. It isn't her turn yet.

But the scarf didn't work the way Carla's ring had. Maybe it was the blood.

Or maybe the almighty Lucinda isn't as powerful as she claims to be.

Whatever.

In the end, maybe it's better that she didn't come.

She's smart. Not as smart as he is, of course. But smart. What if she had shown up, and something had gone wrong? What if he'd had to kill her right then and there, along with Jaime? That would have been all wrong.

That's not how it's supposed to happen.

And so . . . onward.

104.5
39.4

He always plays fair.

He left the coordinates at the scene . . . but will they find them? He made it much more challenging this time. Perhaps too challenging. But if they're smart, they'll figure it out.

If they're not, they'll wonder if he's finished.

And just when they start to think he might be . . .

He laughs out loud.

"What's so funny, Sugar?"

He looks up to see a hooker watching him from a doorway. He stops laughing abruptly. Stops walking.

Stares at her through narrowed eyes as his forehead breaks out in a sweat and his mouth churns too much saliva.

"How about a party?"

She's Latina, young and tiny, with feminine curves.

But she's wearing a muddy shade of brownish lipstick. Still . . .

Nah. She probably has a watchful pimp lurking nearby.

Don't bother. You'll never get away with it.

"Party, Sugar?"

He spits into her face.

Then he walks away, trembling, as she screams after him in outraged Spanish.

And just like that, the euphoria is gone.

Upstairs, phone in hand, Neal closes the bedroom door behind him and sinks onto the double bed he's shared with Erma for nearly forty years.

This can't be happening.

It can't.

There must be some mistake.

He raises the phone to his ear again, hand trembling.

"I'm in a private spot now, Frank. I need you to repeat that for me."

On the other end of the line, Santiago coughs, clears his throat. "I said, we ID'ed the strands of hair that were found in Carla Barakat's hand. . . ."

The first time Santiago said that, Neal responded, "I didn't know you'd found strands of hair."

"There's a lot you don't know," Frank replied.

Then he told him whose hair it was.

Now Neal is asking him to repeat it, afraid to speak, afraid to breathe, until he does.

He must have heard wrong the first time.

He must have.

"The hair belongs to Lucinda Sloan."

Thoughts whirling, Neal takes a moment to regroup.

He knows Lucinda. He loves her like a daughter, believes in her.

He'll accept that her hair was clenched in the fist of a dead woman. He has no choice. There's no way around it. But there's got to be a reasonable explanation.

Of course there is.

"She was on the scene, Frank."

"Yeah. No kidding."

"No, but we already knew that. The fact that her hair—"

"She denied having gone anywhere near the body, or even into the house," Frank reminds him with exaggerated patience. "But somehow, she told my investigators to look in the bathroom, and guess where the body was?"

"She's a psychic!" Neal responds, not nearly as patiently. "For the love of God, Frank, you know that. You worked with her yourself."

"DNA doesn't lie. Looks like psychics do."

"That's bullshit, and you know it. You and I both know there are plenty of possible explanations for the hair being found on the scene."

"Like?"

"Come on, Frank. Circumstantial evidence. Do we really have to do this?"

Santiago starts coughing on the other end of the line.

"Are you all right?" Neal asks.

Santiago ignores the question. "Lucinda said she'd never been inside that house before. *Never.*"

"Yes. Because she hadn't."

"Yet she had the victim's bloody ring in her possession."

"It's a set-up. The hair, the ring . . . She doesn't know how the ring got into her apartment. And she turned it over to you immediately. Why would she—"

"Her hair was in the victim's fist. *Inside the house.*"

"Frank—"

"Before you get up on your circumstantial soapbox, yes, I

know there are ways for that to happen that don't involve her crossing the threshold herself. Let's say a strand of her hair could have, for instance, been left on her pillow one morning. Let's say her lover brushed against it, got it onto his clothes, carried it into the house where his ex-wife lives."

"Randy isn't Lucinda's lover, Santiago," Neal snaps even as he wonders if *"wasn't* her lover" might not be more accurate phrasing.

He's positive the two of them were platonic a month ago. Well, if not positive, at least pretty sure.

Now—they've been spending an awful lot of time together. Neal's been in their company. The old sparks are flying again.

But that means nothing in the context of this murder investigation. Nothing at all.

If he honestly believes Randy and Lucinda were platonic a month ago, though—and if he buys that they haven't seen each other since August—how did her hair get into Carla's hand?

"So you and Lucinda—you're good friends, right, Neal?"

"Absolutely." He debates the wisdom of mentioning that she's under his roof at this very moment, downstairs washing the dishes with his wife.

"She's in the habit of telling you about her love life?"

"No," he admits. "Not really."

It's just like the first time Neal was third-wheeling around with the two of them, Randy and Lucinda, a few years back. Now, as then, he doesn't ask Lucinda any questions, and she doesn't tell him anything beyond the basics: *Randy is coming to go to a movie tonight*, or *Randy and I went shopping yesterday*.

"But," he tells Santiago, "that doesn't mean I believe for one instant that Lucinda and Randy were involved with each other when Carla was killed."

"You don't."

"No."

"It might interest you to know that on February 23rd, the day Randy flew back from Tahoe, the two of them spent the night together."

"I already knew that. I'm the one who told her to stay, because of the weather. She stayed in his room; he stayed on the couch."

"How do you know?"

"She told me," Neal bites out. "How do *you* know any of this?"

"You don't think we had a squad car patrolling the streets after a woman was slaughtered in that neighborhood?"

Okay. Of course they were patrolling.

"Lucinda's car was there all night, parked in front of the house Randy's renting."

"So? That doesn't mean anything."

"It doesn't mean anything for a woman to spend the night with a former lover who's just learned that his wife has been murdered in cold blood?"

"The Barakats were separated, and Lucinda is one of Randy's closest friends."

"Who hadn't seen or had any contact with him in months. Yet she showed up out of the blue on the day his wife was murdered?"

"She's—"

"A psychic. I know, Bullard."

So now they're on a last name basis.

Fine.

"She's been helping us with this case, Santiago. She's the one who figured out that those numbers we had were the latitude and longitude of Beach Haven."

"We were working on it. We'd have come up with it. Anyone could have."

"Why would she have let you know about it, though, unless she wanted to help?"

"To throw us off her trail more quickly."

"And the Ava Neary connection? What does that have to do with anything?"

"Exactly. What does that have to do with anything?" Frank sounds smug. "Smokescreen."

Through clenched teeth, Neal asks, "Look, why don't you just come right out and tell me what it is that you think Lucinda did."

"I think she got into that house using the key that was so conveniently hidden under the mat, and I think she killed Carla Barakat."

"Because . . ."

"Because she wanted Carla's husband all to herself."

"They were separated."

"But not divorced. Maybe she was worried he'd leave her and go back to Carla. He did once before, didn't he?"

So he's done his homework. How did he find out?

"Randy and Lucinda were never a couple," Neal tells him.

"Never a public couple. There's a difference."

"Look, you're going down the wrong path, Santiago."

He's seen it happen before.

Not long after he made detective back in the mid-eighties, Neal encountered his first serial killer: the Frankford Slasher. For a good five years, the shadowy figure raped and murdered victims in the blighted northeast neighborhood.

Officially, the case was solved: an arrest was made; the suspect was convicted—for just one of the murders, and based on damned skimpy evidence, as far as Neal is concerned. He wasn't involved; by then, he was off the case and onto something else.

But to this day, he remains convinced that the real Frankford Slasher evaded capture while the investigation focused on someone who, while he might have murdered the victim in question, could very well have had nothing to do with the rest.

"I'm going down the wrong path?" Frank Santiago echoes.

"I'm looking at the people who had a connection to the victim. How is that the wrong path?"

That, of course, is what you do first in any murder investigation.

But there are other factors at work here.

"This was no crime of passion, Frank. I've worked on a number of serial murders, and—"

"And so have I. And so has Lucinda. We're all experts, agreed?"

"I didn't say—"

"Who better than an expert to pull this off?"

"I don't follow."

"Someone who knows how a serial murderer's mind works. Someone who went to a lot of trouble to make it appear that Carla was a random victim. Right down to figuring out the longitude and latitude of Beach Haven, like that's the reason Carla was murdered—just because she was there."

"I think you're wrong. I *know* you're wrong. It's not just about Carla. According to the second set of numbers we got and that package that was sent to Lucinda, we should be looking at Chicago."

87.7
41.9

"We *have* been looking at Chicago. There hasn't been a similar murder there."

"That we know of."

"The CPD is on it. They combed their files. If any case in Chicago history came close to our killer's M.O., don't you think we'd be on it and so would they?"

"Yes."

"Good, Neal."

Ah, they're back to first names. Frank Santiago must think he's coming around to his way of thinking.

Like hell, he is.

"Why did you call me to tell me this tonight, Frank?"

There's a pause. "To give you a heads up that we're bringing her in for questioning and you, too."

"I'm a suspect, too?"

"You're a witness. You need to be there."

"When is this going to happen?"

"As soon as possible."

"Tomorrow?"

A hesitation. "I'm not sure yet. I'm tied up early in the day."

"Does Randy know this is going on?"

"Randy is not assigned to this case."

"I realize that. But the victim was his wife. And the woman you're about to interrogate is his friend."

"Interview. Not interrogate. There's a difference."

"Does Randy know about this?" he repeats.

"Not yet. And it's not up to you to tell him. Or her, for that matter."

That's true.

It doesn't mean he won't . . . but he has to weigh the consequences.

Neal rakes a hand through what's left of his hair. "You know, it could still happen, Frank."

Santiago doesn't ask what could still happen. A good investigator follows all the threads—conversational and otherwise.

"Hypothetically, yes," he agrees. "But—"

"There's always a cooling off period."

"Granted. Thirty years is a bit much, don't you think?"

"Thirty years?"

"Since Ava Neary."

"That's not what I meant." *And you know it.*

"Look, this case couldn't be more different from Ava Neary's. No one made it look like Carla Barakat slit her own throat, okay?"

"An M.O. can change over the years, Frank. You and I

both know that. The signature doesn't, but the M.O. might. The murder victims she saw in that scrapbook—"

"So-called murder victims she *said* she saw," Frank interjects.

Neal ignores him. "They were all young and pretty, with long hair. So was Carla Barakat, and—"

"You're reaching, Neal."

Yeah, he knows. He can't help it.

Frank's on the wrong path, dammit.

"At the very least, you should be looking into those suicides," Neal tells him.

"Which suicides? The only person who saw this scrapbook is Lucinda Sloan, and she claims it disappeared."

"I saw it, and it did disappear."

"But you told me you never saw what was in it. You don't have any information on these supposed murder victims."

"Lucinda gave you two names she remembered."

"We checked them out. They are two very sad cases of women who killed themselves many years ago."

"So you talked to their families? You made sure their deaths weren't suspicious in any way?"

"We checked them out," Frank repeats. "Without something more to go on . . . What else do you expect me to do? Your friend plucks two names out of the past and expects us to reopen investigations into their deaths? This isn't even our jurisdiction."

"But—"

"Listen, Neal, trust me, if this does happen again—if this so-called serial killer strikes again using the same M.O.— I'll be on the first plane to O'Hare, but . . ."

Neal sighs. "But what?"

"That's not going to happen. Because there is no serial killer."

* * *

Frank hangs up the telephone and allows the painfully suppressed fit of coughing to overtake him, along with a rip tide of self-reproach.

What the hell did he just do?

He shouldn't have called Neal. Of course he shouldn't have.

He leans back in his chair, trembling, sweating cold.

Folding his arms across his wheezing chest, he feels pain as the movement tugs the latest scar there.

His ego got the best of him, dammit. His ego, and his weakening physical state, and his personal grudge against Lucinda Sloan.

Thanks to her, no doubt, both Randy and Dan Lambert have recently asked him—on separate occasions—about his health. When he assured them that he was fine—just getting over a touch of pneumonia, as he'd said all along—he could tell neither believed him.

Because of Lucinda Sloan.

She knows, just as he thought. She knows, and she told his colleagues.

What right does she have to delve into his personal business?

What right does she have, for that matter, to walk free?

When the DNA evidence came back, he gloated.

No longer does the psychic have the upper hand.

All right, so he should never have called Neal Bullard just now, but he couldn't seem to help himself.

He let his personal agenda get in the way of his professional one.

Dammit. This could have serious repercussions. His judgement is going to pieces.

Dr. Rubin said to anticipate that. Said that now is probably the time for Frank to wind down his career.

But I'm not ready to give up.

I'm not ready for any of this.

Frank massages his throbbing temples with his fingertips.

He screwed up royally.

What if Neal tips off Lucinda Sloan, and she bolts?

Or what if you're wrong about her?

He tries to ignore the nagging voice, just as he's been doing for weeks now.

What if he really is going down the wrong path?

What if that guy who contacted him a few weeks ago was onto something?

Victor Shattuck.

Frank had swiftly Googled the name before he even took the call. He found out that Shattuck was a retired FBI agent, like he claimed—and also that he was writing a book about a decades-old unsolved serial killer case.

Frank promptly dismissed him as a publicity hound.

So why did he take the call anyway?

Because it's what you do.

You examine every possible avenue.

You listen to every possible lead, no matter how unlikely.

It would really be reaching to think that a long-dormant— or probably dead—murderer would resurface now. Especially here. The entire county sees a handful of murders a year at most. What are the odds that this bucolic island town would be the scene of two separate serial murder cases in a matter of months?

Then again, there was so much press about the first case. . . . Is it so hard to believe that it attracted unwanted attention from a killer?

Yes.

Damn right, it's hard to believe.

About as hard as it is to believe that Lucinda Sloan happened to show up at Carla Barakat's doorstep because of a psychic vision . . .

Even though she does have a way of knowing things she couldn't possibly know?

Frank sits up abruptly, wondering why he's even bothering to question any of this.

There isn't a decent detective in the world who would give her paranormal, intangible so-called explanation the benefit of the doubt over solid DNA evidence.

As far as he's concerned, they need look no further.

She's guilty as hell.

If he had his way, he'd haul her in here right now. Arrest her.

But there's procedure to follow, and paperwork to do. . . .

And, yes, the morning's ordeal to get through.

Filled with dread, Frank covers his mouth with a handkerchief and gives in to another fit of coughing.

When it's over, the handkerchief is spattered with blood.

Lucinda's BlackBerry rings as she walks the last stretch of slush-pooled sidewalk toward her building, carrying a couple of bags filled with groceries she bought when she got off the subway.

Erma's home-cooked meal tonight—culminating in a sour cream coffee cake, still fragrant from the oven and swirled with crumbly sweet streusel—reminded her that her own cupboards and fridge are shamefully bare. And the Bullards' parental insistence that she try a salad reminded her that she really does need to eat more healthfully now that she's in her thirties.

So much for that.

She went into the store intending to shop the perimeter— fruits and vegetables, dairy and poultry. She wound up in the aisles and came out with chips and soda, Ben and Jerry's, Oreos, and a busload of Easter candy.

Juggling the bags, she reaches into the pocket of her parka for the phone, certain it's Neal.

Maybe he's got something on Isaiah Drew.

Or maybe he'd gotten information earlier, when he took that phone call upstairs, but didn't want to say anything in front of Erma.

He'd been awfully subdued when he returned to the kitchen, quietly eating dessert and letting Erma do all the talking.

That wasn't unusual in and of itself, but something was wrong.

Lucinda even asked him about it at the door.

"We'll talk in the morning, Cin," was all he said, looking weary.

But when she looks at her phone, it isn't Neal's number in the Caller ID window.

Man, her psychic skills really are shot lately.

Which is why she probably shouldn't be concerned about the nagging sensation that's grown stronger all evening . . . as if something's about to happen.

Something violent.

Not to her. She's pretty sure of that—though she's not positive about anything.

No, it's going to happen to someone else. Maybe it already has.

Maybe to a stranger.

Not here, though.

Somewhere . . . else.

Way to go, Lucinda. There's violence somewhere in the world tonight.

Brilliant deduction.

Cam takes one last look at her sleeping infant in the glow of the A.A. Milne honey pot-shaped night light.

Then she tiptoes from the nursery and closes the door, pretty sure she won't share another waking hour with Grace until the day after tomorrow.

She's leaving for the airport in about seven hours, at four A.M., and Grace is more likely than not to sleep through the night now that she's been on rice cereal for over a week. Under ordinary circumstances, Cam would relish the knowledge that the baby won't be up in the wee hours.

But it means Grace will still be sleeping when she leaves in the morning, and that she'll be sleeping again when Cam gets home late tomorrow.

Down the hall, she knocks on Tess's door and is surprised when she calls, "Come in."

Cam opens the door a crack. "I was expecting you to be plugged into headphones."

"I'm waiting for a call." Tess is at her desk doing homework, phone close at hand.

"I thought you were on the phone with him when I brought the baby up."

She could have sworn they were arguing, too. Tess's end of the conversation had been so loud, even through her closed door, that Cam had to call to her to keep it down in there as she rocked Grace to sleep.

"He had to go help his mom with something. He's supposed to call me back. What?" she asks, seeing the look on Cam's face.

"Did I say anything?"

"No, but you're thinking it. It's not like I get to see him tomorrow morning at school. I can't talk to him every day until late in the afternoon, you know. That's, like, almost twenty hours from now."

God forbid Tess have to wait almost twenty hours to reconnect with her boyfriend, is what Cam is thinking.

And she hates herself for thinking it, because it's not like she was never young, and in love, herself.

Her first boyfriend's name was Alex . . . Nickerson? Nicholson? Imagine, her not being able to remember which, after all these years.

But she still remembers his impossibly long eyelashes—not just for a guy, as they say, but for anyone—and the smell of the tangy aftershave he'd filched from his father's medicine cabinet, and the taste of Strawberry Bubblicious on his tongue when he kissed her.

So, yeah, she knows what it's like to be a teenaged girl and in love—or, really, infatuated is the more accurate word.

And because she herself didn't have a mother around to keep tabs on how much time she spent on the phone with Alex Nickerson—she's pretty sure it was Nickerson—she really should give Tess a break.

Thoughts of her own childhood remind Cam of her earlier conversation with Bernice Watts, and of the reason she has to fly away from her girls and Mike before dawn tomorrow morning.

"Good night." Cam bends to kiss the top of Tess's head.

"I'm not going to bed yet! It's so early!"

She smiles at the horrified look on Tess's face. "I know, but I am. I have to be up in a few hours to catch my flight."

"*Why* are you going to Buffalo again?"

"I told you. To look up an old friend."

"Who goes to Buffalo in the dead of winter?" Tess asks incredulously. "Isn't it, like, buried in snow or something?"

"It's officially spring," Cam tells her—as if that makes any difference. She checked the Buffalo forecast earlier on Accuweather. They're expecting two to four inches of snow by morning.

She only hopes the flight won't be delayed because of it. She can't afford to waste any time. Mike was able to take the day off tomorrow, but no more than that. And, anyway, she hasn't weaned the baby yet, and she isn't ready to. They'll have to make do with bottles of pumped breast milk while she's gone.

"Make sure you help Daddy with Grace tomorrow, Tess."

"I'll be in school most of the day."

"I know. Have a good day. Good luck on that math test." She starts for the door, stooping to pick up a stray sock on the way. Since true love came into her life, Tess has actually started to live up to Mike's affectionate but formerly inappropriate nickname for her.

Messy Tessy actually fits now that she's too caught up in her budding love life to spend much time picking up after herself, let alone anyone else, the way she used to.

Again, Cam thinks of her lost sister, of all the things she didn't know, all the things they could have shared.

"Who's the old friend, again?" Tess wants to know. "The one you're seeing in Buffalo?"

Again? As if Cam has already mentioned the name, and it's slipped Tess's mind.

She hasn't.

"Her name is Janet." She throws the sock into the hamper. "Janet O'Leary."

"O'Leary," Tess repeats, apparently not finding it familiar and losing interest fast. She examines her fingernails.

"Right. Like the woman with the cow."

"What woman with the cow?"

"Mrs. O'Leary. The cow that started the fire. In Chicago."

"Chicago? *Where* are you going?"

"Buffalo."

"Not Chicago."

"No, I just meant—"

"Whatever, Mom. Have a safe trip."

Safe.

There was a time, back before last summer, when Tess probably wouldn't have used that word. A time when, even if she had, it wouldn't have jumped out at Cam like an ominous warning.

"I'll see you late tomorrow night," she says, to reassure her daughter—and herself—that everything is going to be just fine.

"Hey, Bradley," Lucinda says into the phone. "What's up?"

"Are you over the flu? Dare I come visit you, or will I wind up contaminated?"

"I'm over the flu." Not exactly up for visitors, though. She's just had too much going on. None of which she's mentioned to Bradley.

She might have, had she seen him, but she hasn't in ages—and not just because she's been sick. He landed a bit part in a show last month and has been busy rehearsing.

"Hey, by the way, when's opening night?" she asks, setting down her grocery bags to let herself into her building. "Remember to save me a ticket."

Maybe even two.

It's not as if she and Randy are *dating*. But he'd probably like to get away to New York and see a show.

"I will, when and if we actually have an opening night," Bradley tells her as she steps over the threshold and turns on the overhead light.

"*If?* Uh-oh."

"It's not looking good. One of the leads quit today."

"Maybe you can take his role."

"*Her* role, and I don't think so," Bradley says dryly. "Although Lord knows if I become any more desperate for cash, I'll do it."

And Lord knows he could become desperate for cash. His trust fund is long gone, and so are his parents—who left every cent they had to the foundation they established to help stray dogs, the irony of which was not lost on their only son.

"Anyway, rehearsals are on hold now so I thought I'd hop the Acela and come down to see you," he tells Lucinda.

"*Now?*"

"I was thinking in the morning, but what the hey? If you're up for a night on the town, I'll get my dancing shoes and shoot right over to Penn Station. I bet I can be there by midnight."

She can't help but smile. "Sorry, can't do it."

"All right, tomorrow."

"No, I meant I can't do tomorrow. *Tonight?* Are you kidding? Do you know how long it's been since I went dancing at midnight?"

"Don't tell me you're getting old, because that's no excuse. I'm older than dirt, and I frequently go dancing at midnight. Why can't you do tomorrow?"

"I'm having brunch with Bitsy."

"Good Lord. Want me to come down later in the day so that we can drown your sorrows together?"

"I thought you were broke."

"Amtrak takes credit cards."

"You have to pay the bill."

"That's what the other credit cards are for. I love those balance transfer checks they send out. So handy. What do you think?"

"I think you're approaching financial ruin." She fishes her mail out of her mailbox, drops it into one of the grocery bags, then starts up the stairs.

"No, I mean what do you think about my coming to visit?"

She hesitates.

"Oh . . . sure."

"Is it me, or do you not sound thrilled?"

"It's just you. I am thrilled." She does her best to sound it. The last thing she wants to do is hurt Bradley's feelings. "I'd love to see you. Come on down."

"Will do. See you tomorrow." He makes a kissing sound into the phone and hangs up.

Having reached her door, Lucinda sees a yellow Post-it note stuck above the knob.

Have a delivery for you. Peggy

Lucinda wonders whether she dares wait until tomorrow to visit the super's basement apartment to collect her delivery, whatever it is. Probably something she ordered online, then forgot about.

She might as well get it now. Peggy probably heard her come in.

She leaves her bags propped against the door and descends again, only to find Peggy about to start up the flight.

The super, in her fifties and divorced, has short white hair and a broad-boned, well-scrubbed face. She's wearing a T-shirt and white Keds with jeans that are pleated and high-waisted: not the neo-retro style that came back into fashion a year or two ago, but the kind that went out a few decades ago. Lucinda can smell the powdery perfume of her deodorant.

She's holding a tissue-wrapped vase.

"Hi, Lucinda. Who's sending you flowers?"

"Flowers! I have no idea."

Truly, she doesn't, unless . . .

"The florist was here this afternoon. You weren't home, so they rang my bell and I signed for this."

No. The flowers couldn't be from Randy . . . could they?

"Looks like daffodils, doesn't it?" Peggy comments as Lucinda stops a few steps above her and reaches down to accept the vase.

"It does."

Peggy hasn't necessarily struck her as a nosy woman before now. She didn't even ask many questions when the police were here and Lucinda had to have her locks changed last month.

But tonight she does seem curious, and a little wistful, about the flowers. Maybe she's living vicariously. The few conversations they've had, she's mentioned how lonely she's been and how nice it would be if a decent man would look twice at a woman her age.

"Secret admirer, Lucinda?"

"Ha, wouldn't that be nice."

"It would." Still wistful, Peggy waits.

"Well, thanks for grabbing them for me. I've got ice cream melting in my grocery bags, so . . . good night."

Obvious bummer for Peggy. "Good night, Lucinda."

Carrying the vase, Lucinda heads back up the stairs. She

can see the card through the tissue paper, propped amid the blooms.

She just couldn't open it in front of Peggy. Not without knowing who sent it, or how she'll react if it's from Randy.

Maybe she shouldn't be surprised.

Maybe this is his way of telling her he's ready to move on, give it a real try at last.

She opens the locks, including the new deadbolt.

"It can't be picked," the locksmith assured her when he installed it. "You're totally safe now."

She'd love to believe that, but the thing is . . .

She's not convinced her locks were picked the first time, or that someone came in the window—the other theory of Neal's friend Roz, who investigated.

She's had visions that involve someone coming in with a key.

And even more frightening visions of a shadowy figure of a man here, in her apartment, with her. Prowling around in the dead of night, when she's asleep.

A man who steals her keys, slips out to copy them, and slips back in.

When she suggested that to Roz, he said, "That would be one hell of a bold move. And if he got in while you were sleeping, and he's behind Carla's death . . . then why are you still alive? He could have done the same thing to you."

There's truth—and cold comfort—in the fact that he didn't.

If he was even here in the first place.

Roz didn't think a former tenant had kept or lost the keys, reasoning that it would have been a more likely M.O. for a run-of-the-mill thief.

Nothing was stolen from Lucinda's apartment.

It was entered very deliberately, and for a specific reason that has everything to do with Lucinda's past—and Carla's murder.

And she's fairly certain that she'll never feel entirely safe in this apartment again.

Neal thinks she should move.

So does Randy.

"That would be running scared," she's told them both, repeatedly.

They both get her; thus, they both get that.

They just don't like it.

She turns on lights all the way to the kitchen, noting with relief that the apartment feels empty and looks undisturbed.

After setting the vase on the counter, she goes around drawing the blinds she reluctantly had installed over all the windows. Then she returns to the door to collect her groceries from the hall.

For a split second, she thinks the bags are going to be gone.

But they aren't.

Of course not.

They're right where she left them, just as everything else has been right where she left it for going on a month now.

You've got to get over being so jumpy, she tells herself, shaking her head as she returns to the kitchen.

She's dying to open the flowers, but she forces herself to put away the groceries first, prolonging the suspense.

If they're from Randy, she'll call him.

No—she'll drive right out to see him. Not tonight, but first thing in the morning.

No—brunch with her mother. And Bradley's coming.

And all I care about, really, is seeing Randy.

She hates that she's so caught up in him, like a teenaged girl with a crush. She hates that she needs to see him, needs to hear his voice. . . .

Needs him, period.

What I need is a sugar fix.

She tosses a couple of marshmallow Peeps onto a paper plate and microwaves them for thirty seconds.

As she digs into the gooey ooze with a fork, she looks at the flowers.

For the first time in years—or maybe, ever—she feels as if her life has spun beyond her control. The sensation is wonderful and terrifying at once.

At last, she marches over to the vase and rips off the tissue paper.

The envelope bears the address of a neighborhood florist shop.

She pulls out the card.

HAPPY SPRING reads the preprinted message.

No note.

It isn't signed.

All that's on it are a pair of decimal numbers she's seen before.

87.7
41.9

The longitude and latitude of Chicago.

Chapter Thirteen

As the plane descends through a gradually thinning layer of gray, Cam is startled to see how close they are to the ground already. Wet snow whirls past the windows. Wisps of clouds momentarily obscure suburban rooftops symmetrically arranged along ribbons of wet black pavement that intersect against a backdrop of white.

Then they're touching down, and the pilot is welcoming them to Buffalo, and Cam is on her own in this aging industrial city at the edge of a vast gray lake.

It's been so long since she's been on a plane—and she can't remember the last time she took a flight by herself. Years ago, probably, when she was still working as a magazine editor.

It feels strange to be sitting here among solo business travelers, dressed in dark suits and lost in their morning newspapers; they take it all in stride as she once did.

Wearing slacks that have sat in dry cleaner's plastic for a couple of years now, along with a tailored white blouse and black cardigan that, thank goodness, never really went out of style, Cam quite possibly almost looks like one of them.

But she doesn't feel like one of them. She has a feeling no one else is flying to Buffalo to investigate a possible murder.

Who are you? Nancy Drew?

Back at the gate in New York, when she arrived only to find her flight delayed for over an hour, then two, it was all she could do not to turn around and go back home, where she belongs.

Not because the plane she was about to board was being checked and rechecked for some kind of mechanical problem.

But because she kept wondering why she was there in the first place. She's no detective. She hasn't a clue what she's doing.

Only the thought of her dead sister made her get on this plane.

No one else is going to see this thing through for Ava's sake.

Lucinda said the police aren't interested—that they even seem to question whether she ever saw a scrapbook of so-called suicide victims in the first place.

Yet Cam and Lucinda verified that the two college girls whose names she glimpsed in the scrapbook—Elizabeth Johnson and Sandra Wubner—did indeed supposedly commit suicide over thirty years ago. Faced with that evidence, the Long Beach Township police still saw no reason to connect it to the death of Randy Barakat's wife.

As Cam follows the rest of the passengers off the plane, she tells herself that she's doing the right thing. Even though she's scared to death, completely out of her element, and wondering how she's ever going to summon the nerve to do what has to be done.

The brasserie, located in an Art Nouveau building off Chestnut Street, is one of the most elegant restaurants in Philadelphia.

The dining room's soaring ceilings, marble floors, and arched windows bear testimony to its former life as a turn-of-the-century bank. Now cushy banquettes fill the room, along with tables set with linen tablecloths and bone china and vases of roses.

At one of them sits Bitsy Sloan.

"Ah, Lucinda, there you are."

Lucinda.

Not "sweetheart," or "darling," or "honey."

No, Bitsy Sloan is not one for endearments—not unless she's talking to her ridiculous squirrel-sized white dog, whose name Lucinda can't even remember, as if it even matters, because again, her mother calls the dog "sweetheart" and "darling" and "honey."

"Hello, Mother." Lucinda plants a perfunctory kiss on her mother's powdered, papery cheek.

Bitsy Sloan is tastefully, expensively clothed, bejeweled, coiffed, made-up, and perfumed. Her dyed brown pageboy brushes the shoulders of her red Dior suit, which drapes from her size zero frame just as it would from a hanger.

Lucinda, wearing a slightly rumpled black Prada pantsuit she took from the back of her closet, takes the seat across from her.

Immediately, a handsome tuxedoed waiter with slick black hair appears. He pours coffee and fresh-squeezed orange juice and hands them menus encased in rich leather binders, their creamy stock embossed in Old English typeface.

Lucinda surveys the choices. Escargot. Foie gras.

She closes the menu, puts it aside, and amuses herself by fantasizing about treating her mother to breakfast at the Denny's out on Industrial Highway, where she'd have to decide between the "Lumberjack Slam" and "Moons Over My Hammy."

Moons.

Lucinda thinks about the Beethoven sonata that mysteriously appeared on her iPod, and about the movie that was ordered on her online account.

Moonlight Sonata.

Moonstruck.

That DVD was no accident. When she called the online store's customer service department, they told her that the order had been placed around Valentine's Day, and that a receipt had automatically been sent to her e-mail account.

She couldn't find one.

Not until she checked her recently deleted e-mail folder.

She had never seen it—nor deleted it.

But someone had—and from her home computer, right before she went away with Jimmy.

She immediately changed the password for the online store account, and changed her e-mail address as well.

"I wasn't sure you were coming." The words are spoken crisply from behind Mother's menu, jarring her.

In other words, *You're late.*

"I'm sorry, Mother. I had business to take care of."

When she left her apartment, Neal—who had come right over last night with Detective Rozyczka, as soon as she'd called to tell him about the flowers—was back.

Today, he'd brought the detective again, along with a security consultant.

"I want to make sure you're safe here," Neal told her as the consultant went around the apartment with a clipboard, a pen, and measuring tape, shaking his head every now and then.

"I am safe. No one's been here. It was a florist delivery this time, not a personal one."

"I realize that. But he's been here before. He's going to come back."

Not he *might.*

He's *going to.*

He.

Who *is* he?

Neal assured her he'd take the information about the flowers to the Long Beach Township Police. "I'll handle it, Lucinda. You just go to brunch with your mother, like you were planning."

This is the last place she wants to be.

But then, so is her apartment.

Really, the only place she wants to be is with Randy.

She called him last night to tell him what had happened.

"I'll come right out there," was his first response.

"No, please don't. It's not urgent."

"Yes, it is."

"Someone sent me flowers, Randy. That's not exactly an emergency."

"Don't be cavalier. You and I both know you could be in danger."

"Not any more than I was before." She kept her misgivings to herself. He had enough to worry about. "Anyway, Neal is coming. He'll take care of things."

"I know he will."

The leather binder across the white linen tablecloth lowers abruptly, jerking Lucinda back to the present.

Her mother's frosted pink lips are pursed—either because she doesn't like anything on the menu, or because she didn't like Lucinda's reason for being late to brunch.

Probably both.

The hovering waiter is there in a flash. "Have you decided, ladies?"

Mother orders a poached egg on dry wheat toast.

Lucinda, not hungry, nonetheless orders Crepes aux Framboise with caramelized bananas and candied pecans, apple wood smoked bacon, and a side of white truffle frites. And a glass of Laurent-Perrier, Brut Millisime, 1997 vintage.

She is rewarded with a disapproving look from her mother—and an approving one from the waiter.

"We're celebrating, are we? Some champagne for you, as well, madam?"

Madam's lips purse harder, if that's possible. "No, thank you."

"I wish you would, Mother."

"Why? *Are* we celebrating something?"

"No." *It would just be nice to see you loosen up, for once.*

The waiter has discreetly vanished again.

"Tell me what you've been doing lately, Mother." *Because God knows I can't tell you what I've been doing.*

Bitsy tells her about her role in an art auction, a civic restoration project, a charity ball. About having the indoor pool resurfaced, and about trying to replace the chauffeur. Same old, same old.

"Your father sends his best regards."

But not his love.

"How is he?" Lucinda asks.

"He was in the Orient last week. He's in Europe this week and into next."

"No, I asked *how* is he? Not *where*."

Bitsy Sloan blinks her crepey, beige shadow-creased eyelids.

Lucinda sighs inwardly. "I'd like to see him," she says, "when he gets back and has some free time."

"So would I." Her mother's smile is brittle.

Lucinda's BlackBerry vibrates in her bag. She waits a moment, then slips it out and checks it, holding it on her lap, out of her mother's view.

It's a link to a newspaper article, sent from an address she doesn't recognize.

Heart pounding, she blurts, "Mother, I need to use the ladies' room."

Bitsy Sloan starts to protest, but she's already up and striding away from the table.

It smells like a funeral parlor in here.

Neal reluctantly closes the door behind him, shutting out fresh air, and approaches the counter, where a woman with long, frizzy blond hair and wire-rimmed glasses is trimming thorns from long-stemmed roses.

"How can I help you?" She sets the shears aside.

He pulls out his badge. Her pale-lashed eyes widen.

"I need information about the person who placed an order for flowers that were delivered yesterday from your shop."

"Why?"

He just looks at her.

She turns to a computer monitor. "Which order was it?"

"The flowers went to a woman named Lucinda Sloan." He gives her address, and waits while the woman presses keys and brings up the right screen.

"Oh, I remember. The daffodils."

"You took the order?"

"Yes, and I remember it because it was placed weeks ago, on Valentine's Day. We were doing roses, you know, and reds, and pinks. . . ."

"Valentine's Day stuff."

"Exactly. We were just swamped in the shop that day, delivery and carry-out bouquets, and in walks this guy wanting to order daffodils that wouldn't be delivered for a month. And he paid in cash, too."

"What was his name?"

She checks the screen. "Let's see. . . . It was Randall Barakat."

That stops Neal in his tracks . . . but only for a moment.

"What kind of man was he? Young? Old? Middle-aged?" Neal asked her.

"Middle-aged, I think. Maybe."

"You think? Maybe?" *Don't lose patience, Neal.* "So you're not sure?"

"Valentine's Day is our busiest day of the year."

Yes, and I'm sure he was counting on that.

"How old would you consider middle-aged?"

"You know. . . . Maybe in his forties, fifties, sixties."

"That's a broad range."

She shrugs.

Randy, who is closing in on forty, doesn't look a day over thirty.

"Was he handsome?"

"Not that I remember."

As far as Neal has ever noticed, there isn't a woman alive who wouldn't consider Randy Barakat handsome.

"White? Black? Asian? Hispanic?"

"White! Definitely!" She looks pleased with her recall skills. "And, you know, he had gray hair."

"Are you sure?"

"Positive."

"Not black."

"No, I told you, he was white."

"I meant his hair."

"It wasn't white, really. It was gray."

Patience, Neal.

"Can you think of anything else to describe this guy?"

"Not really. I told you, this place was really—"

"Busy that day. Got it. Do you remember anything else about him? Anything at all?"

"Nothing other than the fact that he tipped me."

"He *tipped* you?"

"Yes, with a bunch of ones. Most deliveries don't pay cash, and they don't tip the person who takes the order."

That's interesting.

It doesn't shed much light on who they're dealing with, but Neal would bet his life that it wasn't Randy Barakat.

Buffalo International airport is compact and nowhere near as busy as the metropolitan New York City terminal Cam just left. Without luggage, she's in the rental car about five minutes later, consulting the driving directions she printed from the Internet the night before. According to them, it should take her all of fifteen minutes to reach the Buffalo Niagara Medical Campus.

With the roads slick and a light snow falling, it takes twenty.

Cam arrives wishing it had taken an hour, at least. She doesn't feel prepared to meet Janet O'Leary.

What if she isn't there?

What if she is?

What am I going to say to her?

What if she tells me to get lost?

Worst of all: *What if she doesn't even remember?*

I should just go home. What am I doing here?

Looking for answers.

Answers that have been a hell of a long time coming.

The multibuilding complex, sleek brick and glass and steel, is still under construction, as she had known it would be. She did her homework on that, at least.

But what do I do when I get to where I'm going?

What do I say to her?

I should just go home.

But she parks the car and forces herself to push ahead, through the wet, wind-driven snow. She'd recognize that she's reached the Roswell Park Cancer Institute even without the identifying sign.

Everywhere, there are patients in various stages of the disease: some being helped from their cars into wheelchairs; others painstakingly using walkers or breezing along wearing telltale turbans and wigs.

The lobby is a lovely, four-story atrium, complete with a granite information desk, a cappuccino bar, a pianist playing a jaunty show tune on a grand piano. If it weren't for the fact that the place is filled with obvious cancer patients, along with medical staff wearing laminated ID cards, Cam could be standing in an upscale hotel lobby.

For a moment, she wishes she had done that instead—hopped a plane to some island paradise and checked into a resort where she could hide away and pretend everything is normal, status quo.

But it isn't, and she didn't.

She came here, looking for answers.

Looking for answers where there probably are none.

Looking for a killer where there probably is none.

This is a mistake.

She has no business disturbing layers of dust settled over the secrets of the past. Ava is long gone, like their mother; soon, Pop will be, too. But Cam has a family that needs her now; she has a husband who loves her and a new baby girl and a daughter she almost lost.

Whatever, Mom. Have a safe trip.

This isn't safe and it isn't smart and she should leave well enough alone, get on with her life.

Then a beautifully dressed, utterly hairless woman passes Cam, catches her eye, and smiles. She wears her baldness proudly—not, Cam realizes, having given up the battle, but having brazenly accepted it.

If she can do this, Cam finds herself thinking, *then Lord knows I can do anything.*

Jaw set, she walks toward the information desk.

I'd rather be in Philadelphia.

He read that someplace, a long time ago. Who said it? He can't remember, but the quote has been ringing in his ears all morning, as he walks the familiar streets of Society Hill beneath a dank canopy of clouds, wishing he were somewhere else.

Somewhere other than Philadelphia.

He's spent a lot of time here, but it doesn't feel like home. Nor did the upstate New York city where he settled last June to become an upstanding citizen just long enough for the parole officers to relax a little.

The Bronx neighborhood where he'd spent the first eighteen years of his life might have felt like home at one time— before his father was gunned down on a sidewalk right in front of their building.

He and his mother stayed there, though, afterward.

They stayed until he graduated high school, and Ricky Parker across the hall was murdered in his own apartment, and the killer wasn't caught, and his mother decided the neighborhood was getting dangerous.

He didn't miss the old neighborhood.

Nor does he miss the one that came after, in Yonkers.

He can't think of anywhere that ever really has felt like home—except, perhaps, for the maximum security prison where he was housed with over two thousand other men, most of them fellow violent offenders, career criminals mingling with first offenders. Like him. Ha.

Oh, wait, not the prison—the *correctional facility.*

That was back in the dawn of state prison reform; the governor-appointed Special Committee's decision to change the name of the dismal concrete box didn't change much of anything else.

Still—you spend three and a half decades anywhere, it's going to feel familiar. And as far as he's concerned, when something is familiar, it's home.

It isn't that he wanted to stay incarcerated, or would have if he could have, or would ever want to go back. Hell, no. Thirty-five years was long enough to spend behind bars for the inadvertent, sloppy murder of the only woman who had ever thought twice about him.

He lost control that night.

Never again.

One of the neighbors heard Mother's screams. Almost immediately, sirens wailed.

How could this be happening, he wondered, as he fled into the night, panicked. He had executed so many flawless murders; he had sat back and laughed for a couple of years as the authorities hunted for the elusive Night Watchman.

One impulsive move, and he was living his worst nightmare. They chased him down in the dark like an animal.

They got him.

One of the arresting officers called him a crazy son of a bitch as he slapped on the handcuffs.

He's crazy, all right. Crazy like a fox.

Ha. Fox. Funny.

The law enforcement and judicial powers that be thought they had the upper hand, but right from the start, they were wrong.

A little over a week after he killed his mother, the first Vietnam draft lottery took place for all men born between 1944 and 1950.

The first number chosen was September 14.

He had been born on September 14, 1950.

When he heard the outcome of the lottery, he laughed his head off, knowing that his arrest had saved his life; knowing that the almighty draft board couldn't touch him behind those thirty-foot concrete walls.

Prison was bearable because he knew that one day, he'd get out.

With Vietnam, there would have been no such guarantee.

"I'm sorry about that, Mother."

Bitsy Sloan looks up from her hands, clasped in her lap almost as if she's been praying.

Lucinda knows better than that. She doubts her mother prays even at St. John's Presbyterian, where she appears every Sunday morning without fail just as generations of supposedly pious Sloans have done before her.

It's just for show, as far as Lucinda is concerned.

Why would Mother believe in God when she doesn't believe in her own daughter?

Bitsy nods at the seat Lucinda vacated, and the untouched meal that has appeared before it. "Sit down. Your food is getting cold, and so is mine."

Lucinda remains standing, looking longingly at the untouched flute of golden champagne at her place setting. She could use a swig right about now, to help face what lies ahead, well beyond the inevitable confrontation with her mother.

Needless to say, this is not going to go over well.

"I'm sorry, I have to leave."

Bitsy digests this with all the enthusiasm she has for the food in front of her. "Now? In the middle of brunch?"

"It can't be helped." She hesitates, wondering whether to provide any more information than that.

"Are you sick, Lucinda?"

Would it change anything if her mother knew the truth?

"Yes, I'm . . . I'm not feeling well."

Bitsy sighs heavily, too much a lady to betray her emotions any more animatedly than to say quietly, "I'm disappointed."

Lucinda wishes she could believe it's because her mother is concerned for her health. Or because her mother was looking forward to spending some quality time with her.

But it isn't about that, of course. It never has been.

Lucinda has no illusions; she knows she's as much an obligation to her mother as her mother is to her.

As for her father—well, Rudolph Sloan doesn't seem to feel obligated to either of them.

For a moment, Lucinda really does consider telling her mother the reason she has to leave.

There's been a murder, Mother. Another murder, and the killer is on the loose, and I think he's been in my apartment, watching me, and if we don't catch him, I might be next.

If she says all of that out loud, what difference will it make?

Her mother will worry. She's cold, but she's not inhuman. Beneath the sharp edge lies some semblance of maternal caring.

Her mother will also blame her for what's happened. Blame her being in the press, talking about murder. Blame her having made it her life's work to come into contact not just with victims of crime, but with the lowest life forms imaginable: the criminals themselves.

Is it any wonder, her mother will ask, *that you've captured the attention of a homicidal maniac?*

No, it's no wonder.

But she's chosen to live her life on her own terms. She's chosen her path.

So she owns it. All of it. Even this.

I wouldn't have it any other way, she realizes, and leaves her mother to nibble her cold poached egg and go home alone to a house made of cold gray stone.

Chapter Fourteen

Scrolling through the online edition of yet another newspaper, Vic hears the rumble of the mail truck down the street.

With the exception of his college application era and a couple of lean newlywed years when he and Kitty desperately needed their tax refund money, Vic never spent much time anticipating the arrival of the day's mail.

Things are different now—and not just because the mail recently held his first book contract, or because he expects a check for his on-signing advance any day.

The check would be nice.

Further communication from the Night Watchman would be . . . well, not nice.

But every day, he holds his breath and waits for the mail to come, hoping for anything that might put him on the killer's trail once again.

If the task force down in Quantico has made any progress, nobody's bothered to tell Vic. He wouldn't expect them to.

They're on their own with this thing now—just as he's on his own. The guys from the field office have checked in now and then, and they drive by every so often, too. For all he knows, the house is under constant surveillance, which bothers Kitty. But as he told her, better to be watched by the FBI than by an unsub thirsty for the kill after thirty-five years of dormancy.

Welcoming the distraction of the mail truck, Vic leaves the computer and goes to the front door to meet it. He remembers, this time, to punch in the numbers on the alarm keypad, but sometimes he doesn't.

Darned thing is a pain in the ass, but a necessary evil.

Opening the door at last, Vic inhales the dank, cold air—not quite as biting as it has been, though. Beyond the doorstep lies a drab backdrop of bare branches, sparse grass, and mud, but the crocus bulbs Kitty had him plant last fall are sending up tender, grassy sprouts over by the lamppost.

"Morning, Vic." The mailman climbs out of his truck with a wave.

"Morning, Smitty."

"Feels like spring, huh?"

"Almost." Vic accepts the bundle of mail—quite a few white envelopes today, he notices. Some days, there are mostly catalogues and junk mail.

Anxious to get inside and go through it, he bids Smitty a good day and hurriedly barricades himself into the house again.

Standing in the hall, he flips through the envelopes.

The third one in the stack captures his attention.

It's addressed to him, a plain white typewritten label again, no return address.

It was postmarked three days ago in Chicago.

Waiting beside the secretary's desk in the first floor Pastoral Care Office, Cam rehearses what she'll say to Janet O'Leary.

One thing is certain: the woman has most likely never heard of her, or of Ava. She'll have to start there.

Okay, so . . .

"Hi, my name is Cam, and I think that when you were a little girl, you got a look at the man who killed my sister."

And then Janet O'Leary, a cancer survivor herself who spends her days as a lay minister to patients here, will tell Cam to leave, and rightly so, because she has far more important things to worry about today.

So does Cam. When she called Mike a few minutes ago to tell him she'd arrived, she could hear Grace wailing in the background.

Her heart sank. "What's wrong with her, Mike?"

"She's just a little cranky. She'll be fine."

Cam checks her watch. There's an afternoon flight home. If she leaves here in the next ten minutes, she can probably get on it standby.

"Hi." A small woman enters the office, accompanied by the secretary who went off to locate her on her patient rounds. "You're here to see me?"

A look at her ID badge confirms that. Cam nods. "Hi, Ms. O'Leary. My name is Cam Hastings."

She nods, wearing an expectant expression. When the secretary asked for Cam's name, she asked, "Will Janet know who you are or what this is in regard to?"

"No," Cam said simply. "But it's very important."

Now, she tells Janet, "I know you're really busy, and I'm sorry to interrupt you, but I was wondering if I could ask you about something—in private."

She expects Janet to ask for more information, but she nods.

Then she crosses the small reception area, pokes her head into an adjoining office, looks around, and tells Cam, "Empty. We're in luck. Sometimes it isn't. We all share this office. Come on in."

They settle themselves beside a desk covered in papers, a computer, and a telephone.

Cam looks at Janet, who has a halo of soft brown hair and wide-set eyes the ice-blue shade of a winter sky—somewhere other than here, anyway.

"I'm here because my sister died," Cam blurts—not at all as she had rehearsed.

"Cancer?"

"No. . . ."

How had she intended to phrase it?

The right words have flown out of her head, and she has to be careful here to avoid the wrong ones. She needs Janet O'Leary to listen to her. To help her, if there's any way.

She may be the only one who can. Sandra Wubner's parents have both died, and she was an only child.

"It, um, it happened a long time ago. She'd be in her late fifties if she were still alive. She died when she was twenty, in college. . . . They said it was a suicide."

At the last word, something flickers in Janet's blue eyes, but she says nothing.

"All these years, my father and I believed Ava—that's my sister's name, Ava Neary"—no recognition there—"We believed she had killed herself. There were reasons to think she might have, I guess. My mother had abandoned us—just disappeared without a trace—not long before that."

"I'm so sorry," Janet murmurs, touching her hand.

Cam is unnerved by her kindness, her sympathy.

All those years, Cam and her father had dealt with their losses on their own. A woman like this, a woman who spends her days helping stricken people cope with emotional and spiritual pain, could have made it all so much—well, not easier. But perhaps more bearable.

"Not long ago," Cam goes on, "I was given some information that led me to wonder if my sister really did kill herself. . . ."

"Or?" Janet supplies when she can't bring herself to say it.

"Or . . . not."

Janet digests this. "You aren't saying she might still be alive."

"No."

"You're saying someone else might have taken her life?"

Cam exhales, almost in relief, and nods.

Janet O'Leary tilts her head. "Why are you here to see me, Mrs. Hastings?"

"Please—call me Cam. Your maiden name was Toscano, wasn't it? And you grew up on the West Side."

"How did you know that?"

"Newspaper archives," Cam tells her. "Wedding announcement, an interview you did about your work here, and—really long ago—an article about your babysitter."

Now the recognition dawns.

"She hung herself, Janet, and you found her. Do you remember?"

"Sandy. Yes, I remember." Janet O'Leary's lovely eyes have clouded over.

"And you said you saw her boyfriend with her that night."

"I remember that, too."

"The police investigated. Her boyfriend had an alibi."

Janet shakes her head. "I know that, but I got out of bed for a drink of water and when I looked in the living room someone was there, talking to her. At the time I just assumed it was her boyfriend. He'd come over sometimes."

"But now you think it might have been someone else?"

"I guess it could have been."

"How sure are you that someone was there?"

"At the time, I was a hundred percent sure. But later—well, I guess the police and my parents seemed to think I either dreamed it or imagined it, especially once her boyfriend gave them the alibi. They said I was traumatized and it was understandable. I guess I believed them after a while because . . . well, because it was less scary than thinking someone really was there."

"Looking back, though, now . . . you think someone really could have been?"

Janet nods.

"Did you get a good look at him?"

"No. I only saw his back, and he was wearing a jacket

with the hood up. It was snowing really hard that night. I remember seeing snow melting off his boots, too."

"Did he or Sandy know you were there?"

"No. I was supposed to be asleep. I only snuck a quick peek, then I went back to bed. I still couldn't fall asleep though and later when I got up again . . . That's when I found her."

"Hanged."

Janet shudders. "Yes. It was horrible."

"I can just imagine." Cam waits a moment before asking, "Do you think Sandy killed herself that night, Janet?"

Rather than answer, she says, "*You* don't, do you?"

"No. I don't. I think she was murdered by whoever was there. And I think he might have done the same thing to my sister."

Rounding the corner onto Lucinda's block, he's just in time to see a man exit the building.

Watching with interest, he slows his pace as the man walks over to a white van parked at the curb. Seeing the sign painted on the side of the van, he breaks into a slow grin.

LIBERTY HOME SECURITY SPECIALISTS.

Obviously, Lucinda received his little gift last night and his e-mail this morning.

Feeling paranoid, is she?

Then she should really enjoy the little surprise he's got in store for her next. His lips curve into a smile as he pulls it out of his pocket and looks around to see if anyone's watching.

Still holding his cell phone, Randy sticks his head into the office where Dan Lambert is typing furiously at a computer.

"I need to talk to you."

Lambert looks up, eyes going solemn behind his round-rimmed glasses when he sees Randy's expression. "What's up?"

Someone could be in earshot. Randy closes the door.

"A woman was murdered last night in Chicago. It looks like whoever killed Carla could be responsible."

Disbelief sweeps over Lambert's features. "What do you mean? What's going on?"

He quickly updates Lambert, telling him about the e-mail with the link to a newspaper story this morning about the murder of a twenty-two-year-old woman, and about the note that came with the floral delivery—bearing the Chicago coordinates.

"You say Lucinda got the flowers last night, at home?"

"Yes. Why?"

"So she was home in Philadelphia last night when this woman was killed in Chicago."

"I just told you she was."

"Okay."

Randy looks at his friend for a long moment. He doesn't like what he sees in his eyes.

"I have to go," he says abruptly.

"Go where?"

"Home," he lies, and reaches for the doorknob.

"Randy . . . wait."

"What?"

"We can place her at the crime scene here. Lucinda."

"Yeah, I know she was at the scene. She made the call."

"No, Randy. She was inside the house. Inside the bathroom. With . . . Carla."

His hand frozen on the knob, Randy asks, "Why do you think that?"

"I *know* it. I told you. There's evidence."

Randy turns to look at Dan, his thoughts racing. "Are you saying she's a suspect?"

"I'm saying she might become one."

"Tell me why. Tell me more."

"You know I can't."

Turning abruptly, Randy opens the door and walks out, closing it hard behind him.

* * *

Left alone in Lucinda's about-to-be-newly-fortified apartment, Neal dials Frank Santiago's number.

He needs to be told about the flower delivery. Maybe it'll take him off Lucinda's trail for five minutes—long enough to find some leads that might take the investigation in the right direction.

But Frank's phone rings into voice mail—again, fourth time this morning. Neal hangs up and wonders whether he should just drive out to Long Beach Island. Talk to him in person.

That, or tell Lucinda that she's about to be interviewed again for a crime she didn't commit, because her hair was found in the dead woman's hand.

How did it get there?

That's what they'll ask her.

As if Lucinda would know.

The killer put it there, of course. The killer left the bloody ring in her apartment, and before that, the scrapbook. He could easily have stolen strands of her hair from a brush.

Lucinda is being set up for this murder.

Why, Neal hasn't a clue. But the sooner he can get Frank to accept the possibility, the better.

He snaps his phone closed, and it rings almost immediately. Maybe Frank was screening his calls and is getting back to him right away.

Snapping it open, he looks at the number. Nope. Not Frank.

"Lucinda. I'm still at your—"

"Neal, hold on. Listen to me. There was another murder last night. A woman in Chicago."

He sucks in his breath. "How do you know?"

"Someone sent me a link to a newspaper article about it."

"Who?"

There's a pause. "I don't know. It came from an e-mail address I didn't recognize."

"Are you sure it's a real case?"

"Positive. And it was the same M.O. as Carla Barakat.

The victim lived alone, and she was killed in her apartment early last night. Stabbed to death."

"None of that means it's connected to Carla."

"No. But Neal, someone sent me the link, anonymously. What do you think it means?"

He lets it sink in for a minute. "Does Frank Santiago know about this?"

"I don't know. Randy said he isn't in the office and nobody seems to know where he is."

"You told Randy."

"Yes. He and I are catching a flight to O'Hare right now. I'm in a cab on my way to the airport."

"Are you kidding me? You can't—"

"Neal, this is what I do, remember? If I can go to the scene, I might be able to pick up on some information that will lead us in the right direction to get this guy before he does it again."

She's right. This is what she does. But . . .

"Lucinda, this is different. This time, you're directly involved. He's been taunting you. Don't you think it's possible that he might be baiting you?"

She hesitates. "It's possible. But I have to do this. You know that."

And you can't stop me.

The phrase is unspoken, but it comes through loud and clear.

Neal sighs. "Just be careful."

"I'm always careful."

How he wishes he could believe that were true.

He remembers something. "Oh, and Cin?"

"Yeah?"

"I know this isn't even on your radar right now, but I got a call a little while ago. They brought in dogs and searched Isaiah Drew's dorm room."

"And?"

"And found traces."

"Traces . . . Drugs?"

"Yes. You were right."

To her credit, she doesn't say *I told you so,* though under ordinary circumstances, that's definitely her style.

Neal hangs up, puts on his coat, and heads for the door.

He opens it just in time to see a gray-haired man bending over the mat, something in his hand.

"All right, Mr. Santiago, are you ready?"

Ready?

Ready to be rolled, once again, into that hulking metal coffin of sorts, so that they'll be able to tell just how long it will be before he'll be encased in a real one?

"Yes," he says, only after giving the Magnetic Resonance Imaging technician a look, one that tells her he finds her breezy demeanor insufferable.

A middle-aged grandmother type, her doughy figure encased in scrubs, she ignores the look. "All righty then, I'm going to have you lie down here, and we'll get started. Careful of your IV line, now. There we go, that's it."

He settles himself on the narrow, flexible surface and swallows audibly as he stares at the ceiling. He does his best not to let anxiety take over. Does his best to keep breathing slowly, in, out, in, out, despite the chronic wheezing tightness in his chest.

Doctor Rubin, his oncologist, offered him a sedative, as always, to calm the unpleasant panic sensations most people—even those who are not particularly claustrophobic—experience inside the MRI machine.

Frank turned down the offer, as always.

He turned it down even though he's been fiercely claustrophobic since childhood, when a neighbor girl locked him in the basement while she was babysitting so that she could make out with her boyfriend.

He's going to work as soon as he gets out of here, and he

can't afford to be any more clouded than he already has been on the job.

Particularly since no one at work—or, really, outside of his oncologist's medical circles—is aware that cancer is spreading lesions like lethal black confetti through Frank Santiago's organs.

"How long do I have?" he asked Dr. Rubin back on January 2, when he got the news that the new year would most likely be his last.

Not that Dr. Rubin would commit to that.

"There's no way of knowing at this stage, Frank. If you're asking whether you should get your affairs in order, the answer is yes."

Frank's affairs are always in order. The phrasing, however, sent a stab of panic to his gut.

"If you're asking whether we will continue treatment, the answer is yes again. When we halt treatment, we'll discuss your options at length."

When, not *if*.

Options—as if he has any, other than whether to die at home or in some sterile hospital bed.

Even there, he figures he has no options. Who's going to take care of him at home?

Not his two grown kids, who have families of their own and live in Texas and Florida.

Not Ellen, though she still lives less than a mile away. He's pretty sure her possessive second husband wouldn't appreciate her playing Clara Barton to her dying first.

Friends and neighbors have come and gone over the years—some closer than others, almost like family when they were there. But when they're gone, they're gone. Frank's not one to live in the past or keep in touch much.

When the time comes, then, he supposes, he'll just take a cab—or will it be an ambulance?—to the hospital and check in and wait to die.

Now there's something to look forward to.

First, of course, he'll have to tell his kids. And the people at work.

Something else to look forward to.

Dammit to hell. How can this be happening to him?

He's already made up his mind to keep things status quo for as long as possible. Keep living in his own house, keep going about his usual business, keep working. Even if the condition they call chemo brain is impairing his better judgement.

"Can you hear me, Mr. Santiago?"

The damned technician again, this time filling his entire head with her false cheerfulness, her voice coming in over the earphones she placed on him.

"Loud and clear."

"Ready?"

Ready to be sealed into a space so confining that you literally can barely lift a finger, and your own hot, moist breath boomerangs back at your face?

Ready to be assailed by noise, not just her voice but the lame music they pipe in and the harsh metallic chugging and whirring of the machine as it surveys the cancer-pocked landscape of your organs?

Ready to find out whether you get to die in the near, as opposed to nearer, future?

"Ready," Frank Santiago says grimly, and the process begins.

"Who are you?"

They say it in unison, both Neal and the gray-haired stranger at Lucinda's door.

Instinctively, Neal's hand brushes against his gun, concealed beneath his coat.

"I'm Bradley Carmichael—I'm a friend of Lucinda's."

Neal relaxes just a bit. So this is the famous Bradley. He's a handsome man, probably about Neal's age, with a muscular build and perfect white teeth.

"Who are you?"

"I'm a friend of Lucinda's, too. What is that you're hold-ing?" Neal eyes the brown paper-wrapped package in his hand.

"I don't know. I found it propped against the door just now. Is she here?"

"No, she's not."

Bradley frowns. "Are you sure? Because she's expecting me."

Neal raises an eyebrow at that. Lucinda didn't mention anything about expecting company. But then, she was aw-fully agitated about the flowers earlier, and about Chicago just now when he talked to her.

Maybe she forgot.

Or maybe this guy is up to something.

Either way, Neal isn't taking any chances.

When Bradley says, "I'll just come in and wait for her," Neal steps into his path.

"Why don't I call Lucinda," he suggests, keeping one hand over his weapon as the other reaches for his cell phone, "and check with her?"

Bradley shrugs. "Good idea. Tell her that I just took the train down from New York to see her so she'd better get her butt home."

Neal dials Lucinda's phone and is relieved when she picks up on the first ring. "Cin. I'm still at your place."

"Yeah?"

"Your friend Bradley is here."

She gasps. "Bradley! Oh, no, I forgot!"

"So you were expecting him?" Neal relaxes another notch.

"Yes. It totally slipped my mind. Tell him I'm really sorry, and I'll have to catch him next time."

"She says she's sorry, and she'll catch you next time," Neal tells Bradley, who frowns.

"Where is she? Where are you, Lucinda? Here, can I talk to her?"

Neal reluctantly hands over the phone, hoping Lucinda

knows better than to give anything away. She might trust Bradley, but right now, Neal doesn't trust anyone.

"No, it's okay. I understand. Yes. But I can just wait here at your apartment for you to come back," Bradley offers into the phone. "What? . . . No, your friend let me in, but I have your keys. . . . Oh. I didn't know you changed them. Okay, well, then I guess I don't have your keys anymore. Still, I can stick around. . . . No? . . . All right. All right, fine. . . . Whatever. Whenever. Okay. Good-bye."

"Wait. Don't hang up." Neal reaches for the phone.

"Too late. Sorry." Bradley thrusts it at him.

"I'll take that package," Neal tells him, and Bradley hands it over as well.

"Good-bye," Neal calls after him as he heads down the stairs.

He hears a grumbled response from below before the door to the street opens and slams shut.

"Temperamental actors." Neal shakes his head.

Then he looks down at the package in his hand.

Lucinda's name is scrawled on the plain brown wrapping— in what looks like red lipstick.

When Randy spots her sitting at the airport gate, she looks . . . like someone else.

This, he realizes, is Main Line Lucinda Sloan. How easy it is to forget where she came from when she's wearing jeans and drinking Pepsi from a can, waves of unfettered hair streaming over her shoulders and down her back.

Today, it's tamed in a sedate chignon. Even from here, he can see that she's got makeup on. And she's wrapped in what looks like a woolen blanket—a dress coat, he realizes, as he draws closer.

He slows his pace, watching her, wondering why—no matter how she looks or where he sees her—she always makes him feel this way.

What way? How does she make you feel?

Randy's been asking himself a lot of questions lately—and they always seem to involve Lucinda.

He never has any answers.

But, looking at her across the bustling concourse, he's certain of one thing.

She had nothing to do with Carla's death.

He doesn't give a damn what the evidence says, or what people think.

He'd bet his life on Lucinda Sloan's innocence.

Chapter Fifteen

"Ladies and gentlemen, please remain seated with your seatbelts fastened while we're taxiing toward the gate. If you have a cell phone where you can easily get to it, you're free now to make a call."

Lucinda immediately reaches into her pocket. She finds her BlackBerry, along with a packet of chocolate-covered peanut butter eggs she stashed there this morning.

Nibbling one, she checks her phone and finds an urgent text message from Neal.

CALL ME AS SOON AS POSSIBLE.

She licks the chocolate from her thumb and dials, glancing over the seat back to find Randy. They couldn't get seats together; he's sitting several rows behind her.

Seeing her, he shoots her a questioning look. She holds up her phone, mouthing, "Neal."

He answers on the first ring. "Lucinda, where are you?"

"On the ground in Chicago. We just landed." She speaks in a low voice, conscious that the male passenger next to her has folded his newspaper and put it away. "What's up?"

"There was a package on your doorstep earlier. Not from

a delivery service or anything—just a box wrapped in brown paper with your name on it."

He pauses.

"Your friend Bradley picked it up."

"And . . . ?"

"And we've brought him in for questioning."

Her heart skips a beat. "Why? You don't think—"

"All I know is that he was there, and he handled the package—it's in the Crime Lab now—and we need to rule out that he's the one who put it there."

"It's in the Crime Lab? Why?"

"Your name was written in red lipstick on the box, Cin."

"What was in it?"

"Just a blue tissue stained with a red lipstick kiss."

As promised, Jason Czarniak meets Cam at the door of the machine shop in an industrial stretch of a suburban town called Lackawanna.

The double-chinned man with the graying blond mustache, thick aviator glasses, and Buffalo Sabres cap looks nothing like the good-looking athlete in his yearbook photo taken almost forty years ago.

But the name stitched on an oval patch on his blue mechanic's uniform reads Jason, and when she called him earlier, after tracking him down with Janet O'Leary's help, he told her that he had, indeed, been Sandra Wubner's high school sweetheart.

If he thought it was an odd question, he didn't let on over the phone. He agreed to talk to her and asked that she meet him here at the machine shop when his shift ended.

She's dangerously close to missing her flight home, but she's trying not to think about that right now.

A phone call to Mike on her way over here confirmed that poor little Grace is still miserable.

"She probably wants to nurse," Cam told him, plagued

with guilt. "Are you holding her close to your chest the way I do when you feed her?"

"Yeah, I am. But my chest is missing a key component," he said dryly.

"I'm serious, Mike! I'm worried about her."

"Don't be. She'll get through the day on a bottle. Just do what you have to do in Buffalo."

What she has to do in Buffalo is ask Jason Czarniak about his long-dead girlfriend. Hardly a pleasant task.

"We can talk in here." He leads the way to a break or waiting room that consists of a couple of chairs with plastic seats and two vending machines, one of which bears a handwritten OUT OF ORDER sign. The scent of stale cigarette smoke and motor oil permeates the air.

Cam finds this place is more depressing, somehow, than the cancer hospital was. At Roswell, she felt a sense of real hope amidst the despair—of human beings caring for each other.

Janet O'Leary was a big part of that perception. She told Cam a little about her work, saying, "My job is to accept patients for whoever they are, and to help them to use their faith to accept the losses that come with living with, or dying from, their diagnosis."

Cam couldn't help but think of her father, and the losses he never learned to accept.

If she does learn the truth about Ava's death, it won't change anything for Ike. It's too late now. He's not all there most of the time, and when he is . . . What comfort will there be in learning that his firstborn was murdered?

From Roswell, Cam very nearly drove straight to the airport and headed home, thinking maybe she should just forget about it.

But she couldn't bring herself to do that.

Because while the truth can't help her father now, maybe it can bring her—if not comfort—then closure.

"Have a seat. Want a can of pop?" Jason asks her, gesturing at the vending machine that works. On his grease-stained left hand is a gold wedding band.

"No, thank you." Cam imagines him getting over Sandra all those years ago, moving on, marrying someone else. She wonders if he's ever still haunted by what happened.

Probably.

You don't just get over something like that.

"I'm going to get one. Hang on a second." He feeds in a dollar bill, and then another. The second one spits out of the slot again with a whirring sound.

Jason attempts to get it in several more times, cursing under his breath when the machine won't take it and fishing in his pockets for another single.

"Here you go." Cam hands him one from her purse—which, she can't help but think, retails for more than he must make here in a week.

"Oh . . . thanks." He offers her the crumpled dollar the machine wouldn't take.

She shakes her head. "It's okay."

"No, take it. Unless you're planning to use it in some stupid machine," he adds with a grin.

She smiles back and accepts the dollar, deciding she likes him. Watching him take the Pepsi from the machine, she wonders how he dealt with his loss all those years ago. According to Janet, he and Sandy had gone steady all the way through high school and into her freshman year at Buff State. Jason, she said, went to work right out of high school.

"So you knew Sandy?" he asks, after taking a swig of Pepsi and settling in the chair opposite hers.

"No, I actually didn't."

"Oh. I thought that's why you were here." He looks confused.

"I'm here because I'm looking into her death."

Jason raises a dubious blond eyebrow. "Are you a cop?"

"No."

"Reporter?"

"No! I'm just someone who . . . who also lost someone very dear to me, right around the same time. My sister. They said it was a suicide, too, but . . . I'm not so sure."

"Yeah? Because I wasn't so sure, either. Back then. With Sandy."

Her heart pounds. "You weren't? Why not?"

"No one knew this," he leans forward conspiratorially, "but we were gonna get married."

"Really?"

"Yep. Sandy was real excited about it. After she got through college—she was gonna be a teacher—we were planning to settle down and get a house and have a bunch of kids. That was the plan. When she died, I was saving up to buy her a pre."

"A pre?"

"Pre-engagement ring."

Lost in his bittersweet memories, Jason falls silent.

"You said you didn't think, at the time, that Sandy killed herself, Jason."

"Nope."

"Then you thought someone else killed her?"

"I didn't know what to think. When that little kid she was watching that night said she saw me there, I got scared, you know? Because I wasn't there, and I thought they thought I was. They checked out my alibi—thank God I had one; I was at a Sabres game that night with my dad and a couple of his friends. So then they figured the little kid must have been wrong about someone's being there."

"Did you think she was wrong?"

"I don't know."

"So you thought someone else might have been there with Sandra? Some other guy? Or . . . man?"

"You mean, did I think she was cheating on me?" He looks defensive. "Nope. No way. Not her. We were in love. We were going to get married."

Maybe it really would have happened, Cam thinks—maybe

he'd have married the beautiful college girl who wanted to become a teacher.

Or maybe they would have become more entrenched in their separate worlds over time, grown apart, broken up.

Maybe, when Sandra Wubner died, she was already moving on.

Maybe there really was someone else.

Maybe she, like Ava, had gotten involved at college with something that she shouldn't have.

"If she wasn't cheating on you, but you're not sure she took her own life, who did you think was with her at the Toscanos' house that night?" she asks Jason. "Who did you think killed her?"

"I don't know. A stranger, maybe? Stuff like that happens. Look, to be honest with you, it didn't matter to me back then, because she was gone. And the last thing I wanted the cops to do was start in on me again."

"Why worry, if you were innocent?"

He shrugs. "Innocent people get arrested all the time."

Yes, Cam thinks. *And sometimes, guilty ones go free.*

Lucinda and Randy step out of a cab on a side street off West Division and look around at the dusk-cloaked buildings.

"Over there. That must be it."

Lucinda follows Randy's gaze to a narrow three-story brick facade, fronted by several squad cars, a news van, and a telltale strip of yellow crime scene tape.

Looking up at the building's brightly lit second story windows, Lucinda experiences a sudden flash of violence.

Just a snatch of a scream, a fleeting glimpse of spattering blood, a howl of . . . laughter?

Laughter.

Yes, and the jarring sound makes her skin crawl.

"What's wrong?"

Lucinda blinks and looks up to see Randy watching her.

"Nothing, just . . . that's the place. Definitely." With a shudder, she shakes her head to banish the echoing laughter.

"Did you see something?"

"Not really. Just . . . blood. But I heard something."

"What?"

"Someone laughing." She shudders.

Randy looks concerned. "Do you want to . . . I don't know, wait here while I go speak to them?" He points to a heavyset man in a trench coat smoking a cigarette on the sidewalk in front of the building, talking to a uniformed officer who appears to be barely out of his teens.

"No, I'm fine. You know I'm used to this kind of thing. Let's go."

They make their way over to the two men, who by now have noticed them and are watching warily.

Randy opens his wallet and flashes a badge. "I'm Detective Randall Barakat from Long Beach Township in New Jersey. This is Lucinda Sloan. She works with the Philadelphia police department."

She doesn't have a badge, but she does have ID, which she holds up for their perusal. Neither man bothers.

The one in the trench coat stubs out his cigarette beneath a scuffed black shoe. "What can we do for you today?"

"This is where Jaime Dobiak was stabbed to death last night, right?"

Surprise—and perhaps suspicion—filters into his eyes. "And you know that because . . . ?"

"We read it in the newspaper."

His eyes narrow. "Which newspaper?"

Randy looks questioningly at Lucinda.

"It was the *Chicago Daily Times*," she tells the detective, wondering why it matters.

"That's impossible."

"Why?"

"For one thing, that's a morning paper. There was no information about this homicide available when it went to press." He jerks a thumb at the lone news van parked across the street. "The next of kin was notified an hour ago, and the media is just starting to pick up on the story now."

"It . . . it was the online version," Lucinda says slowly, reaching into her pocket for her BlackBerry.

"What time did you say you read this?"

"I don't know. . . . About a quarter after eleven, maybe?"

The detective is shaking his head before she's even done speaking. "Nope. That's impossible. The victim wasn't even found until almost noon."

"Neal. Frank Santiago," a brusque voice greets him on the phone. "I got your message."

Messages, actually. Neal has left a couple more since he saw what was in the package on Lucinda's doorstep, and since hearing the latest news from her and Randy in Chicago.

Neal gestures to Roz that he's going to step outside to take the call.

"Mmm hmm." Roz barely looks up from the object on the table, under bright lights as the forensics team does their thing.

In the corridor, Neal asks Frank, "Where are you now?"

"I just got into my office. Why?"

"We need to talk."

"About . . . ?"

"About the Barakat case. There's been further communication from Carla's killer. And last night, there was another murder."

There's a pause.

"What are you talking about?"

Neal tells him about the woman in Chicago. Hearing the clicking of a keyboard on the other end of the line, he knows Frank is looking for information.

"You won't find anything about it yet. It just happened."

He doesn't bother to explain how it is that they've known about it for hours already. "We confirmed it with the CPD, Frank."

"You said there was communication. What kind?"

"Lucinda got an e-mail this morning—"

On the other end of the line, Frank exhales loudly—not a sigh, exactly, but close.

"She was with me last night, Frank. In case you were wondering."

"Of course she was."

"Are you saying you doubt me? Do you think I'm covering for her?"

"Did I say that? Where is she now?"

Neal ignores the question. "A package was left at her door today."

"What was in it?"

"A blue tissue stained with a red lipstick kiss . . . and microscopic droplets of blood. Forensics is on it now. Looks like it might have come from the Chicago victim's mouth."

"Vic?"

Startled, he spins around in his chair. Kitty is home from work. He didn't even hear her come in.

As she crosses the room, lit only by the glowing computer screen in front of him, he sees that night has fallen without his even having realized it.

"Why are you sitting here in the dark?" Kitty flicks on a lamp, and he blinks. "Working on the book?"

"Working on catching this guy and hoping that makes it into the book," he says resolutely, as Kitty sits on the love seat and unzips the high heeled leather boots she's wearing. "I heard from him again today."

She looks up, startled. "What?"

He clicks the mouse a couple of times, bringing up on the screen a copy of the latest note, written in red lipstick. He'd scanned it and the envelope into the computer earlier, before dutifully handing them over to the field office agents.

Kitty pulls off her boots and crosses the room in her stocking feet to stand behind him.

"Where were you last night? I thought you might try to rescue her," she reads aloud. "RIP, Jaime. March 20. 7:05 P.M."

Vic silently clicks the screen again, bringing up the *Chicago Daily Times* homepage and pointing to the breaking news item he finally found there a little while ago, after repeatedly checking this and other Chicago news sites all afternoon.

Kitty reads the lead paragraph, about a young woman named Jaime Dobiak who was murdered sometime early last evening in her apartment. "Oh, no, Vic."

"Sick bastard. He mailed this letter three days ago."

"Knowing exactly when he was going to kill her? Right down to the minute?"

"Yes. And that it would be too late by the time I got it. He's taunting me, Kitty."

Clearly shaken, she sinks into a chair. "I don't like this."

"I don't either. But if this is how he's going to play it . . ."

Then game on, he thinks grimly.

It doesn't take long, once Chicago's Bureau of Investigative Services gets hold of the e-mailed link Lucinda received this morning, for them to determine what both Lucinda and Randy instantly realized earlier.

It wasn't a true link to the *Chicago Daily Times*; rather, it led to a convincing dummy Web site featuring not just actual stories from the morning paper, but also a genuine-looking article about a murder that had yet to be discovered.

Noon central time, when the victim was found, would have been one o'clock eastern time.

By then, Lucinda and Randy were already on their way to the airport.

The Bureau's computer technicians are already trying to

trace the origins of the fake Web site as well as the e-mail address, but warned that whoever created them most likely covered his tracks well.

Sitting in a glass-walled room opposite Detective Bob Reingold—now minus the trench coat—Lucinda and Randy have walked him through the events that led them here, beginning with the scrapbook on Lucinda's bed, back in February.

Lucinda expects him to bat a skeptical eye when she admits that she isn't exactly an ordinary detective, but he seems to take it in stride, leading her to believe that he might have consulted police psychics himself. She wouldn't dare ask him, though, knowing it isn't something many law enforcement officials are willing to discuss.

For the most part, the man just listens and nods, taking notes and occasionally asking clarifying questions. Of particular interest to him are the longitude and latitude coordinates left at the scene, the wrist watch, and the red lipstick used on anonymous communication received by both Lucinda and Camden Hastings.

Lucinda suspects similar details might tie Jaime Dobiak's murder to Carla's. Of course, Reingold doesn't offer the information, and both she and Randy know better than to ask about it.

As their tale winds down, a phone rings on the desk.

"Yeah?" Reingold barks into it. Then, after a moment, "This is him."

Another pause, then, "Who?"

Reingold listens. Nods. "Yeah. Hang on a second." He covers the mouthpiece and looks at Lucinda and Randy. "Would you mind stepping outside while I take this call?"

"Not at all."

Welcoming the chance to stand and stretch, Lucinda follows Randy into the corridor.

In the instant before the door closes behind them, she hears Reingold say, "What can I do for you, Detective Santiago?"

* * *

Frank hangs up the phone and looks at Dan Lambert, seated across the desk from him.

Dan nods. "You did what you had to do."

"I know that."

"Don't blame yourself for being misled by that DNA evidence. It's what he wanted. He was trying to throw us off his trail."

"I know that," Frank says again, pissed at Dan for belaboring the point, pissed at himself for . . .

Well, for just about everything, from going down the wrong path from the very beginning of the investigation to being unable—after all the triumphant battles he's fought in his life—to overcome the toxic cells that are making a certain death march through his body.

If the news today that it's time to stop treatment brought him to his knees, then the news that another murder has been committed, ostensibly letting Lucinda Sloan off the hook, sent him sprawling.

He let a serial killer slip through his fingers.

If he hadn't been so eager to bring down the psychic who had worked her way under his skin—and into his thoughts—then he might have caught the guy before he killed again.

A young woman lies dead tonight because of it.

Because of *him*.

It's time for Frank to go.

Time for him to face what lies ahead.

When they asked him to wait around to speak with the doctor after his test, rather than sending him on his way as usual, he knew the news wouldn't be good.

He was right.

And when they told him, Frank Santiago—who hasn't shed a tear since the day his father was killed, on duty, over half a century ago—finally broke down and cried.

* * *

"Neal? Is that you?"

"Yes." He closes the front door behind him and notices a familiar blue parka draped on the coat tree.

Garland Fisher is here. Again.

Hanging his overcoat on the newel post at the foot of the stairs, Neal isn't in the mood to be neighborly. All he wants is to eat the dinner Erma will have kept hot for him, followed by a big piece of coffee cake, then to drop into bed.

Guess that won't be happening tonight.

He scrubs his hands in the half bath under the stairs, then trudges to the kitchen to find Garland drinking tea as Erma reaches into the oven with a mitt. In the center of the table, the baking dish that contained the rest of last night's sour cream coffee cake is now empty except for a few crumbs.

"Neal! Long time no see!" Garland, in plaid flannel, is jovial.

When isn't he? Neal wonders grouchily, and notes that Garland is sitting in Neal's own place at the table. Why didn't Erma tell him to sit in one of the other chairs?

Is it too much for a man to ask, to come home to find his own seat vacant, to eat a meal in solitude, to have his wife to himself?

"Just got back from visiting my grandkids," Garland tells him, "and wanted to stop by and drop off a little something I picked up to say thanks for grabbing my mail and keeping an eye on the house while I was gone. Did you see this?" He holds up the copy of *Meanderings* magazine.

"I sure did. Very nice. Congratulations."

"Garland brought us some fudge, Neal. Your favorite. Isn't that nice?" Erma asks, setting a plate in front of him.

"Very nice. Thank you, Garland."

"Welcome. Rough day?"

"They're all rough."

"Was there another murder?"

"There's always another murder."

"Yeah, but you'll solve it, right?"

Resisting the urge to respond to Garland's question with a sarcastic, "Sure, no problem," Neal picks up his knife.

He cuts into a breaded pork chop and wishes Lucinda would call from Chicago, even though she checked in with him about an hour ago to see what had happened when they'd questioned her friend Bradley.

Neal told her they were going to check out his alibi—that he'd been at home in New York the night before—but had no grounds to hold him.

"Poor Bradley, walking into the middle of this. I need to call him and make sure he's okay," Lucinda said.

"I'm sure he's fine." Other than being outraged at having been questioned in the first place, and wanting to know what, exactly, Neal suspected he had done, other than pick up a package he'd found on his friend's doorstep.

Neal had given him very few details.

His gut tells him the guy is innocent, but he's taking no chances where Lucinda is concerned.

"I'm going to stay here at least until tomorrow," she told him before they hung up, "and see what I can find out."

"What about Randy?"

"He's staying too."

Of course. He wouldn't leave her now. There's no question that she's a target—or that the killer was trying to set her up.

As far as he knows, she doesn't even realize she was perilously close to becoming a suspect. It's not up to Neal to discuss the DNA evidence with her—not until he has more information.

Meanwhile, chances are that Lucinda is safer in Chicago than she would be here. Though the crime lab is still running tests on its contents, the package left at her doorstep today suggests that whoever killed Jaime Dobiak is back in Philadelphia.

"Guess I should get going home now," Garland Fisher says, stretching. "It's been a long day. Thanks for the coffee and cake, Erma. Neal, she's an amazing baker."

"I know she is."

"My wife used to make the best apple pie you ever tasted. I used to tell her she could sell it and make us rich, but she said she didn't want to make it for anyone but me." He looks lost in thought for a moment, then tells them, "Been a year next week."

It takes a moment for Neal to figure out what he's talking about.

"Can't believe she's not here to see this." He holds up the literary magazine. "She would have been proud."

"I'm so sorry," Erma says softly.

"Yeah. They say it gets easier. I keep wondering when."

Neal instantly regrets begrudging Garland the last of his favorite coffee cake.

"One day at a time. That's what I tell myself. Just get through one day at a time."

"That's all you can do, Garland," Neal tells him. "Listen, don't be a stranger. Okay? You're welcome anytime."

"Thanks, Neal."

He can feel Erma's approving smile as he goes back to cutting his pork chop and worrying about Lucinda.

Cam can hear the baby crying the moment she steps into the house from the attached garage, and her heart sinks.

She leaves her loafers in the mud room, then drops her shoulder bag and coat in the kitchen, lit only by the light beneath the stove hood. There are dishes in the sink, and on the counter she sees several half-empty baby bottles, a white takeout pizza box with a grease-stained cover, and a couple of paper plates littered with nibbled crusts.

She bypasses the mess and walks through the darkened first floor. In the foyer, light spills down the staircase from the upstairs hall. She looks up to see Mike standing there barefoot in sweats, looking exhausted, with Grace on his shoulder.

"Hey," he says, over her wailing. "You're home."

"I didn't want to call when we landed because I thought it might wake up the baby. Guess it didn't matter." She takes the stairs two at a time and holds out her arms. "Come here, sweet girl. Mama's home. Yes, she is."

"Thank God for that." Mike hugs her, then rubs his tired eyes. "How'd it go?"

"I think I have something to go on." Engorged and already unbuttoning her blouse, she carries the still sobbing baby into the bedroom to feed her, with Mike on her heels.

"What do you mean you have something to go on?"

"I spoke to a couple of people who knew Sandra Wubner and said that A, they don't believe she killed herself and B, there was probably someone with her that night. Some guy, and it wasn't her boyfriend."

She sits on the rumpled king-sized bed, leans back against the pillows, and guides the baby to her breast. Grace immediately stops crying.

Cam and Mike sigh in simultaneous relief.

"Are you going to call the police, then?" Mike asks Cam, after a minute.

"About Sandra Wubner?" She shrugs. "I'm going to call Lucinda first."

Mike sits beside her and pushes her hair back from her face. "Call Lucinda, and call the police, but that's it."

"What do you mean, 'that's it'?"

"I don't want you getting involved."

"But I've got to try to get in touch with Elizabeth Johnson's family. There are—"

"There are a million gazillion Johnsons in the world, and you haven't been able to find them. Let the police do it, Cam."

"But they won't—"

"This could be dangerous, and you can't go taking any risks. We need you here." He kisses the top of her head.

"You just don't want to be stuck here with a screaming baby again."

"You got that right." He leans back and closes his eyes with a weary smile.

She sighs. "Where's Tess?"

"In her room."

"How'd she do on her test today?"

"She had a test today?"

Cam sighs inwardly. Mike does his best to hold down the fort, she knows. He's just not as tuned into the details. Again, Cam feels a flicker of guilt for having left her family today to go chasing down clues in a decades-old death.

But you found some, didn't you? That's important. You did what had to be done.

"All I know is that Tess said she has a lot of homework tonight," Mike tells her. "She only came out to eat, and then she went right back to it."

"Good. That's responsible of her. She's growing up, isn't she?"

"She is. Thank God we get to do it all again."

Cam looks at her husband, thinking he's being sarcastic, then sees that he's gazing down at their baby girl with affection.

"I think I'll wait and call Lucinda in the morning," she decides, yawning deeply. "She's probably sleeping at this hour anyway."

She finishes nursing and carries her drowsy, sated baby down the hall to her room.

After settling Grace in for the night, she sees that the light is still on beneath Tess's door.

She knocks. "Tess? It's Mom. I'm home. Can I come in?"

There's a sound from the other side of the door—not a yes, not a no, maybe not even an actual word.

Opening the door, she sees her daughter sitting on her bed, still fully clothed, her face tear-stained.

"Tess! What's wrong?"

"We broke up."

"Oh, sweetie . . ." Cam goes to her, puts her arms around her.

"I don't know what happened. I thought he loved me."

"I know."

"It hurts so bad."

"I know." Cam strokes her daughter's thick brown hair, grown out for her boyfriend's sake.

Cam knows better than anyone that in the grand scheme of things, a breakup isn't the worst thing that could happen to a fifteen-year-old girl.

But for Tess, right here, right now, tonight, it's the end of the world. And all Cam can do is hold her tight.

"Are you ready?" Detective Reingold asks Lucinda as they step out of the squad car in front of the brick apartment building where Jaime Dobiak died.

Lucinda looks up at it, remembering what she saw—what she *heard*—when they were here earlier.

The eerie laughter was unsettling enough then, at dusk.

Now it's the middle of the night, with mist rolling in off the lake several blocks away, and the streets are shiny from a cold rain that fell earlier.

Like London in some movie about Jack the Ripper, Lucinda finds herself thinking uneasily.

A uniformed officer still guards the building's entrance. Across the street, a small crowd of curious bystanders has gathered along with reporters, a camera crew, and several news vans.

Flashbulbs flash as Lucinda, Randy, and the detective walk from the car to the steps of the building.

"Detective, who are they?" a female reporter calls.

"Wouldn't she love to know," Randy mutters under his breath to Lucinda, flashing her a grin.

Glad no one seems to have recognized her huddled in a scarf and coat, she can just imagine how the press would react if they knew that the Soothsayer Superhero—the Sexy part definitely being negligible in this getup—is here to try to pick up the killer's trail.

It was, surprisingly, Frank Santiago's suggestion that she visit the crime scene. Reingold agreed only after thoroughly checking out her credentials with Philadelphia and Long Beach Township.

Before heading over here, he waited while Lucinda and Randy checked in for the night at a nearby hotel. They had no luggage; the desk clerk raised her eyebrow when they asked for two rooms.

Clearly, she'd thought they were stealing away for a late night tryst.

It isn't appropriate, in the midst of all this, for Lucinda to devote even a moment's wistful thought to Randy and what might have been. She's only human, though, and her emotions are raw. She couldn't help but wonder, fleetingly, what it would be like if the clerk were right.

Then, of course, grim reality came crashing back in, and they were off to the murder scene.

"I'll need you to stay out here while I take her up," Reingold tells Randy. "Sorry."

"It's okay." Randy touches Lucinda's arm. "You good to go on your own?"

She nods.

"Okay. I'll wait right here for you."

Reingold holds the door open, and Lucinda steps inside. Several closed doors line the first floor vestibule.

She heads for the vintage staircase and begins climbing, the wooden treads creaking loudly.

"Lucinda?" Reingold asks, behind her.

Halfway up, she pauses and turns to look down at him. "Yes?"

"I didn't tell you Dobiak's apartment was on an upper floor, did I?"

"No."

He nods. "Just checking."

There are two flights, but she stops after the first, looking down the second floor hall at more closed doors.

There's no mistaking which apartment is Jaime Dobiak's: a strip of yellow crime scene tape straddles a door halfway down the hall.

Reingold removes it, and they cross the threshold.

Lucinda hears a burst of static in her head—like a radio not tuned into a clear frequency. Startled, she goes still, listening for something more.

"What's going on?" Reingold asks after a minute.

She shakes her head. "I'm not sure. I heard . . . something."

"What was it?"

"I'm not sure. It's gone."

She looks around the room. Mismatched furniture, framed posters on the walls, a smell of stale cigarette smoke mingling with the telltale scent of bleach.

"Can I touch her things?" she asks Reingold.

"Go ahead. But wear these." He passes her a pair of rubber gloves. "They've already taken pictures and dusted for prints, but just in case . . ."

She nods and pulls on the gloves, then looks around, settling on a black wool coat tossed over the back of a chair. She picks it up.

It smells of perfume and cigarette smoke.

Reingold stands by in silence as she hugs the coat against her and closes her eyes.

"He came in through the door," she says quietly after a minute. "He had her key."

"How did he get it?"

Lucinda shrugs. "It wasn't hard. He was waiting for her when she came home from work."

She walks through a doorway, into the bedroom.

"He was waiting here. This is where she died. On the floor. He stabbed her."

"Yes."

At Reingold's affirmation, she looks directly at him. "Was she wearing a watch? Engraved on the back with the date she died and the longitude and latitude?"

"Is that what you're seeing?"

"No. It's what I'm guessing, because that's how Carla was found. It was a Freestyle watch. The battery had run out, and the hands were stopped."

"Same brand. But there *was* no battery," Reingold tells her. "Not here, anyway."

Closing her eyes, Lucinda sees a gloved hand removing a watch battery with a pair of tweezers.

"You're right. It was deliberately stopped."

"Looks that way."

"At what time?" she asks.

"About five after seven. Why?"

"Is that what time she died?"

"Around then."

"Same thing with Carla Barakat."

"So you're sure it's the same guy."

"I'm positive."

She looks at the clock radio on the bedside table. Walking over to it, she notices that the volume dial is turned off all the way. She turns it clockwise, and immediately, the room is filled with radio static.

Frowning, she looks up at Reingold. "This is what I heard. Was the volume on when they first found her?"

"Not that I know of. I'll check."

Lucinda leans over to look at the dial. The radio is tuned to FM 104.5.

"What do you think it means?"

"It could mean nothing at all. She's got an iPod on the table here, see? And the clock radio has a docking station. I'm guessing she must listen to the iPod, not the radio."

"Then why isn't the iPod plugged into it?"

Lucinda shrugs. "I think we need to look at this more

closely. Check out places that have 104.5 as a longitudinal coordinate."

"There have to be hundreds. Thousands. Doesn't it seem far-fetched that he'd leave us just the longitude without the latitude?"

"Maybe. But we can't overlook anything. The radio setting might mean something. We need to check out places that broadcast radio stations on 104.5, too, and look at them as potential locations for his next murder."

Lucinda examines the other items on the table: a box of blue tissues and a stack of magazines with subscriber labels attached: *Cosmopolitan, Glamour, Vogue.* On the bottom of the pile is a trade publication, *Journal of Social History,* dated Summer 2006. There is no subscription label.

Puzzled, Lucinda picks it up, thumbs through it. There are articles about AIDS, war, illegitimacy. At a glance, none of it is meaningful.

"Did Jaime have an interest in social history, do you know?"

"I'm not sure."

Lucinda replaces the journal and looks thoughtfully at it. "It doesn't go. I feel like he put it there."

"Why?"

She shrugs.

"It would really help if you could give me some idea of what he looks like," Reingold tells her.

"I'm trying." She stands in silence for a few minutes. Then she walks over to stand in a spot beside the bed, looking down at the floor where it happened. Sinking to her knees, she presses her palms against the hardwood, now scrubbed free of blood.

A burst of ugly laughter fills her head.

"I can't see him. But I can hear him."

"What is he saying?"

"He's not saying anything." She looks up at Reingold in shock and disgust. "He's laughing. He thinks it's funny. He's laughing while he's killing her."

"If you can tell us what he looks like . . . anything at all . . ."

She closes her eyes, and an image comes to her.

But it isn't the killer's face.

"I see her—Jaime. She . . ." She takes in the oddly grotesque image, wondering if she possibly has it right. "She's wearing red lipstick—too much lipstick, it's everywhere, all over her face, and she didn't put it on herself."

"No," Reingold says quietly, "she didn't. And neither did Carla."

Lucinda opens her eyes.

"I didn't know," she tells him, her voice taut with emotion. "I didn't know about the lipstick."

"That's because the lead investigator kept that information classified. It cannot leave this room, Lucinda."

"It won't."

"You have to swear to me. You can't tell anyone. Not even your boyfriend down there."

"My . . . ? Oh. He's not my boyfriend."

Reingold shrugs; obviously he couldn't care less what Randy is to her.

"Listen," he says, "I really wish you could get a picture of this guy so we'd know who we're looking for."

"So do I. All I know is that he's still laughing, wherever he is now. He's laughing at how he fooled everyone. And he's going to do it again."

"When? Where?"

She shakes her head helplessly. "I don't know."

PART III

7:44

Chapter Sixteen

"Ms. Sloan, I don't know how we can ever thank you for what you've done." Desiree Drew clasps Lucinda's hands in her own.

"I'm glad I could help." Lucinda never knows what else to say when victims' families insist on meeting and thanking her in person.

You're welcome feels trite in the light of what it is, exactly, that she's done: help this devastated single mother locate the decomposing remains of her beloved, promising, twenty-one-year-old son who had his whole life ahead of him.

Isaiah Drew was located in the morgue last month—shot through the head, stripped of his wallet, and left to die anonymously on a crack-infested street in North Philly.

His family and friends, Lucinda knows, have come up with every imaginable reason he might have ventured to that neighborhood. They refuse to accept the reality: that he was a closeted junkie in search of a fix.

Neal, seated behind his desk, clears his throat. "Ms. Drew, Lucinda would like to give you something."

She's already reaching into her purse for the envelope. "This is a contribution for the scholarship fund you've set up in Isaiah's name."

"Thank you."

Lucinda expects the woman to put the envelope away and is dismayed when she tears it open, then gasps at the sizable amount written on the check.

"Oh, my goodness . . . This is . . . I don't know what to say." She looks up, tears shining in her brown eyes. "Thank you. Thank you."

This time, Lucinda's equally heartfelt "You're welcome," is more than appropriate.

A few minutes later, Neal returns to his office after escorting Isaiah's mother out.

"You did well, Cin." He knows she always dreads meeting the families after all is said and done.

She shakes her head. "I wonder if it might have been better if she hadn't known what happened to him."

"You don't really believe that."

"Maybe I'm starting to. Maybe it's better to hold onto hope for as long as you can."

Neal sits down and looks closely at her from across the desk "Are you okay?"

"Not really."

"What's up?"

She shrugs. "For the past day or two, I haven't been able to shake the feeling that something bad is going to happen."

"To you?"

"Maybe. Maybe not. To someone. Somewhere."

She tells him how she's been haunted by bursts of fiendish laughter. By blood, and flashes of a shadowy figure, but never his face.

"You wouldn't be human if you weren't shaken up after what's gone on."

What's gone on, she now knows, is that strands of hair with DNA matching her own were found in Carla Barakat's cold hands.

She was horrified when she met with Neal and Dan Lambert and learned the news. "Someone had been in and out of my apartment," she told them. "He must have taken my hair from—I don't know, the bathroom, or a brush, and planted it—"

"We know," Lambert said. "Don't worry. You're not a suspect."

Not anymore, was what he didn't say.

Not with a second murder halfway across the country.

The Chicago police called in the FBI almost immediately. Notwithstanding an age-old rivalry between the two law enforcement agencies, they're now working together and in conjunction with the Long Beach Township police, having determined that Jaime Dobiak and Carla Barakat were killed by the same person.

Lucinda has been half-hoping—or maybe half-expecting—that an arrest would be made once the FBI got involved.

But the weeks have unfolded without any news on that front.

Detective Reingold, with whom Lucinda has directly kept in touch, doesn't seem to think anything is imminent—though, as he cautioned her, he's not at liberty to give her the details.

"We're working on a theory," was all he told her. He promised to pass along the possible Ava Neary/Sandra Wubner connection to the FBI, but again, warned that he couldn't share the follow up.

He did say—because it directly involved her—that his technicians had traced the e-mail Lucinda received to a stolen laptop. The owner was a college student who said it had gone missing from a Starbucks not far from his Loyola campus. Nobody there recalled seeing anything, and the laptop has yet to resurface.

Another dead end.

"I should go," she tells Neal, picking up her khaki raincoat from the adjacent chair.

"Let me take you to lunch. We'll go get a salad, now that you've decided you like your veggies after all." He grins.

"You know, I never should have told you that you were

right—or that I actually like something that's really good for me."

"And deny me the chance to say *I told you so?*"

She rolls her eyes. "On that note . . ."

"I was serious about lunch."

"No, thanks. You're busy, and . . . I've got to get going."

"What are you doing today?"

"Let's see. . . . Sitting at home, reading magazines, eating stale marshmallow Peeps, and waiting for something terrible to happen," she admits with a shrug. "That's pretty much it."

"That's not good."

"I like them stale. I leave the packages open on purpose. They get this crunchy crust of sugar that I really—"

"I'm not talking about the Peeps. I'm talking about the waiting for something terrible to happen."

"Oh—I'm just kidding, about that, Neal."

"No, you're not."

"You're right. I'm not." She sighs.

"Hey, listen—if you weren't kidding about reading magazines . . ." Neal opens a drawer and hands her something.

She looks at it. "*Meanderings.*"

"Garland's got another story out. He gets paid in copies. He gave me five of them, Cin. What am I going to do with them? Take it. Toss it into the garbage, leave it on the subway, whatever."

"Maybe I'll read it," she tucks it under her arm, "while I'm waiting for the something terrible."

"You know, I moved here last year because it was supposed to be a great place to meet guys," Danielle Hendry tells her friend Alicia as they walk out of their office building onto California Street, heading toward the light rail station at 16th Street.

"You've done nothing but meet guys since I've known you."

"Maybe, but every single one of them has had even more baggage than the losers I left behind in L.A. Including my ex-husbands."

They stop at a crosswalk, waiting for the light to turn. It's rush hour, and the streets of Denver are teeming with office workers—on foot, in cars, on public transportation, on bicycles, roller blades, and even skateboards.

At this time of year, it could be snowing, and Danielle has heard that it often is. But this particular April late afternoon is balmy, thanks to warm air blowing up from the Gulf Stream. The sky is overcast with the threat of the season's first spring thunderstorm.

Danielle turns to watch a strapping businessman walk by, noting that he's probably in his first year out of college, maybe second. A good generation younger than her, maybe just a few years older than her son.

But hell, she's well preserved for forty-three, thanks to Botox, dramatic makeup, Preference by L'Oreal, and the elliptical trainer parked in front of her television set.

The young businessman makes eye contact with her, smiles. She smiles back.

"What about that guy you met skiing a few weeks ago?"

Distracted by Alicia's question, she turns. "You mean Ethan?"

"Yeah. I thought you said he was normal."

"I did. But he's got an ex-wife who's still got him wrapped around her finger, plus two little kids who call him up crying every ten minutes. I told him I couldn't deal with all that baggage. And right after that, he started stalking me."

"What?!"

"Yeah. I wasn't going to say anything about it, but . . . it's kind of freaking me out."

The light turns, and they cross the street.

"What's going on?" Alicia asks.

"First it was just calls at night, when I'm alone—someone breathing into the phone."

"You're sure it's Ethan?"

"The number comes up on Caller ID as Private. That's how Ethan's number came up whenever he called."

"A lot of unlisted numbers do, though."

"Guess what? I'm unlisted, too—and I haven't given my number out to very many people around here."

"Maybe it was random. Kids make crank phone calls."

"It isn't just the phone thing, though. A couple of times when I've been driving home at night, I'm pretty sure some-one's followed me." Seeing Alicia's dubious expression, she amends, "I mean, I *am* sure."

"What kind of car?"

"I can't tell, exactly. All I can see is headlights."

"Maybe someone just happens to live in the same neigh-borhood you do. I wouldn't worry about it."

That's easy for Alicia to say. She lives in the suburbs with her husband, three teenagers, and a big dog. She doesn't know what it's like to be single yet again, living on your own in an unfamiliar city.

The divorce wasn't her idea.

The move was.

She came here on a whim, looking for a fresh start.

Now, eight months in, she wonders if it was the right thing to do after all: leave her hometown of Los Angeles behind, with all her friends and family. . . .

And all the memories of a husband who cheated on her, and the dream house he forced her to sell . . .

It was the right thing to do.

She likes it here in Denver. Likes her administrative job, the friends she's made, the apartment she's renting, and the guys . . .

Likes looking at them, anyway.

She turns her head to see if the cute businessman is still there.

No, but someone else is. A man, wearing jeans, a sweatshirt with the hood up—despite the mild temperature—and big sunglasses. Despite the fact that the sun is nowhere to be seen.

Something about him is unsettling.

She turns back to Alicia, grabbing her arm. "Hey, see that guy?"

"What guy?"

Danielle starts to point—then realizes he's slipped away.

"Never mind," she murmurs, wondering if Ethan is the one who's been following her after all.

"Lucinda? What are you doing?"

Greeted by Cam's voice on the other end of the telephone line, Lucinda hesitates before admitting the truth: "Nothing."

Lying on the couch in her apartment with the blinds drawn and the lights on, staring off into space, feet propped on a coffee table littered with an empty Fritos bag, several Fudgsicle sticks, and an unread literary magazine. You can't do much less than this. And she's been doing it ever since she got home from Neal's office hours ago.

It isn't like her to sit and brood.

But something is wrong. She can feel it, a sense of doom hanging in the air.

Cam doesn't ask her to elaborate. "Then I need you to come. Can you?"

"Come where?" Struck by the urgency in Cam's voice, Lucinda sits up straighter.

"Montclair. My house. How soon can you get here?"

"I'm two hours away. What's going on? Are you okay?"

"I'm fine, I just need to show you something. Remember I told you about my sister's old friend?"

"Bernice. I remember."

"Well, she finally went to visit her brother and look through a bunch of boxes from her mother's house, and she found Ava's letters. She sent them to me—I just got them a little while ago—and I think I found something. I can tell you about it over the phone, but I thought you might want to see for yourself."

"I do." Lucinda is already on her feet, hurrying to the bedroom to change out of the ancient sweats she threw on when she got home.

It's about time they got a break involving Ava.

Last month, thanks to Cam's digging around in Buffalo, the police there—while skeptical—agreed to look into the possibility that Sandra Wubner had been murdered.

So far, there's been no new information—nor any definitive word from Chicago or Beach Haven on whether Ava's death was connected to Jaime's and Carla's.

As Randy pointed out, there's absolutely no hard evidence to link the Wubner case to Ava's, let alone to the new murders.

"What about the scrapbook?" Lucinda asked.

"If we had it as evidence, that would be one thing. But you're the only one who saw it."

"Just like I'm the only one who saw Ava on the rooftop with someone the night she died. I get it. No one's going to take my word for it that those girls didn't kill themselves, or that all of this is connected somehow."

"I take your word for it," Randy told her. "But I'm not part of this investigation."

How well she knows that Randy remains frustratingly out of the loop in Beach Haven. With Frank Santiago out on medical leave, reportedly hospitalized with pneumonia for over two weeks now, and Detective Lambert stepping up in his absence, Randy had hoped things might change. But nothing has.

"All I can do," he told Lucinda, "is keep trying to convince them to look into it and hope that they're listening."

And all Lucinda can do is investigate the so-called suicides on her own, with Cam's help.

"I'm on my way," she promises her friend.

"Why don't you stay over so you don't have to drive back there alone late at night?"

"Maybe I will. Thanks, Cam. See you soon."

She disconnects the call, then dials Randy's cell. He's been calling her nightly to check in.

"Hi, it's me," she says. "Did I catch you in the middle of something?" He'd said he was going to be cleaning out Carla's house over the next couple of days.

"I'm at work, investigating a check fraud. What's up?"

She tells him about Cam's phone call, and that she's headed to Montclair.

"Now? I thought you said you were staying close to home today because you felt like something bad was going to happen."

Yes, and she shouldn't have told him that when he called earlier.

"I have to go up there, Randy. This is important."

"But it's not exactly so urgent it can't wait. You're trying to find out about someone who died years ago."

"I'm trying to find out about Ava because that seems to have something to do with what happened to Carla and Jaime and someone is still out there and he's going to kill again, okay?"

"Okay, calm down," he says in a maddening tone. "First of all, if that's the case, you need to stay safe and not go running off in the night. Second, I'm still not entirely convinced that Ava Neary's death has anything to do with Carla and Jaime's. The M.O. is drastically different, not to mention all the time that's passed—"

"What about the scrapbook in my apartment, and the note Cam got in the mail? It was written in red lipstick," she points out—yet again.

Red lipstick, as they both know, is a peculiar fetish of the killer they're seeking.

"It doesn't mean you're dealing with whoever killed Ava—or even that anyone did. It means that someone is using your interest in Ava's case to manipulate you."

He could be right.

The modern-day killer could have seen her and Cam on

television and thought it would be fun to play games. For all she knows, whoever it is never even heard of Ava Neary before last summer.

"Well, we're never going to know," she says, "unless we get to the bottom of this. I'm going, Randy."

"At least wait until I get off my shift, and I'll go with you."

"That's ridiculous," she tells him, bristling at the implication that she needs some kind of . . . bodyguard.

Or maybe, she realizes, what she doesn't like is that for a moment there, she had a flash of pleasure at the thought of unexpectedly seeing him tonight.

"Why is that ridiculous?"

"Because by the time you leave work, drive from there to here, and here to Montclair, it'll be midnight. That's why."

"What's ridiculous," he returns, "is your chasing off at night by yourself instead of listening to your instincts and staying at home where it's safe."

"Yeah, well, sometimes people who stay at home where it's safe find out that it isn't so safe at all." She pauses to let that sink in. "And if I don't do whatever I can to find out what happened to Carla and Jaime—and Ava—then I'll never be able to forgive myself if someone else dies."

"And I'll never be able to forgive myself if that someone else is you."

She shakes her head.

She isn't used to having someone trying to take care of her. She isn't used to this growing sense of attachment, a sense of mutual need and dependence. She doesn't welcome it. It complicates things.

"Look, Randy, you're my friend"—*and nothing more*, she reminds herself, before saying to him, "and I appreciate your concern. But I'm going to go do my thing, and you're going to let me. Okay?"

"Not okay. I don't have to sit by while you run around taking stupid risks."

"Are you calling me *stupid?*"

"You know I'm not. But unless you have a death wish, you should stay home, behind locked doors, until this feeling passes."

Again, she wishes she hadn't told him about her nagging premonition.

In fact, she wishes she hadn't bothered to call and tell him where she was going tonight.

Then why did you?

"Randy, I've got to get on the road. It's getting late."

"Call me when you get there, okay?"

She frowns. "Why?"

"To let me know you made it."

No. This doesn't work for her. This isn't how she rolls. She refuses to be accountable to anyone.

"Trust me," she says, "I'll make it. Bye, Randy."

She hangs up before he can protest.

Throwing a couple of things into an overnight bag, Lucinda decides that a change of scenery will do her good.

If nothing else, it will get her out of this routine of talking to Randy several times a day, and thinking of him as the only bright spot in her life right now. She refuses to be one of those women who sits around waiting for the phone to ring.

She has other things to do. Other interests. Other friends.

In fact, maybe from Montclair, she'll go surprise Bradley in New York tomorrow.

The few times they've spoken on the phone or e-mailed lately, he's been terse.

She can't tell whether it's because his play rehearsals still aren't going well and opening night still hasn't been set, or if it's something that has to do directly with her. Maybe he's still upset over having been brought in for questioning back in March—even though he was subsequently cleared. Or maybe he's merely miffed that she forgot about his visit. Even though she's since explained—several times—that she'd had to leave town suddenly as part of an investigation.

She didn't tell Bradley the details, and he didn't ask. She

isn't sure it would make a difference even if he knew. All the pain Bradley's family caused him has left him both deeply scarred and easily wounded.

Regardless of whether she can see Bradley in New York, and whatever it is that Cam has to show her in Montclair, Lucinda is certain it will do her good to get away for a day, or maybe even two.

Not because you're running scared, though. No way.

Still . . .

She doesn't believe for one moment that whoever killed Carla and Jaime has forgotten about her just because she hasn't heard from him.

He's out there somewhere.

He's going to strike again. Soon.

And there's nothing she can do to stop him.

Pausing in the doorway to the living room, she looks at the mess on the coffee table. At least she can pick up the wrappers and crumbs before she leaves for a day or two. Otherwise, she'll come home to mice.

There are worse things to come home to, she thinks with a shudder as she gathers everything from the table.

Her gaze falls on the literary magazine.

Meanderings 19.04.

Something occurs to her.

It's far-fetched, but . . .

I've got to check it out. First chance I get.

He impulsively ducked into a clothing store a few minutes ago after Danielle Hendry spotted him on the street, but maybe he shouldn't have.

Maybe he should have just kept walking boldly behind her, even after she knew that he was there.

It wasn't as though she would recognize him. With her, he'd carefully kept his distance for the last few weeks, dogging her steps from afar, keeping her under surveillance, messing with her head.

But for some reason, this wasn't nearly as much fun as it might have been.

"Can I help you, sir?"

"No, just looking," he tells the young salesgirl, a fresh-scrubbed, wholesome-looking type.

There are a lot of those out here in Colorado: outdoorsy girls who hike and ski, shunning heels and perfume and lipstick.

He'd chosen Denver arbitrarily out of all the metropolitan areas that fit his preestablished criteria: large, urban, with a relatively transient population. A place where he can get lost. And, most importantly, located in the mountain time zone.

Maybe he should have picked a different location, though. Phoenix. Salt Lake City.

Too late now.

He's here.

He's found *her*, set the stage.

Anyway, it's almost time.

He turns his back on the salesgirl and pretends to browse through a stack of clearance sweaters.

But he's beginning to wonder what good it is, any of it, if Lucinda Sloan isn't involved. With Long Beach Island, he'd struck close to home, setting her up, playing her and the police.

Then, in Chicago, he'd given her clues, expecting her to piece it all together and show up there looking for him.

She didn't—not until he fed her the information via that wonderfully realistic Web page he'd constructed using a laptop whose owner had conveniently turned his back on it in a public place.

The fake Web site had been a stroke of genius, he thought. And she—who claimed omniscience—had bought it.

How he'd relished her arrival in Chicago in the aftermath,

though he wasn't there to see it firsthand. He could well imagine how frustrating and horrifying it must have been for her to realize she could have stopped him—if only she were smart enough.

The clues he'd left on Jaime Dobiak's nightstand were too challenging. He should have known nobody would be smart enough to figure it out. He should have remembered that no one is as intelligent as he. Next time, he'll dumb it down a little.

Now that a month has passed, and she's half a continent away from him—and from his unsuspecting next victim—it all feels diluted somehow.

The chase, he's decided, isn't nearly as thrilling without the feeling that he himself is being chased.

It's far more exhilarating to be just one step ahead of her than ten.

It would be far more rewarding to get away with yet another murder right under her nose.

Especially if she had everything she needed to solve it.

She would, if she were as smart as people think she is.

If she were as smart as I am.

Chapter Seventeen

Sitting beside Lucinda on the chintz couch in the sunroom, Cam watches her friend fold Ava's last letter, written just a few weeks before her death. It chronicles her sister's growing concern over her affair with a man who was not only her geology professor, but married.

Poor Ava, vulnerable, away from home, still hurting over their mother's abandonment. It's not hard to imagine how she might have been swept into something so wrong—or how it might have escalated into something far more dangerous than forbidden passion.

"I think you're right," Lucinda tells Cam. "This might mean something."

Cam carefully tucks the letter back into the yellowed envelope, addressed to Bernice Watts in her sister's loopy penmanship.

"Mom?"

They both look up, startled, to see Tess in the doorway leading to the kitchen.

"Tess! How are you?"

"Hi, Lucinda. I'm okay."

One glance at Tess is enough to reveal that's not true. Cam's daughter has dark circles under her red-rimmed, bloodshot eyes, her hair looks matted, and she's wrapped in a bleach-stained sweatshirt that looks several sizes too big for her frail, scrawny body.

"I need index cards for a project, Mom. Do you have any?"

"I think so." Cam goes to the computer desk across the room and opens a drawer.

Behind her, Lucinda asks, "What's new, Tess?"

Cam winces, hoping Tess won't get into the breakup. Whenever she talks about it she cries, and it appears she's done her share of that already tonight.

"Not much," Tess tells Lucinda in the monotone she's developed since her heart was broken four weeks ago.

"How's school?"

"Too much homework."

"Yeah, well, I'm sure you're learning some great stuff."

"Not really."

"Here you go, Tess." Cam hands her a packet of index cards.

"Thanks."

She and Lucinda watch Tess slouch away.

"What's going on with her?" Lucinda asks as Cam settles herself on the couch again.

"She's been really depressed lately. Not eating, not sleeping, her grades are down. . . ."

"Does it have something to do with what happened last summer?"

"No, nothing like that. Her boyfriend broke up with her."

"Wow. It looks like she's taking it pretty hard."

"You have no idea." Cam shakes her head. "Nothing Mike or I say or do seems to help. I'm really getting worried. All she does is sit in her room and cry. If it doesn't get better soon, I'm going to take her to see someone again."

"You mean back to the shrink? Isn't that a little extreme for a broken heart?"

"I don't know. . . . I'm worried."

It isn't that Cam thinks her daughter might be suicidal. Not really.

But if there's any chance Tess is going through something more than ordinary breakup depression, Cam needs to know.

And if suicidal tendencies run in families, Cam needs to know whether Ava really did take her own life when she was just a few years older than Tess.

"Let's get back to this geology professor thing," she tells Lucinda.

"Right. The first thing we need to do is find this Bill Zubin. And when we do—"

"I already did."

"You found him? Where?"

Handing Lucinda a couple of sheets of paper, Cam tells her, "I've been searching for him online ever since I called you earlier, and I printed all this off the Internet right before you got here."

She watches Lucinda scan the first piece, an article about Dr. William James Zubin, retired from the NYU faculty back in 1999, conducting geological research in a remote part of Antarctica.

"He's in Antarctica?" Lucinda looks up, shaking her head. "Antarctica is one hell of an alibi, Cam."

"He wasn't there when my sister was killed, he was—"

"No, I meant for Jaime Dobiak, and Carla."

Oh. Right.

Cam hasn't lost sight of the reality that whoever killed her sister might also be responsible for the rash of recent murders. But for her, the mission is a personal one—made all the more meaningful after seeing Tess spiral into a deep depression these last few weeks.

"But the article is old," Cam points out. "I think he's back in New York. Look at the next page. It was just a few weeks ago."

"He gave a talk at the Museum of Natural History."

"Yes, and check out what I found in the Manhattan white pages."

Lucinda flips to the last sheet of paper and looks over the directory listing for W.J. Zubin, on East Seventh Street.

"Are you sure this is him?"

"Probably. It's in the Village near NYU, and anyway, how many W.J. Zubins can there be in New York?"

"It's a big city, but . . . I bet you're right. Who have you told about this?"

"Just Mike." He's up in the master bedroom, watching the Yankees game and keeping an eye on Grace.

"What does he think?"

"He thinks I should turn the whole thing over to the police and forget about it. I've been trying to tell him all along that the police don't seem to care, and that if we don't look into this, nobody else will."

"You're right about that. Okay, let's write down what we know about him from reading Ava's letters." Lucinda opens her bag and pulls out a notebook and pen.

She begins to scribble down the basics.

"We know that Ava was starting to feel like he was using her," Cam contributes. "We know she told at least one person—Bernice—about what was going on."

"Right, and she might have told her friends at school, too."

"I don't think so. I heard from a couple of the closest ones last August, and no one mentioned it. The thing is, Bernice did say she thought Ava had ended the affair before she died—but it doesn't say anything about that in the letter. She must have told her that over the phone."

"All it says in the last letter is that she was thinking about taking Bernice's advice and talking to someone in the school counseling office about it."

"Maybe she told the professor the same thing," Cam suggests, "and maybe he got worried that she was going to get him into trouble with his wife, or—I don't know, blackmail him? Maybe he realized he'd lose his job if it got out, so he . . ."

"Threw her off a rooftop?" Lucinda looks up from her notes, and they stare at each other for a long moment.

"Stranger things have happened," Cam tells her.

"What about the other girls? Sandra Wubner and Elizabeth Johnson?"

"As far as I can tell, Zubin wasn't ever on the faculty at Buff State. And I still haven't been able to track down any more information about Elizabeth."

Lucinda shakes her head. "I wish I remembered more than just those two names from the scrapbook."

"I've been trying to research newspaper archives from that era to find other young female suicide victims, but it's like searching for a needle in a haystack. But at least I found Zubin."

"You know what? I was planning to go to the city tomorrow anyway to visit a friend of mine. Before I do that, I'll go over to that address and look him up."

"What will you do if you find him?"

"I'll see what my instincts tell me about him, and we'll take it from there."

She paces across the living room of her apartment as the phone rings in her ear, hoping he'll pick up.

Yet when he does—with a wary "Hello?"—she immediately wishes she hadn't called. He's never going to admit to anything.

"Ethan, it's Danielle Hendry."

"I know."

"I need you to stop, Ethan."

There's a moment of silence. "Stop what?"

"You know. The phone calls, the tailing me in your car, and now leaving me this crazy kids' book that makes no sense whatso—"

"What?!"

"Why are you doing this to me?"

"What are you talking about?"

"Oh, come on," she says impatiently. "You know."

Don't you?

Fresh doubt slithers into Danielle's mind.

"I'm talking about the package you left on my doorstep. It was wrapped in brown paper, and my name was written on it in some kind of red greasepaint, and—"

"Danielle, I don't know what's going on with you," Ethan says, "but whatever it is, I promise you that I have nothing to do with it."

"You're saying you haven't been calling me and hanging up? Following me?"

"No! Why would I do that?"

"You tell me."

There's a pause. When he speaks again, his voice is kind— which is somehow more insulting than if he were sarcastic or even irritated.

"We only went out a couple of times. You really need to move on, Danielle. I have."

"Really? Because it doesn't seem that way to me!"

Even as she lashes out at him, she can hear an echo of her ex-husband, Ron, saying in disgust, "*Oh, here we go. For Pete's sake, Danielle, don't you ever get tired of making a scene?*"

Yes, she got tired of it. That's why they're divorced.

But Ethan isn't Ron, and she's not going to make a scene.

"You know what?" she says abruptly. "I have to go. Just forget I called."

"Believe me, I will."

Danielle disconnects the call, curses, and tosses the phone toward the couch across the room. She misses, and it lands on the floor. She leaves it there.

Walking back into the kitchen, where she opened the package she found on the doorstep, she wonders if maybe Ethan didn't leave it. Maybe it's some kind of joke, played by one of the neighbors, like the overgrown frat boy type a few doors down.

But if it's a joke, I don't get it.

Or maybe there was an invitation tucked into the pages of the book—like, to a baby shower or kiddie party or something. There are a lot of young families in the townhouse community.

She picks up the book and turns it so that the pages flutter face down as she holds the covers.

Nothing falls out.

Maybe there's a message written inside. She checked before, but not all the way through.

With a sigh, she begins reading.

Goodnight, Moon . . .

Vic's progress on the manuscript, which almost seemed to write itself for the first few months he worked on it, has all but ground to a screeching halt.

In recent weeks, he's plodded his way through to the final chapter . . . three times.

He was set to begin a fourth try this evening after dinner, with Kitty's encouragement.

"You'll get it right," she said, like she still believes in him.

But he's not so sure he will, and he's not so sure she should.

He's been sitting at the computer for a good six hours already, but he isn't working on the book, because no matter how he approaches the damned thing, it doesn't feel finished.

That's because it isn't.

There's only one way to create a satisfying final chapter: by apprehending the Night Watchman after all these years.

Vic is certain the communication he received last month was from the elusive serial killer—and that Jaime Dobiak is one in a new crop of victims.

But if the FBI is on board with that theory, they're not admitting it to Vic—and they haven't let on to the press, either.

Every day, Vic scours the Internet looking for new murders, new clues, to no avail.

It seems as if the killer has gone underground again.

But Vic's profile tells him he won't stay there for long this time.

The fact that he's made direct contact tells Vic he's far more daring these days. He won't be able to stay silent—or inactive—for very long.

Serial killers typically don't just stop.

They keep killing until they themselves die or are caught or taken into custody for an unrelated crime.

That, Vic suspects, might be the key.

He's been combing newspaper archives for every arrest that took place in the metropolitan northeastern corridor from D.C. to Boston at the end of 1969 and beginning of 1970, during the weeks following the murder of Judy Steinberg, the Night Watchman's last known victim.

Not misdemeanor arrests, but major crimes that would have brought an extended prison sentence.

He'd be willing to bet that the unsub might be found somewhere among them, though weeding through the data is a time-consuming, painstaking process. Once he's identified suspects who became incarcerated in the late 1960s, he'll check prison records to narrow the field to those who were recently released.

And by then, we'll all be dead of old age.

Hearing an e-mail click in, he removes his fingers from the keyboard and laces them at the nape of his neck, stretching.

At this late hour, it's probably just an advertisement, or spam. Still, he welcomes the intrusion, any excuse to take a break—or maybe even call it a night.

The e-mail is from an unfamiliar address, one that sets Vic's heart pounding.

The screen name is nightwatchman.

That doesn't mean it's from him, he reminds himself. *The whole world knows you're writing a book about the guy.*

But when Vic opens the e-mail, he suspects this might be the real thing.

Full moon on the rise.

That's all.

Full moon—as if Vic didn't know.

He's been dreading it for a month.

With good reason, by the looks of this e-mail.

But there's still time.

The full moon isn't until tomorrow.

For some reason, Lucinda had expected that she might sleep better tonight, away from home.

But it's three in the morning, and she's lying in the Hastingses' guest room, still wide awake, staring at the pattern in the stucco ceiling.

She can't stop thinking—not about Ava Neary or Jaime Dobiak or Carla Barakat—but about Randy.

About how she all but hung up on him earlier, just because she couldn't deal with the fact that he was concerned about her.

Maybe that's not such a bad thing, having someone in your life who cares. Maybe it's time for her to stop—

She hears a bedroom door open and close and footsteps tiptoe down the hall.

It's probably Cam, going to check on the baby.

But the footsteps move past the nursery, past the bathroom, too, creaking down the stairs.

Lucinda gets out of bed, pulls her Princeton sweatshirt over her head to ward off the wee-hour chill, and opens the door. Peering out into the hall, she sees that all the bedroom doors are closed. A faint glow of light is coming from somewhere downstairs.

Not daring to turn on a light, she hurriedly makes her way through the shadows and descends the stairs.

On the first floor, she follows the source of the glow to the kitchen, expecting to find Cam there.

But it's Tess who sits at the table, in a long-sleeved thermal T-shirt and plaid pajama bottoms, stirring something in a mug.

She looks up, startled, when Lucinda quietly utters her name.

"Oh . . . hi."

"Is everything all right?"

"Yeah, I just couldn't sleep." Tess shrugs. "I thought maybe some tea would be good. It's chamomile. Want some?"

"I'd rather have chocolate. Do you think your mother has any stashed away?"

"Top shelf in the pantry, behind the cereal boxes."

Lucinda finds a bag of miniature Kit Kat bars. "Perfect. Want some?"

Tess hesitates.

"Chocolate helps, Tess."

"Helps what?"

"Everything. Catch." Lucinda tosses her a candy bar, grabs a couple more, puts the bag away, and joins her at the table.

"Did my mother tell you what happened to me?"

"You mean the breakup?"

"He totally dumped me."

"She told me. I'm sorry. It's hard."

"You have no idea." Tess glumly takes a bite of chocolate.

Lucinda debates the wisdom of telling her that she does, indeed, have some idea. That she's been through her share of teenaged breakups.

But, thinking back, she realizes that she never was the one who got dumped. She always got herself out before that could happen.

Including with Randy, last time.

If she hadn't been so quick to pull back, if she had let him break his engagement for her sake, they'd have been together all these years.

Or not.

You weren't ready for that back then. You weren't ready to

*take a chance. And even if you had been, you probably would
have lost him anyway, and then where would you be?*

Exactly where I am now.

"What?" Tess asks.

She blinks. "Did I say something?"

"No, but you have this look on your face like . . . I don't
know, like you just remembered something."

No. It's more that she just realized something.

She shrugs. "Want another Kit Kat?"

"I guess, but it's not really helping."

"I'm sorry. Give it time."

"I wish I could be like you," Tess says abruptly.

"What do you mean?"

"You know—a psychic. My mom told me that's what you
do."

Clearly, Cam didn't tell her daughter that she herself is
similarly gifted.

"Why do you wish you were a psychic, Tess?"

"Because I would have known right from the start that I
was going to get dumped, and I would have protected myself."

"How?"

"By not falling in love."

"But then you would have missed out."

"Yeah, on getting dumped."

"No. On falling in love."

"So? Better safe than sorry."

"Sometimes," Lucinda tells her, "you can be safe *and*
sorry."

Unlike Lucinda Sloan, Danielle Hendry doesn't sleep
with the lights on.

Her bedroom is pitch black, other than the glowing digits
of the clock on the nightstand.

Luckily, he has a pen light attached to the key ring where he keeps her duplicate key—along with Lucinda Sloan's, Carla Barakat's, and Jaime Dobiak's. Comes in handy for these late-night missions.

He moves stealthily to the bed and shines the light on her.

She's huddled beneath the quilt, snoring softly; blond hair strewn across the pillow is all that's visible of her.

He arcs the beam over to the bedside clock.

Reaching out with a gloved finger, he turns off the alarm.

"Sleep tight," he barely whispers, and leaves her to prowl back down the stairs and through the first floor of the townhouse, having familiarized himself with the layout on earlier visits.

He was struck, each time, by how bland the place is, compared to Lucinda Sloan's apartment. White walls, beige carpet, stock cabinets, generic-looking furniture.

He had assumed, when he first spotted Danielle at a light rail stop back in March, that her home would have as much pizzazz as she does; she's a flashy blonde, heels and hose and hair spray every time he's caught sight of her. And, of course, red lipstick.

Just like Scarlet.

Coming here tonight wasn't originally on his agenda, but then the brainstorm struck and he knew what he had to do. It was perfect.

He creeps into the kitchen and shines his pen light along the white laminate countertop between the microwave and the ceramic crock full of cooking utensils she doesn't bother to use, existing mainly on yogurt and Lean Cuisines, as far as he can tell.

Aha. Her BlackBerry is there, attached to a charger she leaves plugged into the outlet, just as it is every night.

Like Lucinda, Danielle is a creature of habit. Only he doesn't find most of hers nearly as captivating.

I miss you, Lucinda.

But I'm sure I'll see you soon.

A burst of laughter escapes him. He clasps a hand over his mouth and stands frozen, listening.

Did she hear?

All is still above.

But he's not taking any chances. Swiftly, he grabs what he came for and slips out the door, disappearing into the night beneath the light of a moon that's almost full.

Back in the lamplit guest room, feeling slightly sick from too much chocolate, Lucinda climbs into bed. She can only hope Tess is doing the same thing in her room down the hall, poor kid.

Wondering what time it is, Lucinda looks around the room for a clock. There isn't one.

It's too early to call Randy, that's for sure. No matter how tempting it is to connect with him on the heels of her conversation with heartbroken Tess.

Not that Lucinda is planning to tell him she's realized she's willing to take a chance on an actual relationship with him.

It's still too soon for that.

But hearing his voice right now wouldn't be such a bad thing.

She fishes in her bag for her BlackBerry to check the time.

Definitely too early.

Leaning back against the pillows again, she closes her eyes, willing sleep to come. Her throat is starting to burn from exhaustion, and she can't afford to lose her voice when she's headed to Manhattan in the morning to see what she can find out about William Zubin.

No—don't think about that now. Don't think about anything upsetting.

The trouble is, she can't think of anything, at this point, that's not.

So she does her best not to think at all, focusing instead on deep breathing, the way she does when she's trying to conjure a psychic vision on the job.

When at last sleep overtakes her, she dreams.

At first, it's the puzzle dream—the puzzle is almost done, and there's a missing piece, and she's looking for it.

Then she's in a big, deserted factory of some sort, looking everywhere for the puzzle piece, but she can't find it because it's pitch black.

Somewhere along the way, the dream shifts gears again the way dreams have a way of doing, and someone is chasing her through the factory, but she doesn't know whom. She keeps trying to scream for help but her voice is gone.

At last she rounds a corner and sees a big round beam of light up ahead.

Moonlight, she thinks at first—knowing, with that omniscient dream logic, that the moon is full.

But there are no windows in the factory, and she sees that it isn't the moon at all.

She can make out the silhouette of a man, holding a flashlight.

It's the night watchman, she realizes.

She bolts toward him, blinded by the beam, certain she's about to be saved.

Just before she reaches the man, he turns the light to illuminate something he's holding in his other hand.

A butcher knife, dripping with blood.

He starts to laugh, that horrible, crazy laugh that's been haunting her by day now echoing through her nightmare.

Chapter Eighteen

Walking into the lobby of the sprawling downtown Denver hotel, Vic finds himself surrounded by conventioneers wearing vinyl badge holders advertising some type of marketing conference.

How easy it would have been for the unsub to blend into this crowd, perhaps even borrowing a conference badge just long enough to work his way into the business center and send Vic that e-mail from one of the hotel's public use computers.

But the Night Watchman isn't a legitimate guest here, not even under an assumed name—of that, Vic is certain. His risks, so far, have been much too calculated for that.

Vic makes his way to the business center and finds the double glass doors locked, with a hotel security guard outside.

"Sorry, sir, the center is closed right now," the guard tells him.

"Why is that?"

"Repairs," the guard says tersely.

Uh huh. Vic can see Annabelle Wyatt inside, along with several other agents.

Maybe he should let her know he's here. Just in case . . .

*Just in case she wants to remind you—again—that you're
retired, and she doesn't need or want your help?*

It's not that he'd blame her, or would expect any other response from the Bureau.

It's just . . . ironic, that the predator he spent so many years
trying to catch would reappear only now that it's too late for
Vic to be a part of the investigation.

Well, then, why are you here?

Because, clearly, the Night Watchman wants him to be.
That e-mail he sent from this hotel was no reckless mistake.
He had to know that Vic would trace it and come running;
had to know, too, that Vic would be obligated to turn it over
to the FBI and that they, too, would be here in a heartbeat.

But it's not as though the guy is going to appear out of
nowhere to say, "You're probably wondering why I've called
you all here today. . . ."

"Sir? If you need to use a computer, there's one at the
bellman's desk," the security guard tells him.

In other words, *get moving, bub.*

"Thanks." Vic walks away.

He has no idea where he's going, but it isn't the bellman's
desk.

"Randy?"

In the midst of examining an online bank account as part of
the check fraud investigation, he looks up to see Dan Lambert
in the doorway.

"What's wrong, Dan?"

"What makes you think something's wrong?"

"The look on your face. Don't ever play poker. You'd lose
your shirt."

"I have, and I have." Dan walks into the office and closes
the door behind him. "Got a minute?"

"Yeah."

Randy closes out the computer screen. For a split second,

he worries that this is about Lucinda—that something's happened to her.

But she's not on the island or even in Philly, so why would Dan be the first to know?

And anyway, she'd called Randy just an hour ago.

Seeing it was her, he hadn't picked up, still stung by the way she'd lashed out at him last night when he was only trying to help.

She left him a message that she was leaving Cam's and headed for New York.

"I want to talk to you, Randy. I'm really sorry I hung up on you last night. I just didn't want you to worry about me."

Too bad, he'd thought, hearing it.

That's what you do when you care about someone. You worry about them.

He hasn't called her back.

"I just talked to Frank."

"Yeah? When's he coming back?"

"He isn't." Dan sits in the chair beside the desk. "He's dying, Randy."

I knew that, Randy realizes, even as the words catch him off guard. He's surprised, yet somewhere deep down inside he had realized something was seriously wrong back when Lucinda asked him about Frank's health. At the time, he was too caught up in Carla's death to give much thought to anything else.

Yes, he had asked Frank how he was. Frank had said fine, other than pneumonia. Again, Randy'd had a twinge of misgiving, wondering if it was something more—but he didn't press the issue.

"It's stage IV lung cancer," Dan tells him.

"Did you talk to him?"

"I got an e-mail. I tried to call, but he's not picking up."

"Maybe he's still in the hospital."

"I called. He was released yesterday."

"And what? Sent home to die?"

Dan shakes his head. "I guess so. And the worst of it is, he's all alone. His kids are all far away—and they don't spend much time with him as far as I know. I've always had the impression they blame him for the divorce."

"I've always had the impression Frank blames himself, too. He told me, when Carla and I split up, not to make the same mistake he did, or I'd wind up like him—alone, with regrets."

Randy didn't tell Frank that it was the marriage that had been a mistake. It was the marriage that had left him feeling alone, with regrets.

"I just remembered something," he tells Dan, sitting up and reaching for the phone.

"What?"

Not what—*whom.*

"I have to make a phone call, Dan."

If you see something, say something.

Gazing at the poster plastered above the window of a downtown Number 6 local—courtesy of New York City's Metropolitan Transit Authority and Homeland Security—Lucinda can't help but think, with a hefty slice of irony, of Bitsy Sloan.

The slogan brings to mind all those years, growing up, that Lucinda would see something—something no one else could see—and say something, much to her mother's mortification.

People would react any number of ways, depending on the vision she'd shared. Sometimes, with shocked recognition of some personal detail Lucinda couldn't have possibly known, they'd start asking questions. Questions her mother refused to let her answer, of course.

Mostly, though, those to whom she described her visions were confused, and looked to Bitsy Sloan, who would nervously laugh it off.

"Lucinda is always making up little stories in her head," she would explain with forced affection, as if she considered her daughter's so-called creativity a charming quirk of character rather than a ticket to the looney bin.

God forbid Mother bring her to a child psychiatrist who might actually diagnose a distasteful flaw in the sole heiress to the Sloan fortune.

If you see something, please don't say anything.

That was Mother's credo.

Lucinda learned, eventually, temporarily—for the sake of survival in the stone mansion—to live with it.

And when at last she left the stone mansion, she learned not only to trust her visions but to channel them into her own unique brand of Sloan philanthropy.

If you see something, don't just say something. Do *something.*

She hasn't seen her mother since the day of their curtailed brunch. Nor has she called—but maybe she should, one of these days.

Her mother isn't getting any younger.

No, she isn't getting more tolerant, or easygoing, either.

Bitsy Sloan is who she's always been.

And so am I, only . . .

Lucinda watched Cam this morning as she nursed and bathed and cuddled little Grace, then as she kissed a bleary-eyed Tess good-bye and sent her out the door to school. For the first time, she found herself wondering what it would be like to have children of her own.

She found the concept both terrifying and intriguing. And she wondered what kind of mother she would be.

Nothing like my own mother was the first thing that popped into her head.

Then it struck her that a young Bitsy Sloan, when imagining what her future daughter might be like, probably hadn't envisioned one like Lucinda, either.

I am who I am.

She is who she is.

Yeah. Maybe she'll call her mother, one of these days.

The subway pulls into the Astor Place station, and Lucinda disembarks with a horde of other passengers, many of whom appear to be NYU students headed for late morning classes.

She emerges onto the street. Spring is in the air today: sunshine, and a comfortable breeze blowing off the nearby East River.

As she looks around to get her bearings, she hears her phone beep, indicating that a new voice mail came in while she was underground. She pulls the phone from her pocket and examines the screen. There's not just a voice mail; there's a text message, too, from an unfamiliar number.

Voice mail first—because she knows who it's from.

"Lucinda, it's Randy. I've been thinking about you—not worrying, *thinking*, okay? Call me when you get this."

She will call him—but not now, from the street in Manhattan.

She opens the text message.

Reading it, she realizes that the nightmare has begun again, just as she'd known it would.

Danielle awakens to the ringing of the telephone—and a bedroom splashed with too much sunlight sneaking in through the cracked blinds.

Groggy, she fumbles for the phone on the bedside table. "Hello?"

"Danielle! Are you all right?"

"Alicia?" She rubs the sleep from her eyes. "What's going on?"

"I just found out you weren't here, and I was worried."

"Here . . . Where?"

"Work! H.R. said you didn't call in sick. After what you

told me last night about, you know, that guy Ethan stalking you, I thought I'd better check on you."

Ethan . . . ?

Stalking . . . ?

Oh! That's right.

It comes back to her.

She talked to Ethan last night, after she found that book, *Goodnight Moon*, on her doorstep. After determining there was no message or invitation within the pages, she poured herself a glass of wine and tried to watch TV for a while to unwind. A little later, still vaguely uneasy, she took an Ambien before bed. A pharmacist's label on the orange prescription bottle warns that you're not supposed to combine the medication with alcohol, but she knows from experience that it's not going to hurt her. Not just one pill, after just one glass of wine; it was her own personal sleep prescription back during the stressful post-divorce days.

Works every time.

Maybe too well, she realizes, glancing at the clock and startled to see that it's past ten.

"So *are* you sick?" Alicia is asking.

"No, but I must have forgotten to set the alarm last night. Tell them I'm on my way, okay?"

She's already out of bed, heading toward the adjoining bathroom.

Ten minutes later, showered and dressed in a pale yellow spring suit, she hurriedly throws mascara, eyeliner, and lipstick into her bag to apply on the commuter train. Then she shoves her feet into a pair of heels, dashes down the stairs, and hurries into the kitchen to grab her BlackBerry.

It isn't there.

Momentarily taken aback, she eyes the black charger cord dangling empty from the kitchen outlet where she always keeps it. Then she remembers how discombobulated she was when she got home last night, because of the package. She apparently forgot to plug in her BlackBerry. It must still be in her bag.

She's good to go.

She all but runs out the front door, but takes the time to be doubly sure it's locked behind her.

You can't be too careful, Danielle Hendry thinks, just before she hears the voice directly behind her.

"Oh, dear, it looks like someone overslept."

Then the laughter begins.

104.5
39.4

Lucinda stares at the text message.

Jaime Dobiak's bedside radio had been tuned to 104.5.

She'd known it was no accident.

And that magazine . . .

All this time, she's been wondering about the strange trade journal found on Jaime Dobiak's nightstand. Was a girl who subscribed to *Cosmopolitan* and *Glamour* also interested in social history? Or had the killer left it there as a clue?

The latter.

She should have checked last night, when she'd seen that *Meanderings* magazine on her coffee table and it had occurred to her.

19.04

Volume 19. Issue 4.

Journal of Social History, Summer 2006, Volume 39, issue 4.

She can see it so clearly; even now.

39.4.

How could I have missed it?

Lucinda reaches Neal on the first try, pressing the phone hard against her ear and sticking her finger in the other one to drown out the sirens racing down the Bowery.

"Lucinda, where are you?"

"On the street in New York. Where are you? Are you near a computer?"

"I'm at my desk. What do you need?"

"I just got a text message from a number I don't recognize."

"What's the area code? I'll check it."

"No, wait, first check these numbers against a longitude and latitude chart. 104.5 and 39.4. That's all that was in the message."

He curses under his breath. "Just the numbers?"

"Yes."

He asks her to repeat them. "All right, I'm looking them up. Hang on."

She looks around the bustling street, suddenly feeling vulnerable out in the open like this.

What if he's here somewhere, lost in the crowd, watching her?

She pulls her sunglasses from her bag and puts them on.

Oh, great. Great disguise. He'll never find you now.

"I've got it," Neal announces in her ear. "It's Denver."

"Denver." She immediately steps onto the curb, facing oncoming traffic, and starts looking for a vacant cab. "He's moved on again."

"Looks that way."

"Something's going to happen there, and it's going to be today."

"Are you sure?"

"Pretty much. Last night, I had this crazy dream, about a bloody knife and a night watchman and the moon was full— the moon is going to be full tonight, I checked when I got up, and—"

"Wait a minute. *What* did you say?"

"I said I had a dream about the full moon and a bloody knife. . . ."

"And a *night watchman*?"

"Yes, a—" All at once, the phrase slams into her. "Oh my God, Neal."

"There was a serial killer, years ago—"

"I know. Everyone knows."

Not *a* night watchman.

The Night Watchman: a transient serial killer who snuck into random victims' homes in the night and stabbed them to death. He was never caught.

"He struck on nights when the moon was full," Neal tells her.

"Are you sure about that?"

"Positive. I studied that case. It was early in my career, and I remember—"

"Neal, check the dates," she cuts in hurriedly. "Jaime died on March twentieth, and Carla was about a month earlier."

"I know, I know, I'm checking. . . ."

A yellow cab pulls up beside Lucinda. She opens the back door, hops in.

"Where to?"

She gives the driver the address of the midtown garage where she parked her car.

"The moon was full on March twentieth," Neal says in her ear, "and on February twenty-first."

It was. She knew it was.

Moonlight Sonata.

Moonstruck.

Goosebumps creep over her skin.

"Do you think this is the Night Watchman again?" she asks Neal.

"Could be. That, or a copycat. It was all over the press that the guy killed at night, during a full moon."

"What about the wrist watches? Or the red lipstick—see if you can find anything about the Night Watchman . . . using it to write messages."

She almost slipped about the victims being found with red lipstick smeared on their lips.

But Reingold told her that it was classified information, and true to her word, she hasn't told a soul.

"I'm looking," Neal tells her, as she watches buildings and cars and people flash by out the window of the cab.

Lucinda herself has already searched the Internet repeatedly, looking for clues to past crimes with links to red lipstick or watches. She found nothing.

Surely if the notorious Night Watchman had a lipstick fetish or left his victims with watches that were stopped at the time they died, she'd have found it.

"You still there, Cin?"

"I'm still here."

"Nothing about red lipstick, but I got a bunch of hits about an ex FBI agent who's writing a book on the case. His name's Vic Shattuck."

"Can you find out how I can get in touch with him, please, Neal? But first, I need to know my options for getting to Denver."

"What? When are you going to Denver?"

"*Now*."

Blondie's out cold, lying in the back of the van with BOB'S CARPET CLEANING emblazoned on the side of it.

He'd found it parked on a relatively secluded neighborhood driveway one morning a while back, and had been keeping an eye on it, noticing that no one ever seemed to use it during the day. The owner, who lives alone, works nine to five somewhere else, and uses the van for his part-time business at night and on the weekends.

He figured no one would notice if he borrowed it for a little while. Nor would anyone think twice if they spotted a carpet cleaning van parked right in front of her townhouse with the doors wide open.

Sure, there was a ten, maybe fifteen second window when he did risk being discovered as he approached Danielle Hendry at her front door, delivered his strategically placed blow to her skull, and tossed her into the van.

In broad daylight, anyone could have seen.

Yes, and it was all the more thrilling for him to drive away, confident that no one had.

He hadn't been sure he was going to like doing it this way—going to all the trouble of transporting her away from home. But once he decided to let his friends back east know where to look for him, he knew he had to shake things up a little.

They'll be expecting him to do what he had always done.

They have no idea that he's much too smart to be that predictable at this stage of the game.

He takes a detour to the commuter lot where he parked his own car earlier, in convenient walking distance to the van owner's driveway. At this time of morning, the lot is full, and there isn't a soul to catch a glimpse of him transferring his human cargo from the back of the van to the trunk of his car.

She's dead weight, and he checks her pulse below her ear to make sure that she *isn't* dead.

No. Thank goodness. That wouldn't be any fun at all.

For the first time today, he gets a good look at her face and notes that she isn't wearing lipstick.

What a shame.

"I'll fix that for you soon, I promise," he croons, before closing the trunk and leaving her there while he returns the van, knowing Bob will never be the wiser.

"Frank, my name is Mary," the heavy-set, jolly-looking woman on his doorstep announces. "It's good to meet you."

He shakes her hand, but says nothing.

What is there to say?

It's not good to meet her.

It's a nightmare to meet her, the woman sent by the hospice to help him die.

They have other names for it—palliative care is one—but that's what it comes down to. Why sugarcoat the truth?

"Come on in." He leads the way into the condo, conscious of his shuffling footsteps but unable to do anything about it.

He tried to clean up the place this afternoon, in anticipation of his first visitor in months. But he was too exhausted to do much more than load the dishwasher and stack the newspapers on one end of the coffee table.

"Do you want to be in the living room? Or at the kitchen table?"

"Wherever you're most comfortable, Frank."

Comfortable? Ha.

Where he's most comfortable is in his office down at the police station. But he hasn't been there in a couple of weeks now, and this morning he was forced to announce that this is no temporary medical leave of absence. That he's never going back.

He sent the e-mail, signed off the computer, and has no intention of going back on. At least not anytime soon. He can't bear the inevitable awkwardness, or, far worse, the pity.

"We can sit in the living room," he decides, and asks, just to show her that he's no invalid—yet, anyway—"Can I get you something to drink?"

"Double Grey Goose martini straight up, no olive."

Frank's eyes widen.

Mary laughs a booming laugh and jabs him with a chubby index finger. "Gotcha."

"Oh—good one." He manages a smile.

To his surprise, Mary's little joke actually makes him feel better—unlike the overt cheer of the MRI nurse, whom he had the displeasure of seeing again the other day.

But Mary isn't here to kid around, he knows. She's here to talk to him about what lies ahead. To discuss a DNR and getting his financial affairs in order and appointing a health care proxy—perhaps the trickiest part of the process, as Frank has yet to tell his family what's going on.

It just doesn't seem appropriate to break the news over the phone.

He supposes he'll have to, since the kids have no plans to visit any time soon. He doesn't intend to be a burden on them, though. On anyone.

That's why he agreed to hospice care, at Dr. Rubin's urging.

At yesterday's appointment, he again pressed the oncologist to tell him how much time he has left. Again, the doctor punted. All he would say was that, statistically speaking, Frank's odds of being here six months from now are about fifty-fifty.

Numbers.

Again.

Frank's thoughts automatically flip to the murder case he turned over to Dan Lambert.

The FBI has been brought in, under the assumption that Carla Barakat's death was the work of a serial killer.

Just as Neal Bullard suspected in the first place.

Frank supposes he owes him a phone call, one of these days. Just to clear the air. Settle affairs, as it were.

But not today.

"Well," Mary says, "shall we get started?"

It's been a bad morning.

It has been since everyone left, anyway: Mike and Tess headed for work and school; Lucinda on her way to Manhattan not long after.

Left alone in the house with the baby, Cam had called her father to check in.

Sometimes when she calls him, he's surprisingly lucid.

Not today.

She couldn't understand what he was saying, and she's pretty sure it was mutual. When she promised to come visit him in a day or two, he said that would be good—then asked who she was.

After hanging up the phone, she did her best to distract herself with housework, only to be interrupted by a premonition.

She hasn't had one in a while.

The vision involved a stranger, as they almost always do: this time, a pretty girl in her late teens, maybe college-aged.

But she looked as though she had stepped out of an era long past. Her brunette hair was done up in an old-fashioned style—like something out of "I Love Lucy." She had on a vintage-looking dress with shoulder pads, and dark red lipstick.

Terrible, bloody things happened to the girl in the vision.

As Cam, shaken, wrote down all the details in one of her marble notebooks, she wondered whether it was a true premonition. Or had she seen something that happened decades ago? If so, why now?

And why does she feel such an odd sense of connection to the girl? Has she seen her before, maybe?

Whatever the case, the experience left her unsettled and drained, as such visions always do. She's spent the last couple of hours absently tidying the house and playing with the baby, and is about to feed her when the phone rings.

She recognizes the number: Lucinda, calling from her cell phone.

Cam's first thought is that she must already have news from NYU.

Then she looks at her watch and realizes Lucinda would have gotten to Manhattan less than an hour ago. Not enough time for her to have tracked down Professor William Zubin—particularly if she'd used the parking pass Mike had given her for a midtown garage, and taken the subway down from there.

Maybe she's still on the road, having car trouble or something.

Cam picks up the phone. "Lucinda, where are you?"

"In the car. I'm on my way to the airport."

"What? Why?"

"I got a text message a little while ago with the longitude and latitude coordinates for Denver. That's where I'm going."

"But . . . who sent the message?"

"Neal is getting the number traced. I guess it's from him."

Cam doesn't have to ask whom. "Lucinda, you're crazy to go running out there. That's what this guy wants."

"I know, and I'd be crazy *not* to go out there. This is a chance to catch him, Cam. I've got to do whatever I can. It's better than idly sitting around here waiting for something horrible to happen to someone."

Cam thinks of the girl in the strange vintage clothing and hairstyle. "You're right. It *is* better. Just be careful."

Vic is sitting in a café nursing his third cup of coffee when his cell phone rings.

The call is from his editor in New York. Oh, geez. He doesn't feel like dealing with book business now, when he's here in the middle of . . .

Well, nothing, really.

What else have you got to do?

"Hello?"

"Victor, it's Janine."

"Hi, Janine. What's up?"

"I just got a call from someone wanting to get in touch with you, and I didn't want to give out your number."

"Thank you, that's appreciated." He lifts his coffee to his mouth and asks, before taking a sip, "Who was it?"

"I wrote down her information in case you want to call her back. Her name is . . . Let's see. Lucinda Sloan."

"Lucinda Sloan," he repeats, wondering why that name rings a bell.

"She said to tell you to please, please call her back. She said it's about the Night Watchman."

Vic promptly lowers the coffee cup, digs a pen out of his jacket pocket. "What's the number?"

Janine gives it to him, and he jots it on a slightly rumpled napkin.

"Oh, and she said that if you're going to call her, you should do it right away, because she's on her way to the airport to catch a plane."

"Thanks, Janine." He all but hangs up on her.

He dials the number written on the napkin, processing the name through his brain like he's feeding data into a search engine.

Lucinda Sloan . . . Lucinda Sloan . . .

Definitely familiar, but he can't figure out why.

She picks up on the first ring, sounding breathless. "Yes? Hello? Hello?"

"Ms. Sloan? This is Victor Shattuck."

"Thank you for calling me back. Listen, I'm in the car so if I lose you, I'll call you back, okay?"

"Okay. Do we know each other?"

"No. I'm contacting you because I know you're writing a book about the Night Watchman murders. I'm a detective and I'm working on a case now that has some similarities, and . . . Look, let me just cut to the chase, because I'm about to drive through the Midtown Tunnel."

Midtown Tunnel. So she's in New York.

Lucinda Sloan—detective—New York. Still no connection.

"This guy has been contacting me."

"Which guy?" He holds his breath.

"I'm pretty sure it's the Night Watchman. He's been in my apartment, and he was monitoring my computer, and he planted my DNA at the scene of a murder. . . . It's a long story, and complicated, and we should talk. But I'm about to fly to Denver because I—"

"Denver?" he cuts in. "Why are you flying to Denver?"

"Because that's where he is."

"That's where *I* am." Victor Shattuck feels as though he's just gotten the biggest break in his FBI career—until it hits him that he doesn't have one anymore. "When do you land?"

"Five o'clock your time. I'll call you when I get there. Here comes the tunnel. I'm about to lose you."

"Which airline?"

"United," he hears, and then the connection is broken.

"So I talked to Victor Shattuck," Lucinda tells Neal over the phone, as she strides toward the terminal from the parking lot. Long term—which pretty much sums up her level of optimism that she'll be promptly winging her way back home, case closed.

"Good. What did he say?"

"That he's in Denver."

"No."

"Oh, yes."

"What is he doing there?"

"Same thing I am, I'm sure. Did you get an address from that phone number that sent the text message?"

"We're working on it. It's registered to a woman in Los Angeles."

"A *woman*?" she echoes. "In *Los Angeles*?"

"Yes, a woman, in Los Angeles, but anyone could have used the phone to send a text message."

"So it was stolen?"

"Not reported to be. Anyway, we'll track her down and—"

"What about the phone? Where is it now? Can you have the signal tracked?"

"Working on that, too. Call me when you land. Have a safe flight, Cin."

"I will."

It's not the flight she's worried about.

* * *

Regaining consciousness, Danielle smells exhaust and mildew. Her skull throbbing with pain, she tries to open her eyes, but somehow, can't. Then she realizes that they *are* open, and it's pitch black, and the bed is vibrating.

No—she isn't in her bed; she feels thin, rough carpet against the side of her face. Bewildered, she tries to make sense of it.

Is she in a car? A moving car? The trunk of a moving car? But how . . . ?

It comes back to her slowly.

She overslept. . . .

She was leaving for work. . . .

She walked outside, heard an unfamiliar voice, turned, and saw the van sitting just steps away from the door. . . .

And then . . .

Nothing.

This can't be happening. Not to me.

Please let it just be a dream.

Oh, God. Oh, God. The horror of it swirls around her, settles over her like a clammy tarp.

Someone knocked her out, abducted her. It *isn't* a dream.

It's a nightmare.

And she's not going to wake up.

Chapter Nineteen

"Lucinda?"

Startled to hear someone call her name as she walks into the Denver airport terminal from the gate, she looks around for a familiar face.

There isn't one.

For a split second, she wonders if it's *him*—lying in wait for her here, about to ambush her.

In the middle of a crowded airport, surrounded by security and even uniformed cops?

Not likely.

Spotting an older, unfamiliar man waving at her, she approaches hesitantly, looking around to make sure there are plenty of big, strong guys in the vicinity.

"Lucinda Sloan."

"Yes."

"Victor Shattuck."

Relieved, she shakes his hand. "You came out here to meet me?"

"I had time to kill. No pun intended."

She can't help but smile at his wry expression.

"How did you know it was me?" she asks him.

"Like I said, I had time to kill. I looked you up on the Internet. You have an impressive record, Ms. Sloan. And as soon as I saw your photo, I knew why your name sounded so familiar. I saw you on television last year when you were looking into that old suicide case."

"You have a good memory."

"Goes with the territory. Did you find the information you were looking for back then?"

"No." Does she dare tell him that the suicide might be tied into this case as well?

Not yet. Take it slowly.

Former FBI or not, the man is a total stranger—and right now, her instincts are telling her not to trust anyone.

"Did you check luggage?"

She shakes her head and shows him the overnight bag she'd brought with her to Cam's yesterday. "This is it. I left in a hurry."

"So did I."

"What brought you out here?"

"He sent an e-mail from a hotel in Denver."

"And . . . ?"

"And the FBI is on it. I'm just an author these days, so I have no clue what they've found so far."

"How about you? Have you found anything yet?"

"Working on it. I was at the hotel earlier. I've got a rental car. Come on."

"Where are we going? Back to the hotel?"

"We could . . . but something tells me you might have a better idea."

She looks at him, wondering whether to trust him with the address Neal gave her when she called him right after she landed.

"The police and the FBI will be there," Neal told her. "They'll be expecting you."

"As a potential witness, or as a psychic?"

"Probably a little of both."

"I don't know," she tells Vic, who's neither. "I was going to rent a car of my own—"

He reaches abruptly into his pocket, and she instinctively winces—before she sees that he's merely pulled out his wallet.

"What? Did you think I was going for a weapon?"

"Yes," she admits.

"Good. Your guard is up. It should be." He opens the wallet. "This is my ID. Just so you know that I am who I say I am and not . . ."

"The Night Watchman." She leans in to inspect his identification.

"Satisfied?"

"How do I know this isn't fake? How can I be sure you're not really him, trying to trick me?"

"I guess you can never really be sure of anything, where he's concerned. And you shouldn't assume anything . . . except that he's going to kill again, and again, and there's not a minute to waste."

She thinks that over for a long moment.

Surely her instincts would warn her loud and clear if she were this close to the killer himself.

Remembering that another woman's life might be hanging in the balance, she makes up her mind.

"All right. Let's go."

As he drives high into the mountains west of Denver, with the radio turned up to drown out the sound of thumping from the trunk, he has plenty of time to think.

He thinks about Scarlet.

She moved into the building when he was seventeen and beginning to think that he'd never have what the other boys had.

Sure, he wanted a girlfriend. Had wanted one for a while by then.

But girls didn't like him.

He was too tall and gawky-looking, and he never knew what to say or how to behave when he was around them, other than to laugh. His laughter made them nervous. Anyway, he was rarely around girls because he didn't have the freedom everyone else on the block had.

Mama's boy, the kids always called him, when they weren't calling him Hyena.

He didn't mind so much when he was younger. Why would he? His mother took care of him—cooked for him and disciplined him when he was bad and kept him locked inside to protect him from all the scary things that were out there, beyond the door of their South Bronx apartment.

She couldn't protect his father, though. He'd been gunned down on the street one sunny afternoon.

He remembers how they were walking along one minute, holding hands. And then there was a loud explosion, and then his father pulled him down as he fell. He remembers his father's blood everywhere, on the sidewalk, a red river spilling into the gutter.

He remembers it, warm and sticky on his hands. Remembers putting his fingers into his mouth to get it off, remembers the salty taste of his father's blood.

Remembers the sirens and his mother's screams.

She wasn't the same, after that day.

Neither was he. He was bad—really, really bad. His mother had to discipline him all the time, for his own good.

"Don't you cry," she'd warn him. "Only babies cry."

He remembers the salty taste of his own blood, too.

Blood.

Red.

Scarlet.

It always comes back to her. Beautiful Scarlet, as tall as

he and a few years older, with a throaty, sexy voice and long, flowing hair and exotic false eyelashes and red lipstick to match her skintight dresses.

"Do you wear red all the time because of your name?" he asked her one day, as he helped her carry her groceries up the stairs to her apartment.

"I have my name because I wear red all the time," was her cryptic answer.

"You mean Scarlet isn't your real name?"

She smiled. "No."

"What is it?"

But she refused to tell him. He'd beg and tease, and she'd laugh at his guesses. It became a game with them.

"Is it Agnes?" he'd ask. "Helga? Hortense?"

He never got it right. He was hoping he wouldn't, because then the game would have to end.

Once, when he picked her a bouquet of wild sweet peas he found growing in the vacant lot, she kissed his cheek.

"Thank you, lover boy," she said.

Later, he looked in the mirror and saw that her red, red lips were imprinted there, on his skin. He didn't wash it off.

Then his mother came home and saw it. "What is that?" she demanded suspiciously, gripping his jaw in the vise of her thumb and forefinger. "Where did it come from?"

He pretended he had no idea.

Of course, she didn't believe him.

Of course, she punished him.

For once, he didn't even flinch. It was worth it, because he had Scarlet now.

Then the punishment was over—or so he believed—and his mother made him get up off the floor.

"You can march into the bathroom and wash that away right this instant," she told him, and he thought she was talking about the blood coming from the slashes on his arms where his father's old belt had ripped open his skin.

But she was talking about the lipstick on his face.

When he wouldn't, couldn't move, she dragged him to the bathroom, and she scrubbed his face with scalding hot water and soap until the red lipstick kiss was gone.

Only then did he flinch.

Only then did he feel as though he was being punished.

Still, he didn't cry.

Only babies cry.

And besides, he had Scarlet.

Lucinda gradually allows herself to relax as Victor Shattuck drives along the streets of Denver in the glare of late day sun, heading for the address Neal had given her.

Danielle Hendry, the woman whose phone sent the text message, has gone missing.

She overslept this morning, told a friend she was on her way to work, then never showed up. The friend did say that she had an acrimonious relationship with her ex-husband back in L.A., and that a former boyfriend had been stalking her.

Vic Shattuck, of course, had known about none of this.

He, in turn, has information for Lucinda: she isn't the only one who's been hearing from the Night Watchman these past few months. He's received several messages, the first of which coincided with Carla Barakat's death.

"How did you know it was from him?"

"Red lipstick."

"Of course." Lucinda nods, glad he can't see her expression behind her sunglasses as he darts a glance at her.

"Of course?" he echoes.

"The Night Watchman smeared it on his victims' lips."

"How did you know that?"

She didn't, for sure.

Not until now.

"And there were no exceptions," she guesses, her thoughts racing.

"No. Why?"

Before she can reply, he follows up with a question of his own. "The victims in Beach Haven and Chicago—they were smeared with red lipstick too, weren't they?"

She hesitates.

Then she levels a look at him. "How did you know that?"

He gives a satisfied nod. "Touché."

"So we have a pattern. He strikes when there's a full moon, women who live alone, and he has a red lipstick fetish. No sexual contact with the victims, though. Isn't that unusual?"

"No. It's a myth that serial killers are always sexually motivated. Most are, but some aren't."

"So he's unusual."

"In more ways than that. Most serial killers tend to stick fairly close to home—within their comfort zone. The Night Watchman never did. He struck randomly up and down the East Coast. This time, he appears to be moving east to west instead, but he once again favors metropolitan areas—probably because the population is transient and he'll be less visible."

"And did he leave an engraved wristwatch on the wrists of his victims?"

Vic looks at her, and she has her answer. He didn't know about this.

"That's a new trick. *Watch. Watchman.* He wants no mistake made about who is behind this new wave. What does the engraving say?"

"Date the victim was killed, and the longitude and latitude. And he removes the battery after the victim dies so that the watch stops."

Looking thoughtful, Vic asks her to repeat that. Then he shakes his head decisively.

"He isn't removing the battery *after* the victim dies. He's removing it before."

"What do you mean? How do you know?"

"Because three days before Jaime Dobiak died, he sent me a message that gave not just the date, but the exact time of her death. Did she die at 7:05 P.M.?"

"Around then." Her thoughts tumble over each other. "So he's planning the murders right down to the minute?"

"It looks that way. The numbers have some significance to him."

"We have to tell the FBI."

Vic flashes her a grim smile. "Trust me. They're on it. They have all the pieces and the technology and manpower and resources to put them together. I guarantee you they're way ahead of us."

Maybe so, she thinks. But they're operating with just five senses.

Lucinda has six.

"Can I ask you something about the Night Watchman's crimes in the past, Mr. Shattuck?"

"Call me Vic."

She tells him, briefly, about Ava Neary, and her original suspicion that she might have been one of the Night Watchman's earliest victims.

He's shaking his head before she even finishes speaking. "I don't think so. You said he threw her from a rooftop."

"Yes."

"Too many things don't fit. The Night Watchman always used a knife, he always killed the victim in her home, and he always staged the victim with the lipstick. It would be awfully challenging to stage a body that's fallen out of the sky, for one thing. And for another, this took place a while after he killed his last known victim, Judy Steinberg. He never let more than a month or two go by between murders. Unless he committed a bunch of murders that were undetected between Judy Steinberg and Ava Neary—and unless he completely changed his M.O.—I'd say there's no way in hell he killed Ava."

Then who did? Lucinda wonders grimly as they turn onto Danielle Hendry's street.

* * *

"Hello?"

"Is this Dr. William Zubin?"

"Yes, it is."

It is. It's him.

Cam grips the edge of the kitchen counter to steady herself.

"Who's calling, please?"

Ignoring the question, she tells him, just as she practiced, "I attended a discussion you recently gave at the Museum of Natural History, and I was wondering if you would mind meeting with me to answer a few questions I have."

She holds her breath, praying he'll say yes, knowing that it's a long shot.

"Are you a student?"

"Yes."

"And your name is . . . ?"

"Clair Montgomery." She was prepared for the question.

*Mont—clair. Clair—Mont*gomery.

The lies are stacking up, but she doesn't dare tell him any semblance of the truth, mindful that if he really did have anything to do with Ava's death—and any inkling that she's Ava's sister—he'd never in a million years agree to speak with her.

It might even be dangerous.

"I could meet with you at your convenience, Dr. Zubin, and I won't take up much of your time at all."

"My dear, I have all the time in the world these days," he tells her with a good-natured chuckle.

Hearing it, she wonders if she's barking up the wrong tree. Does she really believe this kindly-sounding old man is a coldhearted killer?

You believe—no, you know—that he cheated on his wife and took advantage of an innocent young girl.

Okay, true. But everyone makes mistakes. A lot of people are immoral. It doesn't make them murderers.

"Why don't you name the time and place, Ms. Montgomery?"

She hesitates, wondering if she should just forget the whole thing.

But regardless of whether he had anything to do with her sister's death, he was involved with Ava shortly before it happened.

He might know something.

She suggests meeting at the Starbucks on Astor Place at seven-thirty. Mike will be home by then. Ordinarily, Cam wouldn't hesitate to leave the baby with just Tess, but she isn't sure Tess can handle the responsibility. These days, she can barely take care of herself.

"I'm afraid I have other plans this evening," Dr. Zubin tells her. "I could meet you there tomorrow, though, at noon, if that works."

"That's fine." She'll just have to bring Grace with her. Maybe that's better. In broad daylight, with the baby in tow . . . It's probably safer.

She hangs up the telephone.

"We're going to find out what happened to your aunt," she tells little Grace, who looks up solemnly from her bouncy seat on the floor beside the desk. "One way or another."

Vic slows the car as they cruise alongside a row of brick townhouses—their destination ahead made obvious by a couple of dark Suburbans and a police cruiser parked at the curb.

A rugged cop, who looks like he'd be right at home in a saddle out on the cattle range, steps out into the road, holding out his hand.

Vic rolls down the window.

"Do you live down this way, folks?"

"No, but we know there's an investigation—they're expecting us."

"Who are you?"

"My name is Victor Shattuck. Retired FBI." He shows I.D.

"And I'm Detective Lucinda Sloan," she says, leaning across from the seat beside him.

"Wait here."

As the cop steps away from the car and speaks into his radio, Vic reminds her in a low voice, "They're not expecting *me.*"

"They need all the help they can get. You'll be fine."

"Is that a psychic observation?"

She hesitates, then flashes him a grin. "Sure. Why not."

Moments later, the cop simply waves them past.

Vic looks at Lucinda. "You're either the real deal or your name has some serious pull."

"Both," she tells him with a satisfied smile.

The scene in front of the townhouse is discreet, as Vic expected. It isn't a crime scene—yet. He suspects they'll be canvassing the neighborhood if they aren't already.

As Vic pulls into a parking space, he spots Annabelle Wyatt stepping out of the townhouse in a tailored black pantsuit, wearing an expectant look on her face.

"Who's that?" Lucinda asks.

"My old boss."

"Strictly no nonsense with her, huh?"

"Is that a psychic observation?"

"No," Lucinda says flatly, "that's obvious."

Annabelle strides toward them, arriving just as Vic turns off the ignition.

"I didn't realize you two knew each other," she greets him as he opens the car door.

"Lucinda and me? Oh, we go way back."

"Really?"

"No. That was a joke."

She just looks at him.

I see she hasn't lost her sparkling sense of humor, Vic thinks.

"Actually, we just met." He gestures at Lucinda, coming around from the other side of the car. "Lucinda, this is Special Agent Annabelle Wyatt. Annabelle, Lucinda Sloan, the famous psychic detective."

Annabelle, he notices, doesn't bat an eye. So she knows exactly who—and what—Lucinda is. Interesting.

"I don't ordinarily work with psychics," she tells Lucinda, "though some agents have. But your colleague Detective Bullard tells me that you've got quite a track record with missing persons and frankly, we've got nothing to lose. I'd like you to come inside and see what you can tell us."

"Absolutely."

Annabelle turns to Vic. "I'd appreciate your input, as well."

He raises an eyebrow. "Really?"

"I heard what happened last night—the e-mail. We know who we're dealing with. He's back, and he's obviously playing cat and mouse with you—with both of you." She sweeps a long, elegant hand to include Lucinda. "His moves are growing bolder. So will ours. Let's go."

Sitting on the rug before the open bureau drawer, Randy packs the last of Carla's jeans into a cardboard box to be donated to a women's shelter.

He saved the bedroom—her clothes—for last.

The rest of the house was relatively easy. There wasn't much to pack up, other than in the kitchen. Nothing sentimental about pots and pans, plates, and utensils. No memories there.

In the bathroom, where she died, he hurriedly swept the contents of the medicine cabinet and vanity into a black Hefty bag. Cosmetics, cleaning supplies, medication—everything went, even the shrink-wrapped new bottle of cough medicine and unopened box of Advil. He simply couldn't bring himself to linger there long enough to sort through anything.

It's different in the bedroom, with Carla's clothes.

He's made a separate little pile of things to keep: her favorite sweater, crocheted by her mother, that she pretty much lived in every winter; the tennis bracelet he'd given her on their first anniversary; her wedding dress and veil, of course.

He was surprised to find that she hadn't gotten rid of them. How could he be the one to toss them?

There's no one upon whom he can bestow these things, but it would feel wrong to give them to strangers. He supposes he'll keep them as mementos of the woman with whom he shared his life for a while.

The box is full.

The drawer is empty.

He closes it, stands, and looks around.

Tomorrow, they'll come to cart the furniture away into a storage unit he rented. He'll have his cottage through Memorial Day weekend. After that, the owners return, and he'll have to find a new place to live. It won't be easy, during the high season on the island.

Maybe he should move away.

To the mainland.

Back to Philly, maybe.

But Lucinda made it clear that she isn't ready to let anyone—not even him—into her life.

It's just not time yet, Randy thinks, as he walks back through the empty house. *It's still too soon.*

"Still too soon," he informs Danielle Hendry, who lies, bound and gagged, on the muddy ground.

Relishing the terror in her eyes as she looks up at him, he taps the face of his watch.

"You've got about ten minutes left. Do you have any last requests? I'll be happy to oblige, if I can."

She grunts.

He cups a hand behind his ear. "What's that? You'll have to enunciate, dear. I can't understand a word you're saying."

She writhes violently at his feet, spattering and smearing her pale yellow suit with even more mud.

"You know what you look like?" he asks. "An overripe banana!"

Delighted laughter bubbles out of him, mingling with the sound of the rushing water of a nearby stream rippling down the mountainside. The release feels good after all the long hours of self-restraint.

She struggles on the ground, trying to roll away from him—as if she can actually go anywhere.

He gives her a hard, sharp kick in the soft flesh between her hip bone and rib cage and is rewarded by a primal howl.

Primal—primate, he thinks, and laughs even harder.

"You sound like a wounded ape! Ape . . . banana. Get it?"

The laughter pours out of him, loud and strong, echoing in the Colorado wilderness where there's no one to hear it.

Just as there will be no one to hear her screams when she dies, nine minutes from now, at precisely 7:44.

Lucinda stands on the small balcony off Danielle Hendry's bedroom, gazing at the fiery ball of orange sinking low in a glowing sky over the distant Rockies.

Somewhere inside, Vic and Annabelle and the others are following up on the information Lucinda was able to give them.

It wasn't much to go on, though.

She felt that Danielle had been abducted close to home, but not from inside the house—which was consistent with the fact that they'd found things undisturbed, no signs of a struggle.

Yet when Lucinda walked through the house—through the kitchen, up the stairs, into the bedroom—she could feel him doing the same thing.

"He was inside," she told the agents.

"Before he abducted her?"

"No, earlier. She was abducted during the day. He was inside at night. In the dark. And she was here, too, in the house."

"Did he take her hostage?" Annabelle asked.

"No. She didn't know he was here." Lucinda shuddered, remembering her own vision, back at home, of someone stealing into her bedroom while she was asleep.

It was so chilling that she found it difficult to focus on Danielle Hendry, though she tried her best, for over an hour.

There were framed photos around the house—of Danielle with friends, and with her college-aged sons.

In all of them, Lucinda noted, she wore red lipstick.

She pointed it out to the others, speculating that it might have been what captured the Night Watchman's attention.

Now, having stepped outside to get some fresh air and clear her head, she thinks again about what Victor Shattuck told her in the car.

If the Night Watchman didn't kill Ava Neary—or, for that matter, Sandra Wubner and the other so-called suicides—then why did he want Lucinda to think he did?

He could be playing with her.

Taunting her.

SOLV IT AND IF YOU ARE WRIGHT YOU WILL FIND ME.

It's almost as if . . .

Can he be giving them a clue to his own identity, rather than letting them know that he killed Ava and the others?

Maybe he *doesn't* want her to think he did it. Maybe he's trying to tell her that in solving the mystery surrounding Ava's death, she'll unlock the key to the Night Watchman murders.

As she watches the last sliver of sun disappear behind a distant peak, she hears a female scream so bloodcurdling that she spins around in horror, thinking it came from right beside her.

There's no one there.

Beyond the French doors, which are ajar, she can see the others, can hear the murmur of their voices spilling out into the night.

They obviously didn't hear the scream.

Okay.

So it came from inside your head.

And so, she realizes a moment later, as another sound reaches her ears, *did that.*

He's laughing, again.

He's killing, again.

Right now.

Where? Where is he?

Is he with Danielle? Is he killing Danielle?

Lucinda squeezes her eyes shut, desperately trying to focus, trying to see her, to see him, to hear more than just that heinous laughter.

She has to get into his head.

Who is dying, dammit? I need to see her. I need her name.

Only one word comes to mind.

Scarlet.

The ground is soaked with Danielle Hendry's blood.

It's likely to draw a good many creatures from their lairs now that night has fallen.

He swings his flashlight beam over her face, admiring the fixed expression of terror in her eyes and the way the blood dribbling from the corner of her mouth is the precise shade of her lipstick.

He used her own this time, having found it conveniently located in her purse. He even made her put it on herself, but her hand was shaking so badly that she made a real mess of things.

He waited until she was dead to touch it up, and to fasten the watch around her wrist. Now everything is just right.

It's a pity to leave her here, where she won't be found before the nocturnal animals come out to feed and destroy his *tableau*.

"But leave you I must," he tells her. "It's time to move on."

"Is she finally asleep?" Mike looks up from the opening pitch of the baseball game as Cam walks into the master bedroom.

"Which 'she'?"

"Grace. Isn't she the one you were putting to bed?"

"She went right down. Then I looked in on Tess. I've been in with her this whole time."

"Did you talk some sense into her?" Mike moves over and pats the spot next to him on the bed. He's shed his jacket and tie but is still wearing the suit pants and dress shirt he'd had on when he walked in the door from work a half hour ago.

Cam sits and pulls off her gold post earrings. "I mostly just listened while she talked."

"About him?"

"About why he doesn't love her anymore."

"Did you tell her that there is no such thing as love when you're fourteen?"

"She's fifteen," Cam reminds him, "and no, I didn't say that, because I don't believe it."

"I hate seeing her this way." He unbuttons his cuff links.

"So do I. Do you think I should make an appointment for her to talk to someone?"

Mike looks at her. "Not yet. Give it another couple of days and if she doesn't pull herself together, then we'll see." He shakes his head. "I still can't believe she managed to get through being abducted by a maniac and seeing someone die right in front of her with no problem, but this little jerk breaks her heart and she falls apart."

"I'm wondering if everything is catching up with her now, though. Maybe this is a delayed reaction to all the stress of last summer. Speaking of which . . ."

"Uh-oh." In the process of stripping off his shirt, he looks up expectantly.

"I'm going to talk to my sister's old geology professor tomorrow in the city."

"Cam, you know I don't—"

"I have to do this, Mike."

"It could be dangerous."

"It won't be. My gut feeling about him is that he had nothing to do with Ava's death. Maybe it really was a suicide, who knows?"

"Lucinda doesn't seem to think so."

"Lucinda might be wrong."

"Do you think she is?"

"I don't know," she admits. "But I am pretty sure that if this Dr. Zubin were dangerous, I'd have a sense of it. And I don't."

"You could be wrong."

"I rarely am," she reminds him with a smile. "And anyway, I'm meeting him in a public place, at a Starbucks in the Village. Don't worry."

"When tomorrow?"

"Noon. Why?"

"I'll go with you." He stands and tosses the shirt into the hamper.

"You'll be at work. How are you going to get away in the middle of the day? You're lucky you got out of there at a decent hour tonight."

"I'll work it out. There's no way I'm letting you go talk to this guy alone."

"Because *you* have a sense that he might be dangerous?"

she asks, rubbing her temples, thinking she's starting to feel a little bit dizzy.

"Because I don't know what to think, and because you're my wife and I love you." Mike steps out of his dress pants and reaches for a wooden hanger.

"But I'm sure I'll be—"

"I'm not taking any chances on my family, ever again. I'm coming with you, and that's that. Okay?"

She nods, watching him fold the pants onto the hanger, snap the dowel over the fold, hang the pants in the closet.

"I'm going to go take a shower," he tells her.

"Um . . . I made dinner for us."

"Okay, I'll be quick."

Cam leans back against the pillows as he leaves the room. She's definitely dizzy, a telltale sign that she's about to experience another premonition.

Sure enough, closing her eyes, she again sees the girl with the old-fashioned hair and dress and lipstick. She's crying, cowering as the tall figure of a man stands over her with a knife.

He's laughing, Cam realizes. Laughing hard, as if it's all a big joke.

But it isn't.

He brings the knife down, and the girl's anguished scream mingles with his laughter, and Cam glimpses his face.

Weathered-looking features, cold black eyes, and gray hair.

Then the vision dissolves, leaving her to wonder, helplessly, who—and where—the girl is.

"All right, ladies, let's take it again from the top."

Still winded from the duet, Kelly Patterson crosses the stage to her mark.

Christina Hazelwood, who's playing Miss Adelaide, the second female lead, calls, "Wait a minute."

Watching Christina hurry down the steps and over to the

piano to confer with Gary, the student director, Kelly mutters "*Now* what?"

Hearing a snicker from the wings, she realizes that one of the male leads overheard her. Oops.

"Hey, Kelly, what's up? Did you upstage poor Christina again?" Julian Dodd—wearing a rakish grin and a Mariners' cap backward over his wavy dark hair—wags his finger at her. "You know she's the real star."

Kelly grins and rolls her eyes.

Five minutes pass.

Julian sits on the floor, cross-legged.

Five more minutes pass, and Kelly joins him as the stagehands sneak off for a smoke break.

"At this rate we're going to be here all night," Kelly says, watching Christina consulting so fervently with Gary over the script that you'd think this was Broadway, rather than a college production.

Granted, U-Dub is no small-scale school. But still . . .

"Got someplace better to be?"

"My room. I've got to finish a paper for Modern American Lit."

"Yeah, well, showbiz ain't easy, Doll," Julian tells her in his best Sky Masterson accent.

No, it ain't.

Maybe she shouldn't have auditioned, on a whim, for the musical production. It's not as if she's set foot on a stage since her friends coaxed her to sing a Backstreet Boys song with them in a middle school talent show.

But back in January, entering her second semester, feeling homesick for Spokane and lost on the vast campus, Kelly decided to take her parents' advice. It might help to be a part of something—even if it was just a small chorus part in a musical.

To her shock, she landed the plum lead role of Sarah Brown—coveted, and wrongly reported to have been sewn up, by campus diva Christina, a senior.

It doesn't take a casting director to see that vampy, campy Christina is perfect as Miss Adelaide, the hot box dancer. Kelly—a slight, brown-eyed brunette—may not be perfect as Sarah, but she's doing her best. She enjoys being in the spotlight for the first time in her life, and it's brought her out of her shell. People who never even knew she existed have been noticing her lately.

"All right, Kelly, everyone, Christina would like to try blocking the scene in a different way," Gary announces from the shadows in front of the stage.

Julian groans aloud.

Kelly groans inwardly.

This is going to take forever. She's going to be up all night finishing her paper.

Oh, well. In a few weeks, she tells herself, it'll all be worth it, when she's standing on this stage in the spotlight before a live audience, singing "Marry the Man Today," wearing Sarah Brown's vintage 1950s dress and hairstyle and red lipstick.

Chapter Twenty

Watching the numbers on the digital clock on the hotel nightstand roll over from 5:59 to 6:00 in the glare of a too-bright bedside bulb, Lucinda realizes she's not going to fall asleep.

She's been trying since she got into bed an hour and a half ago, her body aching with exhaustion and the relentless tension of a night spent waiting around for something to happen.

Nothing had.

No sign of Danielle Hendry, no leads, no communication from the Night Watchman.

Just as she's wondering whether to get up, or stay in bed and hope that sleep will overtake her, she hears the distinct rumbling sound that means her BlackBerry is about to start ringing.

At this hour?

Then she remembers that it's a decent hour back on the East Coast, and no one—other than Neal and Cam—is aware she's not there.

She gets out of bed and fishes the ringing phone from her bag.

It's Randy.

Again.

He called Lucinda's cell phone a few times last night, too, wondering why she hasn't called back yet, wanting to know where she is. And worrying.

"I can't help it," he said in the last message, late last night. "I'll admit it. I'm worried that I haven't heard from you. Look, maybe you're still mad at me. That's fine. Be mad. Just call and tell me you're okay."

She didn't call.

But she did send him an e-mail that said simply, I'm fine, busy on an investigation, will explain all later.

She can just imagine what he'd say if she told him the case involves staking out a serial killer halfway across the country, on the heels of the killer's texting her from the phone of a woman who has now gone missing.

She lets the call go into voice mail again. Partly because she's just too exhausted to deal with a potentially emotional confrontation right now, and partly because she's pretty sure her voice is all but gone by now. It was hoarse when she climbed into bed.

Sleep would have helped, but it's too late for that.

She crosses to the window and parts the thick vinyl-backed curtains to see if it's light out yet.

No, but almost.

The eastern skyline's rectangular silhouettes sit against a blue-black backdrop streaked orange along the base.

Remembering last night's spectacular mountain sunset—and the chilling omen that came with it—Lucinda thinks about Danielle Hendry.

The glowing rim of the sun appears in the distance—and that's when it hits her.

Walking out to the edge of the driveway on a gray morning amid the steady beeping of a truck in reverse, Neal glances down the street at the latest neighborhood construction zone.

Two doors down, next door to Garland Fisher's house, they're putting in a massive two-story addition. What are they thinking? The old houses on the block sit close together on modest lots just big enough for a patch of lawn, a few shrubs, and a driveway. Who needs that much house?

Shaking his head, Neal picks up his newspaper and unfolds it to read the front page headlines, one of which involves a case he'd been working on. A guy who has a questionable source of income and whose name might as well be Pauly Walnuts disappears from his house in South Philly, and everyone around him—including his wife—denies mob ties. Everyone—including his wife—claims he probably ran off with a mistress.

Now he turns up with a bullet through his temple, execution style. As far as Neal's concerned, his friends and family are either seriously deluded, or bold-faced liars.

"Morning, neighbor!"

He looks up to see Garland Fisher waving through the open window of his car, pulling into his driveway beside a bank of forsythia in full bloom. He gets out, picks up his own newspaper, then looks over at the construction vehicles.

"Crazy over there, isn't it?" he calls to Neal.

"It sure is. What are you doing out and about so early? Did all that noise wake you up?"

"How'd you guess?"

"Because it woke me, too."

"Should be some kind of ordinance against starting at that hour."

"There is," Neal tells him, just as Erma sticks her head out the front door. Her hair is in the curlers she sleeps in, and she's wearing her robe.

"Neal! Lucinda's on the phone! Oh, good morning, Garland."

"Morning, Erma," he calls back, before saying to Neal, "Lucinda—I've met her. You didn't tell me she was a psychic, though."

"Who did?"

"Erma. Said she helps you solve cases. Does she ever, you know, get in contact with dead people?"

Already on his way toward the door, Neal is struck by the odd question and turns back.

"Dead people? Why?"

"Seen it on TV—you know, those people who can talk to the dead. Was thinking maybe I could get someone to put me in touch with my wife."

At a loss for words, Neal simply shakes his head.

"Oh, well. Worth a try. Have a good day, Neal."

"You, too." He closes the door.

"You make sure you get that tea with honey and lemon," Erma is saying into the phone. "Feel better. Here's Neal."

He takes the receiver. "What's the matter, Cin? Are you sick?"

"No," she rasps.

"You sound awful."

"I didn't get to bed until after four."

"I won't bother to ask you if you've heard anything new since then," Neal tells her. "I probably know more than you do right now." He's already been up for a while, keeping apprised of the situation from this end.

"Did Danielle Hendry turn up?"

"She's still missing, as far as I know. We've been checking out the name you mentioned—Scarlet."

"And . . . ?"

"And nothing. There are no reports anywhere of a missing person by the name of Scarlet, first or last."

"All right. I figured it was worth a shot."

"It was. Are you sure it's a name, though?"

"No. But it felt like it. Listen, Neal, I need you to look up something for me. I don't have access to the Internet right now."

"What is it?" He's already on his way into the den, where the computer is.

"Check the sunset time for Chicago on March 20."

Not bothering to ask her why, he sits at the desk and does a quick search. The information comes up within seconds.

"7:05 P.M."

"He killed her at sunset. That's why he knew in advance. Check the sunset for Beach Haven on February 21."

Catching on, Neal types in the request. "5:40."

"That's what time Carla's watch stopped. That's when she died. At sunset. On the night when the moon was full. That's the pattern."

"Cin, spare your voice. I get it."

"It happened again last night. I was watching the sun set over the mountains, and I heard it—I heard what he was doing."

"Killing Danielle Hendry."

He hears her try to clear her throat, but all that comes out is a whispery squeak. "I should go."

"Tell the FBI about this, Cin. Right away. Oh, and wait— Randy called me last night. This morning, too. He didn't get me, and I haven't called him back yet. I wasn't sure how much he knew."

"He doesn't know anything."

"He's going to ask me what's going on."

"Then tell him," she says simply, with all the voice she can muster.

"How long are you going to stay out there?"

"As long as it takes."

"As long as it takes for what?"

"To find Danielle Hendry. To find out who or what this Scarlet is. To apprehend this sick bastard before the next full moon."

He hangs up to see Erma watching him from the doorway.

"I worry about her, Neal."

"So do I." He shrugs. "What can I do? She's got a mind of her own."

"She shouldn't be so alone. Nobody should. But sometimes people don't see that until someone points it out for them."

He knows immediately where she's going with this . . . and he's not going along.

"You know I'm not the type to interfere in someone's personal life, and even if I were, Lucinda isn't the type to listen."

"She tried salad. She liked it."

"We're not talking about salad."

"We're talking about things that are good for her." Erma pauses. "Are you seeing Randy Barakat any time soon?"

Neal sighs. "Even if I saw him, I wouldn't—"

"All right. I know, I know. You wouldn't get involved."

Pushing the baby stroller into the Astor Place Starbucks at noon, Cam immediately sees that the place is jammed with students from the NYU buildings down at the opposite end of the block. Every table is full, and there's a long line from the wide counter to where they stand at the door.

"How are we going to find him in this zoo?" she asks Mike, dismayed. "I wish we at least knew what Zubin looks like."

She couldn't ask him that when they spoke on the phone yesterday. Not after telling him she'd been at his museum lecture.

"I think we can safely assume he'll be the one without the tattoos, piercings, or ponytail," Mike tells her.

"This isn't really a good time to be cracking jokes."

"I'm serious. That rules out ninety-nine percent of the people in here."

She looks around. Okay, he's right about that.

"You stay here with Grace. I'll take a walk through and look for an older guy."

Watching her husband make his way through the crowd, looking authoritative in his dark business suit, she's glad he came with her. She's out of her element here—in the Village, in the city. It's hard to believe there was ever a time when this was her home, her life. She belongs across the river in the Jersey suburbs now. Then again, when Mike moved out last year, the house in Montclair felt foreign to her too.

Thank God he came back.

Thank God we have this beautiful baby.

Thank God Tess wasn't hurt by that lunatic who abducted her.

Thoughts of Tess lead, as always lately, to thoughts of Ava.

The courtyard beside the academic building where Cam's sister fell to her death is just a few blocks away from here.

Mike reappears in the doorway of the glassed-in section that faces the sidewalk along Astor, waving her over.

So he found Dr. William Zubin.

Cam pushes the stroller through the crowd, steeling herself for whatever lies ahead.

Vic Shattuck never went to bed.

Why bother at four in the morning?

Instead, he used the wireless Internet in his hotel room to search for clues about Scarlet.

Lucinda seems to think it's the name of a recent—or even future—victim of the Night Watchman.

Vic isn't so sure.

Now, as he heads down to the hotel restaurant to meet Annabelle Wyatt for coffee, he's surprised, again, that she agreed.

When he called her an hour ago—having waited until a decent hour—to tell her he wanted to run something by her, he expected her to say she was sleeping, or busy, or leaving town . . . some excuse.

But she asked him when and where, and told him she'd be there.

Maybe he shouldn't be surprised. Last night, as they went over the details of the case beginning with the Jersey Shore murder, she treated him almost as though he'd never left.

Don't call us, we'll call you.

Annabelle Wyatt didn't call him—but he's here. And she needs his help, whether she knows it or not.

He walks into the hotel restaurant and sees her immediately, sitting in a secluded booth near the window with a cup of coffee. Her back is to him, but she turns when he's a few yards from the table, makes eye contact, nods.

"Good morning," she says briskly. "Let's get right to it. I have a lot to do."

He slides into the bench opposite hers, orders a cup of coffee and two eggs over easy.

"Aren't you getting anything?" he asks, as the waitress hurries away.

"I ate breakfast three hours ago. Don't be offended if I leave before your food comes."

"I won't."

Annabelle steeples her fingers beneath her chin. "Tell me."

"You know that Lucinda Sloan came up with the name Scarlet last night."

"Yes. It doesn't match any current missing persons records."

"You checked?"

"We check everything."

"I know that. But did you check past records? As in, forty years ago?"

"No. Explain what you mean."

"My profile on the Night Watchman told me the unsub was likely reenacting the same murder over and over. Which you know."

"Which I know."

She isn't impatient, just efficient, he reminds himself. He has to get used to her again, after eighteen months away.

"If that were the case," he goes on, "it would follow that he might—in the act of killing—consider every victim to be the original. Correct?"

"Possibly."

"That means he would be thinking of the original victim whenever he kills."

"You just said that."

"Which means we should be looking for a woman named Scarlet who was killed forty years ago somewhere on the eastern seaboard."

Annabelle Wyatt stares at him for a long, satisfying moment.

"Is that all?"

"That's all."

"Good." She stands, checks her watch. "Good work, Shattuck."

"Is that all?" he shoots back at her. "Just 'good work'?"

"No. How soon can you get to Quantico? I'll arrange the clearance."

Vic Shattuck breaks into a slow grin. "My bags are packed, and I'm on my way. Is that quick enough for you?"

She's already on her feet. "Don't forget to eat your eggs first. And Vic?"

"Yes?"

"Breakfast is on me."

The first thing Cam notices is that Dr. Zubin is completely bald. Fashion statement? Or simply age?

Before she has time to decide, Mike gestures in her direction, and the man turns expectantly toward her.

The glint of recognition in his eyes is unmistakable.

He knows, Cam realizes. *He knows I'm related to Ava.*

Remembering what Bernice said about seeing Cam on television last summer, she acknowledges that the resemblance to her sister would be unmistakable to the few people who have seen both Ava at twenty and Cam as a grown woman. The last pictures of her sister look very much like Cam does now. They have the same long, straight dark hair, the same big round dark eyes, the same olive complexion.

He knows, and yet he doesn't look fearful, or suspicious.

He just looks surprised. And, incredibly, fondly nostalgic.

There's no need to go on with the ruse.

"Dr. Zubin, my name isn't Clair Montgomery. It's Cam Hastings. Cam *Neary* Hastings."

"Camden. Ava's little sister."

Her given name on his lips catches her off guard.

"She spoke of you often."

Cam's eyes widen. Her throat unexpectedly clogged with emotion, she looks at Mike.

He asks, "You were close to Ava, then, Dr. Rubin?"

"I was in love with Ava."

Shocked by the unabashed admission, Cam had expected to confront Dr. Zubin with the photocopies of Ava's letters she tucked into her purse—having left the original packet of envelopes safely at home. Just in case, she thought at the time, the professor somehow grabbed hold of them and made off with them.

Now, the idea seems preposterous.

"Why don't we all sit down?" he asks, then leans toward the baby, asleep in her stroller. "And who have we here? She's precious."

"That's Grace," Cam manages, and he smiles an avuncular smile.

"You're blessed. I always wanted children. My first wife couldn't have them, and my second had three of her own, in their teens already when we met."

Cam doesn't know what to say to that. Of all the scenarios she'd imagined, this warm, fuzzy one never came anywhere near her mind.

She doubts Mike expected it either, but he's recovered more quickly. "You said you were in love with Ava—was that before or after your first wife?"

Anticipating a lie, Cam is surprised once again.

"It was during. That's not something I'm proud of. In fact, of all the missteps I've made along the way, getting involved with Ava is my biggest regret. She was young, and so was I—only a couple of years older than her. I was in an unhappy marriage. She was getting over losing her mother—did you ever find out what became of her?"

Cam tells him, quickly—in as little detail as possible. Then, getting the conversation back on track, she asks, "What do you know about my sister's death, Dr. Zubin?"

"I know that she took her own life. I was heartbroken— on some level, I blamed myself for what she had done."

"Because of the affair? Do you think she killed herself because of it?"

"No—we had parted ways by then. It was a mutual decision. We were on good terms. But I regretted not being more aware of just how troubled Ava was. I knew that she was still hurting over her mother, and feeling guilty for having left you and your father alone at home. And I knew that one of the young men she knew had been bothering her, too. But I was in the midst of separating from my wife, caught up in my own problems, and I didn't—"

"Wait a minute—someone was bothering her?" Cam cuts in.

"Yes. Ava was a beautiful girl. A lot of young men were interested in her. But this one wouldn't take no for an answer, she said, and he was driving her crazy."

"Who was he?" Mike asks. "Do you remember his name?"

The professor shakes his head. "Jack, maybe? Or John. Something like that. He was in one of her classes that semester."

Cam and Mike look at each other.

Dr. Zubin knits his gray brow. "Why do you ask?"

Ignoring the question, Cam says, "Ava didn't mention anything about this in her letters to a friend she was in touch with at the time. How long was it going on before she died?"

"Oh, not long. A few weeks maybe, as far as I know. Why do you ask?" he repeats.

"Because we're not sure my sister took her own life. There's some evidence that someone was on the rooftop before she jumped that night."

The professor's expression is grave. "Are the police aware of this?"

Cam can't tell him that the only evidence is a psychic vision—and a scrapbook, from an anonymous sender, that disappeared into thin air.

"Dr. Zubin, is there any way I could get my hands on the old school records that would list the other students in Ava's classes during her final semester? I'd like to try to identify this Jack or John person who wouldn't take no for an answer."

"You, personally? That would be a complicated process, unless you had a police—"

"What about you?" Mike cuts in. "Would you be able to help us?"

"Again, that would be—"

"Dr. Zubin, you knew my sister. You loved her. I loved her, and I needed her, and I lost her. All these years, I've believed she left me, like my mother did. I need to know the truth. Please help me find out how Ava died. Please."

The old professor looks at Cam for a long time, watches her take the napkin Mike silently hands her to dab at the tears running down her face.

"It might not be easy, and it's going to take some time," Dr. Zubin says at last, "but I'll see what I can do."

Neal is well aware that there are more than two thousand homeless teenagers in shelters across Philadelphia. Acting on a tip that a runaway foster kid he's been looking for might be somewhere among them, he's covered a lot of ground already today, with no luck.

It's been exhausting—to say nothing of disheartening. The youth doesn't want to be found. The city is full of lost souls who consider themselves no better off in foster care than they were before or would be on their own. They may be right.

Yet Neal doggedly pursues them, same as always. It used

to be because he cared. But somewhere along the way, that changed. Now he does it because it's his job.

Devouring a cheese steak at a lunch counter in a section of town that, like many, has seen better days, he allows himself to think about Lucinda.

And Randy.

Specifically, Lucinda and Randy, together.

Thank you, Erma.

Why am I worrying about this? It's none of my business.

When Neal called Randy back earlier and told him where Lucinda was, he wasn't thrilled. Nor was he surprised.

"She's done a lot of foolish things in her life, but this takes the cake."

"I wouldn't say that."

"She's done worse?"

"She's no fool, Randy. She knows exactly what she's doing, and she knows how to take care of herself better than anyone I've ever known. Myself included. So if I were you, I wouldn't go scolding her for running out to Denver. She does what she has to do. Always has, always will. Whoever tries to tell her to do anything different gets burned. Nobody knows that better than me."

"And me," Randy said ruefully. "Thanks for the reminder."

Neal isn't sure it'll do much good. Randy has a fierce protective streak about him, and it clashes with Lucinda's even fiercer independent streak.

Maybe they can meet each other halfway this time around—but Neal won't believe it unless he sees it.

And again—it's none of his business. No matter what Erma says.

His phone rings as he washes down the last bite of cheese steak with thin, lukewarm coffee. He throws a ten and some ones on the table and stands, striding toward the door with his phone in hand.

He'd love for it to be Lucinda calling, but it isn't.

"Neal? This is Frank."

"Frank who?"

"Frank Santiago," comes the reply—at least, that's what it sounded like. But with all the din in the luncheonette, Neal is sure he must have heard wrong because the weak voice on the other end of the line sounds nothing like Santiago.

"Hang on a minute, I'm in a restaurant." He steps out onto the street, waits for a garbage truck to pass. "That's better. Now *who* is this?"

"It's Frank Santiago."

"Frank—what's wrong? Are you okay?"

"Funny you should ask, Neal. I'm actually not okay. In fact, I've never been less okay in my life. That's probably a good thing, considering it's almost over."

"Considering what's almost over?"

"My life."

Neal is about to ask him if he's joking, but Frank coughs. Hard and long. It doesn't sound good. He isn't joking.

"I haven't got much time left, Neal. I'm getting my affairs in order. You're not on the top of my list, so don't flatter yourself. But this call is a helluva lot easier than some of the other ones I've had to make."

"What are you talking about?"

"Cancer. Ask your friend Lucinda. She figured it out. I'd ask her how much time I've got left, but I have a pretty good idea. So I wanted to let you know that I'm sorry about what happened. I should have listened to you, but I let my pride get in the way."

He stops talking, starts coughing again.

Listening to it, Neal can feel Frank's helplessness. Hopelessness.

"Listen, Frank, you don't have to—"

"Hear me out. I went down the wrong path because your friend Lucinda figured out that I was dying before I was ready to admit it, even to myself. I was angry at the world, and I took it out on her."

"That's not the only reason. There was evidence—"

"No, but you were right. I should have looked harder at Chicago. I wouldn't listen to you. If I had, that second girl wouldn't be dead."

"You don't know that's the case, Frank."

"I don't know that it's not. I have to live with that. Not for much longer, but still . . . So, I'm asking your forgiveness."

"Frank—"

"Hear me out, I said." That Frank is as cantankerous as ever makes Neal smile and tear up at the same time. "I can only swallow so much pride in a day. Do you forgive me, Neal?"

"I forgive you."

"Thank you."

"What can I do for you? Is there anything you need?"

"Yes. But other than forgiveness, it's nothing you can give me. Thank you, though."

"You're welcome. And Frank? I'm sorry."

"That was my line." Frank goes into another coughing spell. When it's over, he says, "You know, there is one thing you can do for me, after all."

"What is it?"

"Make sure somebody catches the son of a bitch who killed Randy's wife."

After Scarlet kissed his cheek with her red lipstick lips on that long ago day, he knew she was his girlfriend, even though he hardly got to see her because she worked nights and slept days.

His mother worked days and slept nights and didn't meet Scarlet, didn't even know she existed across the hall, as far as he could tell.

The boys at school knew, though.

They knew because he told them, one day just before graduation, when they were heckling him in the locker room as always, calling him the usual names: candy ass, Mama's boy, Hyena.

But this time, he held up his head, and he told them defiantly, "I have a girlfriend, and she's better looking than all of your girlfriends put together."

Of course, they didn't believe him, so he told them all about Scarlet, and how she was an older woman, and how she'd kissed him wearing red lipstick.

They still didn't believe him, so he told them to come over after school, when his mother was at work, and he'd introduce them.

He remembers how excited he was that hot June afternoon when the boys showed up and he led them across the hall to her door.

He remembers knocking, remembers the door opening, remembers Scarlet standing there, beautiful and statuesque, wearing a silky ruby-colored robe and a turban and, of course, her red lipstick.

"These are my friends," he told her. "I wanted them to meet you."

"Oh, how nice, Lover Boy," she said in her throaty voice, and she shook all their hands.

Then she kissed him—again!—on the cheek. Right in front of the boys.

"I have to go take my bath and get ready for work now," she said, and sent them on their way.

He turned to the other boys after she closed the door, all set to say "I told you so."

But before he could get the words out, they were laughing.

Laughing hysterically, the way he did sometimes.

Only they weren't laughing at nothing.

They were laughing at Scarlet. And at him.

"You idiot—that's no woman."

He had no idea what they were talking about.

They found that even funnier.

"Come on," suggested Nicky Colletti, who had already enlisted and would die in Saigon seven months later, "let's sneak up the fire escape to her window."

Afraid of what they might do, he accompanied them.

He'll never forget the heady thrill of that first moment he glimpsed her through the window, left wide open in the heat, as she soaked in a tub full of bubbles with no idea that she was being watched.

He'll never forget the sheer horror of the next moment, when he spotted her beautiful, luxurious hair sitting on a wig stand on the vanity.

Even then, he tried to convince himself that the boys were wrong. That it didn't mean anything. That a lot of women wore wigs when they got dressed up; that she had a beautiful head of hair beneath the turban.

He kept watching, and he calmed himself down, and for a little longer, he reveled in the forbidden pleasure of spying on her.

Then she stood and climbed out of the tub.

The humiliating truth hit him like a train, and he couldn't breathe.

The other boys were laughing so hard they had to scramble down off the fire escape before they fell.

He could feel the emotion welling up inside of him, aching in his throat, stinging his eyes.

Only babies cry.

So he laughed.

He laughed until it hurt, and then he laughed until it didn't hurt anymore.

Leaving for work later, Scarlet didn't close the window. It was too hot that night.

The moon was full.

And when Scarlet came home early in the morning, he was waiting.

PART IV

8:26

Chapter Twenty-one

"In another week or two," Randy tells Lucinda as they climb out of his car and start walking toward the sandy path to the beach, "you won't be able to get close to this parking spot."

"Even at night?"

"Maybe—if there's a monsoon or something. Otherwise, forget it. Memorial Day to Labor Day, this place is jammed."

Memorial Day, Lucinda knows, is exactly two weeks from today.

The next full moon is exactly one week from today.

She looks up at the wedge of moon riding in the black night sky amid thousands of stars.

Randy follows her gaze. "I know what you're thinking. Don't."

"I can't help it."

He's still out there somewhere, undoubtedly plotting his next murder.

She'd spent an entire week in Denver in a futile wait for something to surface. Sensing that Danielle Hendry was murdered in a mountainous, wooded area, Lucinda tried her best to pinpoint the locale for the searchers.

She couldn't come up with anything. Failure has been a bitter pill to swallow.

Neal tried to comfort her when she got back home, reminding her that she was out of her element. She's never been to Denver before. The city is surrounded by vast stretches of mountainous, wooded terrain.

But Lucinda knows her failure had nothing to do with that.

She's worked cases far from home before. Once, in the Berkshires, she successfully narrowed a search party's wilderness efforts to within a few yards of where a hiker's body was discovered near the fork of a mountain stream.

The problem this time wasn't that she was *physically* in unfamiliar territory.

It was that she was *emotionally* in unfamiliar territory.

She's not accustomed, when working a case, to feeling vulnerable, fearing that her own life might be in danger.

Nor is she accustomed to letting her personal relationships interfere with her work.

The truth is, she was distracted because she missed Randy. She didn't want to miss him, but she had.

She didn't want to feel accountable to him when at last she returned his call and admitted she was in Denver, but she had.

She didn't want to go running to him practically the moment she returned to the East Coast, but she had.

They didn't discuss what had—and hadn't—happened between them up to that point, and they haven't since. There seemed to be an unspoken agreement to forgive, and to forge ahead—as friends, if nothing else.

So far—nothing else.

They cross between the grassy dunes and tilted board fences toward the surf pounding at the end of the path. Lucinda's fear of the dark tries to get the better of her, but she can't let it. Randy is with her, and there's some light from the moon reflecting off the water.

"I just can't believe we're no closer to finding this guy than we were last month."

"I thought we said we weren't going to talk about that tonight, Lucinda."

"That was over dinner. And we didn't."

Sharing a pizza and a pitcher of beer, they'd talked about the closing this week on Carla's house; Lucinda's plans to attend Bradley's opening night—at last—this coming weekend; the new apartment Randy had found to rent for the summer on the mainland; Cam's hopes that she'll uncover the name of the male student who may have been stalking Ava before she died.

The last topic was as close as they got to discussing the Night Watchman—which isn't close at all, really, because thanks to Vic Shattuck's insight, Lucinda now agrees with Randy that the notorious serial killer wasn't responsible for Ava's death.

The Watchman seemingly wants them to make a connection—but as Vic pointed out, he could be deliberately misleading them.

She and Randy emerge from the dunes onto the wide beach, where they came to walk off the tiramisu and cannoli they'd shared for dessert.

The salt air is balmy tonight, and there are a few people on the beach, most of them with dogs and flashlights. She reaches for Randy's hand as they walk south along the water, the lights of Atlantic City glowing reassuringly in the distance.

He squeezes her hand, then laces his fingers with hers. The warm contact with his skin brings a burst of longing.

"The problem," she tells him, to keep her mind from wandering to forbidden places, "is that we can guess when he's going to strike again, but we have no way of knowing where."

"Or whom."

"I thought we were onto something with the lipstick theory."

Danielle Hendry's friends confirmed that she always, *always* wore red lipstick.

Jaime Dobiak occasionally had.

"Carla never wore red lipstick, though," Randy reminds Lucinda.

"I know. That's why it doesn't fit."

So it's little comfort that she herself doesn't wear lipstick at all. If she's been targeted by the killer—as even the FBI suspects she has—there's little she can do to protect herself.

Yes, she's frightened. But that doesn't mean she's lost every last ounce of the courage that got her this far in life.

She's as safe as she can be under the circumstances, short of going into hiding—which she refuses to consider. They've got her building under surveillance, are monitoring her phone calls and her e-mail for further communication, and her apartment is equipped with an alarm, multiple locks and deadbolts—and a pistol.

That was Randy's idea, backed up by Neal.

Yes, she knows how to use it. She learned years ago at a range and proved to be an excellent shot.

She just never imagined that she might actually have to use a gun in her own home to protect herself.

"Stay with me, Lucinda. Just for tonight. Please."

"I'll be fine driving home, especially after all that espresso. It's not even that late. I'll be home at a little after midnight if I leave in a half hour, and—"

"No," he stops walking and turns toward her, grabbing her other hand to make her face him, "that's not why I want you to stay. I know you'll be fine if you go. I know you can take care of yourself. But, Lucinda . . ."

She realizes that he's going to kiss her in the split second before he does.

His lips are against hers, and the years fall away.

If this were a movie, she finds herself thinking, it would end right here—credits rolling over the couple in each other's arms at last.

But it isn't a movie, it's real life, and in real life, kisses end and relationships end.

Randy pulls back, still holding both her hands. "I'd say I'm sorry, but I'm not."

She smiles faintly, but before she can answer him, her BlackBerry buzzes in the pocket of her jacket.

She pulls it out. "I have to see who it is."

"You could say you're sorry—but I bet you're not."

Maybe.

Maybe not. Maybe she was tempted to see where this was going to go. Maybe the spell doesn't have to be broken, she thinks—until she checks the phone and sees who's calling.

"It's Vic Shattuck," she tells Randy. "I need to take this."

"Saved by the bell, huh?"

Bell . . .

If I were a bell I'd be ringing. . . .

That's a song, an old one. Funny how the line popped into her head out of nowhere.

"Hello? Vic?"

She hears his voice, but she can't make out what he's saying above the static and the sound of the waves.

"Vic, I've got a bad connection. Can I call you back in a few minutes?"

He speaks again.

She shakes her head, frustrated.

To Randy, she says, "I've got to get better reception. Something's going on. It sounds urgent."

Randy sighs. "Come on. Let's go."

"I'm sorry," she tells him as they walk back toward the path to the road, "and I really do mean it."

"*If I were a bell I'd go ding dong, ding dong diiiiing!*"

Whirling across the Havana nightclub set, breathlessly concluding her big solo, Kelly falls into Julian's arms.

"That was almost perfect!" Gary announces from beyond the footlights.

Almost.

Kelly and Julian look at each other.

"Just remember, you guys have just realized you're in love, but Kelly, Sarah's supposed to be rip-roaring drunk in this scene. Play it just a little sloppier. Julian, Sky is telling himself that he's *not* going to take advantage of her. For a minute there, you looked like you were going to jump her bones. Take it down a notch. Got it?"

"Got it," Julian tells Gary. To Kelly, under his breath, he says, "I won't jump your bones till later."

She wishes Gary and the crew and the lights would disappear.

Who'd have guessed that she'd fall in love, for real, with her leading man?

And he with her?

Yesterday, there was a huge color photo of the two of them in the newspaper. It was snapped at a full dress rehearsal. In the photo, Julian, wearing Sky Masterson's baggy suit and fedora, is gazing adoringly at Kelly. She's smiling demurely into the camera, looking glamorous in a silky blue 1950s dress, her hair done up with sophisticated waves, her face made up with sexy eyeliner and red lipstick.

Christina, obviously jealous that she hadn't made the papers, had tried to convince Kelly that Julian gets involved with all his leading ladies. But she doesn't know how he treats Kelly when they're alone together; hasn't heard the things he says; hasn't seen the way he kisses her.

She doesn't realize this is the real thing.

The timing couldn't be worse. Julian's a senior. He's graduating in a few weeks, going on to grad school in California. Kelly's heading home to Spokane for the summer, then will be back here in the fall—without Julian.

Just when her life is finally getting interesting, it's going to come crashing down around her.

But she doesn't want to think about that now.

They still have a whole week of dress rehearsals to look

forward to, opening night on Friday, the weekend run, the cast party Sunday. . . .

Then comes Monday. That's what I'm dreading.

Monday, it'll be all over.

Gazing out the window at the lights that dot the Quantico campus, waiting for Lucinda to call him back, Vic is struck by the irony that he's homesick.

Not homesick for New England and the new house, but for Kitty, of course, and for the simple things that have lately filled his retirement days: slippers and sweats, home-cooked meals, quiet days spent working on his book.

The deadline that seemed so distant now looms uncomfortably close, but he hasn't found a moment to work on finishing the manuscript. Since he's gotten here he's eaten, slept, and breathed the case.

It's what he thought he wanted—what he missed so desperately, in those early months after forced retirement. It isn't that he doesn't want to be here now. He wants, more than anything, to locate the unsub and bring him down.

But once he does, Vic suspects he'll no longer look back wistfully at his career. He'll be grateful to go back to his new life, far from the intense bustle of Quantico.

"Maybe we should think about taking a cruise with the Gudlaugs this summer," Kitty suggested when he spoke to her last night. "I've been looking through that brochure Dave sent, and I think we might have fun."

"Maybe," Vic told her, thinking salsa dancing, bingo playing, and buffet-eating sound pretty good compared to what he's been doing lately.

The phone rings. Lucinda.

"I'm sorry," she says breathlessly. "I couldn't hear you at all when you called. I'm in a better spot now. What's up?"

"Danielle Hendry turned up."

She gasps. "Alive?"

"No."

It doesn't take her long to absorb that. She never believed Danielle would be found alive.

"Where was she?"

"In a wooded part of the mountains—like you said. Some boy scout took a tumble off a steep trail and landed next to what was left of her."

"What a nightmare for the boy."

"No kidding." It wasn't pretty, Vic hears. She's been out there with the wild animals for a few weeks now. The poor kid will never be the same.

"Was she wearing the lipstick?"

"No way to tell. But she was wearing a watch."

"Freestyle," Lucinda says, "and engraved with April 20, and the longitude and latitude, and stopped at 7:44."

"You got it."

"Are you going out there, Vic?"

"No," he tells her. "I'm going to Seattle."

"Seattle! Why?"

"Because its coordinates are 122.3 and 47.6 . . . and those numbers were carved on a tree next to Danielle's remains with the bloody knife that killed her."

A few days ago, Dr. Zubin called and gave Cam three names.

"You didn't get them from me, all right?"

"Of course. Thank you for helping."

"If you find out what happened to your sister," he said before hanging up, "will you let me know?"

She promised that she would, when—not if—she finds out.

There were three boys named John—one of whom was known as Jack—in Ava's classes that last semester at college.

One of them, John Amarind, died—as had so many young men in that era—in Vietnam.

Cam has already met with John Hubbard, an investment banker who lives in the Jersey suburbs not far from Montclair.

He said he remembered Ava—but only because of her shocking death. "I didn't even realize she was in my accounting class until I saw her picture in the paper and recognized her."

He could have been lying—but Cam chose to believe him.

"I wish I could tell you more about her," he said, "but to be honest, we were total strangers. I'm sorry for your loss."

Finally, she tracked down a John Ruzzoccino, who had been in Ava's psych class and is now a partner in a law firm in Boston.

When she reached his office this afternoon, she got a secretary who wanted to take a message.

She opted not to leave one, preferring not to try to explain to the secretary the reason for her call.

Tonight, with Mike working late and both girls upstairs asleep, she dials his office again. If she gets through to an automated directory, she'll go to his voice mail and leave a message there.

She does get an automated directory, but after entering the first few letters of his last name, she finds herself transferred to a line that is picked up by a human voice on the first ring.

"Jack Ruzzoccino."

"Mr. Ruzzoccino! You're there."

"Yes. . . . Who's this?"

She launches into the speech she'd been prepared to rattle off on his voice mail. "You don't know me, but you knew my sister, Ava Neary, back at NYU. She was in a psychology class with you for a few months before she died."

"I remember Ava," he interjects quietly, when she pauses to take a breath. "She was a sweetheart." With his Boston accent, it comes out *sweet haht.*

"So you knew her?"

"Sure, I knew her. What a tragedy. I'm sorry for your loss. . . ."

"Cam," she supplies. "Cam Hastings."

Now what?

Does she ask him if, by any chance, he was dangerously infatuated with Ava and might have thrown her off the rooftop?

Maybe it was John Amarind. If that's the case, she'll never know.

"I didn't really get to know your sister until a week or two before she passed away," John Ruzzoccino tells her. "The class was in a big lecture hall, but we sat near each other. She was having a hard"—pronounced *hahd*—"time in that class because of some idiot kid."

Cam clenches the receiver. "What do you mean, having a hard time?"

"He kept bugging her, saying she thought she was too good to go out with him, saying all kinds of stuff that was making her nervous. So I picked up on it and started walking her to her next class—I'm a big guy, and he was a little weasel, this kid. I told your sister to let me know if she wanted me to take care of him."

"What was his name? Do you remember?"

"Sure I remember. We had the same first name, only I've always been called Jack. He was John. John . . . Stockman. That's it. I remember because he was stocky, and the name fit."

"John Stockman," Cam repeats, writing it down.

There was no John Stockman on the class list, according to Dr. Zubin. Maybe it was a mistake.

Or maybe he doesn't exist.

"Do you remember what he looked like?"

"Oh, yeah. Like I said, he was stocky. Short. He wore thick glasses with black frames. He had very bad acne all over his face. Your sister was so out of his league it was a joke. Yet this guy walked around like he was hot stuff. It was bizarre."

"Thank you so much, Mr. Ruzzoccino. One last thing. Do you know whatever happened to John Stockman?"

"I never saw him again."

"After that semester."

"No—I mean, after your sister died. He stopped coming to class. I figured, he was probably just going to the lectures to be near her, and once she was gone . . . he didn't bother anymore."

"That's interesting." To say the least.

"A lot of people didn't go to lectures. As long as you had the syllabus and showed up for the tests, you could get by."

"Did he show up for the tests, after that?"

"Like I said, I don't remember ever seeing the guy again. But to tell you the truth, it's not like I was looking for him. The only reason I ever noticed him in the first place was because I saw how he was bugging your sister."

"Well . . . thank you for your time. I'm really glad I got a hold of you. I didn't think I would."

"I'm here late tonight, working on a case. Mind if I ask why you went to the trouble of tracking me down after all these years?"

Cam hesitates.

What if he made up the whole story?

What if John Ruzzoccino was the one who was stalking Ava, the one who killed Ava?

Realizing she doesn't dare trust him with the truth, Cam says, "I was so young when my sister passed away that I feel as though I never knew her. I thought maybe if I tracked down people who had, they could share something about her that I might not have known."

"I'm sure you'll find lots of people who knew Ava a lot better than I did. In fact, after she died, I realized I must not have known her at all, because she struck me as someone who had her act together—not someone on the verge of checking out. She hid it well. I was shocked when I heard."

"Thank you for telling me that, Mr. Ruzzoccino."

Hanging up the phone, Cam goes straight to her desk and brings up a search engine.

She types in *John Stockman*. . . .

And comes up with over 99,000 hits.

This is going to take a while.

Leaning against a bike rack in the dark, Randy watches Lucinda sitting in the passenger's seat of his parked car, talking on the phone to the FBI guy. It's obvious by her expression, by her movements, that something's up, like she said.

He sees her open the glove compartment, take out a fast food napkin, and use the dashboard as a desk as she jots notes on it.

Maybe he should be sorry he kissed her—sorry for himself. It only made him realize how crazy he is about her. How crazy he is, period, to think he's ever going to get over her this time if they give their relationship a shot, and it doesn't work.

This time?

Hell, he didn't get over her last time.

When she left, he married Carla out of guilt and pity, thinking it was the right thing to do. Even though he knew that she didn't love him any more than he loved her. Carla needed him.

Lucinda didn't need anyone.

Maybe she still doesn't.

And maybe Randy is a guy who needs to be needed. Not as fiercely as Carla did. But needed.

Just wanting someone—desiring them—isn't enough. Because when you come right down to it, you can survive without the things you want. You'll fight to the bitter end for something you need.

Lately, he's glimpsed a crack in Lucinda's armor—a sign that maybe things are changing.

All those years, stuck in a dying marriage—he'd dreamed about finding his way back to Lucinda. He'd dreamed about making her see that they belong together.

Now, his only chance is to convince her to take one.

At last, she hangs up the phone. When she opens the car

door, he thinks she's going to rejoin him, but she calls, "Randy, come here!"

He hurries over. "What's going on?"

"I need to get back to my car."

His heart sinks. He'd been hoping, after that kiss, that she would stay tonight. Or longer. Say, forever.

He should have known better.

"What happened?"

"I'll tell you while we drive."

"Why the big rush?" he asks, getting behind the wheel.

"I have to get home and pack for an early flight."

"Where are you going?"

"Seattle. That's where he is."

"The Night Watchman."

"Yes."

No, he thinks. *No!*

"It's my job, Randy. I'm a detective. Like you," she adds pointedly.

"No," he says, "not like me. This is *not* your job."

He sees the storm brewing in her eyes, but he can't stop himself.

"You're going to Seattle because you *want* to, not because you have to."

"I'm going because Vic said—"

"I don't care what Vic said. You don't work for the FBI—and neither does he, for that matter. You're not assigned to this case with no choice but to jump when they say jump."

"They didn't say jump. This was my decision."

"It's a bad decision. This guy is a cold-blooded killer. He wants to get to *you*. He wants to do to you what he did to Carla, dammit, and you're going to play right into his hands!"

She stares at him. He waits for the inevitable: for her to lash out at him in return, telling him she'll do whatever she damn well pleases.

To his shock, the retaliation doesn't come.

"They think he killed Carla to get to *me*, Randy. And now

he's killed two other women—that we know of. How am I ever going to live with that unless I stop him? Don't you see? I do have to go to Seattle. I don't *want* to. Trust me, it's the last thing I want to do. But I have to."

He shrugs. "Then I'm coming with you."

"You can't do that. You have a job, and you're moving, and—and you have the closing on the house this week. You can't just drop everything to come out there and . . . what? Wait around with me for something to happen?"

I can protect you, he wants to tell her.

But that, he knows, would be a mistake.

She's right. He can't go, and he can't stop her.

Silently, he starts the engine.

"Randy?"

He looks up at her.

"I'm going to go to Seattle. And when I come back, you'll be here. And—we'll talk. Deal?" She holds out her hand.

He reaches for it, sees that it's trembling.

He takes it in both his own. "Deal."

"Hello?"

"Ms. O'Leary, this is Cam Hastings. Do you remember me?"

"Of course," she says around a yawn. "Call me Janet. What can I do for you?"

Cam glances at the microwave clock in her kitchen. Oops. She should have checked it before dialing. "Have you ever heard the name John Stockman?"

"No. Should I have?"

"I'm wondering if he went to school at Buff State with Sandra. Is there any way you can find out if he was a student there when she died?"

"I know a few people. I can check into it. Let me get a pen. . . . What was the name again?"

Cam repeats it, then quickly explains what John Ruzzoccino told her—including the physical description of the guy who was harassing her sister.

"I didn't get a look at him," Janet reminds her.

"What about his build, though? Was he short and stocky?"

"Remember, I was a little girl. . . . If he was, he didn't strike me that way."

That doesn't mean much, Cam realizes. Adults all look big when you're a child.

"See what you can find out about him," she tells Janet, "and let me know if he was a student there."

She hangs up, certain Janet won't find him even if she does manage to gain access to the registration records.

There are many John Stockmans in the world, she knows, having spent the better part of the past hour clicking through search engine hits on the name. None of them, as far as she can tell, has ties to Buffalo, Sandra Wubner, NYU, or Ava.

Cam looks again at the clock.

When she spoke to Lucinda earlier today, she was headed out to Beach Haven to have dinner with Randy—whom she refuses to acknowledge, at least not to Cam, as anything more than a friend.

Chances are, she's still there.

Sorry to interrupt your date that you claim isn't a date, Cam thinks, dialing her friend's cell, *but I need to fill you in.*

Driving across the causeway toward the mainland, Lucinda is consumed by if onlys and coulda-shoulda-wouldas.

Why is it that every time she and Randy part, she's filled with regret over the things she didn't do or say?

Next time, she vows, *I won't hold back.*

Next time, I'll—

Her cell phone rings.

She reaches eagerly for it.

No, she's not supposed to answer it while she's driving, and no, she doesn't have a headset, and no, there isn't a place to pull over to take the call.

But maybe it's him. Maybe she can tell him right now how much he means to her.

"Hello?"

"Lucinda, it's Cam. I'm so glad I got you."

Hopes deflated, Lucinda asks, "What's wrong?"

"Does the name John Stockman ring a bell?"

Ring a bell . . .

Again, that old song pops into her head.

If I were a bell I'd be ringing . . .

"No," she tells Cam, "it doesn't ring a bell."

But this song does. Why?

Maybe she heard it at Neal's house when she was there for Sunday dinner. He's always got the radio tuned to show tunes or old swing music. Yeah, that was probably it.

Cam tells her she's found out that a student by that name was stalking Ava before she died, and that he doesn't seem even to have been enrolled at the school at the time.

"I'm wondering if he was just some guy who wandered in off the street, posing as a student. It was a big lecture hall, and I'm sure it wasn't as though the instructor took attendance or counted heads."

"And back then, campus security wasn't what it is today. I bet people came and went pretty freely."

"I've got to find this guy, Lucinda. Want to help me?"

"I can't. I have to go away for a while."

"Where to?"

She quickly explains the situation.

"I don't think that's a good idea."

"You and Randy both. But I have to go, Cam. And, listen, I have to hang up now because I'm on the road. Will you let me know what you find out about this guy?"

Cam promises that she will, and hangs up.

If I were a bell I'd be ringing . . .

That old tune is stuck in her head now.

That happens sometimes: a song will pop up out of nowhere, and she'll find herself humming it for a few days.

She wishes she could be sure it were just one of those random things.

But she has a feeling it isn't—and she has no idea what it means.

Chapter Twenty-two

Leaning on the pipe railing at the edge of a wide, weathered wooden pier, Lucinda gazes out at Elliot Bay, holding a thin red and white-checked cardboard container of fish and chips.

Crisp and fragrant when she got the meal at a seafood kiosk down the way, the coated fish is now sodden, the french fries unappetizingly cold and mealy.

She bought the food because it smelled good, its aroma mingling with the briny sea air, and because she hasn't eaten a thing all day—unless you count about a gallon of coffee plus another of Pepsi—and because it was something to do.

After a week in Seattle, this is the day she's been dreading. Something's going to happen tonight when the full moon rises.

The more anxious she's become as the day wears on, the less able she is to focus. The less she's able to focus, the more anxious she becomes.

When she could no longer sit in her hotel room, caught in the vicious cycle, she forced herself to go out for a short walk around nearby Public Market to clear her head. It didn't work: not the change of scenery, not the fresh salt air, not the vigorous climb from Alaskan Way to the market perched high above the water on Pike Street.

From there, she had a bird's-eye view of a vast ocean liner sailing out of the bay.

She's seen quite a few of them, staying here on the waterfront. She even spotted the enormous *Norwegian Star* moored across from the hotel, and mentioned to Vic that she was supposed to sail on it last summer.

"Why didn't you go?"

"Something came up with a case. I had to postpone it."

"Story of my life. Kitty wants to take a cruise when I get back home."

"You should." Lucinda opted not to tell him that in just a few weeks, she's scheduled to be back here in Seattle, departing on the *Star*, bound for Alaska at last.

Back here . . . or *still* here?

She's all but put the cruise out of her mind for the past few months, fairly certain that she's not going to be going anywhere unless this case is solved.

Even if it is solved—a solo cruise might not be her idea of the best way to celebrate.

Maybe by then, a vacation for two will be more fitting.

Okay, you need to put that right out of your mind, too.

Focus.

Watching a fat white gull bobbing in the water, she notices droplets landing on the choppy blue-gray surface and realizes it's raining again.

She flips up her hood and tosses a couple of fries toward the gull. With a swift glide and a fluttering of wings, he devours them and eyes her, waiting for more.

"Here you go." She tosses the contents, scattering the meal across the surface of the bay.

Instantly, the gull is joined by several others, screeching and flapping and dive-bombing their way to the food.

Lucinda watches the feeding frenzy for a few moments,

reminded of a day with Randy last summer at a beachside grill on Long Beach Island.

It was the first time she'd seen him in three years, lured to Beach Haven because of a missing persons case. That day, as they ate mango water ice and funnel cakes sitting across from each other on a sticky picnic table, she realized he was flirting with her and fought hard not to flirt in return.

She didn't know, then, that his marriage was troubled.

She never dreamed, then, that she stood a chance in hell of revisiting a relationship with him.

Now, after a week on the opposite coast, talking to him several times a day and longing to see him, she's more than ready to put aside her misgivings and give it a try.

She hasn't told him that, though. They've mostly talked about the case and his having sold Carla's house and his upcoming move.

That's fine with Lucinda. She doesn't want to discuss a relationship over the phone. It can wait till she sees him again.

Whenever that is.

With a sigh, she throws the container into a nearby trash can. She should get back to the hotel and check in with Vic.

Somewhere in the gleaming high-tech city sprawled on a series of steep hills behind her, someone is going to die in a few hours.

Lucinda can't save the woman's life unless she figures out who and where she is—but it seems less likely with every minute that ticks by.

"What are the chances he'll be glad to see us?" Randy asks Neal as they climb out of their respective cars in front of Frank Santiago's condo building.

"I'd say around—zero," Neal tells him, and is surprised that Randy looks surprised. "He might be dying, but I'm guessing he's still Frank."

"Arrogant, cranky, impossible?"

"Exactly. In my experience, it's only in the movies that dying people turn sweet and saintly." Neal opens his car trunk and takes out the bouquet of fresh lilacs Erma cut from the yard, then adds, to be fair, "I don't know, I guess there's always a chance the guy has mellowed a little."

"Good. Then maybe he'll just be arrogant and cranky." Wearing a wry smile, Randy tucks a manilla envelope under his arm and aims his keys at the car. It chirps twice as he locks it. "Ready?"

"Let's go. What's in the envelope?"

"Cards and notes from everyone at work, and some mail that got delivered with his name on it. I wanted to bring him something else, but . . . nothing seemed appropriate. Those lilacs are nice, though."

"Erma's idea."

"They smell great."

"Yeah." Neal hesitates. "You know who loves lilacs?"

"Who?"

"Lucinda. Every year when they're in full bloom, she comes over and parks herself next to my shrubs and inhales them for a good long time."

"I didn't know she liked lilacs."

"Loves them. I bet there's a lot you don't know about her." Randy raises an eyebrow. "Like?"

"Did you know she never liked salad until recently?"

"No." Randy shrugs.

"Yeah, she knew it was good for her, so she made herself try it every once in a while, just to see if she'd changed her mind. A few months ago, she tried it again—and what do you know?"

"She liked it."

"Yep. And now she eats it all the time. Says it makes her feel good."

"Huh."

Neal nods. *And that,* he thinks, *is all I'm going to say about that. I did my part. He can take it from there.*

They head up the walk, into the vestibule, ring Frank's apartment.

"Ever been here before?" Neal asks Randy, who shakes his head.

A female voice answers the intercom. "Who is it?"

"Friends of Frank's."

"*Who?*"

They look at each other. Neal knows Randy's thinking the same thing he is: that maybe Frank doesn't *have* any friends.

Neal leans close to the intercom. "Tell him it's Randy and Neal."

There's a long pause, and then the door buzzes.

It's been nearly a week since he read online that Danielle Hendry's remains were found.

By now, they'll have converged here in Seattle: the FBI, Vic Shattuck, and—with any luck—Lucinda herself.

Unless they're utterly stupid, they know that tonight's the night.

Full moon.

They probably know, too, what time he's going to make his move: sundown—not that there's any sun today in the rainy Pacific Northwest.

So yes, they know. They're not stupid.

But he's not stupid, either. Far from it.

They've been waiting, no doubt, for some kind of communication from him—some indication that he's here, waiting to strike.

He's given them nothing, nothing at all.

This time, they're feeling their way through utter darkness; this time he'll blindside even the victim. As much as he's enjoyed playing with the others, letting them know someone was watching them, sensing their growing apprehension, he doesn't dare indulge himself again.

There's only one way to play this one smart: he's in; he's out; it's over.

And then it will be Lucinda's turn.

Julian Dodd emerges from the library at last and starts across Red Square.

It's about time, he thinks, checking his watch before falling into step behind him.

Starbucks cup in hand, Lucinda knocks on the door of Vic's room, two floors below her own.

The door opens immediately. "That was fast."

"I was about to get into an elevator when you called my cell," she tells Vic, framed in the doorway of a room littered with papers, files, and an empty pizza box sitting open on the bed.

"Were you on your way out?"

"On my way in—with this." She holds up the mocha latte. "Want a sip?"

"What I want right now has a lot more kick, and I don't want to sip it."

Lucinda glances at the window to ensure that it's still daylight. "Did something happen already?"

"If you're asking whether he's killed anyone yet, the answer is no. But yes, something's happened. Sit down." He closes the door behind him, locks the bolt and the chain, and indicates the lone chair.

Lucinda sinks into it.

He clears a spot on the bed by sweeping the pizza box and a bunch of newspapers to the floor, then sits facing her and hands her an envelope.

"What is this?"

"Take a look."

Lucinda pulls out an old black-and-white mug shot. "Who is he?"

"He," Vic tells her, "is Scarlet."

* * *

"There. How does that feel?" Angie, the hospice nurse, slowly raises the back of the bed they've set up in Frank's living room.

"Hurts like hell."

"I'm sorry." Angie starts to lower it again, but he stops her with a bony hand that looks, to him, as if it belongs to someone else. And not just because he can barely see it.

"Don't. Everything hurts like hell. I might as well be able to look at them."

"It's so nice that you've got company, Frank, isn't it?"

"Funny, I was just thinking that now I know how all those perps felt when I chased them down. Cornered by the cops, no place to run."

Angie laughs, and he manages a weak smile.

"Turn that off, will you?" Frank gestures at the television, where a couple of overly made-up middle-aged women are crying about something as violin music rises in the background.

He doesn't want anyone thinking he's lying here watching the soaps. Angie likes them, so he lets her turn them on in the afternoons. When he's not sleeping, he watches with the eye that isn't yet blind. It makes the time go by.

"I'll go make some more coffee."

She's the only one who ever drinks it now that Frank has such a hard time swallowing—except for the one other day he had visitors.

The kids came to see him, with Ellen and her husband. That was a barrel of laughs. Ellen and the kids cried a little, and the doofus Ellen married had the nerve to tell him not to worry, that he'd see that Frank's family was taken care of.

When was that? A few days ago? A few weeks?

His mind used to be so sharp. Now it's mush—because of all the medication, Angie and Mary and the others say.

The medication?

Who are they kidding?

It's the tumors. Cancer cells choking out brain cells, killing them off, killing him.

Most of the time, he just wants it to be over.

He hears the knock on the door, the rumble of voices: Angie introducing herself to Neal and Randy, speaking to them in a hushed tone.

For all he knows, she's telling them he'll be dead by tonight, or tomorrow, or next Monday . . . whatever the case may be.

Then again, she'd probably tell him too, if he asked. These hospice people aren't like the doctors. They're honest. If you ask them a question, they'll answer it. No bullshit.

When Frank realized that, he stopped asking. Maybe he doesn't really want to know when it's going to happen, after all.

"Hey, Frank." He hears Neal Bullard's voice, knows that he's standing over him, but he can't see him.

"He's blind in that eye," Angie whispers, "and it's painful for him to turn his head. If you go over there, he'll be able to see you."

"I'm blind, but I'm not deaf," Frank manages to say.

Then Neal appears, with Randy beside him. He feels one of them touching his hand.

"Hey, Frank."

"How are you, Frank?"

He wants to tell whichever of them asked the question that it's a stupid one, but he can't, because he suddenly has a lump in his throat. Both his eyes are swimming with tears, dammit.

He doesn't want them to see him lying here crying, wasting away, dying.

But here they are, and here he is, and he might as well make the best of it.

He coughs away the fluid in his lungs, then asks, "You catch that guy yet?"

They don't ask who.

"We're closing in," Neal tells him. "We'll get him."

"Let me know when you do."

"I will."

Randy speaks up. "I brought you some cards and notes from everyone at work, Frank."

"I'll read them to him later," Angie's voice says. He can't see her, but he can feel her, doing something with the IV bag hanging above him on his blind side. "And, Frank, they brought you some beautiful lilacs. I'll put them in a vase where you can see and smell them."

"Better hurry up, while I can still see and smell," he quips, then coughs again, painfully.

"Is there anything we can do for you, Frank?" Neal asks, so concerned that Frank is moved all over again.

"Not for me," he tells them. "But you can do something for yourselves. Live."

"Live?" Randy echoes.

"Yeah. Don't just exist. *Live.* Every damned beautiful day. Don't forget. Got it?"

He sees Neal and Randy exchange a glance.

"Got it, Frank."

"Good."

Worn out, he closes his eyes.

"Is he . . . ?" someone asks.

"He's just tired." Angie tells them. "You take a nap now, Frank."

"Bye, Frank. We'll come back."

Good-bye, he thinks, and drifts off to the dark place where it doesn't hurt.

"Hi, you've reached the voice mail of John Ruzzoccino. I'm unavailable to take your call at the moment, but if you'll leave a message, I'll get right back to you."

"Mr. Ruzzoccino, it's Cam Hastings. Ava Neary's sister? We spoke last week. I'd appreciate it if you could call me as soon as possible. I just found something interesting, and I wanted your take on it."

Cam hangs up the phone and turns back to Grace, watching her in the baby swing that rocks gently with a rhythmic clicking sound.

"I wish I could call Lucinda," Cam tells her. "But we can't bother her, can we? Not today, of all days."

Grace gives her a drooly smile.

"I didn't think so." Cam dabs at her daughter's chin with a burp cloth. Poor baby is teething like crazy.

"It's almost time for us to go get Tess at the train station, Gracie." She unstraps the baby from the swing and lifts her out. "What do you think? Will your sister be happy or sad today?"

Grace gurgles.

"Happy? I hope you're right, baby girl."

Cam's caught fleeting glimpses of the old Tess this past week. They've got a long, long way to go, but she seems to be coming out of her depression. Yesterday, Cam even caught her playing peekaboo with Grace, laughing at her baby sister's gales of giggles.

Holding the baby against her shoulder, breathing her sweet, clean smell, Cam crosses the room to the arched windows.

Spring is in full bloom out there: the rhododendron and azalea border at the back of the deep lot is laden with splashy pink and purple blossoms.

For Mother's Day last weekend, Cam went to the nursery and came back with flats of annuals. She planted them right away in the flower beds at the front of the house, remembering all too well that she'd skipped the ritual last year. Mike had just moved out, and she was alone here with Tess, secretly pregnant, enmeshed in A.A. . . .

What a difference a year makes.

Her gaze falls on the weathered wooden play set in the far corner of the yard, next to the shed. Tess wouldn't let them get rid of it as they had planned when she became a teenager. Not that she ever used it—but Cam guessed she was clinging nostalgically to one of the tangible reminders of her not-so-distant childhood.

None of them ever dreamed that another little girl would one day play there. But next year at this time, Grace will be gleefully sliding down the slide just as her big sister once did.

Cam's own girls are as far apart in age as she and Ava were.

Thinking of her sister with a pang of regret, as always, she again wishes she could call Lucinda to share what she discovered on the Internet a little while ago.

Any other day, she would. But Lucinda's still on the opposite coast staking out a murderer who's supposed to strike tonight.

And really, all Cam has is a hunch, based on . . .

What?

A name that's fairly common, a physical description that could apply to thousands of guys, and circumstantial evidence.

It's not much.

But it's something.

Finally, something.

A few days ago, Janet O'Leary had told her that there was no student by the name of John Stockman enrolled at Buff State when Sandra Wubner was there.

Cam wasn't surprised.

She just kept searching the Internet, checking out every John Stockman she could find.

Nothing.

She tried plugging in *Stockman* and *NYU*, *Stockman* and *Neary*, *Stockman* and *Buffalo*, *Stockman* and *Wubner*—hoping to trigger a relevant search engine hit.

Still nothing.

Today, struck by inspiration, she typed in Stockman and murder.

And there it was.

* * *

"Scarlet was a man?" Lucinda is incredulous, as Vic expected, gazing down at the old mug shot in her hand.

The guy is young and handsome, with big dark eyes fringed by sooty lashes.

"His name is Ricky Parker," Vic tells her. "He was arrested in New York a few times back in the sixties."

"For what?"

"Soliciting, among other things. He was a drag queen, lived in the Bronx, but he danced in a club down in Greenwich Village. His stage name was Scarlet. He always wore red gowns when he performed—and red lipstick."

Vic watches Lucinda's eyes widen.

"How did you find him, and what does he have to do with our case?"

"Annabelle's had a team combing old cold case files, crimes occuring in the Northeast back in the sixties, looking for early unsolved murders that might have been connected to the Night Watchman."

"So you think this guy is the Night Watchman?"

"No. I think this guy is one of his victims. Ricky Parker was hacked to death in his apartment back in June of 1967."

"They didn't catch the killer?"

"I'm not sure how hard they tried. That wasn't long before Stonewall. Tough city cops didn't exactly think highly of transvestites back then."

He doesn't elaborate, but she nods, seeming to get the picture.

"Some prints were lifted at the scene," he tells her. "They couldn't come up with a match back then."

"What about now?"

"We're sure as hell going to try."

Cam wasn't sure, at first, that there was a connection between her sister and the search results for *Stockman* and *murder*.

Now that she's had time to process what she found, she can't imagine that there *isn't* a connection.

In 1970, shortly after Ava died, a twenty-five-year-old drifter and draft dodger named Andrew J. Stockman was arrested in Syracuse for the murder of a young Syracuse University student named Sheila Wright.

I KNOW WHAT HAPPIENED TO HER. SOLV IT AND IF YOU ARE WRIGHT YOU WILL FIND ME.

The first few misspellings were meant to throw them off. The last was no accident.

Trying to study for her chemistry final at her desk in her dorm room, Kelly can think only of the chemistry she'd shared—or at least, *thought* she'd shared—with Julian Dodd, both onstage and off.

"Ask me how do I feel from this chemistry lesson I'm learning . . ."

Last night, when she'd sung that line to him during her giddy "If I Were a Bell" solo, he'd looked at her as though he couldn't wait to be alone with her.

Obviously, he was acting, because after the final curtain call, Julian left.

She had assumed they'd go over to the cast party together. She looked for him everywhere, even venturing into the men's dressing room. When she couldn't find him, she finally went alone to the party, thinking he must have figured he'd just see her there. Disappointing, but not devastating.

Devastating was when he never even showed up. Somebody said that his hometown girlfriend had been in the audience, that he'd gone off somewhere with her after the show.

How could that be?

At least Christina didn't bother to say *I told you so.* She was too busy basking in the adulation of fawning under-classmen.

Bewildered, Kelly went back to her room and cried herself to sleep.

This morning, she'd told herself she was not going to call Julian.

Then she had.

Three times.

She texted him, too, asking **Are you okay?**

Who knows? Something horrible might have happened to him when he was walking from the theater to the party.

She knows.

Something horrible definitely happened to *her*.

She'd ignored the little voice in her head that told her a smooth older guy like Julian could not possibly fall in love with a nerdy freshman like her. Now she can't wait until the semester is over and she can escape to her parents' farm near Spokane. She never wants to see Julian Dodd again.

"That's it. I can't do this anymore." Lying on her loft bed, Kelly's roommate, Renee, snaps her textbook closed. "I'm starving. Want to go get something to eat?"

Realizing she's starving too, Kelly nevertheless shakes her head. "I need to study."

"That's all you've done for the past three hours."

No.

All she's done is think about Julian.

"Come on, Kel, take a break."

"I—"

She breaks off as her phone signals a new text message. She checks it. "Oh my God! It's from Julian!"

Sheila Wright—like Cam's sister and the others—was a beautiful girl with long hair parted in the middle.

Cam learned, from reading several articles about him online, that Stockman had been stalking Sheila for a week or two before she died.

Stockman had a gun. The girl fought hard for her life. Her screams roused campus security, and an officer arrived in the midst of the struggle, just in time to see Stockman's gloved hand close around Sheila's fingers as she grasped the gun. He twisted the barrel so that it aimed at her temple, and pulled the trigger.

Sheila Wright died instantly.

Andrew J. Stockman went to prison.

Attica.

Cam found a photo of him online.

He was stocky, with black-framed glasses and pockmarked skin.

But he couldn't have written the red lipstick note to her, because a little over a year after his arrest, he'd been killed during the infamous prison riot.

Sitting on the bed in her hotel room, Lucinda mutes the local news on television and calls Randy. It's almost eleven o'clock. He's probably getting ready for bed.

He answers the phone immediately, as though he'd been holding it in his hand when it rang. "Are you okay?"

"How was Frank when you went to see him, Randy?"

"He looked awful. Emaciated. Barely alive. It really makes you think, seeing someone like that."

Then he told her again to be careful, and she promised him, again, that she will be.

She's keeping her promise, all but barricaded in her hotel room for the past few hours, just in case . . .

The FBI has stationed a guard on the corridor outside her room tonight, too, just in case . . .

Just in case Lucinda Sloan is the Night Watchman's intended victim in Seattle.

The sun sets in less than a half hour.

"I'm fine," she assures Randy now. "Just thought I'd call and say good-night."

"What are you doing?"

"Same thing I was doing last time we spoke. Keeping an eye on the local news in case something happens. Waiting for the killer's face or the victim's name to pop up in my head so that we can reach her before he does."

"You're not getting anything?"

"Nothing at all. Although . . ."

"What?"

"Did you ever hear this song?" Feeling a little ridiculous, she sings the only line she knows: "If I were a bell I'd be ringing," then hums the melody for a few more bars.

"I've heard it. I think it's old, but I don't really know it. Why?"

"I don't know. . . . It's been stuck in my head on and off for a while now. Today it's on again."

"That happens to me sometimes. You must have heard it someplace."

"I guess."

Any other day, she wouldn't think much of it.

But today . . .

"Randy, I have to go. I'll talk to you in the morning."

"Wait—do me a favor. You don't have to stay on the phone with me, but call me back at eight-thirty."

"Why? It'll be so late there."

"I'll be awake. Just . . . call me. Okay?"

"Okay."

She knows why.

He wants to make sure she's survived sunset.

Renee climbs down from her bed and comes over to read the text message over Kelly's shoulder.

Can you meet me on the trail by the stream out near Graves Field?

"No way," Kelly says.

"Wait, maybe he wants to explain what happened last night."

"Now? After he ignored me all day?"

"You never know. There might be a good reason."

Frowning, Kelly texts back, Why?

"Good," Renee says. "See? At least give him a chance to explain."

It doesn't take long for the reply: I want to ask you something.

Trying to tamp a flutter of anticipation in her belly, Kelly turns to her roommate. "What do you think he wants to ask me?"

"I don't know, but you're crazy if you don't find out."

Kelly responds, Ask me now.

She holds her breath, waiting. It doesn't take long.

In person. Please. I want to see you.

Neal knows from experience that a telephone ringing in the dead of night never means anything good—unless one of your daughters happens to be in labor.

His aren't.

He's sitting in front of the eleven o'clock news when the phone rings, not because he cares about what's going on locally, but because he's still haunted by seeing Frank today, and consumed with worry about his extra daughter—Lucinda.

He crosses himself quickly, praying it's not bad news, and picks up the phone.

"Neal, I'm so sorry to call you this late."

Lucinda.

She sounds breathless, in a rush, but she's okay. Thank you, God. Neal crosses himself again.

"It's okay," he tells her. "I was up. Anything yet? Did they get a print match on that drag queen case in the Bronx?"

"Nothing yet. You like old music. What song is this? I only know one line. Here, I'll sing it."

She does.

Relieved that she's obviously doing just fine—and puzzled that she called him for this—Neal asks, "Are we playing Name that Tune?"

"Do you know the name of the song?"

"Sure. So do you. You just sang it."

"If I were a bell I'd be ringing . . . That's the title?"

"Yup. It's from one of my favorite musicals. *Guys and Dolls*. When the girls were little, Erma's mother came to stay one night, and I drove her up to New York to see it on Broadway. It was—"

"*Guys and Dolls*—Broadway," she cuts in. "Oh, no . . . Neal."

"What's wrong?"

"I don't even want to say it, but . . ."

"Cin, what's going on?"

"Bradley," she says. "Bradley was in *Guys and Dolls* on Broadway. That song's been going through my head for days now, and I didn't know why. Maybe it doesn't mean anything, but—"

"Maybe it does."

Sitting by the computer, Cam waits for a response from John Ruzzoccino.

She spoke to him a little while ago and asked if she could e-mail him a photo to look at. She had saved it as a separate jpg attachment, not wanting to send any information about the murder of Sheila Wright, or Attica. Nor did she mention who it was—or whom she suspected it was, anyway.

She just asked that John open it as soon as possible and let her know his reaction.

"Will do," was his jaunty reply.

Mike is a few feet away, on the couch, ostensibly watching a post-game report on the Yankees. On an ordinary night, he'd be dozing in front of the television at this hour.

Not tonight.

She sighs.

"Anything yet?" he asks, glancing her way.

"Trust me, you'd know."

"A watched e-mail box never boils . . . or something like that." He yawns.

"Why don't you go to bed? You have to be up at five-thirty."

He shakes his head. "I want to see what this guy has to say."

"What if he doesn't get back to me tonight?"

"You asked him to."

"I know, but what if . . ." She shakes her head. She can't bring herself to say it.

Her instincts tell her that John Ruzzoccino is a good guy.

That's not all her instincts are telling her today.

Earlier, she had another vision of that girl in the 1950s get-up. All along, she'd been thinking she was having a vision of a long ago crime victim—which isn't typical, because she usually sees things before they happen.

Only this time, she realized the scene might be contemporary—that the girl might be wearing some kind of costume. In the vision this time, she was text-messaging into a cell phone—and they certainly didn't have cell phones fifty years ago.

Cam doesn't know what to make of the vision, but it's troubling.

"You've got mail," the computer announces.

She hurriedly drags the cursor over to the mailbox icon.

"Mike, it's from John Ruzzoccino."

Hanging up the phone with Neal, Lucinda immediately dials Vic's number to tell him what's going on.

"*Guys and Dolls?*" he echoes. "You think your friend might be the Night Watchman because he once was in *Guys and Dolls?*"

Bradley. The Night Watchman?

It's preposterous.

And yet . . .

"For some reason, I'm making some kind of connection, Vic. Can you have someone look into it?"

"Of course. Sit tight. I'll call you back."

She hangs up, releases the mute setting on the television. On the local news channel, they're discussing the weather. Rain.

What else is new?

"The sun sets tonight at eight-twenty-six P.M." The cheery meteorologist spews the statistic along with several others, but all Lucinda cares about is the sunset.

It's eighteen minutes away.

Dammit.

Bradley.

What if it's him?

She can try to reach him, right now—see where he is, and what he's doing.

What are you going to say? she asks herself, even as she dials his cell phone. *Bradley, if you're about to kill someone, please don't.*

His phone rings a few times before he picks up, sounding sleepy.

"Bradley—where are you?"

"Home. In bed. Where are you?"

"Working."

"I wish I could say the same." He yawns. "I thought you were going to make opening night."

"I meant to—I'm so sorry I missed it. I'll catch it as soon as I get back."

"Back? Where are you?"

"Away. On business."

"Well, don't rush home to see the show, because you already missed closing night—which, actually, you could have attended, because it was opening night."

"Oh, Bradley . . . I'm sorry."

"Not as sorry as I am."

Now is not the time to comfort a once-again-out-of-work actor.

The clock is ticking.

Suddenly, there's a loud pounding on Lucinda's door.

For a moment, she's seized by panic.

Then she hears Vic's voice calling to her.

"Open up. Lucinda, it's important!"

"Bradley, I have to go."

"Now? But I was going to tell you about—"

"I'm sorry, Bradley. We'll have to talk later. Something is going on here, and . . . it's important."

"Isn't it always. Thanks for calling, Lucinda."

His tone is sarcastic. She can't worry about that now.

She hangs up, throws the phone onto the bed, and hurries over to the door.

"Lucinda!"

It sounds like him, but she checks through the peephole to make sure it really is Vic at the door.

Yes, of course it's Vic. You heard Vic's voice.

Who else would it be?

But it's 8:11, and she's not taking any chances.

"I'm here, hang on. . . ."

She opens the locks, opens the door. "Did something happen?"

"*Guys and Dolls* . . . That show just played all weekend at U-Dub."

"U-Dub . . ."

"University of Washington. A body was discovered on campus about an hour ago."

"An hour ago? But—that's too early."

"It was a guy. They think he was mugged."

"Then why—"

"He was in the show, Lucinda. *Guys and Dolls*. Let's go."

* * *

The rain stopped earlier, leaving the dense foliage along the path dripping and the bugs rattling and chirping. Cars rumble on the distant road, and Kelly's own breathing sounds oddly loud in her own ears.

This is a bad idea.

A very bad idea.

And yet, here she is, walking along a deserted path at dusk, against her better judgement.

"Julian?" she calls, wishing he had told her where, exactly, they were supposed to meet.

No reply.

All right, this is really stupid. She doesn't know this part of campus very well; in fact, she's never been down here alone, and certainly not at night.

Maybe she should have asked Renee to come with her. But that wouldn't have been very romantic, and—

Hearing a footfall behind her, she spins around.

"Julian?"

"No," a male voice croons, "not Julian."

Terror grips her. "Who is it?"

The only reply is laughter, harsh and high-pitched.

She tries to run but he grabs her by the hair, jerks her head back so that her neck is arched, and she can see nothing but the dark silhouette of tree branches far overhead.

Seeing the glint of something silver coming at her, she's certain it's a knife, and he's going to hold it to her throat and . . .

Dear God, please don't let him rape me.

But it isn't a knife.

She feels something pressing against her mouth, a waxy substance smearing across her lips, and it's bizarre, and thank God, thank God it isn't a knife. . . .

Then she sees the knife coming toward her.

"There's no time to waste, Kelly. You have to die right—"

The world goes black.

* * *

Cam highlights John Ruzzoccino's e-mail and clicks the mouse to open it.

The document contains three words.

That's John Stockman.

Phone in hand, Randy paces through the cottage, from the Captain's Quarters to the Galley and back again, doing his best not to let his imagination take him to a dark place.

Lucinda is fine.

She promised she'd stay in her room.

But it's almost eight-thirty, and she hasn't called.

He can call her . . .

No.

She said she'd call at eight-thirty. In one minute, the phone is going to ring and everything will be fine.

Just don't think about it.

Think about something else.

The move.

He's moving in a few days. He'll be glad when he doesn't have to look at this nautical crap anymore, glad to be in a generic mainland condo.

Who cares if it'll take him forever to get to work and back for the next few months with summer traffic?

He'll be closer to Lucinda.

Okay, it's eight-thirty.

Wait one more minute, and if she doesn't call, you can call her.

He waits.

She doesn't call.

He calls her.

The phone rings, rings, rings. . . .

Randy's chest is starting to constrict.

"Hi, you've reached Lucinda Sloan. I'm not able to take your call right now. Please leave a message."

"Lucinda, it's me. Where are you? You said you'd call!"

He hangs up abruptly, dials 411.

"Seattle," he says in response to the automated voice. "The Marriot Hotel."

"Which Marriot in Seattle, sir?"

"I . . . I don't know." She said something about being able to see the bay from her room. "Is there one on the water?"

"The Marriot Waterfront. I'll connect you."

Moments later, the hotel operator is on the line.

"I need to be connected to a guest room," he tells her. "Lucinda Sloan."

"One moment, please."

For a split second, he's grateful to have gotten the right Marriot on the first try.

Then it occurs to him that anyone wanting to see if she's registered in that hotel would have been able to confirm it, just like that.

The Night Watchman knows she's in Seattle. All he'd have had to do to find her would be to call one local hotel after another asking for her until he was connected to a room.

The phone rings.

Rings, rings, rings . . .

No answer, and a cyclone of panic engulfs Randy.

She said she'd be there; said she wasn't going anywhere; promised she'd call him.

There's only one explanation.

Something's happened to her.

Racing toward the campus, seated with Vic in the back seat of a black SUV, Lucinda stares at the dashboard clock.

A few minutes ago, as she watched it turn from 8:25 to 8:26, she could see it all.

The knife, the blood, the red lipstick. She heard it, too: a man laughing hysterically as a woman gasped her dying breath.

Lucinda doesn't know who, or where, the woman is.

She couldn't get a good look at her face or any identifying characteristics—other than her mouth, contorted, bleeding . . . grotesquely smeared with red lipstick.

All she knows is that it's too late.

Again.

Riding across campus, head bent low over the handlebars of the bicycle, he sees telltale flashing lights in the distance, right where he left Julian Dodd with his throat neatly slit and a book of Ibsen plays clutched in his hands.

He left the kid's backpack there, but took his wallet along with his cell phone, making it look—at least, for now—like a random mugging.

By the time they find Kelly Patterson and make the Night Watchman connection, he'll be hundreds of miles away from Seattle.

"There are sixty-five thousand people on this campus," Al Butirski tells Vic and Lucinda, sitting across the desk from him. "Since I came here in the late eighties, there have been three murders. None of them were random. This looks like it might have been."

Vic wants to remind him that looks can be deceiving, but that would put the burly head of the university police department on the defensive.

"Did this boy have any enemies? Was he dating anyone that you know of?"

"I hear he was dating everyone." Al flashes them a wry smile. "And I don't know about enemies. But his wallet and phone were taken, so again, this looks like a random mugging."

Vic isn't so sure about that at all. "Was there anything unusual about the way the body was found?"

"Not really. He had just come from the library this afternoon and he was holding a book in his hands."

"What book was it?" Lucinda asks.

"A collection of plays by, let's see . . ." He consults a notepad. "Henrik Ibsen."

"Ibsen. He wrote *A Doll's House.*"

"Very good, Agent Shattuck." Butirski smiles briefly. "Were you a lit major? Theater?"

"No, but I know a little about it."

A *Doll's* House.

Guys and *Dolls.*

Coincidence?

Glancing at Lucinda, Vic sees that it hasn't escaped her, either.

A uniformed officer sticks his head into the small office. "Hey, Al?"

"What's up?"

"Sorry to interrupt, but we've got a girl out here who says her roommate went to meet that Dodd kid a little while ago."

Vic feels Lucinda stiffen beside him.

"Bring her in," Butirski commands the officer, then looks, belatedly, at Vic. "Is that okay?"

"Sooner the better," Vic tells him.

Moments later, a shaken-looking girl is escorted into the office. She has a blond ponytail, a round face, and frightened-looking brown eyes.

"This is Renee Danziger," the officer informs them.

"Have a seat, Renee. Who's your roommate?"

"Her name is Kelly Patterson." She sinks into a chair.

"And you don't know where she is right now?"

The girl shakes her head. "She went to meet Julian a little while ago."

"Was she dating him?"

"*She* thought so. They were in the show together."

Lucinda's head snaps up. "*Guys and Dolls?*"

Renee nods. "Kelly had the lead. She was really into Julian, but everyone knows he's a player. That's why I was surprised he wanted to see her tonight. So was she. Then after she left, one of my friends called and told me he'd been killed. I am so freaked out." She starts crying.

"Renee—" Al Butirski plucks a tissue from the box and hands it to her. "That doesn't mean something happened to her. Maybe when he didn't show up she went somewhere else, or—"

"No, you don't understand. She got a text message from him, saying he wanted to meet her."

"When?"

"I don't know—maybe an hour ago?"

Butirski looks at Vic and Lucinda.

"The kid's been dead longer than that. We found his body before seven o'clock."

"Renee," Vic says urgently, "do you know where your friend was supposed to meet him?"

"On the trail by the stream behind Graves Field."

Speeding along on a bicycle through the dark streets of Seattle, he can almost hear his mother telling him to be careful.

Story of his life—until that late November day in 1969.

The coldest crime of all, the prosecuting attorney called matricide during his closing arguments. The jury stared at him, and he knew they were going to convict.

He was right.

He's always right.

They deliberated for less than an hour.

Found him guilty of manslaughter: the taking of a human life without premeditation.

Ha.

If they only knew.

But they didn't.

They had no idea who he really was, nothing at all to link him to the murders of all those women.

That, and being safe from the draft, were what kept him going for all those years, gloating as he kept tabs from behind bars on both Vietnam and the news that law enforcement officials from Maine to the Great Lakes, including the FBI, were continuing their search for the Night Watchman.

What power there was for him—from his safe haven behind thirty foot high, gun-tower topped concrete walls—to observe the bumbling, ongoing search for a serial killer!

What power in the fact that he alone knew their search would remain fruitless!

What power in knowing the guards had no clue to his true identity!

In prison, it was all about control. The guards had it. The prisoners relinquished it.

Or so it usually went.

Not for him.

He was in control, always. Even if nobody realized it but him.

In prison, when they weren't ignoring him altogether, they were treating him like a nobody.

How he gloated over that.

Idiots had no clue that he was Somebody.

Somebody to be feared. Somebody to be reckoned with.

But they would know, one day.

The whole world would know.

For the time being, he would serve his sentence, with time off for good behavior. He would take advantage of every class—academic and vocational and, in particular, computer technology—offered at Attica. Someday, he would get back to his business, and no one would ever be the wiser.

No one, that is, except Stockman.

Standing a few yards from Kelly Patterson's corpse in the floodlit thicket just off the trail, Lucinda desolately watches the investigators take measurements, snap photos, bag potential evidence found nearby on the path: a soda can pop top, a coin, a plastic hair clip.

Kelly's throat is slashed.

Her mouth is smeared with red lipstick.

And on her wrist is a Freestyle watch, the hands fixed at 8:26 P.M.

Less than an hour ago.

It could have ended so differently.

If only Lucinda had figured out sooner what that song meant.

If only they'd gotten to Kelly before he did.

They could have intercepted the message sent from Julian Dodd's stolen cell phone. They could have been here waiting for him when he showed up to kill her at sunset.

Could have . . .

If only . . .

Randy!

She forgot to call him.

Immediately, she reaches into her pocket for her cell phone and realizes it isn't there. Did she leave it behind in her room? She ran out of there when Vic showed up.

She hurries over to where he stands talking intently to a couple of guys from the local field office.

"Vic, can I borrow your phone, please? It'll only take two seconds."

He tosses it to her without missing a conversational beat, and she steps away to make the call. It's after midnight there now, but something tells her Randy didn't calmly drift off to sleep when he didn't hear from her.

"Hello?" She can hear the dread in his voice when he answers, on the first ring.

"It's me."

"Oh, God . . . Thank God . . . When I saw that this call wasn't coming from your phone I thought . . ."

"No. I'm okay. I'm so sorry I couldn't call you to let you know, but—"

"You're okay," he echoes raggedly.

She quickly brings him up to date, telling him the tragic story of Kelly and Julian.

"Where are you now?"

"I'm at the crime scene, and I'm on Vic Shattuck's phone—"

She breaks off, seeing Vic and the agents hurrying toward a couple of investigators who are positioning more spotlights to illuminate the path. They must have found something there.

"I have to go, Randy," she says hurriedly. "I just wanted you to know I was okay. I'll talk to you tomorrow. Good—"

"Wait, there's something I want you to know, too. Don't say anything, okay? Just listen to me. I love you, Lucinda. I've been waiting to say that for so damned long. I love you. Now go."

Stunned, she stands holding the phone against her ear.

"Lucinda!" Vic calls. "Come over here and look at this!"

In a perfect world they would burst into the room at the Motel 6—registered to a John Knight and paid for in cash— to discover the unsub there, asleep in his bed.

But the world is far from perfect.

There's no doubt that the key card they discovered on the path near Kelly's body belongs to her killer; there were drops of blood on it.

But when the agents storm the room, it's empty.

Summoned to take a look, Vic and Lucinda cross the threshold to see that the bed hasn't been slept in. There's no luggage.

"Maybe he'll be back," one of the agents speculates, as another calls in the forensics team to start dusting for fingerprints.

"He won't be back."

"How do you know?" Vic asks Lucinda, who merely shrugs.

Yeah. Stupid question.

How does she know anything?

He's still amazed by the way she made the *Guys and Dolls* connection.

Amazed that they'd come so close to saving the lives of those two kids; so close to catching the unsub that if Vic allows himself to dwell on any of it, he'll be physically sick.

"Look at this!" On his hands and knees, one of the agents holds up a yellow slip of paper clamped in a pair of tweezers. "This guy's getting sloppy."

Sloppy.

Vic tilts his head thoughtfully

The agent examines the slip of paper. "This is a mail order receipt, dated back in January. From Star Jewelers in New York, for five watches, plus engraving."

Sloppy, indeed.

"No." Vic shakes his head. "No way."

"What's wrong, Vic?" Lucinda asks.

"The unsub is highly organized. Meticulous. Why would he suddenly have gotten sloppy enough to not only leave the hotel room key at the scene, but a receipt in the room?"

Lucinda stares at him. "He wouldn't. He wanted us to find both. Is that what you're thinking?"

"That's exactly what I'm thinking. At every scene, he left us a clue to where he's going next. That receipt," he tells her resolutely, "is going to give us the answer."

Chapter Twenty-three

The nurses in the hospital corridor greet Cam by name and fuss over Grace as she pushes the stroller toward her father's room.

"How is he today?" she asks.

"Pretty good." Pearl, a no-nonsense old school nurse, gives a satisfied nod.

Glad to hear it, Cam rolls Grace into her father's room. He spots them immediately—which is a good sign. Sometimes it takes him a while to tune out the television or whatever else he's absorbed in.

"Well, well, well. Look who's here."

Sitting up in his hospital bed, Ike Neary looks better, if anything, than his old self. His gray hair is clean and combed into a neat ponytail, his frame has filled out thanks to a steady, healthy diet, and his eyes aren't bloodshot courtesy of booze and pot.

Yet looks can be deceiving, Cam knows. In one of life's bitter ironies, her father is fading away even as his body bounces back from years of hard living.

"Who's here, mon?" Nigel, the Jamaican male nurse asks, nodding a hello to Cam as he finishes writing something on a clipboard chart.

"What's the matter, you don't have eyes? My daughter!"

Which daughter, though, Pop? Cam wants to ask—because you never can tell where his mind is at.

He pats the bed. "Sit down over here with your old man, Cam, and let me get a look at that beautiful grandbaby."

Relieved, she looks at Nigel.

"It's okay," he says, "I'm finished. Enjoy your visit. Good to see you, Cam. See you tomorrow, Ike."

"Where are you going?"

"It's three. My shift is over."

"All right. Give me some skin, brother." Cam's father holds up his hand.

With a grin, Nigel slaps it, then gives Grace a little pat as Cam rolls the carriage over to the bed.

"She's getting big."

"Yes, she is. See you later."

As he leaves, her father says, "He's one cool cat, that Nigel. What a surprise to find him working here."

"What do you mean, Pop?"

"He used to play sax with Bruce, down in Asbury. Called himself Clarence back then."

Cam's heart sinks. She doesn't let her father see her face as she lifts Grace, dressed all in pink, out of the stroller.

"Look at you. How's my beautiful girl?" Ike holds out his arms. "Come to Granddad."

Cam gently places the baby on her father's lap, then sits beside him.

"You look good today, Pop."

"I feel good." He tickles the baby and is delighted when Grace rewards him with a big smile.

"You know who she looks like when she smiles?"

Cam nods. "Tess."

"Yes, Tess. Who else would I be talking about?" He gestures at the baby. "She looks like Mike."

Momentarily confused by his phrasing, Cam grasps it when

her father goes on to tell Grace, "Yes, you do, Tessie. You look just like your daddy."

Cam sighs inwardly.

When she came here today, she was considering telling her father what she had learned last night. She wondered whether it might bring him some peace to know that Ava didn't abandon the two of them the way Brenda had.

Momentary peace, anyway. He doesn't retain much these days.

And he spends enough time, as it is, living in the past.

It's probably best not to dredge up old pain.

Not when the truth is as ugly as the lie they've lived with for all these years.

"Ladies and gentlemen, welcome to Philadelphia International Airport. The local time is 10:42 P.M. Please remain seated until we reach the gate, but if you have a phone close at hand, you're welcome to use it now."

Lucinda is already dialing.

Vic picks up immediately.

"I just landed." She clears her throat in a futile effort to make her tired voice a little less hoarse. Several cups of hot tea on the flight didn't help, though she was able to catch a few hours' sleep—her first in almost forty-eight hours.

"Did you find out anything?" she asks Vic.

"Yes. The jewelry store is in midtown Manhattan. Hordes of people coming and going. No one remembers him. But the watches were all Freestyle, and they do have a record of what was engraved on them."

"And . . . ?"

"And they match the four we've got so far."

"What about the fifth? If we know where he's planning to go next, we'll have a head start figuring out who the victim might be."

"We believe we already know." Vic's voice is oddly subdued.

With a jolt, the plane arrives at the gate, and the captain sounds the bell.

"What do you mean? You believe you already know the place, or who the victim might be?"

"Both."

Dread creeps over her.

"Lucinda, the fifth watch reads June 18, 39.5, 75.1."

"Where is that?"

"Philadelphia."

Lucinda's flight landed fifteen minutes ago, according to the Arrivals board.

Randy waits beside the passenger exit with a bouquet of roses—white, not red. He figures she saw enough red last night in Seattle to last her a lifetime.

She sounded so beaten down when they spoke this morning—rather, *he* spoke. She tried, but her voice was shot.

He didn't bother to ask whether she'd slept last night. He knew she hadn't.

In a whisper, she told him how they'd gone from the crime scene to the hotel where the unsub had been staying, only to discover he'd vanished. But the desk clerk remembered him as an older man, tall and lean, with gray hair, glasses, a beard. Now, at least, they have a description to go by.

Her voice barely audible, Lucinda told him she'd be flying home to Philly tonight. "I'll call you when I land—it'll be around 10:30," she rasped.

He decided to surprise her at the airport.

Now, as Randy keeps an eye on the stream of passengers exiting the gate area, he thinks about what he said to her last night, fresh from Frank's deathbed and the advice to not just exist, but to *live*.

I love you.

The words just fell out of his mouth impulsively, but he meant them.

He didn't give her a chance to respond then—even if she'd wanted to. He told himself it was because she was in the middle of a crime scene investigation, but that's not the only reason.

He was afraid of what she'd say in return.

"Please don't love me," or *"Well, I don't love you,"* or God only knows what.

He didn't want to hear it over the phone.

Let her say it to him in person.

And if that's not what she was going to say—well, he'd prefer to hear the alternative in person, too.

Suddenly spotting her face in the sea of faces coming toward him, he realizes he almost missed her, and no wonder. This is Lucinda as he's never seen her.

Unaware that anyone's watching, she's let down her defenses for the first time since he's known her. Ordinarily, her commanding presence makes her stick out in a crowd; tonight, she's lost herself in one, intentionally or not. She walks slowly, shoulders hunched as though she's cold—or afraid—making her look smaller than she is.

Not just smaller. Vulnerable.

She glances around as she walks, as though she's searching for someone—not for Randy, of course; she doesn't expect him to be here. For a moment, he wonders if she arranged for someone else to meet her. Then she draws closer, and he sees that her expression isn't one of anticipation, but apprehension.

He hurries toward her, wanting to let her know that she isn't alone. That he's with her, and he'll take care of her.

"Lucinda!"

She freezes, darts a glance in his direction. He waves, watches her face register shock, and relief.

As she hurries toward him, he realizes he can't say any of the things he was about to. The vulnerable Lucinda he glimpsed just a moment ago has vanished, replaced by a woman who stands tall, radiating strength. A woman who clearly doesn't need—or want—anyone to take care of her.

So.

Her boyfriend decided to surprise her at the airport, did he?

Leaning against a pole behind an open newspaper, he watches the couple embrace.

She looks thrilled.

Personally, he's never cared for surprises—not unless he's the one planning them.

He must always, *always* be the one in control.

And you always have been.

Even back in September, 1971, when a tense situation spiraled into utter chaos for the other two thousand-odd inmates at Attica prison.

Control amid chaos. That was the key.

He seized the opportunity to do what had to be done.

When the uprising was over, over forty men lay dead, inmates and correctional personnel.

As far as the rest of the world was concerned, all were casualties of the bloodiest clash in prison history.

He alone knows that one among them was not.

After hanging up with Lucinda, Vic presses a speed dial key to connect to a number he'd erased from the phone's memory a while back, never imagining he'd need it again.

Funny how things work out.

"Annabelle Wyatt."

"I told her."

"How did she take it?"

"In stride. She's a tough cookie. I told her we'll do every-thing possible to keep her safe, but not to let on that she knows what's going on."

"Good. You didn't give her any classified information, did you?"

He sighs inwardly. "No. I didn't."

"Remember. She's not a part of this investigation."

And you're lucky you are.

Annabelle doesn't say it, but the message comes through to Vic, loud and clear.

"I'll be clearing the decks here and flying to Philadelphia as soon as possible," she says crisply. "You do the same."

"Absolutely."

But only after a quick detour to see his wife.

In the old days, he was used to all the travel, used to being apart from Kitty for weeks at a time. Not anymore.

When this case is resolved, he'll be ready for retirement at last, and this time, there will be no wistful backward glances.

"All right, Vic. Good work."

"Did you determine whether anything else found at the scene was significant?"

"It's hard to tell. We're working on it. This is all classified, got it?"

Meaning, *don't tell Lucinda.*

"Got it."

"The soda can tab has probably been there for a while. The plastic clip might have flown off the victim's head. The strands that were caught in it look like a match to her hair. We'll do DNA testing on it, of course. The coin was foreign. A krone."

"A krone! From Norway!"

"Yes. A krone. Why? Does that mean something to you?"

"Henrik Ibsen was from Norway."

There's a moment of silence as she digests that.

"So you're thinking . . ."

"Norway, Annabelle. That's where he's going. Not Philadelphia. He was trying to throw us off his trail. He's going to Norway."

"We don't know that for sure."

"No. But I'd say there's a pretty good chance."

"We'll start looking into it. And remember. This is classified."

Classified.

He can't tell Lucinda.

But if the Watchman is headed overseas, it looks like she might be safe, for now, after all.

Lucinda prolongs the hug, keeping her face safely buried against Randy's shoulder until she's certain she's regained her composure.

She probably shouldn't be so damned glad to see him but the truth is, after what Vic just told her on the phone, she was feeling shell-shocked and alone in the world.

Then, miraculously, there was Randy—just what she needed, though she hadn't realized it until she saw him.

"What are you doing here?" she asks, finally daring to pull back and look up at him.

"Surprising you."

"How did you know—"

"Shh, don't talk. You barely have a voice. How did I know which flight you were on? You told me you were landing at 10:30. It wasn't hard to figure out."

"You're amazing."

"Well, I am a detective," he says with fake modesty.

"No, I mean—that you're here. I'm so glad to see you."

Oops. That just popped out. Should she have admitted that she's glad to see him, even after he told her he loved her?

Probably not—considering that she has no idea how she feels about the revelation. It's not something she's spent a whole lot of time thinking about in the last twenty-four hours—

or will be able to think about in the weeks ahead, now that she's the Night Watchman's next target.

Vic said they'll be laying a trap for him, and that they'll keep her safe.

Lucinda just wishes she could believe that.

A knock on the door jars Vic's attention away from the laptop screen.

"Housekeeping," a male voice calls.

Irritated by the interruption, he goes over to the door.

Opening it, he realizes belatedly that he should have checked through the peephole, just to make sure it really is housekeeping.

A man stands there beside a cart loaded with towels, sheets, toiletries.

He has gray hair.

"You want turndown?" he asks in broken English.

"No, thanks."

The guy reaches into his pocket.

Vic immediately goes for his gun—then sees that the man is holding out a couple of chocolate pillow mints.

"Oh—thank you." Blindly removing a couple of bills from his pocket instead of his weapon, as if the money were what he'd been going for in the first place, Vic thrusts it into the man's hand.

Oops—one of the bills is a ten.

Grateful he didn't shoot the guy, Vic can't help but smile at his delighted expression.

"Oh, thank you, sir, thank you! Thank you very much! Here!" He reaches into his pocket again, and this time, pulls out a big handful of chocolate mints. "For you. Thank you!"

"You're welcome." Watching him trundle off down the hall with the housekeeping cart, Vic is momentarily amused, and glad to have made the guy's night.

Then he turns back to the computer screen, where he's researching Norway.

Otherwise known as the Land of the Midnight Sun.

"The worst part," Cam tells Mike, curled up beside him on the chintz sofa in the sunroom, "is that we'll probably never know whether he killed my sister and the others. There's no way to prove that anyone was even on the roof with Ava the night she died, and Lucinda said the figure was hooded in her vision, so she didn't get a look at his face."

"I'd say there's enough circumstantial evidence to assume he did it, though."

"No, I know. I just wish there were proof." Cam leans her head against his shoulder and yawns.

"At least the police said they'll look into it."

"Right, but unless they come up with a long lost signed confession in Stockman's handwriting, I don't see what good it's going to do." She yawns again.

"You should go to bed," Mike tells her. "It's been a long day."

It has, what with digesting the truth about Stockman, enduring the visit with her father, and hearing from Lucinda that two more people were murdered last night. When Cam went online to read the Seattle newspaper's account of the victims, she was stunned to recognize Kelly Patterson in a photo of her and Julian Dodd snapped during their performance in *Guys and Dolls*.

Kelly was the girl Cam has been seeing in her visions.

If only she had known . . .

But how could you have known?

Exhausted, she stands and stretches. "Are you coming up, Mike?"

"I'm going to stay here for a few minutes and check the score on the game."

"Isn't it over?"

"Didn't start till ten. They're playing on the West Coast tonight." He reaches for the remote.

"And here I thought you were being so noble, spending the whole night playing Scrabble with me and Tess instead of watching baseball."

"I *was* being noble. I was trying to take your mind off everything. And it worked—for a while. Until you lost."

"Yeah, well, you try to win with an *x* when you can't use it to spell *s-e-x*."

Mike snickers. "You could have. It's not like Tess has never heard of it."

"True. I just hope she isn't thinking about doing it."

Mike covers his ears. "Stop that. Go away."

With a yawn, she picks up their empty tea mugs and starts toward the kitchen. In the doorway, she turns back. "Mike?"

"Yeah?"

"There's just one thing that's bothering me."

"You mean besides our fifteen-year-old daughter and *s-e-x*?" He's already flipping channels.

"I'm being serious here."

"So am I."

"Mike."

He looks up and sees the look on her face. "Okay. What is it?"

"Someone sent me that note wanting me to make the connection between Sheila Wright and my sister. Before he died, Andrew Stockman must have told someone what he did. That person is out there somewhere—and he knows what happened to Ava."

He decides not to follow Lucinda Sloan as she leaves the airport with Randy Barakat. No reason to, really.

He knows what he came to find out: that she's already aware that she's next.

Fear was vivid on her face when she walked through the airport, before she spotted Barakat and put on the fake bravado.

She's a sitting duck.

But she's smart.

She'll try to escape.

He's smarter.

He won't let her.

"Vic. Did I wake you?"

"Yes." Dazed, he sits up in bed, turns on the lamp, sees that it's three in the morning. "What's going on, Annabelle?"

"We've got a match on those old prints."

PART V

10:24

Chapter Twenty-four

"I still don't understand why the FBI didn't just put this Eugene Fox on 'America's Most Wanted,'" Cam tells Lucinda as they stroll through the Reading Terminal Market with little Grace in a baby carriage, a federal agent trailing discreetly behind.

"He was on the wanted lists after he violated parole last fall," Lucinda tells her around a mouthful of apple dumpling she bought at the Amish stand down the way, "but no one realized he was the Night Watchman for all those years he was in prison, so it wasn't necessarily a big deal. Parole violators are a dime a dozen."

"The whole story is unbelievable."

Lucinda couldn't agree more.

It's been three weeks since Vic told her they'd matched the fingerprints found in Ricky Parker's—a.k.a. Scarlet's—Bronx apartment to Eugene Fox, a mild-mannered young man who lived across the hall with his mother.

Born on September 14, 1950, Fox had led a low-key life before and after, with one exception: as a little boy, he'd been holding his father's hand when a stray bullet hit him during a botched holdup. The father died right there on the sidewalk in front of his son.

Something like that will scar a kid for life.

Eugene and his mother moved from the Bronx to Yonkers not long after Parker's death, which was, of course, officially unsolved. Eugene worked as an elementary school custodian, kept to himself, took care of his mother.

Until, in November of 1969, he was arrested for killing her.

"How sure is the FBI that this Fox guy is the Night Watchman?"

"Let's put it this way. The date he killed his mother coincides exactly with the murder of Judy Steinberg, the Watchman's last known murder."

Neither law enforcement nor the press made a connection between Eugene Fox in Yonkers and Judy Steinberg less than thirty miles—yet a world—away, on Long Island.

"Why didn't the FBI make this information public, then, when they got the fingerprint match?"

Lucinda had wondered the same thing, at first.

Now she tells Cam what Vic and Annabelle told her.

"They don't want him to know they're onto him. They're almost positive he's going to lay low until June eighteenth. They know when and where he's going to strike. This is their chance to get him."

"And put your life at risk in the process."

Lucinda doesn't reply, spooning the last of the dumpling and rich cream into her mouth, then tossing the plastic bowl into a trash can.

She wasn't really hungry—hasn't been, lately. But you don't come to the market, with its dozens of food stalls, without indulging. So she did—to show Cam, and the agents, and *him*, if by chance he's watching, that she's just fine.

"Lucinda, I'm worried about you."

"It's fine. Trust me, I've got so much security right now that whenever I leave my apartment I feel like the president."

"Why do you leave at all? If I were you, I'd hole up until they catch the guy."

"No way am I going to be a prisoner in my apartment for

almost a month," Lucinda says staunchly. "If there's anything I know for sure, it's that this guy doesn't strike in broad daylight in public places. And anyway, the FBI wants me to go about my business as usual, in case he's watching."

"Do you think he is?"

Lucinda hesitates, then admits it. "Yes. I can feel him sometimes."

"Now?"

"No. Not now."

"Have you seen him?"

"No. But sometimes I just sense that he's nearby. You know what I mean."

Cam nods. She, alone, knows what Lucinda means.

"Aren't you terrified?"

"Now? No. Like I said, we know when, where, and how he's going to make his move. And these guys are with me all the time."

"You're willing to trust them with your life."

"They're the FBI, Cam."

That doesn't answer the question—but it's the best she can offer.

"This is your life, Lucinda. And I don't want anything to happen to you now that everything has finally fallen into place."

Lucinda can't help but smile. "Oh, sure, it would have been fine for something to happen to me before, when I was lonely and single. But now that Randy and I are . . . well, whatever we are—"

She has yet to put a label on whatever it is they've been doing since she got home from Seattle.

"Dating," Cam tells her with a firm nod, then checks her watch. "For that matter, so is Tess, and it's getting late."

"Late? I feel like you just got here!"

"That was almost two hours ago. It's three o'clock, and I don't want to hit rush hour traffic. I've really got to get going home."

"So Tess is dating again? She and Mr. Wonderful got back together, then?"

"No, I think she's actually getting over him. This is someone new. His name is Chad, and he invited her to his junior prom. She's been practicing walking around the house in the shoes she was going to wear, but they're giving her blisters so I promised I'd take her to look for a new pair tonight."

"Wow, that's nice of you. My mother would have told me to get out the Band-Aids and suck it up."

Her mother.

She's been meaning to call Bitsy before . . . well, before tomorrow. Since she got back from Seattle, she hasn't had a chance.

Who are you kidding? You've had plenty of chances.

But maybe it's better this way. One less person to have to lie to.

"I'm so glad to see Tess smiling again," Cam says, "that I'd buy her Manolo Blahniks if I didn't think they'd hurt her feet worse. Anyway, the prom is tomorrow night."

"They're having a prom on Friday the thirteenth?"

"I know, crazy, isn't it? But I didn't want to say anything about it to Tess. I don't think she's noticed the date. Anyway, she's had enough bad luck."

She's not the only one, Lucinda thinks grimly.

They make their way toward the exit. Lucinda finds herself scanning the crowd, just in case.

She's seen a photo of Eugene Fox, taken just before he was released from prison last June.

She made it a point to memorize his features: weathered face, gray hair—and the coldest, hardest black stare she's ever seen in her life.

She wants to believe she'd know him if she ever saw him again, but the truth is, he looks like thousands of other middle-aged men.

She'd recognize those stony dark eyes anywhere, but the rest of him would be easy enough to disguise simply by gaining or losing weight, dying, shaving, or growing his hair, adding a beard or mustache. . . .

Wearing sunglasses.

Outside Reading Terminal, Cam gives her a hug. She's parked in the garage across the street.

"Please be careful."

"I really wish people would stop saying that to me," Lucinda tells her as she bends over to press a kiss against little Grace's downy hair. "Trust me, I don't have a death wish."

"I just hope that when they get this guy," Cam says, "they take him alive."

Lucinda doesn't have to ask why.

She knows the whole story. Knows that Eugene Fox and Andrew Stockman were in Attica together—in adjoining cells, according to the records Vic found.

Eugene Fox might very well be the only person on earth who can confirm their suspicions that Ava Neary was murdered. Ava, and Sandra, and all those other girls pictured in the scrapbook he sent Lucinda.

If they get him, perhaps they can offer answers to all those grieving, bewildered families, including Cam's.

But something tells Lucinda that when June 18 comes, Eugene Fox will never let himself be taken alive.

And that he's going to do everything in his power to bring Lucinda down in a blaze of glory with him, FBI or no FBI.

Unmasking the Night Watchman was a bittersweet triumph for Vic Shattuck.

He never imagined that with a name and a face at last, the killer—no longer an unsub—would remain free.

Now, with June 18 just six days away, Vic is ensconced in the field office on Arch Street in Philadelphia, working on the Norway angle—which seems to be a frustrating dead end; missing Kitty like crazy; worrying about Lucinda Sloan like crazy.

Annabelle Wyatt assured him and reassured him that they

won't let anything happen to Lucinda, but there are no guarantees.

Annabelle knows it, Vic knows it, and he has no doubt Lucinda knows it, too.

If she has any misgivings, though, they're hidden away as effectively as the Watchman himself is.

She's willingly going along with Annabelle's plan to set a trap for the Night Watchman on June 18, using Lucinda herself as the bait.

"Why not consider a decoy?" Vic asked. "We can get an agent who looks like you to take your place."

"Do you think that will work?" Lucinda asked Annabelle.

And Annabelle, damn her, shrugged.

"I'll stay," Lucinda decided. "We can't let him slip through our fingers."

Either she's the bravest woman Vic has ever known in his life, or the most foolish.

Possibly a bit of both.

Maybe Lucinda still, somehow, doesn't get it. Maybe she doesn't understand just how clever and cold-blooded a killer the Night Watchman is. Maybe she doesn't grasp how much danger she's in.

But Vic does.

And he's not going to let another innocent woman die.

He tried, early on, to talk her out of this, tried to convince her to go into hiding.

She flat-out refused.

"Something tells me Annabelle wouldn't be thrilled to know you'd even suggested it, Vic," she'd said, wearing an amused little smile.

She was right.

But he could not, in good conscience, let a woman put her life on the line without at least giving her an out.

He suspects he'll live to regret that she didn't take it. She won't, though.

Not because Vic might be wrong about what's going to happen on June 18.

Lucinda Sloan won't live to regret it because she won't live at all.

Hearing her mother's heels tapping briskly across the marble corridor, Lucinda turns to see Bitsy Sloan in the doorway of the drawing room. She's dressed—in the middle of a weekday—in a navy silk dress and pearls.

Nice to know that some things never change.

"Lucinda! What in the world are you doing here?"

"Hello, Mother. I was in the neighborhood so I thought I'd stop by."

And so the lies begin. Reading Terminal is hardly in the neighborhood.

Yet after Lucinda left Cam, she decided that if ever there were a time to reach out to her mother, this is it.

Her mother looks at Magdalena, who escorted Lucinda into the mansion after she rang the bell.

"Can you please bring us some tea?"

"Right away." The maid nods, then flashes Lucinda a smile. "It's nice to see you again, Ms. Sloan."

"You, too, Magdalena."

"Let's sit down." Bitsy arranges herself on an eighteenth century French sofa and indicates the chair opposite. "What's wrong?"

What isn't?

If Bitsy were a different kind of mother—and, to be fair, if Lucinda were a different kind of daughter—she might be tempted to pour out the whole story. She might even be tempted to stay.

Behind the stone and ivy walls of the Sloan mansion, she feels unreachable, untouchable. That, of course, is the whole idea.

Generations of Sloans before her actually believed that the real world, with all its problems, couldn't penetrate the fortress.

But Lucinda never bought into the illusion, and she isn't going to start now. She's here not because it's a safe haven, but because she has something to say.

And not much time to say it.

It might be now or never. So talk.

"I wanted you to know that I've been thinking about how little time we've spent together over the years, Mother, and I want that to change."

Bitsy Sloan's perfectly arched eyebrows disappear beneath the bangs of her perfectly styled pageboy, yet she maintains her composure as she replies, "I see. What made you start thinking about that?"

"Who knows? Maybe, now that I'm in my thirties, I'm finally growing up."

It was a joke, but her mother's response is unexpectedly heartfelt.

"You've always been grown-up, Lucinda. Maybe that was part of the problem."

"What do you mean?"

"You never really needed me."

"Oh, Mother, don't—"

"Please." Her mother holds up a hand. "Just let me speak. And then you can speak. Who knows? Maybe we'll have an actual conversation." She flashes a grim smile.

Again caught off guard, Lucinda returns it.

"You were always independent, Lucinda. You were determined to take care of yourself from the time you were very young. You didn't need me. And I was relieved, to be perfectly honest, not to be needed. I had my life; your father had his; you had yours. For a very long time, I thought it worked quite nicely."

"I guess maybe it did."

"But now, sitting here shocked to see you appear out of nowhere in the middle of the day, I realize I don't know a thing about what it is that you do, exactly. Or where and how you live. Or . . . who you are."

"I really didn't think you wanted to know, Mother."

"I didn't." Bitsy shrugs. "I'm not going to pretend any differently. Just as I'm sure you don't really want to know what it is that I do, day in and day out, or who I am."

Lucinda opens her mouth to tell her that she does know.

But do you?

"Maybe we can try to spend some time together then," she tells her mother. "Maybe Dad will even join us."

"I doubt that. But maybe. He'll be home on Sunday night for a few days. Why don't you come to dinner while he's here?"

"Next week? I can't." Seeing the flash of disappointment in her mother's eyes, she adds, "But soon. I promise."

Even as she says it, a little voice warns her, *you shouldn't make promises you aren't sure you can keep.*

"All right, Frank, I'm going to give you something stronger for the pain. Can you hear me, Frank? If you can hear me, squeeze my hand."

He squeezes Angie's hand.

Or is it Mary?

"Frank, if you can hear me, squeeze my hand."

He's squeezing, dammit.

"He probably can, whether he's squeezing or not," another voice says. "Hearing is the last thing to go."

"Frank, we're making you comfortable, okay, honey?"

Her voice is very far away.

"I need ten more cc's, Angie."

Ten.

Numbers. It's always about the numbers.

"Frank, I know it hurts. . . ."

Her voice fades before he can tell her that she's wrong.

It doesn't hurt.

Finally, it doesn't hurt at all.

* * *

As they climb the steps to Neal's house, Randy squeezes Lucinda's hand. "I'm starved. How about you?"

"You know me. I'm always hungry."

Lies.

He doesn't know her. He thinks he does, but he doesn't.

And she isn't hungry. How can she eat, knowing what's going to happen tomorrow?

For once in her life, Lucinda wishes she were enveloped in darkness.

That way, Randy wouldn't be able to see her face and perhaps sense that she's hiding something from him.

But the sun is still riding high in the sky, though it's early evening now. Lawnmowers hum, a group of boys play street hockey on a neighboring driveway, and children ride tricycles on the sidewalk as watchful parents chat.

It's all so ordinary—such a far cry from the insulated stone mansion Lucinda left behind a little while ago. Fresh from the unexpectedly candid conversation with her mother, she finds herself craving something she didn't even realize was missing.

Family ties.

Roots.

Ordinary—and thus, for her, extraordinary—everyday life.

Neal opens the door, wearing slacks and a polo shirt. "Lucinda. Randy. Glad you could make it. Come on in."

Looking around the front hall, Randy hands him the bottle of wine they brought. "You know, it's been years since I was here, Neal."

"Oh, well, it hasn't changed much—except that there's a lot more clutter, and some things are a little more worn out, just like the people who live here."

"Hey, speak for yourself." Erma appears from the kitchen. "It's good to see you again, Randy."

"You, too." He hugs her. "I hear you retired. Congratulations."

"A year ago, but thank you. I just wish Neal would join me. It gets lonely around here."

Randy turns to Neal. "You hear that? Your wife is lonely. Don't you think it's time you threw in the towel?"

"Not yet," Neal says gruffly.

"Then when?" Lucinda asks.

"When it's time. And that's all I have to say about that."

Erma shakes her head, then gives Lucinda a quick hug. "How are you, sweetie? Hanging in there?"

She must know what's been going on. Lucinda figures there are few secrets between Neal and his wife.

Before she can assure Erma that she is, indeed, hanging in there, Garland Fisher steps out of the kitchen. "Erma, don't shoot the messenger, but your rice just boiled all over the stove."

"Oh, no!" She scurries past him.

"Lucinda, I know you've met our neighbor." Neal gestures at Garland. "He popped over so I invited him to stay for dinner. Garland Fisher, this is Randy Barakat."

"Nice to see you again, Lucinda. Good to meet you, Randy." Wearing cargo pants and a khaki fishing hat, Garland shakes both their hands warmly.

Lucinda flashes back to the night it all began, remembering how she suspected Garland of stealing the scrapbook.

But his eyes are anything but cold and black. How little she knew back then.

To think that Eugene Fox was here, in this house with them, that night. He brazenly came in the front door, knocked over the vase and frightened the children, then crept into the kitchen while they were all distracted here.

He could have followed Lucinda home, or been waiting in her apartment when she got there.

He could have killed her right then and there, but he didn't.

He wanted to wait.

Timing, after all, is everything.

For him.

And for me.

Looking at Randy and Neal, Lucinda can only hope that when the time comes, they'll understand.

Trust.

That's always been an issue for her.

For three weeks now, she's been thinking about the handful of people with whom she's entrusted her keys, her secrets, her safety, her heart.

Neal. Cam. Randy. Even Vic.

But when you get right down to it, there's only one person on the face of this earth she's willing to entrust with her life itself.

That person is Lucinda Sloan.

Chapter Twenty-five

On Friday morning, Lucinda calls Randy early, before he can call her.

That's unusual.

"Hey, why aren't you sleeping in?" he asks, hearing her voice.

"Didn't feel like it. Are you at work?"

"Yes, and I definitely could have stood to sleep in after getting home at one in the morning. I wish you had let me call in sick today and stay at your place last night like I wanted to."

"Another time," she tells him.

"Are you still coming out here tomorrow to go to the beach? It's going to be a gorgeous day."

She hesitates. "We'll see, okay? I have to go. I'll talk to you later."

Uh-oh.

Something tells Randy she's going to back out.

"Lucinda?"

But she's already hung up, and Dan Lambert is standing in the doorway of Randy's office.

"What's up, Dan?"

Seeing the look in his eyes, Randy bows his head.

He knows what's coming, but still, it's a blow to hear the words.

"Frank Santiago died last night."

"Tess? Did you get the dress on? Do you need help?" Cam calls through the closed door of her daughter's room.

"No. You can come in."

She opens the door.

Tess stands in front of the mirror, wearing a coral-colored chiffon cocktail dress and the new high-heeled sandals they bought last night, her face made-up and her hair in layered waves that fall past her shoulders at last.

"Oh, Tess."

"Do I look okay?"

Cam shakes her head.

"I don't look okay?"

"No, you do! You do. You look beautiful. And so grown up I just . . . I can't believe it. Five minutes ago, I was pushing you on a swing."

"Um, Mom? I think that was Grace."

"No, that was you. Trust me."

"Well, you know what they say. Time flies."

Yes. It does. Whether you're having fun, or not.

Looking back over Tess's childhood, Cam thinks of all she missed, lost in a haze of booze and anxiety. And now look. Tess is a woman. In no time, she'll be gone.

Time does fly. It's more precious than Cam ever knew.

That's why she's not going to waste another minute dwelling on what happened in the past. What's done is done.

You know the truth about Ava. You don't need to hear it from a sick, depraved human being like Eugene Fox. Why give him the satisfaction? It won't change anything. It won't bring Ava back.

It's been thirty-five years. It's time to let go.

Cam wipes a tear from her eye.

"What's wrong, Mom?"

"Nothing," she tells Tess. "Nothing at all."

And she means it.

On her knees pulling weeds from the flower bed beside the front door, Erma looks up in surprise—immediately followed by dread—when Neal pulls into the driveway.

"What are you doing home in the middle of the afternoon? Did something happen?"

"Yes." He steps out of the car. "I've made a decision."

Erma stands and pulls off her gardening gloves, brushing dirt from her shorts. "What is it?"

"I'm going to retire."

Erma breaks into a grin. "Why now?"

Neal hesitates.

He could tell her about all the missing persons who will never be found, with or without him.

He could tell her that last night, just before he crossed the yard to his own empty house, Garland Fisher told him how lucky he is.

Or he could tell her about Frank Santiago.

Someday, they'll talk about all of those things.

For now, he just shrugs and says simply, "Because it's time."

"Lucinda! There you are. I've been trying to call you for the last two hours, at home and on your cell. Where have you been?"

She ignores Randy's question. "I got your messages. Is everything okay?"

"I wanted to tell you that Frank passed away last night."

"Oh, no." For a moment, her own troubles disappear. "I'm so sorry to hear that."

"Yeah." He sighs. "I've been thinking about something he said to me the last time I saw him. I want to tell you about it.

Why don't you drive out here tonight instead of waiting until tomorrow?"

"Randy, I can't. I'm sorry."

"You can't come tonight or you can't come tomorrow?"

"Both. I just need some time, okay?"

"Time for what?"

She clutches the phone, wishing she could tell him, wishing she could see him, wishing she could say that she loves him, too. . . .

And wishing he knew the truth.

But he can't.

Not yet.

Not until it comes to an end, one way or another.

"Vic, it's Annabelle. I have news, and it's not good."

"What is it?" He sits on the bed in his Philadelphia hotel room and braces himself for the worst.

"She's gone."

"Excuse me?"

"She's missing, Vic. We have no idea what happened to her. Nobody's seen her since she got home late last night."

"Who?" he asks in dread, though he already knows.

"Lucinda Sloan."

Elliott Bay is bathed in a pink glow tonight as the sun sinks low in a purplish-blue sky, with the frosty tip of Mount Rainier visible in the distance.

Lucinda knew it was out there when she was here last month, but she never got to see it, as it was perpetually shrouded in dense gray clouds. The weather has been beautiful since she landed in Seattle a few hours ago. Maybe it's a good omen.

Considering that today is Friday the thirteenth, she won't count on it.

Last night, for the first time in her life, she turned off her bedside lamp.

Under cover of darkness, she strapped on her backpack and slipped out the window, closing it after her.

As she scuttled away into the night, she expected someone to fall into step behind her: the FBI—or him. The Night Watchman. Even though the full moon is still a few days away.

But no one followed her. The agents weren't expecting her to turn off the alarms and sneak out the back, giving them the slip.

She didn't breathe easily until she'd gotten through security at the airport.

Before dawn, she flew from Philadelphia to Chicago.

From Chicago, she changed airlines, then flew to Denver.

There, she changed airlines for a third time, and flew to Seattle.

If, by chance, they trail her, they'll think she's retracing the Night Watchman's steps, and that her journey ends here.

This is where they'll look for her.

But they'll never find her—and neither will the Night Watchman.

Chapter Twenty-six

"Vic? Are you even listening to me?"

Jarred back to his telephone conversation by Kitty's voice, Vic turns away from the view of Philadelphia's night skyline beyond his hotel room window.

"I'm listening."

No, he isn't.

He's thinking about the fact that across the ocean in Norway, June eighteenth has already dawned.

Vic is almost convinced that Eugene Fox has abducted Lucinda and somehow taken her overseas. They've got her photo plastered from Oslo to Nordkapp, but so far there hasn't been a single sighting.

The trouble is, it doesn't make sense for a killer who murders at sundown to transport his next victim to a place where the sun doesn't set at all during the summer solstice.

And he was moving from east to west across the United States, from one time zone to the next. If he planned to keep going now that he's finished this continent, wouldn't Alaska or Hawaii be next? Why Norway? Even crossing the Pacific to Asia would make more sense than that.

"Vic! Did you hear me?"

"No," he confesses. "Sorry, Kitty."

She sighs. "I'll just let you go. It's late, and it's a work night, and you're busy—"

"No, wait, don't hang up yet." He needs the connection to his wife. He needs to be reminded that there's a normal life out there waiting for him when this is all over. "What were you saying?"

"How much did you hear?"

"Not much."

Kitty sighs. "Well, for one thing, Dave Gudlaug called today."

"Did he ask where I was?"

"Of course."

"What did you tell him?"

"That you went away to finish your book in peace and I'm under strict orders not to tell anyone where you are."

"Well, it's not a total lie. The second part is true."

"He wanted to know if we've given any more thought to a cruise with him and Louise this winter. I said we have, and we'd love to go."

"Kitty, I don't know."

"Come on, it'll be fun."

"It doesn't *sound* fun, playing bingo with a bunch of old farts and eating at buffets and—"

"You don't *have* to play bingo or eat at buffets."

"Oh, right, you can play bridge instead, and eat in a tuxedo at the same time every night with strangers at your table."

"Dave said it's not like that on this cruise line. Norwegian has freestyle dining. You eat wherever you want and when-ever you—"

"*What* did you say?"

"I said, it's not like that."

"Freestyle."

"Yes, that's what they call it in the brochure. Didn't you read it?"

"Freestyle . . . Norwegian . . . Kitty, I have to go."

"What? Vic—"

"I'm sorry. I love you. I'll call you back later."

Freestyle.

That was the brand of all five watches.

Norwegian.

Ibsen was a Norwegian playwright.

There was a Norwegian krone next to Kelly Patterson's body.

All this time, Vic had been thinking of Norway . . . land of the midnight sun.

Heart pounding, he dials Annabelle.

June eighteenth.

Not the longest day of the year, but almost.

And it sure has felt like it.

All day, she's been uneasy.

All day, she's felt as though he were here with her, watching her.

But that, of course, is impossible, unless he's out there floating on an iceberg.

Standing on the balcony of her suite, the doors open behind her so that she can listen for the steward's knock, Lucinda watches the sun sink low over the vast Gulf of Alaska.

It's almost over.

Not just the day.

The nightmare.

The sun set hours ago in Philadelphia.

By now, the FBI will have the Night Watchman in custody.

They would have been staking out her apartment since she left, regardless of the fact that she's not in it. Perhaps they even sent in a lookalike decoy to pose as Lucinda for the past few days.

They were undoubtedly lying in wait tonight for the Night Watchman to make his appearance.

And when he did, they would have gotten him.

She hopes Vic Shattuck was there to personally slap on the cuffs—or pull the trigger, if that were the case.

With any luck, the story will be in the press in a day or two. She'll pick up a newspaper in one of the ports of call.

For now, though, she'll stay hidden away in her cabin, where she's been from the moment the ship set sail from Seattle on Saturday morning. Not because she doesn't feel safe here, miles out at sea. This is the last place anyone would ever think to look for her. She never mentioned the rebooked cruise to anyone, having resolved not even to think about it, much less discuss it, until the case was solved.

For five days now, she's been thinking of Randy—and Neal, too—constantly. She knows how worried they must be, wishes she could reach out to let them know she's all right.

She doesn't dare. Not yet.

Not telling anyone where she was going—or even that she was leaving—has been the most difficult thing she's ever done in her life. It doesn't matter that it was for their own good as much as—or perhaps more so than—her own. It felt wrong.

Yet she could never ask or expect Randy or Neal to lie to the FBI. Never.

That would have been even more wrong.

Hearing a knock on her cabin door, Lucinda steps inside the stateroom, leaving the doors to the balcony open to let in the cool sea air. She's been doing that as much as possible, not accustomed to being cooped up in a small space day after day like this.

She keeps the lights on, of course, as always. All day, all night. The television, too. She likes to keep it tuned to the station that broadcasts the ship's position, the weather, the time. It's nice to keep track of how far they've come, where they are—and how far they still have to go.

"Room service," a voice calls.

Lucinda peers through the peephole to make sure, feeling

a little foolish. As if the Night Watchman could suddenly beam himself to a ship three thousand miles away from Philadelphia.

Nope. It's the cabin steward who's been taking care of her for four nights now.

Lucinda opens the door. "How are you, Eduardo?"

"Just fine. You're eating late tonight. I thought you were upstairs at the big chocolate buffet, but maybe you have other plans, eh?" He gives her a sly look. "Maybe you're expecting company? I could bring some wine, some champagne. . . ."

"No, it's just me."

He gives her an "if you say so" shrug that she doesn't really understand. Does he think she has a secret lover stowed away on board?

"Well, if you change your mind, the buffet is the highlight of the cruise. Everyone on the ship is there. Well, *almost* everyone. It's really something. Chocolate-covered strawberries, chocolate-covered everything you can imagine, chocolate sculptures, chocolate fountains . . . Don't you like chocolate?"

"I love it."

"Then you should go."

"Maybe I will, after dinner."

After sunset.

As if reminded why he's here, Eduardo rolls the room service cart, elegantly draped in white linen, into the suite. "Where would you like this? Would you like to dine outside and watch the sunset? It's beautiful tonight, isn't it?"

She follows his gaze to the balcony.

High overhead, the endless arc of midnight blue sky is filled with swirls of clouds, melding with streaks of reddish orange as the sun descends toward shimmering water. A vivid strip of yellow rides across the horizon, radiating from the sun's fiery dome.

"In just a few hours, the sun will be rising again," Eduardo tells her. "Have you noticed that it never really gets dark here in Alaska at this time of year?"

"I have definitely noticed, and that's fine with me."

"Why is that?"

"Because I'm afraid of the dark."

He grins at her.

Ha, you think I'm kidding, Eduardo.

"Then if you ever come to Alaska in the winter, you'd better bring someone to hold your hand," he advises, tongue firmly in cheek. "It's just the opposite at that time of year. It never really gets light."

"I'll keep that in mind."

"Will you be needing anything else?"

"No, I'm all set."

As Eduardo moves to leave, something drops out of his pocket.

It's a wad of dollar bills.

Watching him scoop up the money, Lucinda wonders if she should be tipping him now. Obviously, somebody is. She thought it was policy on this line to wait until the end of the cruise. She'd better double-check that with the concierge in the morning.

She locks the door behind Eduardo, and slides the chain.

There.

Safe and sound.

Lucinda glances at the television screen with its convenient statistics.

They're cruising off the Alaskan coast at 20 knots, having just left Skagway's port at 59.75 135.53, over a thousand miles from Seattle—and three times as far from home. It's 10:19 P.M. The sun will set in exactly five minutes.

Thank God she listened to her instincts and fled Philadelphia last week. Thank God she took charge of her own life, the way she always has.

At the open balcony door, the sheer draperies flutter in the stiff wind off the water.

Looking uneasily out at the setting sun, she reminds herself that she's safe here.

Still, maybe she won't leave the doors open tonight after all.

Come on, that's ridiculous. Buck up.

She shivers. It's not just that she's anxious. It gets really cold out here on the water at night. In fact, it isn't all that warm during the day, either.

She's spent hours sitting on the teak deck chair wrapped in a blanket, gazing out at the sea.

Hours thinking about what she'll do when she gets back to Philadelphia.

About the changes she's already made; the changes she'll continue to make.

Her mother was wrong.

She hasn't been grown-up all her life. She's been a child: willful and carefree.

But maybe it's time to grow up.

With a sigh, Lucinda glances at the statistics on the television set.

It's 10:20 P.M.

She looks at the room service cart, wondering why she even bothered to order dinner—and a heavy one at that: steak, potatoes, salad, dessert. . . .

She frowns, realizing there's something extra on the tray, tucked in the shadow of a bud vase amid the silver-domed plates, utensils, cutlery.

It's a gift box.

They really spoil you in first class.

The first night, there was a bottle of champagne from the concierge.

The second, a box of chocolate truffles.

The third, an invitation to the Captain's private reception—to which, of course, she sent her regrets.

Last night, a fruit basket.

Now what?

She eyes the box with apprehension.

Today is the eighteenth. You're confusing premonition with paranoia.

Still . . .

The gift is wrapped in shiny red paper and knotted with red ribbon.

Red.

But lots of gifts are wrapped in red paper. The ship's logo is red. It makes sense.

Lucinda picks up the box, feeling foolish for being so hesitant.

Come on. What do you think it's going to be? A bomb, courtesy of Eduardo and the Night Watchman?

Tick, tick, tick, sunset, boom!

She glances at the open doors.

A wedge of sun still sits on the horizon, but it's sinking fast.

Open the damned present. At least it's something to do. It'll take your mind off everything.

Lucinda slices the ribbon with the steak knife, tears off the paper, opens the lid, and the world skids to a screeching halt.

Randy's footsteps are hollow on the hardwood floors of Lucinda's apartment as he walks through the rooms, taking one last look around as the FBI support agents pack up.

June 18 came and went without a visit from the Night Watchman, without a sign of Lucinda.

Eugene Fox must have abducted her days ago, catching her off guard.

It shouldn't have, though. Lucinda was wary. She knew she was a target.

The FBI was here, ready for anything.

Not Vic Shattuck, though. He'd been taken off the case. That was a surprise. Randy had expected him to see it through, for Lucinda's sake if nothing else. He didn't even say good-bye before he left.

It's been a rough couple of days, coming to terms with the fact that Lucinda is gone.

Randy kept thinking that maybe she had run off of her own accord, that the Watchman would show up here tonight after all.

They were ready. The whole damned neighborhood was staked out; the apartment was occupied by a decoy who, at least from a distance, looks like Lucinda.

At 8:32, they waited, all of them, holding their breaths.

Waited.

Waited.

All night, into the morning.

Randy stops pacing, leans his forehead against the wall in despair.

Lucinda.

How the hell did the Watchman get to her last week, when she was under surveillance, behind locked doors? How did he slip past the agents? How did he disarm the alarm?

Does it matter?

It's June 19.

The sun will rise in a few hours.

It's too late for Lucinda.

Trembling, Lucinda lifts the wristwatch from the box.

The hands are stopped at 10.24.

She turns it over.

June 18
135.5
59.7

"Surprise!" a voice croons out of nowhere, and she looks up to see a figure standing at the balcony door, silhouetted against the setting sun.

*   *   *

Cam cracks the door to the nursery.

She can see Grace, asleep in her crib, bathed in the nightlight's pink glow.

Satisfied, she closes the door and slips over to Tess's room.

No nightlight here, but the shades are up. Light from the fat full moon illuminates the room. Tess, too, is sound asleep in her bed.

She looks so sweet and innocent in slumber. Like a little girl again.

So different from the young woman who, just days ago, attended her first prom and came home head over heels in love—again.

Cam closes the door and tiptoes past the master bedroom where she left Mike snoring.

All is well in the Hastings home tonight.

She just had to be sure. Even though she was well aware that the reason she hasn't been able to sleep tonight has little to do with anything going on under her own roof.

It's Lucinda.

Sometime after Cam left her on Thursday afternoon, she disappeared.

Neal Bullard told Cam that the FBI believes she might have been abducted by the Night Watchman.

No.

That's not what happened. Cam is certain Lucinda took matters into her own hands. She's alive, gone into hiding.

Cam has a strong sense that she's somewhere out West.

Somewhere overlooking the water.

But she hasn't told a soul about her psychic impressions. Not even Neal Bullard or Randy Barakat.

There's a reason Lucinda didn't tell anyone where she was going.

If Cam is right, and Lucinda is safe, then they'll all find out soon enough.

And if she's wrong . . .

Until tonight, she didn't think that was possible, so powerful was her intuition.

But as she lay in bed trying to fall asleep, an equally powerful sense of foreboding crept over her.

Be safe, Lucinda. Wherever you are.

Of all the great moments in Eugene Fox's life—his vengeance on Scarlet; his release from prison; his initial discovery of Lucinda Sloan—this is, by far, the greatest.

Even she, the all-knowing psychic detective, with all her supernatural powers, is no match for him.

She thought she was so smart, running away.

She thought she had outwitted them all.

But she herself has been outwitted by the master. Her brilliant idea was his own; he controls not just her movements, but her thoughts, as he set out so long ago to do.

He booked the cruise for Lucinda months ago and reserved a room for himself right next door, with the adjoining balconies separated by a thin plexiglass wall. Crossing over the rail from one to the other was laughably simple.

He knew all along that he'd have her right where he wanted her when the time came.

Knew her better than she knew herself.

So distracted was she by his other maneuvering that she didn't think to question the letter from the cruise line. She accepted it as authentic.

The night she called him, directly, to confirm, it was all he could do not to burst out laughing right then and there on the telephone.

He controlled himself then.

And so he will now, until it's over, though laughter is already beginning to bubble inside him as he stands face to face with her at last, seeing the look of sheer dread and shock on her beautiful face.

He moves toward her.

"What's the matter, Lucinda? Didn't you know that I always get the last laugh?"

"Do you want some more coffee?" Erma asks Neal, sitting beside him on the couch in their living room.

"No, thanks." He checks his cell phone for the thousandth time, as if he could possibly have missed a call. "If I have any more coffee, I think I'll be sick."

"Do you want to try to get some sleep?"

Neal shakes his head. "I don't think I can."

Erma rests a hand on his shoulder. "You don't know that Lucinda isn't out there somewhere, waiting it out. It would be just like her to take matters into her own hands."

"I wish I could buy that she'd just take off without telling us."

"You don't?"

Neal shrugs.

Something he heard Lucinda say a while back has been echoing through his thoughts for days now, since she vanished.

"A secret isn't a secret unless you're the only one who knows."

"I wouldn't do that if I were you."

About to make a run for the door behind her, Lucinda sees the gun in his hand and goes absolutely still.

"Move a muscle, and I'll shoot you dead."

"No, you won't."

"What?" His cold, dead eyes gleam with interest. "You don't believe you're about to die? Why do you think I'm here, then? To share the view?"

He laughs.

Her blood runs cold. She knows that sound. She's heard it for months now, echoing through her thoughts, through her nightmares.

Keep him talking.

"You're not going to shoot me. That's not what you do, Eugene."

The laughter subsides. "So we're on a first name basis, are we?"

"Absolutely. Call me Lucinda. Unless you'd prefer Scarlet."

The black eyes narrow.

"You don't want to use a gun," she tells him, noting the sliver of sun just barely visible above the water behind him. "That wouldn't be any fun. You want to stab me. I know you have a knife."

"You think you know everything. Guess what? You don't."

And neither do you.

Keeping her voice, her gaze, her hand steady, she eggs him on. "Oh, I think I do. I know things about you that nobody else on earth knows."

"Like what?"

"I know that you're the Night Watchman. I know that you watched your father die at your feet when you were a child. I know that you killed your own mother. And Ricky Parker. And Andrew Stockman."

Only at the last name does he raise an eyebrow.

It was a guess on her part, but clearly a good one.

"He died during the uprising. Dozens of inmates did. You don't know anything."

"Really? I think you seized the opportunity to kill him yourself and make it look that way."

It's a hunch she's had ever since Cam told her about Stockman. Judging by Eugene's expression, she's on the right track.

"Why would I kill that nobody?" he asks in disdain.

This is your chance to learn the truth for Cam.

But when this is over, will you even be alive to tell her?

Over his shoulder, she sees the sun slipping dangerously close to the horizon.

Keep him talking.

"Maybe you killed him because you felt threatened by him, Eugene. He was bigger and stronger and smarter than you."

"That's a joke! He was a peon. He bragged about all those girls he'd killed, every detail, went on and on about them all day, all night, talking like he was so bold."

"He *was* bold. Brave, too. Lucky. Not like you. He got away with it."

"That shows how smart you are," he scoffs. "You know why he went after them? Because they wouldn't give someone like him the time of day. So you know what he did? He made them all look like suicides. Didn't even have the guts to own it."

"Not like you."

"Damn right."

The last rays of the sun have all but disappeared.

"I bet you told him how to do things the right way."

"Hell, yes, I told him."

And then you realized he knew too much.

So you killed him.

Suddenly, Fox follows her gaze, over his shoulder.

Sunset.

"It's time, Lucinda."

He moves toward her.

She forces herself to stand her ground, seeing the knife that's replaced the gun in his hand—and the lipstick.

"It's time for you to die."

Back in Philadelphia, Vic learned that being FBI doesn't mean you're granted immediate access to the ship's manifest.

By the time he'd landed in Alaska, Annabelle had confirmed that Lucinda is, indeed, a passenger on the *Norwegian Star*.

"What about Eugene Fox?"

"That's anyone's guess," Annabelle replied. "Who knows what name he's traveling under?"

Even now that Vic is here on the ship, having gained the necessary clearance to board in Skagway before they set sail an hour ago, there's a hell of a lot of red tape involved in getting to Lucinda. He had expected to reach her well before sunset.

It didn't happen.

As he races up the wide staircase toward Deck 11 with the head of security by his side, Vic looks at his watch.

It's 10:24.

Lucinda remains motionless until the last possible second.

Then she makes her move, lunging right toward him, not away.

Caught off guard, he instinctively raises the knife.

So many times, in her visions of the women murdered by the Night Watchman, Lucinda's ears have been assaulted by the dull, sickening sound of a blade thudding into human flesh.

Now she hears it for real; feels the blood spatter over her; sees her hands red with blood.

It's too late.

"Where is it? Where's her cabin?" Vic demands, taking the last flight two steps at a time.

"That way," the security guard pants. "To the left."

Vic races toward it, praying that it's not too late.

Eugene Fox staggers back, looking bewildered. Glancing down, he sees the steak knife's blade protruding from his chest.

He looks up at Lucinda, raises the gun, aims it at her, pulls the trigger.

Nothing happens.

"Maybe I don't know everything," Lucinda tells him. "But I knew there was no way you could have gotten a real gun on board this ship. And like I said, I know that isn't how you operate."

A sound comes out of him.

For a moment, she thinks it's a sob or a cry of pain.

Then she sees the look on his face and realizes that he's laughing—even as he collapses on the floor of her cabin.

The sound seems to chase her as she dashes out into the hall, looking for help.

Incredibly, help appears.

Lucinda stops short in disbelief. "*Vic*?"

"Lucinda, are you hurt?"

She follows his gaze, looks at her hands. "No, this is his— he came at me, and I stabbed him. He's in my room."

Vic doesn't ask who she's talking about.

"All right, stay here. You, too," he instructs the security guard who's caught up with him.

Vic moves stealthily past her and stands with his back against the wall, gun poised, beside the open doorway.

After a few moments, he peers around the corner into the room.

He takes in the scene for a moment, then crosses the threshold.

Heart pounding, Lucinda waits outside her room with the guard, expecting Eugene Fox to emerge bleeding from his chest wound, like something out of a horror movie.

A minute passes.

Another.

Just when she can no longer take it, Vic calls her name, tells her to come in.

Fox must be dead.

Thank God.

Lucinda walks into the room to see Vic standing just inside the door, facing the open balcony doors.

"He's gone."

"What? He can't be gone!" Lucinda looks around wildly. "He was right—"

She sees the bloody steak knife, lying on the floor where she left him.

Sees the trail of blood from there to the balcony.

Sees, beyond the drapes billowing in the sea breeze, against the backdrop of the twilight sky, the railing smeared with red.

Epilogue

Vic can hear Kitty vacuuming the living room as he sits down at his desk.

"Will the noise bother you?" she asked when he announced he was going to go work on the book.

"The only thing that could bother me right now," he told her, "would be my being anywhere other than here with you."

She smiled. "It's good to have you home."

"It's good to be home."

He boots up the computer and opens the document he left behind weeks ago, when he went off to try to alter the ending in real life.

Now, facing the final chapter again, he thinks about Eugene Fox, the man who seemed to fall off the face of the earth, only to resurface and begin killing again.

What if . . . ?

No.

Still . . .

"You don't really believe the Night Watchman survived . . . do you?" he asked Lucinda on the phone last night.

"No," she said. "I don't."

"Because you're a psychic?"

"Because I can't let myself believe he's out there somewhere," she said firmly. "I refuse to go through life always looking over my shoulder. It's time to move on."

Yes, it is.

Scrolling to the last chapter, Vic thinks of the ending he'd wanted to write. The one in which he, Vic Shattuck, brought the Night Watchman to justice at last.

He thought it would have made a great final scene for the movie.

His agent thinks that what happened in real life will make a better one.

"This way, it's open-ended. The guy is stabbed in the chest, staggers to the railing, and falls overboard, lost at sea. Or is he?" she added ominously.

"Oh, come on. You don't really think anyone's going to believe the Night Watchman survived the fall into the ocean, do you?"

"His body still hasn't been found."

"That doesn't mean he's still alive out there somewhere."

"No. But it leaves one helluva good opening for a sequel."

"Well, you'll have to find someone else to write it," Vic told her. "Because I'm going to be busy."

"Doing what?"

He grinned. "A whole lot of nothing."

"You've been so quiet tonight," Randy tells Lucinda as they walk the beach hand in hand beneath the light of a waning moon. "Don't tell me you've lost your voice again."

Lucinda smiles. "Not this time."

"I guess you've just said all there is to say, then."

"I guess so." She squeezes his hand. "Except one thing."

"Yeah? What's that?"

"Remember a few weeks ago, when I was in Seattle and we were on the phone and you told me something you'd been waiting to say for a long time—but you didn't give me a chance to respond?"

"I remember."

"Can I respond now?"

"That would be good. That would be really good."

They stop walking. She looks up at him.

"I love you, Randy. I've always loved you. I just didn't know it, or maybe I just didn't know how to say it, or maybe the time wasn't right—it was too late, or too soon . . ."

"Not anymore."

"No, not anymore."

He kisses her. "Stay with me, Lucinda."

He doesn't say *tonight*.

He doesn't *mean* tonight.

She knows that.

Knows, too, that there are no guarantees.

"I'll stay," she says softly, and the tide comes in, washing over their bare feet as they head back.

That night, climbing into bed beside Randy, she turns off the bedside lamp.

"You're not afraid of the dark anymore?" he asks, surprised.

"I'm not afraid of anything anymore."

Lucinda falls asleep in Randy's arms, dreaming again about the wooden jigsaw puzzle.

Only this time, all the pieces are there.

As she fits the last piece into place, she sees the complete picture at last.

It's Lucinda herself, smiling, as behind her, the sun rises over the Atlantic.